THE NIGHT BIRD'S FEATHER

By

JENNA KATERIN MORAN

Dedicated to:

	Elane Imgoven	Various Maginns
Cync Brantley	R'ykandar Korra'ti	Andrey S.
Rand Brittain	Angela Korra'ti	Amy Sutedja
Cheryl Couvillion	AJ Luxton	Chrysoula Tzavelas
Jim Henley	Jenn Manley Lee	Raymond Wood

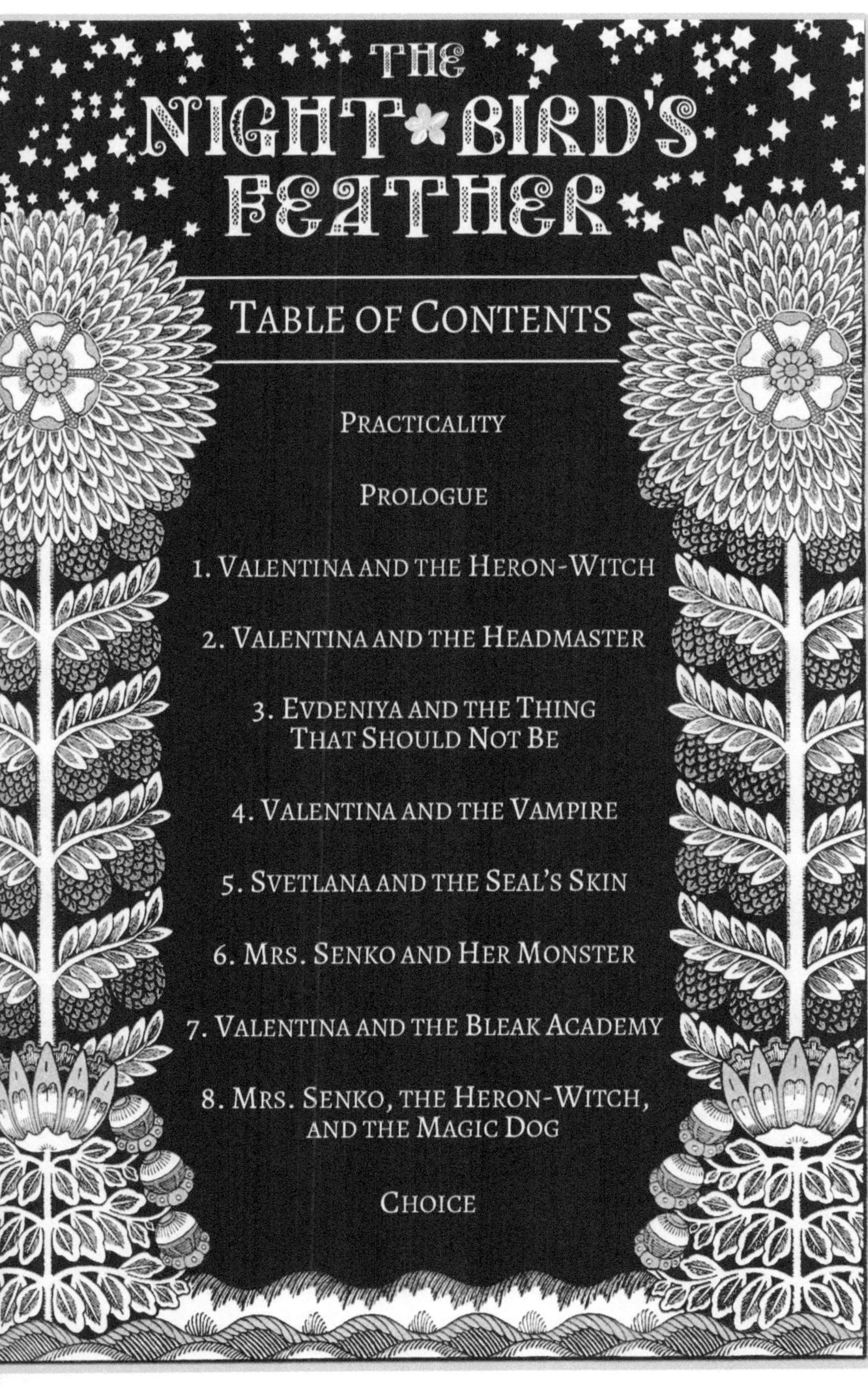

THE NIGHT BIRD'S FEATHER

TABLE OF CONTENTS

In the late 1300s, three ships of refugees from the Mongol invasion of Kievan Rus' found their way to an isolated, demon-haunted otherland. They settled at the edge of its lake and founded the human settlement of Fortitude. To deal with local conditions, certain of its families developed strange talents. One such was the Sosunovs, who practiced the arts of lucid dreaming, spiritual combat, and communicating with their loved ones (across arbitrary distances) through shared dreams.

"THE TOPIC of this class is practicality," she said. "And I am Mrs. Senko, and I will devour all your dreams."

She looked down. She stared at the desk blankly. She sighed, and blew a strand of hair away where it had fallen down over her eyes.

"And yet, for some reason, some among you have failed to grasp this lesson. When your life is troubled, you come to me, as if I am expected to care. When you face these ridiculous mirage-problems of childhood, you expect me to understand them. To assist. Even as recently as this morning, I was approached by one of my students, asking me, 'Mrs. Senko, Mrs. Senko, what do I do if I am haunted by an evil witch?'"

She turned to the chalkboard. She started by writing, neatly, midway down on the right side of the board, *Witches do not exist.*

She footnoted it, after a moment.

"Obviously," she said, "there are those who call themselves witches, and those who are called witches by others. Yet, this fundamental principle remains valid. The word has a meaning. In the fervid, overworked imaginations of the rustics, there is a totemic ideal, an ideological complex, a false image, which is the 'witch' ... and yet, however rich in association that ideal may be, it is a concept without referent. What does one do about witches? Nothing. *Witches do not exist.*"

She stared at the board, in satisfaction, for a moment, then she turned.

Devin's hand was raised. She stared at him for a long time, as if willing him to lower it, but he did not lower it. After a moment, she said, as if clarifying a point for the most obdurate of minds, "I am, therefore, not a witch."

There was scattered laughter, and Devin's hand inched back, slowly, down.

"This is not our topic for the day," Mrs. Senko said. "I wouldn't waste your time on something like that. There are no witches; thus the practical matters of the disposition of witches, or the defense against witches, boil down to ... nothingness?

"No.

"Today's class is not about witches," she said. "Today's class is on the ethics of self-sacrifice."

Aprosinya sat up, and then leaned forward, and there was fury in her face—but it raised little reaction from Mrs. Senko save a slight twist of her left upper lip, very close to being a smile. "Aprosinya," she said softly, then corrected herself—

"No. ... Ms. Sosunova. Could you tell us a little about your family's obligations?"

Aprosinya had missed the moment of its appearance, but Mrs. Senko had written BATTLING WITCHES high on the chalkboard.

Aprosinya turned her face to the side. She looked at the window.

Finally, she said, "There is no way to put this that you will accept, Mrs. Senko, but I cannot make corrections to my family's duty as if it were a paper."

"Well-said," noted Mrs. Senko. "Very well; present it as if I were a stranger."

A bitter smile flashed across Aprosinya's face.

"Oh," she said, falsely, "you really must come by the compound sometime! Father would be delighted to tell you the family history."

"Aprosinya," said Mrs. Senko.

"Less of a stranger than that?"

"Work with me."

Aprosinya sighed. She breathed out. "From time immemorial," she said, softly, "they have come in off the waters of the Lake: the witches, and been a trouble to the citizens of Fortitude. They are wicked creatures, arising from and in that state of wickedness. They are beings of malice, and they live primarily in dreams. They ... infect them. And this is scary because there are very few people in all the world who are strong in their dreams. If you train your body for a thousand years, still in your dreams a witch can catch you and render you helpless with one hand. If you train your soul to resist hardships and temptations, still they can walk in your dreaming mind and twist you, turn you bad. You can be as careful and practical as you like—"

Here she glared at Mrs. Senko, as if daring her to say anything, and in fact made it blatant by adding: "*and I told you that you would not accept this—*

"... you can be as careful and practical as you like, and yet, they can make everything in your life go all awry. For most people, there is nothing to be done. Thus, the family Sosunov. Thus, it is our duty to patrol the dreams of Fortitude. To protect the vulnerable sleeping minds. That is our obligation and our magic."

"One oddity," Mrs. Senko said, "leads to another."

Aprosinya tilted her head.

"Accept one fanciful notion and three others crowd the line ..." Mrs. Senko twitched. "But no. That is not the topic for the day. Let us, for now, accept this lacework of fanciful follies at something approaching its face value. Would you say, Aprosinya, that this obligation extends to you?"

"I would."

"*You* are obligated," said Mrs. Senko, "to spend your nights, regardless of your own interests, and even on occasions where there is homework to be done, papers to be prepared, tests to study for, classes the next morning—in an unlimited futile struggle to defend the dreams of others from the idiosyncratic manifestations of malisons like these?"

Aprosinya pulled a face.

"That is my destiny," she said. "Though, I am not very good at it."

"Mm," said Mrs. Senko. "I have found in life, you know, that when children speak of destiny, it tends to speak not so much to destiny as to an ideological indoctrination, an unwarranted fascination with adult topics, or, a failing on the part of the adults around them. Mm?"

She turned to the chalkboard. She thought for a moment, then wrote PRO and CON under the heading of BATTLING WITCHES, with *Witches do not exist* already roughly centered a ways beneath the label CON.

"You see," she said, "it is my opinion that you ought not be having such adventures, even were we to accept their existence, but rather should be developing your character here, within this institute. There is time enough to be crushed under the faceless malevolence of irresistible monsters when you have been released from here into the broader world."

After a moment, Mrs. Senko added the following entries to the column on the right:

- *Loss of sleep*
- *Adverse side effects*
- *Detrimental influence on mood*
- *Potential suicidal behavior*
- *Risk of death*
- *Risk of transformation*
- *Risk of failed apotheosis, followed by laying waste to large portions of the afterlife and troubling he the lord of Death's dominion*

The last one took up two lines and squeezed itself unpleasantly close to *Witches do not exist*, still below.

"Mrs. Senko," Devin asked, "wouldn't 'adverse side effects' be too general?"

"Well, it's a term for generic poor outcomes in clinical trials," Mrs.

Senko said. "I can't write down everything that happened to just *one* person who fought a witch."

"Ah," said Devin, awkwardly. "But—"

"Fine," said Mrs. Senko. "Fine."

She erased the last entry.

"As Devin has reminded me," she said, seemingly put out, "'laying waste to large portions of the afterlife' has only even allegedly happened once. Now. More importantly. Does anyone have any pros?"

Bluntly, Aprosinya suggested, "Inevitability."

"Ooh," said Mrs. Senko.

She wrote *Depressive ideation* in the space that had opened up inside the CONs.

"That is not what I meant," said Aprosinya. As Mrs. Senko held up the chalk, Aprosinya added, "if you write 'snippiness' or 'denial of reality' up there I will bite you."

Mrs. Senko hesitated. "... oral fixation?" she asked, apparently wondering if she should add this, but Aprosinya only slapped her notebook against her desk.

"What I meant," Aprosinya said, "is that on certain occasions, it is not necessary to *do* Sosunov magic in order to attract the attention of witches. If they've had previous encounters with the family, or are willing to follow the prevailing trends of expectation? It is sometimes enough simply to be Sosunov."

Mrs. Senko still had not recorded anything under PRO. She stood there for a moment, and then she turned, and she looked straight at Aprosinya, and there was something hard in her gaze. "Ms. Sosunova," she said, "if I may ask, what is the point of having a family of dedicated dream guardians, if in the end the witches can bother whom they will?"

Aprosinya was silent.

"Perhaps I am misunderstanding?" said Mrs. Senko. "Are you the last survivor of your esteemed family? The only one west of the Lake and all its waters who can intercept the pains of others' dreams? Are you alone, Ms. Sosunova, so that if a witch should bother anyone *else*, well, you can choose whether to fulfill your 'duty' or to leave them to suffer it, but if a witch should bother *you*, then, there is nothing to be done? Is *that* the case? For certainly if that *is* the case—ignoring for the moment that witches, again, do *not* exist—I should be more sympathetic to your plight than I have been."

"That isn't," said Aprosinya.

She looked away.

"That isn't," she said, as if it were a whole sentence, and complete.

"Then," said Mrs. Senko, "I will not write down that it is inevitable. Your family could perfectly well guard you from this, and most likely should. Have you asked them to?"

Silence.

"Have you informed them?"

This provoked a reaction: "They have to know," said Aprosinya.

"...then?"

"It's in *my* dreams," said Aprosinya. "It's *my* job. I ... I want to be able to handle it. Because I am a Sosunov."

Mrs. Senko waited.

"To be one of the people who protects," said Aprosinya.

"There," said Mrs. Senko, as if she'd been waiting for that. "At last we have one for the PRO column."

She wrote down:

- ❧ *Reducing the burden on the vast unthinking herd we name society.*

"Oi," argued Devin.

"Oh," said Mrs. Senko, "I am not saying that this is a bad thing. As you can see, I have put it under the column labeled PRO. It is *for the best* that a hero takes their stand, shouldering and being crushed under the vast weight of things in order that the milling kine suffer each of them the tiniest bit less. That is a well-established and commonly understood moral principle."

"That characterization isn't convincing," said Aprosinya.

"No?"

Aprosinya frowned. She thought about this. Then she said, "No. I don't know why not."

"Mm."

"There is," Aprosinya said, "a nameless good, you see, in it. You should help people. You should do your duty and have a place. I don't know how else to put it."

"One might say," said Mrs. Senko, "that you're a child, who goes to school. That that is your destiny. That that is your place."

She was scribbling it in, then, at the bottom of the CON column: *Distraction from one's proper duties and one's conduct.*

"I can't be a child before I'm a Sosunov," argued Aprosinya.

"Can't you?"

"I'll be a Sosunov all my life," said Aprosinya. "Even if I marry out of the family, my children will be Sosunov cousins, my magic will be Sosunov magic, my duties will be Sosunov duties. There's hardly any path in life that doesn't leave me a Sosunov. But the only way to stay a child forever is to die."

Mrs. Senko glanced at the *Potential suicidal behavior* for a moment. She looked back.

"Mmm. I will tell you a secret," she said. "It is a ... cheat. It is a way of cheating at practicality. A trick I learned from your ancestress, in fact. It is this. If you ever find yourself saying things like 'I can't' or 'I have to,' or certainly 'it is my duty' or 'my destiny,' then, you stop. You may simply ... stop."

Aprosinya's eyes were on her.

"You are not writing this down, Ms. Sosunova."

"It's not a real lesson!"

"Oh," said Mrs. Senko. "You're going to have *trouble* with your examinations."

Aprosinya hesitated.

"In any case," said Mrs. Senko. "That's all. That is the cheat. That is the trick. It is like crossing off factors in division. 'You can't be a child before you're a Sosunov.' 'You have a destiny.' 'You have a duty.' 'You have a job.' '*Because you are a Sosunov.*' You find yourself saying things like that. And ... stop."

Her lip curled.

"Tonight I will ask you to read pages 233-246," she said, "of *A Guide to Practicality*. It is the section called *Ideological Indoctrination*— ah. Recognizing it. Spotting it. Rejecting it. You can stop before the section on receiving it."

"So that's your advice?" said Aprosinya. "That's it? Just ignore what I'm supposed to be, to do? Have my family come out here to help?"

"It's tempting," said Mrs. Senko. "But you did say one thing worth hearing."

Aprosinya blinked.

"You said 'I want.'"

"Uh," said Aprosinya. She settled lower in her seat.

"I find that interesting," said Mrs. Senko. "Here you are, poisoned. Alleging— and, since we are speaking of dreams and concepts, does it even matter that these are falsehoods? Alleging that a witch haunts you. Alleging that it has *damaged* you, that it has taken away a portion of your life's essential brightness; that it has put you on a path that leads towards only grim despair."

"I didn't tell you that—" Aprosinya started.

"And yet you tell me that you *want* to fight it. You want to be able to handle it. You see your destruction, you see the allure of your own ending, and you rush towards it with a smile. That is, while not precisely the attitude that I am seeking to encourage in this class, *interesting*. That is worth hearing. Is it going to be worth it, Ms. Sosunova? Because I *can* tell you that simply wanting to be able to handle a thing is not enough to do so."

"Of course it isn't," said Aprosinya.

"I could even say," said Mrs. Senko, "that wanting a thing is its opposite: actively detrimental to being able to do it. Something that will prevent you from taking the most effective course of action, and instead bind you into battle with one hand tied behind your back. For there is only one excuse I can imagine that *would* justify your insistence on battling this witch alone, Ms. Sosunova, which is to say, as practice for encountering *later* witches; but you're not expecting that to happen, are you."

Aprosinya went still. Then, softly, she admitted it.

"No," she said. "No, I'm not."

"You're doing this," said Mrs. Senko. "You're letting her in. You're facing her alone. You're letting her *destroy* you. Because you're scared that you won't get another chance to be important, later on."

"That's," and here Aprosinya hesitated.

"They're rare," said Mrs. Senko. "Aren't they? Witches?"

Aprosinya seemed to be having a little trouble breathing.

"So you wake up every morning, now," said Mrs. Senko, "tired; hurt; scared. It's eating into you, it's cutting you, it's filling you up to the brim of you with despair; only, you have to let it, you have to fight it on your own, at most asking a few people for help *so that you can feel like you asked for help*, a few people who are, of course, merely practical, dull, and boring teachers who cannot possibly do more than give you vaguely relevant *tips*—"

And very sharply:

"And don't think I believe for a moment that you *expected* me to say something that would make it all *easy* for you, Aprosinya—"

Aprosinya sagged, and Mrs. Senko finished:

"Because if you don't, if you don't let her pollute you, if you don't let her foul the nest that is your mind, *you might miss your chance,* and then live the rest of your life completely futile, a dream guardian with nothing to guard against, *a magician with no point.* Mm?"

Aprosinya was flushed. She was slouching.

She protested, "It's in *my* dreams."

"I should take her from you," said Mrs. Senko. "Yes. I will do that."

"What?"

She looked straight on at Aprosinya. It was as if she dragged the girl's eyes up to meet hers by will alone. "Witches don't exist, Aprosinya. And if they *did,* they wouldn't be interested in *you.*"

Mrs. Senko reached forward. Her hand was some ways from Aprosinya, but it was in her visual field; its fingernails reached back, not so much from the hand's spatial position as from its place in that visual field, to pinch behind Aprosinya's eyes. It was surprisingly painless as they closed on something; as she pulled it out;

"So I am confiscating the entire notion," Mrs. Senko said, and she pulled her hand away.

There was a silence after that, for a while. Then Devin raised his hand, and she called on him.

"We, ah," he said. "didn't actually discuss the ethics of self-sacrifice at all."

"There are none," said Mrs. Senko. "That is the lesson. That is the extent of it. You are children; you are to be protected; you are not to engage in any form of self-sacrifice. Then, later in your life, you will become adults. You will be untrustworthy and unreliable. You will be part of a great, seething faceless mass of malice, very like unto a witch. You will mill through the world, moon-faced and rotten, and you will not sacrifice yourself then either. But if you wish to engage in self-sacrifice, if you wish to consider it, then first I wish you to remember this—"

And she tapped the board.

"And pages 233-246, like I have said."

"How—" Claire asked.[1] "Ma'am, I mean, how are we supposed to read the sections on spotting and rejecting indoctrination without reading the actual indoctrination section?"

"Don't try to be cute," Mrs. Senko said.

Claire shrank back in her seat. She struggled with words for a moment before finally managing, "but they're the same pages?"

"Ah," Mrs. Senko said. "Right. I had forgotten I had done that."

She'd written the textbook, of course. Or, at least, she had compiled it.

"Well," Mrs. Senko said, and tidied up her own notes, and rapped them on the table. "That's because nothing means anything and all ideas, concepts, and motivations are just hypotheses that somebody or other put together. Class dismissed."

---

1 She was the ghost at the back of the class.

NCE UPON a time, there was a fishing village named Fortitude on the shores of a Big Lake in the middle of an endless, seething nothingness.

It sat towards the southeastern end of a roughly 700-square-mile parcel of reality.

Most of that parcel of reality was taken up by the lake. Most of the rest, by unclaimed land, or the village. To the west, across the hills, there *was* a tented city that strange creatures dwelled in, though; this, in time, would become "Horizon." Beyond *that* lay the Walking Fields.

This haven, as a whole—this promontory of reality—was simply known as "Town."

IF YOU went to the north, across the nothingness, you would find a few more scattered pockets of existence. Schism, and Soma Village. The mountain, Kailas Mantra.

Eastward—'round and past the lake—you might find the Bleak Academy.

The rest ... was lost.

It was nothingness and chaos; emptiness, mystery, and disorder. This, was known as "the Outside."

There was no direct connection between all this and the world we know.

It was a geographically disconnected fragment of existence.

... but, if one knew how to sail the Lake correctly—at the proper times, along the proper courses—one could find one's way to the rivers, lakes,

and seas of Earth. Conversely, if one just knew how, one could sail all the way from Earth to the docks of Fortitude, as well.

If you were to go and sail there now, of course, it would be too late. This story would have already happened. But ... if you'd woken yourself up, a couple centuries back; rolled out of bed; stared up, bright-eyed, at the sky, and caught yourself a ship to Fortitude—there's just a chance that you would have been there for the beginning of all this; caught the moment when all of this was just barely starting:

With Fevroniya Sosunova, and a bird.

ONCE UPON A TIME, then ...

Fevroniya Sosunova was telling a story.

She was telling a story, and a bird started listening. What kind of a bird? It was a beautiful heron, fat-bodied and narrow-beaked, all white with red tips to its feathers.

It listened, but it didn't know that it was listening.

It heard the story, but it didn't know that it was hearing the story. Not at first. But it liked the sound of the words. It liked the sound of the words, and it started wanting to *own* the sound of the words. It started wanting to be the one *making* the sound of the words. And when Fevroniya reached the part of the story where she said, "Like the world was a mirror, which cracked," the bird fluttered its wings, and it echoed those words in its harsh croaking voice:

"... ich cracked ..."

And in that moment, quite entirely by accident, the bird looked down at the waters by its feet, where the ripples broke up its reflection. It caught sight of that broken, cracked likeness. It noticed, in that instant,

that it was thinking a thought, a thought in words, and that that thought had *meaning*:

"*Like the world was a mirror, which cracked.*"

After that, it ... *she* ... couldn't be a heron any longer. She had to give it up. She'd had a thought, with words, that had meaning in it, and from that moment forward the fire of her consciousness was a fire that ate words.

From that moment forward, she couldn't be a heron; she had to be people. Or, at least, a *kind* of people.

She became a witch.

MRS. SENKO, ONE SUPPOSES, must have been wrong, or lying. What with a witch just *existing*, like that—

... which just goes to show (if you've had her class) that even obvious and well-known things can be deceit.

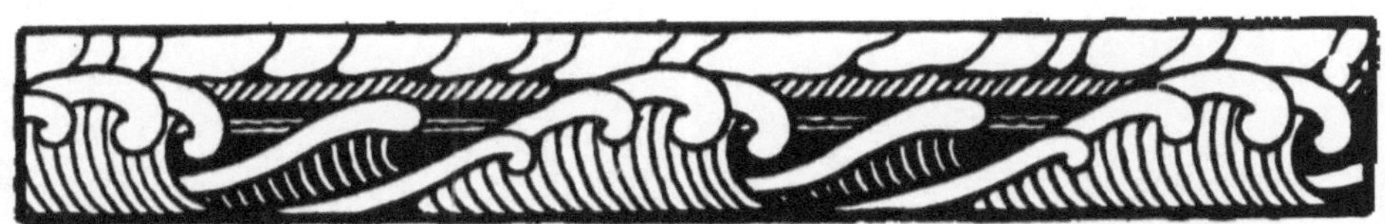

CHAPTER ONE

VALENTINA AND THE HERON-WITCH

Once upon a time, but not so very long ago, Miruna Sosunova learned to see through the back of her eyes like the front of them. She raised up the curtains of the self and went out beyond them, into the territory of nothingness and death. She saw there the secret that was like the rain, that was like a cloud passing over nothingness. She lit up the void, in that moment, like a candle in the dark, and she understood for the first time, then, that she was beautiful.

She held out her hands and this understanding pooled inside them. It became a thing: a chunk of silver; it became a key. ...

— from A Beginner's Guide to the Sosunov Magic,
by Sidonie Sosunova

L ET'S TELL the story of Valentina Grigorievna Sosunova and the heron-witch!

Generations and generations before Aprosinya was born, Valentina was a young girl from the Sosunov family.[2] She'd been trained since birth in how to fight witches, but she hadn't ever been expected to have to actually fight one. Certainly not one like the heron-witch, who was the worst witch the Sosunovs had ever seen.

What did the heron-witch do?

She hollowed people out. She made space for herself inside them and nurtured her own spirit there. She cultivated herself inside her victims like a chick in an egg. And while she was doing this her victims would sleep and sleep and no one would be able to wake them. That was pretty bad, but it wasn't the bad part. The bad part was that she was really *good* at it. She wasn't like most of the horrible witches that the Sosunovs had seen before, who might do pretty bad things but would just fall over when someone with powers of their own stood up to oppose them. The heron-witch was strong, strong enough that the whole Sosunov family, who thought they were pretty darn good at handling witches, didn't stand even the ghost of a chance.

The Sosunovs drifted off to sleep, one by one, and they did not wake again, until only little Valentina was left to care for them, and to keep the house, and to fight alone against the witch to win them back.

It wasn't easy. The fight wasn't easy. She had to work very hard, and for a very long time.

---

2 The "a" on her last name was a local convention.

IT STARTED like this:

It was a warm night in summer and a wind blew in past thick magenta curtains and Valentina's family was having dinner, and among all the clatter of silverware and all the talk at the table, Valentina's great-grandfather found himself nodding off. His eyes slipped closed. He drifted off into darkness. He floated off into dreams. Only, where his dreams should have been, he found a witch waiting instead.

The river of his dreams ran past the two of them. It was a many-colored tumult. It cast up white spray.

She stood athwart that river: the witch.

"Shoo," he said.

She tilted her head. She fluffed and settled her feathers. She took a step forward.

"Don't want to get dragged into the business of witches," he said. "Want to dream of my wife."

The witch didn't understand words like those. The witch could barely understand the words that she *knew*. She wasn't approaching Valentina's great-grandfather to *talk* to him. She was approaching him because there was a nesting instinct waking in her, a hungry witch's instinct, and she wanted to take something that the old man had.

He almost realized that, and started to react, but by then it was just too late.

There was a great fluttering of wings, and a lunging beak, and that beak struck him on the forehead, and his consciousness of the world went out. He fell into the kind of dreams that have no dreamer, deeper and deeper dreams until he was just a shell for her, a dreaming shell to her, and she cultivated her *own* nascent consciousness inside him, like an egg.

He nodded off at the table, and he did not wake.

He was just the first. Valentina's grandmother was next, and her grandfather, and her great-uncles. The witch took them at different places and at different times. Two went to bed. One sat down on the couch. One was out walking around the complex where the Sosunovs lived. ... and the witch found them. She raised up her wing. They fell under the shadow of that wing, and they fell asleep. And in that sleep, no matter how hard they fought, no matter how strong they had believed themselves to be, they fell under her sway, they fell into her power, they were turned into empty containers for her will, and she cultivated herself inside the dreams of them, like an egg.

This wasn't the first time that a witch had troubled the Sosunovs. Chaos blows across the surface of the Lake and roils in the lands Outside the town. From time to time it stirs up something that becomes a witch or monster. That's nothing unexpected. There'd been five or six witches already that century, and all manner of oddnesses to boot. Like weeds, they'd be cut down, and like weeds, they'd spring up again; that a witch would arise to make trouble—well, the Sosunovs weren't all that surprised.

They gathered their strength. They prepared to fight.

Only, this time, they lost.

They might as well have been yelling at starlight. They called up their magic, all the magic that the Sosunovs knew, and they still fell asleep one right after another. Nothing they did had the slightest effect upon the witch or delayed her efforts by the smallest amount. Valentina's Dad fell asleep and he didn't wake up. Her aunts and her uncles, too. Her cousins, one by one, fell asleep.

"Be good," her mother said, as she drifted off. She took Valentina's little hands in hers to warm them. "Be good. Keep the house, and protect it."

And then the whole family slept—save Valentina.

The witch hunted her down. She raised up her wing, and Valentina fell under the shadow of that wing, and she too slipped into dreams. Only, Valentina was young. She was *too* young, the youngest of the Sosunovs, and she was yet to drink deeply enough of the nectar of the world. She had never left the immediate surrounds of Fortitude; never seen the world; never felt the touch of the King of Evil, or of Death's dominion, or of the angel of the Houses of the Sun. The witch sent her to sleep and found that she couldn't *fit* into Valentina's dreams; or, rather, she could fit, she could walk right on in as a bird, but she couldn't turn those dreams into an egg. She couldn't cultivate her spirit and power inside.

Valentina slept, but she didn't stay asleep like the others.

She woke, instead, scared and stiff on the floor.

"BE GOOD. Keep the house, and protect it."

Simple words for a pretty tough job.

It was hard just being alone in the house. It was lonely and difficult just being the last of the Sosunovs. But Valentina couldn't just moon around in the house being lonely.

After the first day or so, taking care of sleeping people becomes really hard on its own.

Even if they're asleep, they still need food. They still need water. You still have to turn them over so they don't get bedsores and check that they're still breathing and take care of all of the messes that they make.

A big modern hospital full of doctors and nurses would have a hard time with fifteen comatose Sosunovs. It would put a strain on their schedules.

Valentina wasn't a big modern hospital. She was just one little girl.

If she'd been left alone there with no guidance at all, she wouldn't have known what to do, and everyone would have died. She would probably have tried to feed them, but she would have forgotten about water; she wouldn't have even thought about turning them; and she wouldn't have had any idea how to keep them all clean.

If they'd all fallen asleep at once, that would have happened.

But they hadn't fallen asleep all at once. It had been slow. So there'd been time for some preparations.

There was a plan.

Valentina's Mom and Dad and aunts and uncles and cousins had had time to write up a plan and a schedule. They'd shown Valentina how to take care of people who were asleep. Everything they could do to make sure that someone left behind to care of things *could* take care of things, they'd done, just in case there actually was. And that would fine if it had been Valentina's Mom and Dad and an uncle, say. It would have even been fine if it had been Valentina and her big strong cousins Donal and Ivan, at least for a couple of days.

She was just one little girl.

She got exhausted just rolling everyone over—never mind changing the beds!

It was too much for her, and to be technical, that meant she really wasn't supposed to do it at all. That was part of the plan too. Her Mom had been clear about that. Towards the end, when it started to look like there wouldn't be enough people left, when it started to seem like keeping things going might be too much to manage, she'd written it into the plan in her big looping handwriting:

"If it's ever too much. If you're ever doing something and it's *just too much*. Even if you've already started doing it. Even if it doesn't seem there's anything you can do *but* to do it.

"If it's ever too much, you can stop."

In a situation like hers, Valentina's Mom didn't expect Valentina to do more than she could ... only, while a lot of the parts of the plan had details spelled out (like how much water to use in the soup, and how often to turn people over in bed), "if it's ever too much" was just aspirational. An *idea*. That part of the plan didn't give Valentina any actual guidance on what exactly "too much" was, or on where the line was between "I can go a bit further" and "this: this is too far."

Valentina didn't do a little bit, then stop, and evaluate how much she could manage.

She just worked very hard.

The first day[3] she managed. She was a tough little thing, and she didn't shrink back from work. She bustled about the house. She kept things tidied up. She made broth and she fed it very solemnly to her family, a sip at a time. She wiped down everyone's brow. She adjusted everyone in their beds. It was a struggle, and she got behind schedule, but she had the energy to give it her best.

The next day it was harder.

The third day she woke up and her whole body hurt and she thought of what she had to do for the day and she burst out crying. She couldn't get up, not until the heaves of her sobs shook free the last of the tears from her eyes.

She got up. She kept going.

She was stronger than she ever thought she would have to be. She was braver than she thought she ever could be. She started slipping, forgetting really important things, but at least she kept going.

She didn't stop, even though it was too much for her; only, it *was* too much for her.

On the fourth day, when she was rolling her dear grandmother over, she fell down. She couldn't get up.

Her hair fell over her grandmother's body like one corpse's over another's. Her eyes filmed over. She fell asleep.

VALENTINA DREAMED. It was a magical dream, but not a dream of the witch. It was a dream of the Sosunov family magic, the magic that was *supposed* to keep them from getting put to sleep forever by miscellaneous witches, the magic that she'd been trained in since she was just a baby in her mother's arms.

Here's what happened.

She dreamed she came out of the rain. She found herself in an old, gothic school. She shook herself and she looked around, but there were

____

3   well, the first "day." We'll go into that later.

no people anywhere around her. There were just the murmurings of ghosts.

She dreamed she walked into one of the classrooms and looked towards the front of it.

There was a teacher, but she wasn't teaching anything, on account of being stuck in an egg.

"Goodness," Valentina said.

She walked to the egg. It was twice the height of the desk, plus a little bit more.

She had an umbrella with her, because it had been raining, so she rapped on the egg with its handle.

"Ah," said a woman's voice from inside. It sounded a bit embarrassed. "Valentina."

"Hm?"

"I cannot talk to you today," the teacher said. "I am stuck in an egg."

"So I witness," said Valentina. "… if you like, then I think I could crack it …"

A snort of bitter laughter. "I am the unparalleled," said the egg. "The great and terrible. The teacher, 'Mrs. Senko.' My students they fear and admire me. The world it resounds with praise for me, for my hard-headed, clear-sighted practicality. I can hardly come spilling out with the egg whites, bits of yolk in my hair."

"Uh," Valentina said.

"The notion is unthinkable; I reject it," Mrs. Senko said.

And it sounded to Valentina like she was thinking that she might just *stay* in there. "… you can't do that, Mrs. Senko," Valentina objected. "An egg's got to crack."

"That's hardly a thing to say to someone who's *in* one."

"It's how you get chickens," Valentina explained.

The egg did not respond for a time. Perhaps its teacher was thinking. Finally, Mrs. Senko said, "I shall allow you to smuggle me out. If you like. Then perhaps one day the students will crack open the egg, and find nothing but its gooey innards, and I can walk in behind them *just* as they all conclude I am dead, clear my throat, and say, 'Why is there a giant hollow egg in my classroom?' And my reputation would, you see, be preserved."

"You're a teacher!" Valentina said. A worm of laughter tickled somewhere deep down in her throat. "You shouldn't pull pranks."

"It would be very simple," Mrs. Senko argued. "You'd just have to poke two holes in the bottom of the egg and drain me out into a bottle—"

But Valentina just shook her head.

"An egg's got to crack, Mrs. Senko," she told her; and that's what she did. ... well, what she almost did. What she *nearly* did. Valentina was *certain*—

But the wing of a dark bird of nightmare passed over that dream; and the egg was, quite suddenly, empty; and Valentina was, just as swiftly, alone.

LATER VALENTINA woke up. When she realized she had woken she cried.

Oh, she didn't want to stay in *that* dream, particularly, staring at a hollow eggshell and a bunch of empty desks. It had gone cold. It had gone lonely.

... but when she was asleep, and dreaming, she could move, and it wouldn't hurt. She could look at things, and her eyes wouldn't hurt.

In her dreams, she wasn't totally defeated.

In her dreams, she wasn't responsible for anything. At most she ought to have studied. Once she woke up, she had a list of tasks as long as her arm.

In fact, the first task was to stagger over to the message board where she kept track of her tasks for the day and start crossing them off, because she wasn't going to be able to do all of them any longer.

No "sweep." No "scrub."

It hurt, but she crossed off her grandmother's bath. She had fallen asleep on the job and now she just didn't have time.

She crossed off going around wiping off everyone's foreheads.

Then she had to find out what had gotten worse while she was sleeping. No one was visibly dying, or anything, so that was good, and the house wasn't on fire, but three of her family had made a mess on their bedding.

That wasn't the catastrophe that it could have been.

Her parents had set up sickbeds for most of the family and she'd remembered, on that first day, how to set up the rest. She didn't have to tear out her hair, lug heavy people around, and change all of the bedding, just because of a mess. She just had to pull her cousin, grandmother, and father over to one side, fold over the sick-pad, change their briefs, wash what she could with a sponge, and put down a new pad to roll them back over onto, before hauling the whole thing off for washing.

Really, all of it was doable, except for the way that there was just so *much* of it, and the way she had to do it surrounded by family who were there and yet not there. How she had to live every moment surrounded by familiar faces and yet completely alone.

It weighed on her like iron manacles and an iron yoke.

She washed her hands. She splashed cold water on her face. She nearly drowned herself because it was hard to lift her head out of the sink.

Then she went and pulled her family up a little bit on the pillows, as many as she could, and gave them all a few sips of water, and prayed that because of the magic nobody would choke on it.

She lugged the stock up from the larder, poured it into a clean pot, and set it to boil.

She chopped up the vegetables, finer than ever.

She didn't bring in the laundry. That was a task she'd actually given up on. This was back in the early days of Fortitude, back when there weren't electric washers and dryers. (Heck, there wasn't even a sun in the sky.) She'd have had to lug the clothes down to the river, scrub them with sand, beat them with rocks, and warm up other rocks in the fire to dry them with, and after the first day it was clear to her that *that* was too much.

So she'd begged a neighbor for help.

He'd been surprisingly kind. Well, it had surprised *her*. He was from one of the branch families, a fourth cousin but not an actual Sosunov, and so there'd been this story running through her head that of course, it was much too much to ask him; but he'd just given her a worried look.

"If that's all you need," he said.

"It's too much," she'd said, and blinked to keep her dried-out face from crying.

Too much or too little, though, he'd done it, so all she had to do was haul the washing down to the gates and leave it there. The clean laundry was already stacked and folded there in its bins.

It was still almost too heavy.

She fell over, halfway back to the house, and she spilled it.

Right in that moment, she thought really hard about turning around, and going back to her neighbors, or maybe the whole town, for help. As she lay there, it struck her that the shame that would bring to the Sosunov family, and to her personally, seemed so *small* compared to how tired she felt.

She released the stubbornness in her that was clinging to her ongoing course, and let go of the inchoate fear of bringing outsiders in, and she felt a kind of lightness as they went, but underneath that lightness was a thing like steel.

Shame and tiredness were important, but they weren't the most important thing. The most important thing was that her Mom had already told her what she had to do.

"Be good," her mother had told her. "Keep the house, and protect it."

So Valentina didn't get up and go get help.

… it turned out she couldn't have gotten up anyway. She tried to get up and her body wasn't responding.

She fell asleep there, all her decisions irrelevant, between the front gates and the house.

SHE DREAMT she was on a ship.

She had her hands on a railing. The ship rolled. The water underneath it surged.

Next to her stood a man wearing olive and purple clothing. There was a bit of silver thread in them.

He had Riders' eyes, which Valentina found quite peculiar—they were twin gates into the night sky and scattered stars, with vague clouds of greenish-gray doubling as irises and nebulae. Where a cosmopolitan person of the modern era would politely avoid making a big deal of this, she found herself sneaking glances at them for a while.

Now and then, one of the stars in his eyes would break free of its place in the welkin and fall.

"I shouldn't be here," he said, eventually.

"You shouldn't?"

"In your dreams," he clarified. "I shouldn't be here, where you are dreaming. But I don't actually know how to get out."

"Well—" said Valentina, and then stopped. Her mother Iskra had taught her long ago how to wake up when she was caught in an unwanted dream. It was very simple. She just had to close her eyes and stand very still, and the wind would pick up and whisk her away from the dream. Ever since she learned that trick, she could get out of any dream she wanted; at least, as long as she remembered she could.

… but just when she was about to talk him through it, she realized that maybe he couldn't actually close his eyes. Maybe he could.[4] But she didn't know!

____

4 In fact, this was so.

So she just stopped there, awkwardly, until she figured out something else to say.

"Are you *sure*," she said, "you shouldn't actually be here? Because this is a rather nice view."

He looked out and up over the railing, out at the horizon.

They stared across the water at the sun.

It's not good to stare at the sun, but Valentina didn't know that. She'd *heard* of the sun, because her family came over from Earth, but she'd never actually seen it before. So she stared.

Eventually he said, "You're not meant to look at it."

"You just don't like to have fun," she said.

He snorted.

She looked at him.

"One day," he said, "you will be sighing at me, because I haven't put in enough time in my studies, and I will remind you that you said that. I will say, 'Ah, but Valya, my darling, you have been very clear that I am an old fuddy-duddy who doesn't even like fun, so I can't imagine what you think I've been doing.'"

She scrunched up her face. She mocked him with the set of her mouth and her eyebrows. "'My darling?'"

"Well," he said, "you'll be ever so old at the time."

"Cre-*e*-py," she said.

She looked away, and he laughed.

"What?"

"You're adorable," he said. "That's absolutely hilarious. May I ask you, when is this?"

"That kind of thing isn't important," Valentina said, because she honestly wasn't sure of the year. She elbowed him. She pointed out at the sun. "Can you tell me, what *is* it?"

He hesitated.

Then he said, softly, "It's a terrible curse."

His face was wistful, maybe with a hint of adoration on it, as he stared at the horizon and the sun. His tone was fond. He didn't look or sound like somebody talking about a terrible curse, but there wasn't any obvious insincerity in his words either; a bit of humor, at most.

"A long time ago," he said, "the sun came to the lands around Fortitude, and from that day, the people of those lands ceased to see things as they truly are, and instead saw—something else. Something dangerous and twisted. A ... sharp and bright knife of dream. But that hasn't happened yet, Valya, has it? You're still in the dark."

"I don't understand what you mean," she said. "I've got lanterns."

"Mn," he said.

Then he laughed.

"I am so terrible at this," he said. "I actually promised you I would wait until you were older, but I don't know how to get out of your dream."

"Oh?"

This caught Valentina's attention. She turned slowly away from the sun and she looked at him. She tried to see his face but her gaze was full of bright spots. She put one thing and another together.

"You're a real person," she said. "Not just a dream-thing."

He nodded. Then he hesitated. For a moment he almost shook his head, too, but he didn't. He nodded again.

"You're here," she said, "by the Sosunov magic."

"I am."

She chewed on her lip. "Tell me where your body is," she said. "I'll have to put you up with the others. Oh, God, I hope you're not totally gross."

"That won't be happening," he said.

"You're—"

She worked out the theory in her head.

"You're some kind of weird cousin," she said. "You have a weird eye problem and you have this dream of the sun. And because you're weird they didn't tell me about you, only now, you're asleep and in the hands of the witch. And you've torn yourself free and we've met here, on this boat, but you still can't wake up. That's fine. So tell me where you *are* and I'll *help* you."

"That's not it," he said.

She frowned at him.

She leaned her head down on the railing. "I'm so tired," she said, even though she wasn't. She felt light. She felt happy and clean. And she almost cried as she realized it. "I'm going to have to wake up."

"There's a witch?" he said.

"It doesn't matter," she said. "You can't be a Sosunov. That was wrong. I'm just dreaming nonsense. God. So stupid. Just look at your *eyes*."

"That's awfully difficult," he sighed.

"Listen," she said. "It's very easy, but I don't know how you'd do it. You just have to close your eyes, like this."

She turned to him. She had her eyes closed, though the light of the sun still shone in brightly right through the lids.

"And then you stand very still."

She could hear the wind roaring. It fluttered the sails, then they went still and taut like her body. Then the wind seized her and it flung her awake.

THE STOCK HAD BOILED over. The kitchen was filthy and the soup tasted awful. She still ate it, and fed it to the rest of her family. She fed it to them in little sips so that they wouldn't choke.

In the modern day you'd want to go to a doctor.

In the modern day if somebody was asleep like that, you wouldn't really be able to feed broth to them. There wouldn't be any good way to do it. They would choke no matter how careful you were. You wouldn't want to try to take care of them on your own. You'd want to take advantage of the miracles of modern medicine.

Valentina leaned on the witch's good graces instead.

She prayed to the witch, quietly, before each of the feedings. She said, "I don't know what you're doing to them. I don't know why you're keeping my family locked up in dreams. But their bodies will die if I don't feed them. So please, miss witch, sir, don't let them choke."

And maybe it was because of that and maybe it wasn't, but they ate OK. They drank OK. There were a few scares, and she had to go outside and scream for a bit after a chunk of carrot almost closed the throat of her mother, but it was mostly OK.

And afterwards, she sat there by her mother's bedside. Even with other things to do, even with other things she *had* to do, she stayed there for hours, and she put her hand in the stiff, senseless hand of her mother, and she cleaned the sweat from her mother's forehead, and she told her mother about the dream.

"There was the sun," she said. "And this man. And it was all, it was all so pretty."

She asked her mother, "Did you ever see the sun?"

Then, because no answer was given, she said, "It wasn't like it was in the storybooks. It was so very bright, and it wasn't painted at all."

She leaned her head against the arm of her mother.

"When I was a child," she said, because she'd forgotten already that she was still a child then, "and you would come into my dreams, and send away all the nightmares, and we'd play in all the strange worlds that I made, you said, 'It's because I love you, Valyusha.'"

She looked aimlessly out around the room.

"That you could use the magic to visit me," she said, "for that you loved me, and for no reason else. That you could tear through the walls between your dreams and mine, no, not tear, simply step over them, lifted by love."

She choked out, "Where are all of you now?"

It wasn't fair. She already knew that. It wasn't fair, from the moment she said it. She knew why none of her family had come to visit her dreams. She *knew* why her dreams had no one in them that she'd ever met. The Sosunov magic was defeated and broken. The Sosunovs were bound, trapped in dreams by a heron, and their love was put to sleep or otherwise kept from breaking them out.

She thought, if anything, it must be the love of her family that served as her shelter.

She tried to think that:

That it must be because her family *loved* her that the heron-witch hadn't claimed her. That it must be because of that love that the heron-witch had backed away from enchanting her. Valentina tried to think that that was because of her family's love.

The thought didn't stick, though. She could think it but she couldn't feel it.

What she *felt* was completely alone.

AFTER A WHILE Valentina stood up. She closed her eyes. She made a fist and put her hand at her chest.

She did something that was very difficult, but also important. It was another task from the crisis manual, and her Mom and Dad had emphasized it over and over again. She took a deep breath and she let go of the shame for everything she'd left undone and was not doing, and she closed her eyes and stood very still until she felt sure it was gone from her.

Then she went back to the endless work that she still had to do.

She managed. Until an hour past midnight, she managed; then she took herself to her bed.

IN HER DREAMS, she was in a natural cavern. The walls were vast, water-slick stone. There was a passage behind her and a gateway before her; the gateway was shattered, the doors of it were broken, and beyond it lay a dusty grey valley under a great golden star.

A teenaged girl stood before those gates. She glanced back.

"Oh," she said, looking forward again. "Great-gran Valentina."

Valentina shuddered. She shook her head.

She stepped forward. She hid behind the older girl and peeked forward, staring out at the star.

The older girl said: "I ought to just go. You know? I ought to step forward. But I can't. I'm afraid."

"My name," Valentina said, carefully, "is Valentina Grigorievna, but I'm not hardly anybody's great-gran."

"Uh-huh?" The older girl looked over. "Really?"

She glanced her up and down.

"Well," she said, "that's as it may be. I'm Aprosya, anyway—Aprosinya Alexandrovna Sosunova."

Valentina mostly ignored her and pointed forward. "What is that?"

"Mm?" Aprosinya looked blankly at Valentina, then out through the gate again. "That? It's ... it's everything, I guess. The richest soil and the deepest dark; the land beyond the boundaries of despair. The land beyond the lands of life where you can crack the egg of who you are."

"Hmm."

"I want to go there," Aprosinya said, in a small voice. "I *do.* I worked so hard for it. Just—"

"Just?"

She gestured broadly.

"I got scared, because it's death, isn't it? I mean—doesn't it have to be? You go there, and you die, and you don't come back.

"I got scared.

"I thought I'd dream about it, before I went forward. I said, I would wake up the magic in me, and I would dream again; and I would find somebody I loved, and I would *ask* them. Not *her.* I would ask *them,* I would say to them, 'o, how can I step forward?'"

She swallowed.

"Because, great-gran Valentina, it honestly feels like I'll rip myself out when I do."

"Huh," said Valentina.

"... what do you think?" Aprosinya said.

"It's pretty," Valentina said.

"Huh? Uh." Aprosinya said. After a while, she said, "Uh, I guess."

Valentina stepped forward. She set her hand on the air between the shattered gates. She left it there; it was supported there, as if it lay against cool stone.

"I'm all alone," Valentina said.

A wry smile twisted Aprosinya's face. "Don't go through those gates because you're lonely, Valya," she said. Like she was quoting, or nostalgic. "—that isn't what they're for."

Then she laughed.

"Sorry."

"Sorry?"

"It's nothing," Aprosinya said, and her eyes were livelier.

"There's a witch," Valentina said.

"Ah?"

"She's got my whole family," Valentina said. "She's got all of them, they're asleep, and she's ... doing witch stuff with their dreams."

"Oh," Aprosinya said, and made a face. "*Her.*"

"Huh?"

"We've met," Aprosinya summarized.

"... oh," said Valentina. "Do you ... do you know how to beat her?"

Her voice was eager, desperate almost. She'd forgotten, by then, that she was only dreaming; had forgotten that this was just metaphors and images; and dared to imagine that Aprosinya was someone real, someone who loved her, or someone that she loved. But Aprosinya didn't seem to catch the desperation in that voice, or maybe she was just too old and too sophisticated to be concerned about it: too blind to the importance of other people, maybe, too focused on the gate and what lay beyond. "I don't know how to beat her," Aprosinya said.

"Oh."

"For years she hurt me," Aprosinya said. "I struggled for *so long* to get rid of her, to be the one that *beat* her, and then—

"It all got taken out of my hands."

"Oh," Valentina said again. She blinked at Aprosinya for a moment. Then her face fell. She felt hope, that had been beating strongly in her chest, fade away. It left her like air out of an unknotted balloon. "That isn't even the same witch."

"No?"

"My witch," Valentina said. "Well, not mine, but my witch, she—she puts people to sleep and they just stay there. She doesn't really *hurt* you."

"... I guess," Aprosinya said.

Her attention drifted back to the gate, and Valentina's followed it. Valentina chewed on her lip. "Right," she said. A resolution formed. She picked up Aprosinya's right hand in one of hers. She pulled her over to the gates. She touched it to the air, where hers had been. "You see," she said, "it's all hard and stopped up anyway—"

But in this she was wrong. It was astonishing:

It astonished her.

Aprosinya's front finger simply passed through.

"Oh," Valentina said blankly. "Uh. This, then. You can just go on."

Aprosinya laughed, a little. "Oh, really? Is that all?"

Then, after a moment, she nodded. She stepped a little forward, turned, and leaned her back against one of the broken gates while she ruffled Valentina's hair.

"Eh, you're so *little*," she said, a goofy smile wide on her face, before she slipped away.

After a few minutes it occurred to Valentina that she was alone again. She stepped forward; or tried to step forward, at least; but just hit her head and arm hard on the air of the gate.

SHE woke to a knocking sound. There were two to three taps, then a pause, then the sound repeated. She licked her lips and shook her head blearily.

The tempo of the knocking varied, now faster, now slower.

It seemed to her that it sounded irritated.

She stumbled to the door and opened it, but there was nothing behind it. She leaned against the handle and looked around. When she finally saw the source of the knocking, outside the great window, she felt a rush of heartache.

It was the beak of a heron, tapping on the glass.

"How—" she said. She realized it couldn't hear her. She licked her lips again. She cleared her throat. She went over and she rolled up the window. "How did you get onto the grounds?"

The bird turned its head and it eyed her. Then, swiftly, it turned and it pecked her hard in the center of her head.

"Pancake fucker," she swore, reeling back. "Dammit. Ow!"

Its wings were spread against the sides of the window. It was coming forward. It was wiggling its way inside, and there was something wrong with that motion. It wasn't natural, it wasn't a bird's proper motion. It came in through the window like a fish, or a worm, and not a bird. It was maybe even like soup bubbling over or like bread surging out of a too-small pan inside the oven. Valentina made a plan in her head where she'd slam the window back down on top of it, but she was too little and the way it moved was too eerie. She wanted to slam the window on it, truly she wanted to, but instead she found herself stuck. Her toes felt too heavy. Her body wouldn't obey her. She just couldn't move.

Then it was inside.

It stalked proudly towards her.

Valentina fell down, and she grasped for her magic to defend her, but she wasn't nearly good enough with the Sosunov magic to do anything useful with it in the waking world, and it's not like it would have helped her much even if she were.

She choked on a sob.

Then she gave in. She lowered her head. She couldn't take any more.

"Fine," she said. "Put me to sleep, then. You win."

She almost looked forward to it. At least, she thought, it would mean she could rest now. But the heron didn't put her to sleep. Instead it stared at her with naked hostility for a long time, and then it spoke, and its words were strange to her: they were like a grinding of the gears of the world, like a voice lain over the world, and finally she realized that she did not so much hear them as *perceive* them, that they were an emanation from her awareness of the witch.

"They will die," said the witch, **"if this continues."**

Quietly, Valentina said, "I believe in them."

The witch looked at her.

"They'll beat you," Valentina said. "Mom and Da and grandmere and great-uncle and great-gran, they'll all *beat* you. They won't die."

"They will die," said the witch, **"at some inconvenience to myself, because you are one small Valentina and not enough to keep this house. Thus I have decided that I shall offer aid."**

Valentina hesitated. She said, "Witches don't do that sort of thing."

Outside, she heard a sound like a helicopter landing, though she had never heard a helicopter; a sound like fire crackling; a sound like thunder, though stranger—and when her ears and head finally wrapped some sense around it, and she looked to the window and she saw, a thousand birds were landing in the yard.

"A thousand birds," confirmed the witch, **"to help you keep this house."**

Valentina stared blankly. She was too tired to really feel any relief;

instead, all she could feel was a sonorous dizziness and a grinding sense of mental incapacity as she tried to figure out how the birds would help. The witch did not wait for her to finish processing the matter; she went stalking through the house, and Valentina followed after her. When they reached the dining hall, the witch looked back at Valentina and added a belated clause to her previous sentence: **"and kindly make a cup of tea for me; I shall be staying in, I think, a while."**

Valentina didn't know what to do, so she bent her head. She turned. She went out into the court. She stared at the birds. She said, "Um," and, "you can start on the sweeping, I guess. And bring in some firewood."

And she met the bright gaze of a little wren that stood staring her eye to eye and asked it, "Do you know how to put on the water for a cup of tea?"

Then she shook her head. "That was a dumb question," she told herself. "Really."

She glared at a heron, because it was both too much like the witch to get any sympathy and because it hadn't even started looking for a broom: "And you," she said, pointing, while it backed up, its wings flapping. "You, can you change the beds?"

This wasn't very good magically summoned domestic helper heron management on her part.

She really should have handled it differently.

By the time she found it later, tugging helplessly against a draw-sheet, its beak was chipped and there were feathers everywhere. That was when she realized that she'd have to make an actual plan.

SHE'D BROUGHT the witch tea, before that. She'd dumped the tea-set on the table, poured tea out into a bird-bowl, and staggered away. She'd gone out and stared at the courtyard full of birds that were sweeping, at the untidy bowl of firewood that others were building, shivered in confusion, and gone in to tend to her family's health.

There were birds everywhere. There were feathers and droppings everywhere.

It seemed a little silly to be doing her own work in the midst of a horde of magical servants, but no matter how hard she tried to be a marvelous heroine who'd instantly know how to handle this kind of thing she still found herself at a loss. She comforted herself with her routine for a while, and *tried*.

Eventually, that led her to the corner of her mother's room, in a chair, with a notebook, having moved on from trying to be a heroine to pretending to be the kind of adult Sosunov who could come up with an elaborate household management plan involving large numbers of birds.

After a while, this effort was interrupted.

A bell rang out through the house, once, twice, thrice. She ignored it.

A wren fluttered down from a shelf and pecked at her shoulder.

"Oh," Valentina said, after a moment. "The witch wants me?"

She pulled herself to her feet. She stared blankly at the notebook she'd been trying to write on. Then she went to deal with the witch.

She had to kick firewood out of the way. There was too much of it in the courtyard.

"There's too much firewood," she said to the witch.

"That's one of your waking world difficulties?" asked the witch.

"... I guess?" said Valentina.

"Well," said the witch, **"I'm sure the birds can do something about it."**

Valentina waved her hands, then subsided.

"Valentina."

"... yes?"

"I will be taking my breakfast in four hours. I should like something with fish. And possibly frogs?"

"OK."

"You will join me," said the witch.

Valentina put the notebook on the table. She shook her hands in the air. "This isn't in the emergency manual," she wailed.

The witch glared at her.

"Four hours," she said. **"Please be prompt."**

WHEN VALENTINA SLEPT it was dreamless. When she woke it was to a sharp pain in her cheek. It repeated, until she slapped at it, and accidentally came in contact with a beak.

She recoiled.

She scrambled across— "Why am I sleeping in the laundry?" she asked, aloud.

"I am not accustomed to waking people," said the witch, irritably. **"And now I have done it twice. You are tempting me to simply banish you to eternal dreams and hope that the birds are wise enough to take care of you all. And where is my breakfast, child?"**

"Um," said Valentina.

Horrible visions of swarms of birds trying and failing to change bedpads and cook broth for breakfast warred in her mind with the opportunity to stay asleep. Her vision, drowning in her tiredness, was full of sparks and lines of light.

"I'm sorry," she said, finally. "I fell asleep. What time is it?"

"More than four hours," said the witch. Then, awkwardly, **"I do not know how to tell time from the clock."**

"I'll ... I'll make something," said Valentina.

She dragged herself to her feet.

"See that you do."

Valentina went outside. She pushed the door open. Firewood fell. "Stop," she said to the birds, helplessly. "Just ... stop. No more firewood. No more sweeping. Someone ... go to the market and get ..."

She looked back at the witch, who only glared at her unhelpfully.

"Eight pounds perch," she said. "And some fish heads. Mind you don't eat any. Eight onions, eight carrots, some parsley and celery and dill. And chop up the firewood and store it in the shed."

The birds were just looking at her.

One or two of them seemed like they were going to move, or at least do *something*, but they didn't. She stared at them blankly. Frustration and anger built up inside her—then faded awkwardly away as she, quite suddenly, understood.

"There's money in the dish by the kitchen table," she said. "Do you need me to write out a list?"

And a tern was brushing against her leg like a cat, and an egret had tilted its head, almost eagerly, to one side.

"Fine," she said, and took a step back as the birds almost swarmed her, as she was suddenly at the center of a swarm before they were perched on her, beside her, around her. "I'll write it out. And you—"

She pointed at a magpie.

"You're smart. You look smart. Figure out which ones can break up the firewood without hurting their beaks. And get someone to bring me a chart."

She found a stub of pencil and paper. She wrote out the list. And before she'd even half-finished it, while her eyes were scanning the kitchen, and while a distant part of the back of her mind was wailing because there is no way to keep anything sanitary when surrounded by hundreds of birds, she realized that the witch was staring at her, in the middle of an empty place in the swarm.

"What?" Valentina snapped.

"I also like biscuits," said the witch.

"Then wake up my Dad," said Valentina. "Wake up my Dad. He's got the best recipe."

"**Kuh,**" snorted the witch. And: "**I will drag it from him. I will give it to you. You will make them.**"

"Fine," whimpered Valentina.

She caught the eye of a gull. "You," she said. "Search the house. Make sure nobody's dying or dead. If someone's in trouble, come tell me. *I don't know how to organize birds.*"

"**Just do as you've been,**" snapped the witch, and she turned, fluttered her wings, and flew to the top of the temple; but Valentina didn't think that would, in the end, be enough.

THERE WAS fish stock left. It hadn't been ruined. When she'd sent the kitchen birds off to the market and went out to drag the stock up, she'd found two vast flocks lined up and waiting, with the wren, so fluffed out and proud she could only think it was smiling, pacing back and forth at their head.

"Oh," said Valentina. "Thank you. Yes. You can be my lieutenant. Did you get someone all started on the firewood?"

It looked at her. It shrugged.

"I need someone to bring up the fish stock," she said. "My arms are like noodles."

The wren thought about this. It turned. It looked at the birds.

Thinking agitated it.

After a long moment, she understood the gist of its confusion. "Clever birds," she said, "to tie string through the handles and put on a cover. Small birds, to keep it from tipping. Tall birds to drag it up the stairs by the strings. And then some more small birds to scrub up the pantry after, with rags and pipe water and soap."

She muttered.

"You're magic birds," she said. "I shouldn't have to figure all of this out."

She stalked away. She dug out some leeks, tossed them in a heavy-bottomed soup pot, and started sweating them in butter. Spotting a sandpiper just standing around watching, she asided, "You'd probably just sauté them if you were cooking these, right?"

The sandpiper piped, *twee-wee.*

"Right," she said. "'Cause the thing about sandpipers is, you don't know proper cooking. But you have to let them sweat. You have to let them cook slowly, in their own juices, not like you barbarian birds and your barbarian shoreline sautéing. If you want a proper ukha anyhow. You don't want them all brown!"

There was a thumping at the door, followed by a thumping at her heart: *the witch!*

But it wasn't. It was six egrets, dragging the stock.

"Oh," she said, disentangling the egrets from the string, which had somehow wound itself nearly entirely around them. "Thank you. I don't suppose you could find some clean wet cloths and wipe down people's foreheads with them?"

She chopped up some celery. She added it to the pot. She wiped her forehead with a sleeve.

"Like that," she said, vaguely, in case the egrets were still watching, and added, "I do hope that they come back from the market all right."

It was a little embarrassing, because she'd hoped to add the onions and carrots right then.

Instead, since she couldn't, she just poured in the stock. She added some salt and some pepper. She looked around for bay leaves and finally banged her head against the counter, twice, because she'd completely forgot.

"You aren't a woodpecker," the witch informed her. She'd come back down to the ground.

"I know that," said Valentina, after a dizzying moment of uncertainty. "I'm going to be at least a three-quarter hour here."

"I have the recipe," said the witch, **"for the biscuits."**

And something in Valentina snapped at that. Something in her broke when she realized that the witch could go in and get her Dad's secrets from him and she couldn't even get him to wake up; and there was a kitchen knife in her hand, and she'd turned, and she'd flung it, right at the witch.

The witch's wings spread. They flared. The knife went past her. The witch danced backwards, hissing, and that was the only reason that it cut her.

Valentina's aim wasn't up to it, Valentina herself wasn't up to it, it wouldn't even have *touched* the witch if she had ignored the throw.

But it isn't safe to throw a knife in a kitchen, not ever.

It just isn't something you do.

The witch danced backwards, fluttering away from Valentina, and when she did so she stepped on the knife, and the knife turned under her foot and it cut her, and her foot began to bleed, ebbing dark blood.

The witch's hissing grew louder. It was like a tea pot that someone'd forgotten. Then the witch kicked away the knife, shrieked, and tucked her head under a wing.

"You shall not kill me," whispered the witch. **"Kill me and they'll die. Every last one, Valentina."**

"Just leave me be!" cried Valentina.

The witch turned. The witch hobbled out.

After the stock had come to a boil, Valentina reduced the heat. She covered it. She set it to simmer. And then, even though she'd told the witch to leave her alone, she stalked out to find her.

"Let me see that," she said. "If you walk on it it'll just get infected."

The witch was crouched on a pile of firewood. Her foot was bleeding all over the wood.

"You have to clean it and wrap it," said Valentina, helplessly. "Not … rub it on dirty wood that a thousand birds have been pooping on."

"I knew that," sulked the horrible witch.

The witch snapped at Valentina anyway the first two times she approached, but on the third approach she let Valentina clean the wound.

Valentina wrapped the cut. She knotted it. She lowered her head, almost leaned on the witch's leg for a moment and rested. But she didn't fall asleep there. Not with the soup already started. Instead she staggered back into the kitchen.

It was just in time for the perch to arrive.

"THIS is not from the market," sighed Valentina. "Did you birds lose the money?"

She cleaned the perch. She gutted it. She threw the guts to her helpers, even though her Mom had always said that throwing fish guts was rude. She sniffed the soup and she thought it was ready, so she tossed in the fish and let it poach in the soup.

The birds brought in the carrots and onions. One of them brought in what she judged to be the grocer's wool cap.

She stared at it for a while.

"Either this is a protest against the grocer's behavior," she said, "or one of you has dramatically misunderstood the making of soup."

She thought it rather too late to add anything to the ukha, so she made a side carrot salad, instead.

Finally she staggered into the dining hall with it.

She set it out.

She set the table.

And she called to the witch.

"THERE'LL BE A SALAD," she said, "in an hour. It's cooling."

"I told you," said the witch. **"I want biscuits."**

"There are a thousand birds in my house," said Valentina, "and everyone's dying."

The witch peered at her.

Then, delicately, the witch sipped at the soup. **"It's good,"** she said, as if in surprise.

"It's 'cause I left the heads in," Valentina said. "You leave the fish heads in, and then you'll know when it's ready because the eyes pop— why am I even *talking* to you?"

"I suppose," said the witch, **"we are now family."**

It was such a dissonant statement that Valentina's grip on reality faltered. She put down her spoon. Tears slipped down her face, she couldn't control them, and the world seemed all of the sudden quite far away, and her ears started ringing, and she put her head on the table very slowly and her shoulders shook and her teeth were gritting together and she made not a sound with her sobs, until:

"Sleep, then," said the witch, and she fell into dreams.

SHE FOUND herself sitting on the edge of a desk, her legs kicking, while a severe-looking woman in black Victorian costume scribbled on a schedule book nearby.

"Ah," the woman said, and Valentina recognized her as Mrs. Senko. "Valentina."

She turned her chair. She set down her quill.

She folded her hands in her lap.

"Mrs. Senko," said Valentina. Then, hesitantly, "You're not in the inside of an egg."

"Certainly not," agreed Mrs. Senko.

There was an awkward pause.

"Yes," agreed Valentina. "Certainly."

She hopped down. She looked around.

"This is—"

"The Administrative Complex," said Mrs. Senko. "I am preparing my lessons. Although, well, I suppose I must be *dreaming* that I am preparing my lessons, on account of:

"You are here."

Mrs. Senko pressed her lips together.

"It is a waste of effort," she said, irritably, "since I shall have to check it all over carefully, and from memory now, once I have waked."

And something in that prompts this from Valentina: "Mrs. Senko, if you had to— I mean, if you were taking care of fifteen comatose people, and a large complex of buildings, and you only had a thousand bird-helpers to do it with, um, I mean—"

Mrs. Senko's eyebrows were up.

"I mean, birds of, kind of, like, various sizes and capabilities, I mean, what would you do?"

"Sell them to the circus," snapped Mrs. Senko, "and use the money to hire hospice workers and maids."

"What?"

"Seriously, Valentina," said Mrs. Senko. "You can't run a household with birds of various sizes and capabilities. The idea is absurd."

Valentina's mouth was open. She closed it. Then she said, "It's not … they're not *my* birds."

"Ah," said Mrs. Senko.

She pursed her lips.

"I stand by my statement," said Mrs. Senko. "Your fairy godmother or whatever else you have that is giving you a thousand birds to work with has gone entirely out of its senses."

"It's a witch," explained Valentina.

"Well, sell her, too," said Mrs. Senko. "Circuses can always use a good witch."

Valentina wrestled with this thought. She squinted with one eye, then the other. She said, "I don't think she'd let me. She's very forceful."

"Valentina," said Mrs. Senko, "you're aware that a coma is a serious thing, aren't you?"

"She's spelled them all to sleep," Valentina said.

"A medical condition," Mrs. Senko emphasized, "requiring more in the way of treatment than this nonsense about birds?"

"I can't *help it!*" wailed Valentina.

"Weak-minded poppycock," muttered Mrs. Senko.

"A doctor can't help somebody that's been witch-got," said Valentina. "And I can't— I don't know who to trust, I can't—"

She kind of trailed off there. The truth is, under Mrs. Senko's skeptical look, she was a little bit embarrassed to say that, because not trusting people was a decision she'd made back at the very beginning of things, based on fears that had broken and situations that had changed, and she'd never gotten around to going back and revisiting that decision, only, now that she did, she couldn't really prove it made sense.

"I ..." Valentina said.

"Valentina," said Mrs. Senko, "I believe that we can both agree that this situation is an exception to the normative Fortitudian housekeeping expectations."

The girl gave her a blank stare.

"I mean," said Mrs. Senko, "while keeping house on your own while your family is off on some senseless adventure is only to be expected at your age, doing so while they are in serious medical extremity is over and beyond the call of duty; for the love of Heaven, get someone there who can help."

"Could you—" started Valentina, and then faltered.

"Complete sentences, dear," suggested Mrs. Senko.

"Could *you* help?"

Mrs. Senko's eyes flicked up and down Valentina. "Unlikely," she said. "I'm fairly certain you haven't looked that young in centuries."

"I've only ever looked younger," countered Valentina.

"What I mean," Mrs. Senko said, "is, I'm afraid that even if I woke up right this second and left before morning, I don't think I'd arrive in time to be of any use. You're going to have to go into town and ask somebody."

There was a knot of pride and fear in Valentina, as she heard those words.

It made it hard to breathe.

"You won't be betraying the pride of the Sosunov family," said Mrs. Senko, almost gently. "You won't be failing your parents. You won't be showing yourself a bad daughter who can't even keep a house under control for a few weeks. They'll be proud of you for trying your best but they won't be ashamed of you for not being able. You're just one small Valentina, dear. It is too much."

"What would you," said Valentina. "I mean, what would you do, if you had a witch?"

"A witch," said Mrs. Senko, thoughtfully, "that came in from the Lake, and cast your family into sleep, so ... she could nurture herself in the dreams of them as if they were an egg? A heron, hungry for human wisdom; a heron that had tasted of *understanding* and *awareness* when it ate somebody's dreams—and who grew addicted to it, then, grew to *crave* it, realized that it could not turn back and fall back into the senselessness of the animals, and so decided to *take* from it what the world had chosen not to give?"

"... maybe?" said Valentina.

"Mm," sighed Mrs. Senko. "I'd probably tell her to come to my school and learn it all properly, rather than stealing it—wisdom, I mean, sense, and the like—from fully-developed adults. I'd say, why use human dreams as your medium when you've already got a perfectly good mind? Then, when she showed up for classes, I'd pin her wings to the wall, cut her throat, point her head so it could look at the blackboard, and let her bleed out while the students were watching. So that they could learn an important lesson, about life."

Valentina shivered. "I wouldn't want you to do that."

"Well, you're a good Fortitude kid," said Mrs. Senko. "You're all basically dumber than rocks."

Valentina laughed. She couldn't help it.

"I guess that's so," she agreed. She kicked her feet.

Mrs. Senko seemed to be struggling against a smile. Then she sighed. "This once," she said, "I will step forward and be the representation and totemic avatar of a cruel, uncaring adult society that will nevertheless throw reluctant bits and scraps of half-hearted assistance to the younger generation, now and then, to keep their loyalty and innocent subservience intact."

Valentina looked puzzled.

"I mean," said Mrs. Senko, "that I can help you. Rather, I *will* help you. Despite your atavistic attachment to family pride and your aversion to blood. The fundamental problems you have are two-fold: that birds are a fundamentally chaotic medium for operation, and, your own inability to grasp the totality of the work before you until after it's slipped out of your hands."

Valentina continued to look puzzled.

"... don't sweat it," said Mrs. Senko. "A thousand birds, you say?"

Valentina straightened. "Yeah!" she said. "They're mostly like titmice and stuff but there's a fair few of the tall 'uns from the mangroves."

"Mm," said Mrs. Senko. "And fifteen sleepers, one young girl, and a witch."

She sketched idly on a slab of white cardboard in front of her; the ink that bled from her pen feathered out from the passing of her hand, coalescing into ever-more-detailed letters, notations, and lines.

"The simplest method," she said, "for getting birds to do paperwork—"

The word "no!" burst from Valentina, in horror.

"Yes," said Mrs. Senko.

"That's not what I need here," said Valentina, with some confidence.

"You'll have to trust me," said Mrs. Senko, the ink flowing out to form a diagram of a prototype bird reporting and record-keeping system. "I could hardly be known everywhere for my hard-headed practicality if I didn't know exactly how to handle a flock of birds. ... though you're probably going to forget all this when you wake up, which makes this whole thing rather pointless—"

"You're just a dream figment, Mrs. Senko," Valentina informed her. "There is no greater devotion."

Mrs. Senko's lips twitched.

"Well, then," she said. The quill pushed harder into the cardboard; the scratching of her hand against it left furrows. She paused for a moment in thought, then brightened. "Ah!"

She scribbled; she made a flourish; she shoved it hard into Valentina's arms.

"Here is my notion," she said. "I am told that it's easier to remember your dreams if you write them down as soon as possible after waking. Herewith, my brilliance: child, go to the classroom and copy this over four to five times *while still asleep*. You shall remember it with such crispness that it shall be even as more real to you than the black behind your eyes."

Valentina stared at it.

"Pardon," she said, "but—"

"It's a complete pluravian patient/facility management plan," explained Mrs. Senko. "Now go! Spit-spot! Time's a wasting, and—as you can see—I've only allocated so many hours for your dreams."

"Thank you," said Valentina. She hugged it to her. She brightened.

"You won't be thanking me," muttered Mrs. Senko, "by the time you're on the fourth copy."

But she was smiling, and Valentina was smiling, and Mrs. Senko spoke louder as she said, "Mind you don't get lost in the Complex, now," and Valentina went scampering away.

THE FUNDAMENTAL BASIS of an avian reporting system is small, smooth river stones. A bird marks the completion of each assigned task by carrying the stone to its bucket; *management*, for the birds in charge, becomes little more than a visual scan of the buckets, which easily reveals which birds and even which task groups are ahead and which are falling behind. If one has access to quality machining—rare in tasks relying on large flocks of birds—then one can even use the buckets for switching, e.g., allowing a certain weight to depress a lever or rotate a wheel to indicate changes in task.

Valentina, of course, did not have access to quality machining. Realistically, without finely-balanced wheels, stones, buckets, and levers, the responsiveness of the system would come mostly from her. *Micromanagement,* Mrs. Senko had written, in her fine, neat hand, *is regrettably inevitable; I can arrange the birds into a smoothly-functioning engine, but eventually there will be a series of critical errors where chaos infiltrates the system and spreads in geometric progression; the birds cannot possibly fix this, and I doubt the witch has a head for it, so resolving that will depend, in each case, on you.*

She copied it down.

The plan filled seven blackboards—thirty, somewhere in the early part of the fifth copy, by the time pigeons sang her awake.

The witch's voice echoed: **"Today there must be something with frogs."**

VALENTINA CLIMBED up to the rooftop, later, where the witch stood staring out at the Lake.

She sat down on the roof's edge.

The witch turned her head.

"If you fell asleep here," noted the witch, **"you would tumble down, down, and crack your head on the courtyard below."**

Valentina gripped the edge with both her hands tightly and looked down.

"Yeah," she said. "I probably would."

The witch looked back away. **"That is why I do not sleep, myself. I** do not have the knack for it, and not doing it has kept my head from cracking."

"I'm told," Valentina said, "that if you don't sleep, you'll get a little bit ..."

"Crazy?"

"Yeah," muttered Valentina.

"That's why it's important," the witch conceded, **"that there be a Sosunov family. To guard the dreams of the people of Fortitude and make sure their sleep is safe."**

"That's what my Dad says," agreed Valentina.

The wind blew a few leaves past them.

"I'm kind of," she said. She thought. "... surprised. I mean, that you got them. We were supposed to be strong."

"What is strength?" asked the witch. **"We are all strong, and we are all weak. We discover what we are when we see something else; it breaks over our horizon, looms above us like ... like a giant star, and shows us by its light that we are dark or by its dark that we are light.**

"When I saw your great-grandfather's mind for the first time, it was the lantern-light to me. It was like the clouds that had been drifting through me, gray and dark, were suddenly brightening; were turning red, pink, gold. The sky that spread inside of me was filling up with light.

"But ... 'strength?' 'Weakness?' I have not seen them. Only the great big field of shiny things that is the world."

"Oh," Valentina said.

She thought about this.

"Why haven't you eaten me yet?"

The witch was still as stone, as if she'd become a gargoyle on the Sosunov roof. Her eyes were the color of the night. There was something brittle in her reply: **"I wish I could."**

"Oh?"

"I am hardly going to squeeze myself into a brain that small,

Valentina. That would be folly. I would pop and my feathers would fly out. And who would cook my frogs?"

"Oh."

"... I cannot eat you," said the witch. **"I cannot devour you, cannot knock you out and culture myself as a thing that grows within your dreams. But I wish I could. I have looked at your dreams; do you know, that they are *vibrant?*"**

Valentina waved a hand, vaguely, being the kind of kid who mostly just approximated what other people were saying in her head when she didn't understand it. "You have a lot of birds," she said.

The witch fluttered her wings in a shrug.

"There are more if you need them."

"I think we're good," Valentina said.

"Oh?"

"Though, I guess, commanding tons of birds wouldn't be so bad."

The witch was still on her previous question. **"You've worked things out, then?"**

Valentina shrugged.

The witch glanced down over the courtyard. She watched the birds bustling about. She said, **"And my meal?"**

"I don't know any frog meals," said Valentina. "So I just asked them to catch some, and I'll stick 'em in pies."

"Eh," said the witch. **"Well enough. In the future, though, I shall expect research."**

"Sure," Valentina said. "I'll put some in the salad."

Later, she realized that research wasn't a vegetable; or at least, not any one that she knew. For right then they just stared out at the Lake until Valentina asked:

"Will you give them back?"

"Eh?"

"Will you give me my family back, Miss Witch? Won't you? Couldn't you?"

And the air was still and quite cold for a while.

VALENTINA DREAMT she stood on a clock tower overlooking a campus on a moonless night—not that she had a proper sense, back then, of "night" or "moon." She dreamt she was older, and taller, and her hair hung down beside her in a sable braid, and her dress was gold, and lamplight glittered through the world below like stars. Great hands counted out the time beneath her; behind her was an airy loft, and bells.

"Oh, goodness," she said. "I'd best not fall."

"Hm?"

He was there behind her. He held her arm and the brace of the window. She turned and she recognized him, in his clothing of olive and purple with its silver piping and his Rider eyes.

"Not *here*," she said, snorting, pulling her arm out of his and leaning forward to stare down at the campus below her. "I mean, in real life. I'm on a roof!"

"Oh," he said. Then, more firmly, "yes. Do not fall off of roofs. What are you doing falling asleep up there anyway?"

"I think," she said, "it's your fault. I got eaten by your dream."

He looked guilty.

"Really," he said, "I didn't think that was possible—"

"No," she said. "I mean—"

She waved a hand around, almost losing her balance.

"I was wishing," she said, "that I knew what to do."

And their words might not quite not be enough here, so I think that I must explain them.

He was picturing dreams eddying through the world and time as some sort of thick purplish fog, and then imagining that a dream of him suddenly reached up its dream-tentacles and grabbed a girl, who was sitting at the edge of a roof, and dragged her into the dream. *He* was tentatively feeling guilty, in other words, and afraid that she would accuse him of suddenly killing her—of grabbing her with his dream and making her fall off of a roof.

But *she* was imagining something different.

She was imagining that a dream with him and the tower and the campus in it had been sitting somewhere out there in an endless mathematical space of possible dreams. That the wobbling edges of her *need* and *wanting* had suddenly lined up with it, like to like, and that her heart and his dream had then locked together.

She was thinking, in other words, of the Sosunov magic:

Of the way that the dreams of two loved ones can be made to connect across all of time and space; of the way that the unformed portions of two dreams could be sort of ... wiggled together ... until they clicked and the dreams were made one; of how she'd always been taught that it was specifically love that allowed that, that made it possible, that bound two hearts to the point where the theoretical consanguinity of dreams became more than an interesting intellectual exercise—but how it seemed to her, in that moment, that maybe *need* could realize that connection too. How it seemed to her in that moment that if there were a dream out there that could help her, maybe it *would* be as close to her heart as a loved one, so greatly desperate was she.

And thus:

"Maybe you can help me," she said. "Because there is a witch, and she has my whole family. And that witch, she won't let them go."

"Oh," he said.

He hesitated.

"This is the Bleak Academy," he said, after that hesitation. "And I am named 'Magister Wan.'"

"What's bleak about it?" she asked.

"Um," he said, as if uncertain. Momentarily he foundered. Then he said, "It is a name. It is what it is called. But if I had to say I think I would say that there is a thing that we study, here at the Bleak Academy, that is injurious to our desired conceits. The bones of the world are a terrible thing to see. The truth that is under the faces of things—it is cold. Do you understand? So we call this thing 'bleak.'"

"You don't know."

He laughed. He smiled. "I don't know," he said. "The name predates my creation."

Wind shook the clock tower.

Valentina spoke: "I am Valya— Valentina Grigorievna Sosunova, and I hold the Sosunov family legacy in trust."

"Yes," he agreed.

"Yes?"

"I mean to say," he said, "that— I mean, I am aware. Your reputation precedes you."

"Absurd," she said.

"Well," he said, after a moment. "It is a dream, after all."

This saddened her. She lowered her head and her hair hung down past her. "I daresay it must be. Tell me, Magister Wan—"

"'Wan,'" he said. "Please. Or, if you must, 'Gylbard.'"

"... Vanya," she decided[5]. "Can you help me?"

"I'd take the stars from the sky for you," he said. "I'd fight Perdition's beast for you. But I don't understand what you'd expect me to do."

"Come out of my dreams," she said, "when I wake. Draw a sword. Kill the witch. She won't be expecting that. I'll be falling, and she'll lunge to catch me with a great fluttering of wings, and you'll burst out of my eyes. She'll brake, desperately, but she'll still be skewered, and I will fall in freedom to the ground."

"Mn," he said. "I think not."

---

5 incorrectly

"Extravagantly loyal," she said, as if in complaint.

"Well," he said, "ask the impossible, and then the unthinkable, and that's the best I can do."

"You can't?"

"Can't," he said. "Also, won't; you'd hit the ground and break your head."

"Oh," she said.

He rubbed at his nose. "I honestly don't know why you'd think I could do that," he said. "I've never heard of anyone who could come *out* of somebody's dreams."

"Great-uncle Hernais," said Valentina, thoughtfully.

A laugh was startled from him: "Ahaha, oh?"

"It's his best trick," Valentina said. "When he's not held in enchanted sleep, I mean. You're dreaming of him, and *pop*, out he comes. 'S how he got Sasha home from that mine."

"Well," said Wan, "*I* couldn't do that, certainly. I can't even imagine where to start."

"I guess," Valentina said.

"I could try," he said, "I mean—"

He hesitated.

"I *could* try to warn you," he said, "before the witch comes. If you like. But then I don't know how we'd be having this dream."

"Before?"

"Well," he said, "I mean— haven't you had those dreams where, like, Kallinik shows up to see you, even though he hasn't been born yet? Or someone who's already dead?"

"I guess," said Valentina, distractedly.

"Like that," he said.

She shook her head. "That doesn't seem like it'd help," she said, "'cause they're all asleep already. But you could maybe break into their dreams *now?*"

"Hm," he said.

"Like you got into my dreams," she said, hopefully. "You could burst into their dreams and—"

"You're younger than you look," he realized, slowly.

She glanced down, shrugged. "Maybe?"

A certain tension occupied his form. "Valentina," he said, "I can't do what you're asking of me, because I've never even *met* your family."

"Oh," she said. And with a twist of a frown, she said, "What good *are* you, then?" and stepped forward off the ledge of the tower.

For a moment everything was shuddering dizziness; then she felt the beak clutching at her collar, then she felt it jerking her backwards, and:

"Don't fall, fishlet," said the witch.

Valentina glanced at her. She glared at her, blinking to clear the doze from her eyes.

Then she slipped carefully forward, in a controlled, proper fashion, and dropped to the ground to land on her feet.

IT SEEMED to her that things were almost good for a little while then.

She organized the birds into an army to take care of her home and her family. They moved with purpose, and their eyes were sharp.

"You're an elite force," she told them. "*Valentina Force.* But it's no good if we don't kill that witch."

This the birds would not do.

They grew curiously unresponsive when she suggested it. Even the most mischievous of cockatiels just looked away.

Nor, she found, was she able to seek help from others.

There was a second, independent guard of crows and swallows around the house. They eyed her when she walked too far from the compound. They croaked and called out malevolently. She feared them, and when that fear snapped in her and she charged out past them, they drowned her in their swarm.

She shrieked. She flung up her hands to guard herself. She blacked out.

At that moment she felt a hand at the back of her collar; she felt herself being pulled back; she woke back up in the dream she'd been having before, in the airy loft of the Bleak Academy's clock tower, dragged back to her footing by Magister Wan.

"You oughtn't do that," he said.

She blinked at him.

"If you do that," he explained, uneasily, "you might fall off of that roof you're on, in real life."

"I'm not on a roof," she growled. "I'm being swarmed by stupid birds."

He blinked.

"Oh," he said.

"It's that witch," she said, sulkily. She let him pull her inwards. She sat against an angled plinth and crossed her hands over her knees. "She won't let me use birds to kill her and now she won't let me out. And she's always wanting me to bake things even when I don't feel like it and she laughed at me because I thought research was a kind of a food."

Magister Wan snorted.

She cast him a glare, causing him to snort a few more times with a faked awful expression as if, instead of making fun of her, he just had something stuck at the back of his throat.

"That's a transparent artifice," she informed him.

"Well, I am somewhat transparent."

"It made sense," she protested. "Like, *radish*."

"You shouldn't let a witch get to you," he said. "You're Valentina Grigorievna Sosunova, after all."

"Ugh."

Then she looked up.

"What would you do?" she asked him. "If there was a witch? If the witch caught all your family, or, I don't know, all your Academy, if she bound them in dreams?"

"A long time ago," he said. "the Headmaster went out to meet a woman who had come to the Bleak Academy with two swords in her hands. He is a terrifying man and he thought he could subdue her with great ease if she dared trouble him, but instead he lost quite terribly quick. She caught his spear's barb with one of her swords and she cut him open with the other, and she would have brought it back around to cut off his head; only, he showed her her reflection, instead."

She looked blankly at him.

"As for me," he said, "I did nothing. I would never have dared to do anything. But when I saw her do those things, the pen and inkpot dropped from my hands as if they'd lost all feeling, and my jacket felt uncomfortable across my shoulders, and I fell in love."

"That is not very much like the experience I am having with the witch," she said.

"No," he agreed.

"I was right the last time," she said, laughing. "You really are useless."

The stars that shone in his eyes twinkled and he smiled with them and he said, "That is what the Headmaster tells me, haha. 'Why do I keep you around, Mr. Wan?' he asks me. 'You are nothing! Disposable! Replaceable! If I killed you right now I could find ten thousand more exactly like you!'"

"Well," she said, "I wouldn't go *that* far, myself."

"Oh?"

"You're the best Wan," she said, "that *I've* ever known."

"Ah," he said, as if touched, "but you are just a young child. I'm sure you'll meet ten thousand more just like myself."

"Please," she said, softly. "Isn't there any way you can help me?"

A tick of the clock, then another; then, "I will teach you a magic," he said, "with which to kill witches, but this may not be for the best."

It confused her. "No?"

"I am under strict instructions never to teach this to anyone," he said. "And *especially* not to Valentina Grigorievna. Only, you might as well learn it *somewhere*, you see."

His forehead pinched for a moment in worry, then it smoothed again.

"Here," he said.

He took a hair from her head; plucked it. He smoothed and straightened it, rolled it between his fingers, bit his lip as the worry recurred again, then shook it off and sighed.

"This I have taken," he said, "because it is real; there is little here that is real, that is from your world, but you are real, and so this is real. Yes? You can see it, yes?"

Valentina nodded.

"If you were to write down a book of the truth of the world," Wan said, "including all the things that are real, there are some that would say, it would include this hair."

"It's just the dream of it," Valentina pointed out.

"Mn," he said. "Well, the hair you have in waking, then. The hair you have in waking, though I don't imagine you've actually kept track of each one from your head. The hair you have in waking, and therefore dream of, with the brain and the mind and the heart and the soul that exist in the waking world, that hold the memories of the waking world, that manifest reality here from reality there; it would, therefore, some would say, include that hair."

She gave the hair a second, speculative look. The light behind him sparkled off of it: a light of stars. "... right."

"But there are others," said Wan, "that would say: no; this is a thing too small to be truth."

He rolled his hand in the air, searching for words.

"How many hairs can you hold in your head at once?" he said. "Not—

on your scalp. But in your thoughts. How many can you *look at*, Valya, *have your attention on*, at once? Not many. Maybe seven? And so you look from hair to hair, and you see each small one of them, and then you back up, you change the focus of your gaze, you look at the whole *head* of hair, and you say, 'Ah: the big things are made of the many little things.' But you can never see that directly, right? You can't ever look at each individual hair, all at once, and find the thing that binds them together into your head of hair.

"It's a cheat, hey? You take one hair, and 'the hair' remains. You take another—well, you still have hair. Pull out as many as you can keep track of, as many as you can hold each individual plucking of inside your head: you still have just as much hair as you started with. This single hair isn't *part* of your head of hair; it's a manifested representative sample. It's one thorn of the thing, but it's not *the thing*."

"You shouldn't pull your hair," she said.

"You could fill a book with all the details of the world," he said, ignoring her. "This hair, and that hair; that nose, and that ear; that eye; the length of that thing, and this thing, and the other; each exact color ... but then you would find that nowhere in that book is the truth of anything. You'd find out to your horror when you gave that book to the celestial librarian that it didn't actually add up to the world—that it didn't add up to *anything*, it was just a bunch of details that you saw, one at a time.

"There wouldn't be any people in that book. There might be another book, just as bad, with people in it— but, enh." He waved a hand to put that thought aside. "The thing is, there wouldn't be any people in *this* book. Not any dreams. Not any schools or great heads of hair. The book of details would just have a bunch of sensory impressions that we *pretend* make up the world. Because when we tell ourselves that the whole is made up of the parts, that's all it is. Pretend. A happy lie. A trick we pull upon ourselves. We are counting, one, two, three, four, five, six, seven, ... many?"

Valentina frowned at him.

"Many," he repeated. "More. ... all."

"You have incorrectly learned your counting."

He laughed. "Caught," he said.

She snorted.

"... there is a thing," said Wan, and his voice was different now; truer, clearer, from his heart and not his head. "There is a thing that cannot be spoken of in words, that cannot be written of in books; a thing the wrong word can't be used for.

"There is a thing that has no details to it; it precedes them: it is noiseless, lightless, tasteless, it has no texture and it has no scent. Before the world we witness there is a void that is lively in its emptiness and a darkness that is impregnated with great light.

"We look outwards at the world, Valentina Grigorievna, and things come out of us. Things come out of the truth of us and the flaws in us: the things that fill our book of details about the world. We learn this habit deeply; so deeply, that we start to imagine, 'oh, the world is just an accumulation of this. It is the thing that you get when you put together all these little details that I have written down.'

"We assemble them back together; and we cheat, we lie, we lose track of *so many* little pieces before we build the whole; only, we do not notice that we have left the original truth behind: that the whole that we have built back up is a new falseness, born from nothing.

"... but if we have seen the True Thing, if we have seen the void that is lively in its emptiness, then we may understand that all ... this ..."

He gestured around.

"Is just our made-up words, in some stupid book; and it may therefore be corrected."

Valentina had been lost for some time by then, but she knew words that were kind of like the words he was using, and so she said them:

"Miruna Sosunova," she recited, "saw the secret that is like the rain;

that is like a cloud passing over nothingness. And when she saw that secret, she lit up the void around her … like a candle lighting in the emptiness!

"And she understood for the first time that she was beautiful."

"Ah," said Magister Wan, and smiled. "*That* is a lesson too advanced for me."

"… oh?"

"I can only teach a lesser magic," he said.

"You aren't teaching *anything*."

"Fair enough," he said.

He set her plucked hair down gently on a ledge.

He cleared his throat.

He took out a little black ink pot from a pouch that was on his belt, and a brush, and with one great slash of ink he struck away the hair that he had taken from her head.

And she thought at first that it had been blown away by the movement, and then that it had blended into the mark left by the ink—though, wait, that was only a shadow; and finally that it had been caught up in the bristles of the brush, but then she saw it:

Not the hair, or the ink, but rather the *absence* of it, where the hair had been.

There was a certain … lively emptiness … to it.

"This is everything that I am worth," said Magister Wan. "The limit of my attainment, and one day you shall exceed me at it. But look:

"When you see that the little things are not the whole; when you can pull them out into isolation—then, they may be *corrected*."

And she *sort* of understood him, and she *sort* of didn't, so she didn't say anything at all; just scrunched up her face a bit in concentration, staring at the void where the hair had been.

"It is a party trick," he admitted. "It is not the True Thing that is behind all things. It is not a great achievement. It is only … changing the focus of your eyes. Seeing that all the little things, like hairs and bread and witches—that they could be any way, or no way at all, and the world would be the same. That they are just words in a book, just little words, and the words are *wrong* ... and so the book can be corrected."

And it all clicked into sudden sense inside her head; or rather, none of it made sense to her, but there was a thing *beyond* it that she saw, to wit:

I could strike away the witch.

"Show me," she said.

Because that is what she understood of all of this:

That:

I could strike away the witch.

"Ah," he said. He laughed a little. "Hahahahuh. Well. There are no words for it, of course."

She made a face.

"But—" he said.

He touched his heart. Then he set his hand on her chest, above *her* heart.

"Stop imagining that the little things in the world add up to the bigger things," he said. "You must sever that conceit. See that the world is not held up on the back of its tiny details, but rather is suspended upon a vast sea of darkness, like deep black ink. That underlying all we see is darkness. See that, and that darkness in your eyes may bleed down from sea onto the little things; they will gasp for air in that empty void, and subside into the nothingness from whence they came."

He drew back his hand.

Where he had touched, a spot of her dress was cold and dark, like he'd spilled wine on it, or ink, or blood.

And for a long moment, she reached for it; then sighed, and slumped.

"You can't just do that," Valentina said.

"Hahaha, no?"

And frustration was like a net around her, binding the pieces of the world around her tight; and then she felt a certain queer acceptance, and she released some portion of that net, and the words came floating through her like a wind:

"If you could ditch things just by being too smart for them," she said, "if you could just *see* them gone, witches, ghosts, or hairs— there wouldn't be anywhere near as much stuff in all the world."

He nodded, after a moment.

"It's hardly anything I can teach in words."

"You keep *talking*," she protested.

"It goes without saying," he said, not seeming to hear her. "It's not enough just to *think* the things they think at the Bleak Academy. It's not enough just to *imagine* that you've recognized an underlying falsehood in the things you see around you and to *tell* yourself that you're dismissing them from your attention.

"There's no way you could be expected to understand anything, to *do* anything, just from that."

He held the brush in his hand, and it was dripping with black ink, and where it dripped, there was no clock tower and no night. Where it dripped there was no air and there was no dream. There was no sight and there was no sound.

"But ... that too can be corrected," he said.

And he swept his brush across the world, and there was no dream, nor neither was there waking.

Her inner eye recoiled.

The dream dissolved; he took every last detail of it, covered it in a darkness that was not darkness and a silence that was not silence. He left her in a void and there was no touch in it, no taste, no smell. She dreamt then a dream that was like drowning, like a suffocation of the body and the mind; with nothing else to look upon, she dreamt the roiling emptiness that is precedent to things.

She experienced choking. She experienced dying. Her eyes railed desperately from side to side within her head but found nothing to latch onto. Her throat was thick with tasteless honey and her ears drank in the ringing, throbbing absence of any sound.

And when the panic peaked and passed she almost tasted of a secret.

In the world stripped of all its little things, for a moment, she almost had it.

She *seized* at it, clutched at it like a lifeline, found a cool clear richness in the void to cling to. She set her mind's fingertip upon the substance of the True Thing that transcends all things and laughed with a brilliant and growing joy; knew it for something that could defeat the witch, knew it for something *better* than that, *better* than just any old weapon against the *witch*, pulled herself closer to it, wrapped herself around it like she'd hug a great stuffed animal, pulled it tight against her heart and she to it, and it passed through her heart and, where her heart had been, *a dark bird fluttered now and spread its wings;* where her marrow had been, starlight filled her from her toenails to her tip; where her *life* had been was a closed neon circle of perfect and eternal light, and *all was well*—

But in that moment the attention of he the lord of Death's dominion he[6], it fell upon her.

In that moment the Headmaster of the Bleak Academy became aware of a young girl in Fortitude and her communion with the True Thing that transcends all things, that is at the center of and beyond his Bleak Academy; and in those days he was a jealous god.

He swept his attention down to join the stream of her thoughts. He merged it with them and turned their flow in ever-so-slightly the wrong direction.

She became aware of a flickering of motion in the dark, and glory became nightmare, and all was lost.

It moved.

---

6   whose title, in its native tongue, reads identically whether seen normally or in a mirror

... something moved, like a snake or a fish twitching in the darkness, and she realized it was the motion of her eyes; and she understood in that instant that she was not looking upon nothingness, no, not precisely, but rather that her eyes had been turned inside out or backwards front within that dream; that she did not look out onto nothingness, but rather inwards onto herself. And in that moment she felt, or was reminded, of the great extent of her; of the bones of her, lying scattered in the nothingness; of the muscles around them, writhing, twisting, gross; of the many layers of her skin.

In that moment she was loathsome to her, gross and visceral and twisted to her in that moment, all that flesh, and she wept into herself. And in that sudden awareness that there was not *nothing* but rather *Valentina* she lost the secret that she'd almost had.

She realized in that moment that she was nothing but a heap of ungainly and unsightly things; that she was a pile of hair and bones and meat and skin that dared to dream of truth and nothingness; and from this she woke up screaming, in the midst of a swarm of birds.

IN THE END, there was no one to discuss this with but the witch herself.

"I asked him how to kill you," Valentina said; and the witch looked at her sidelong, disturbed, but didn't speak. "And he showed me ... this ..."

She gestured vaguely.

It was the time before the sun, so the world was dark; things were lit, inasmuch as they were lit at all, by lanterns, and the light that things have inside them because they are themselves. It was a brooding dark and in that darkness it was impossible for the witch to say whether there was a shadow that followed and dripped from Valentina's hand as she gestured or merely the intimation and concept of such a shadow; whether there was a hint in that gesture at a deeper reality, a thing beneath the things that are assembled to compose the world, or simply the fear or hope or dream of such a thing.

Valentina gestured, waved her hand through the air, and darkness was, and darkness followed, and the sharp eyes of the witch went following that indication of a darkness as it went.

"I lost the whole dream," said Valentina. "It drowned in it. And for just a moment I thought that I had found something beautiful. Something perfect. Something that would cut through you like a knife, miss witch, and end you, but more than that, more than that—"

She hugged herself.

"It would have been amazing," she said. "I think I know, I think I finally know, why Miruna left us. Why she did it. Why she opened the back of her eyes like the front of them and went away. Why they called her a goddess, after that. Because it was so beautiful.

"But then— I moved, and the muscles of me were like grey eels writhing in that darkness, and they left smears of the slime of them behind them on that dark. And I thought, and the thoughts of me were like ants tracking filthy mud across the floors. And everywhere I looked and I saw myself, and I thought, *how horrible. How awful.* And I let it go."

The wind skittered leaves around the courtyard.

A thousand birds went about their chores.

"There is no shame," said the witch, eventually, **"in being Valentina."**

"There is," Valentina protested.

"All of us are piles of unsightly and ungainly things," said the witch. **"They heap up and become us, flesh and bone and dreams. But there cannot be any shame in this, because: it is what we are."**

"There *is*," said Valentina.

The witch shook her body, once, all over, and her feathers fluffed. **"It is a thing that is,"** she said. **"Without comparison. And without comparison there can be no beauty and no filth."**

Valentina hit the witch's wing with an awkward sideways punch. It didn't hurt her, nor was it really meant to. "You shouldn't say nice things," she said, angry. "You're not supposed to be nice to me. You're my enemy."

"Kuh," snorted the witch. **"I'll say what I like."**

Valentina curled in on herself.

The witch rapped her sharply on the head. **"If you want me to be awful,"** she said, **"I can find some task for you."**

"Whatever," said Valentina.

"Go pull some water from the well, or something."

"The birds'll handle it."

"It's too heavy."

Valentina waved vaguely. "They've got teams. Seriously. It's all on the chart. A good manager doesn't interfere with a smoothly running engin—why do you even *care?*"

The witch pondered that for a while. Then she made a harsh, annoyed noise.

"Whatever," she said, and she stalked away.

And Valentina turned her head and watched her go and frowned at that, because there was something in the way it sounded that reminded her of her uncle Ivan—not to be confused with her cousin Ivan—of the way *her uncle Ivan* sounded, when he sulked.

THE SOSUNOV household approached an equilibrium.

Valentina struggled with her anger. The witch wandered the roofs in the shape of a heron. Fifteen Sosunovs slept. A thousand birds kept house.

At mealtimes there was broth for the sleepers, bugs and fish and other suchlike for the thousand birds, and a proper meal—soups, pastries, breads, fruit, and salads—for Valentina and the witch. The last two ate together, sometimes keeping company with the higher ranks among the birds.

Some nights, Valentina tried to break into her mother's dreams, or her father's dreams, or the dreams of her Aunt Fevroniya—to no avail.

And the days went by.

It was a terrible situation but it became the normal one. Valentina got *used* to it. She learned the patterns of it. She developed habits that fit her circumstances. She spent her days wandering the house to check on family, reading the books from the family library, practicing her magic (though, shying away from the thing that Gylbard Wan had shown her), and checking on the reports—well, the piles of stones—that were assembled by the birds.

The witch got used to the situation too—to a greater extent, in fact, than the witch was comfortable with. She was still a metaphysical embryo. She was still *growing* inside the dreams of the Sosunov family. She was still vulnerable, and that made her afraid. She did not like the fact that she was becoming predictable, that she was developing habits, that there were certain specific times that she would stand on the rooftops, certain specific times that she'd follow after Valentina, certain specific times that she would pester the girl for tea. It terrified her that she found herself checking on the sleeping family members herself, that she would brush their heads with cloths, that she would adjust their sheets and blankets, that she would upbraid the birds that had taken poor care of them. She told herself that she did these things only because the Sosunovs were necessary, because they were the *container* for her, but she was not comfortable with it. She knew, deep in her bones, that there was something more to it than that.

She feared that "something more." She hated it.

Most of all she feared the fondness that she was developing for Valentina.

"You are too thin," she told the girl. **"Eat more."**

Or: **"Out! Out of the library, you! You are spending too much time in contemplation. Go ... play by the river. Go, stretch your legs!"**

She would stand over the girl, when Valentina slept, even though she could not invade and steal her dreams.

Once she put out the lantern, in Valentina's room, because she was afraid that the fire would burn the girl, rather than out of any fear for the witch herself.

The witch knew the reason for all of this, of course, but she didn't admit it to herself. Instead she told herself a lie. She told herself, *I am becoming soft because of the comfort of habit. I am becoming soft, because: this is becoming 'home.'*

When that lie was threatened, when something threatened to contradict it, she would grow very angry and lash out.

For the most part, Valentina didn't have the complementary problem. She didn't have to worry that she might grow fond of the witch. Her whole family was asleep and possibly dying when the witch could let them wake up at any time that she wanted instead. Plus, the witch was an alien *thing*. That made it pretty easy, most of the time, to maintain a callous attitude towards the witch. But one day, Valentina was in the twilight between dreaming and waking and she found herself wondering if the witch was possibly lonely.

She woke up choking in horror at herself.

She was viciously angry at herself for thinking of caring at all.

For the most part she hated the witch, anyway; but, now and then, from time to time, sympathy like that slipped in.

That was where things stood, more or less. Then a wren mis-placed its task stone and the ham stock wasn't properly skimmed and a tall bird fed Valentina's cousins soup with gristle in it and her cousin Nikolai choked.

Valentina was walking innocently through the complex when the witch struck her, barreled into her, howling, crying, **"Kolya, Kolya[7]; ah, thou hast killed a part of me;"** and the beating of her wings battered Valentina, and Valentina crawled back, crying, desperate, afraid, and tangled in her clothing and the feathers and her own motion, until the witch said, among her shouting:

"Kolyusha, gone."

---

7 "Nikolai, Nikolai"

And an understanding of what that meant sank in to Valentina in the small and dirty place in her mind that her self had crawled to, and inside her sweating face something hardened and grew cold, and she writhed up in one great motion, struck at the witch, clawed at her as if her fingernails were made as talons, tried to choke her, and for just a moment she touched on it, on that awful magic that Gylbard Wan had shown her, for just a moment when she struck at the witch she was sick at herself for her collaboration in the world that had thrown up the details of the witch's existence; for just a moment the witch was not a *thing* or even a collection of things to her but rather a ghastly pretense that facilitated the pulsing tide of something *wrong*; and where she ripped at the witch bone dissolved, fat melted, and feathers flew away as she dug through the layers of that pretense with her hands to grip at the wriggling bones of the horror underneath; and the witch's beak cracked the temple of Valentina's skull, and her brain shook and her world caught fever, and the sun was rising—though, of course, it wasn't rising—and Valentina was flying, falling, far into the dark.

"I'LL KILL HER," Valentina snarled, and she rolled up out of bed. She landed, tangled in sheets and blankets, on a tiled floor that was not familiar. She lay against a dresser, her head pounding, and she blinked.

A girl was staring at her in shock from the bed she'd just fallen from.

She'd almost placed her, when—

"Great-gran?" Aprosinya asked.

"Ah," said Valentina.

She sank her head down to the floor. She sighed. The girl was younger than the last time, smaller, but—

"I am dreaming," Valentina concluded.

"Oh, this I know."

"But, there's a bed," Valentina protested. She waved her hands vaguely, as if to indicate the sheets and blankets into which they had been tangled. "That's, I—I don't *do* that. Dreaming of beds is like singing to birds."

"... I thought it would help?" Aprosinya said.

"Help?" Valentina levered herself up. She stared at Aprosinya. *So young*, she thought, and then felt a wash of amusement:

No wonder people keep saying that to me.

"Well," said Aprosinya, awkwardly, "I am still new at this."

Valentina tilted her head. "You ... *should* be old enough?" she said.

Aprosinya looked away. She was blushing. "All my life," she said, "I've had dreams. You know. Parents, cousins. People I know. They'd visit. But I'm not as good as ... I mean, you're *special*. I'm just me. This is my first time getting close to *choosing* a dream."

"Oh," said Valentina.

"It's harder!" said Aprosinya.

"Yes," agreed Valentina.

"I mean, I know *how*," Aprosinya said. "I do my lessons. But I'm not *good* at it. So this is ... hey! I did it! I did it my first time!"

"Congratulations," Valentina said, smiling a little.

Aprosinya pulled her legs up onto the bed and folded them tailor-fashion. She stared at Valentina earnestly. "I wanted to talk to you, great-gran," she said, "because I've met the witch."

"Uh?"

"Your witch," said Aprosinya. "She's come back. And she's bothering me."

Her voice was thick with ... uncertainty? Pain? And then a sudden burst of hope:

"And I realized, wait, I could do it. I could ... I could call you up. I could *ask* you."

And Valentina finally put together a thing that she had in one sense known all her life, but never formally considered, which is: "You're from *later*."

"Hm?"

"I mean," Valentina said, "you're dreaming of me. But not *now*. You're dreaming of me ... like, *tomorrow*."

"Oh," said Aprosinya. She looked Valentina up and down. "I guess."

And, brightening:

"Did I get you when you were young? When you'd just fought the witch? That's awesome. That's amazing. I was just trying to get, you know, great-gran. But wow. Yeah. You're like, you're like, younger than *me*. What was it *like*?"

She'd seized one of Valentina's hands. She'd pushed against the wall. She'd slipped down off the bed and was now uncomfortably close: "Were there really a thousand birds?"

"She *killed Kolya*," said Valentina, and Aprosinya drew back.

"Well," uncomfortably said Aprosinya, "um. Yes. And—"

Aprosinya bit her lip.

"Um. I. Um. You are very intense about this, great-gran. Valentina."

Valentina pulled herself out of the sheets and blankets. She pushed Aprosinya away from her. She stood up. She looked around.

"Where is this?" she said.

She opened up the blinds. She stared out blankly at the world, for it was dawn, but it was dawn in *Horizon*—blocked off by buildings and the morning fog—so she could see the light, but not the sun.

"When is this?"

"This is ... um. It's Horizon," said Aprosinya, slowly. "My dorm room, in Horizon. —I don't know whether they called it Night London, or Horizon, or 'the cursed place,' back when you were, um, you. And it's ... well, I'm trying to dream of an early morning, so I don't get too confused when I wake up."

"I had almost gotten used to it," said Valentina. "I can't believe I did that. I almost let her ... I almost got *used* to her. And then she killed Nikolai and attacked me, and when I wake up I will be dead."

Aprosinya shook her head.

"*Yes*," said Valentina. "I can tell. I have such a headache as you only can get by dying. I am going to kill her. I am going to rip her guts out through her throat. I am going to pin her to the wall and cut her throat and let her bleed out all over the table. I am ... going to get mobbed by a thousand birds and get eaten to pieces. You should go. I bet she'll poke her head into the dream and eat us both at any moment."

Her voice went sick: "Right through the window, even."

"She can't, gran," said Aprosinya. Then, as if correcting herself, "Valentina. She couldn't possibly have. You'd have said."

"What?"

"You'd have told me," Aprosinya said, "if she was going to come in through my dreaming about you and catch me. That's the kind of thing you would have *mentioned* to me by now."

"Gran," said Valentina. She tasted the word. Then she blinked. "I'm a grandmother?"

Aprosinya looked embarrassed. "I am in so much trouble," she said.

"What?"

"I can't believe this. I *knew*, you always told me, you always *said* not to dream of you from back before sunlight, and then I *did* it. I bet I'm like messing with the timeline or something."

Valentina stared blankly at her.

That blankness, of course, had much the same explanation as her long-delayed realization about "later," which is to say, she was yet to have such an understanding of time. Timelines? She predated the *notion*. To her time had never been a substance but a *medium*; living before even day and night, she gave no *weight* to the idea of tomorrow save as a thing one grows into:

Today, I am young, but one day, an adult; today, I am studying, and later, will know; today I am a granddaughter, but one day, a grand*mother*—

"It's weird," said Valentina. She grasped at it. She smiled at it, a bit. "I can look forward to that."

She still did not quite understand. On some level she expected Aprosinya to disappear and turn into a little grandchild for her to cuddle in her arms; plus, she'd forgotten the "great" and placed Aprosinya as Valentina's child's own daughter. On another level, she was thinking thoughts like: *I wonder what the child will look like.*

Her thoughts, in short, drifted, which Aprosinya took advantage of, like thus:

"That's not what we're here for, great-gran."

Valentina sighed. A wash of the panic from before came through her, but it was more distant now. She stared out at the fog and the light. "OK," she said. "You wanted to talk about the witch."

"Yeah."

"I can't help you," Valentina said. Her voice was heavy and awkward. "I wish I could get your help, myself."

"What?"

"I don't know what to do," Valentina said. "She's too strong for me. I don't even know. You might just be a dream. I don't think I'm going to live to have grandkids. I'm just, kind of, like, one small Valentina."

"Gran—"

"What would you do?" Valentina asked her. "If you were all alone, with a thousand birds and a witch, and they wouldn't let you leave, and now your family was dy— dy— if he was, if she said, if he was *dead?*"

"I'm just one small Aprosinya," the other girl said, softly.

"Oh?"

"I'd die."

"Oh."

And Aprosinya half-smiled. "What would you do, gran, if it came back afterwards? If it dug its way into *your* mind, didn't even make an egg of it, just ... *crawled in* ... until you could hardly think of anything else sometimes, hardly focus on anything else sometimes, that wasn't just the thinness of your existence, and the pain? And, maybe— and—"

"And?"

"If maybe you want that?"

Valentina turned and looked at her; and it was weird, to feel a brief and angry surge of protectiveness for a grandchild you'd never had, who was more or less your age. And she spoke in an angry mother's tones:

"Care to explain that?" she said.

"If," and Aprosinya looked away, and she was struggling with her words, "if she were your second witch, you know, your *second*. If you were beating even your great-great-great-etcetera-grandmother's record. If you were kind of glad, you know, that—at least, you were worth enough that she bothered to hurt *you*, that she went after you and not somebody else? That you were doing your job, you know, in the Sosunovs? That you were *special* because of it?"

"Because she chose you," said Valentina, "to hurt."

Aprosinya licked her lips. "She said I was like you," she offered. "Nobody'd ever said I was like you before. When we first met she said she would hurt me because I was *like you*."

"I'm just me," Valentina pointed out.

Aprosinya snorted, but let it pass. "If I let go," she said, "—if I make her stop, then I'm just a nobody. A dead end."

And the flow of words kind of clotted up in Valentina, then, because she really wanted to say, *you're not nobody*, but the truth was, they'd barely even met; and it wasn't like Valentina didn't know that pride, that thing that says: *my problem! Mine! Not yours!*

But finally something found its way out of her, which was this: "I had to get help, eventually. I had to. I tried. I couldn't do it on my own. I broke my mother's instructions to keep the house. But the birds wouldn't let me."

"Huh?"

"Maybe," said Valentina, "if you try, it'll be the same."

She made shooing gestures, just a bit half-heartedly:

"Like, if you try to make it stop," she said, "maybe you'll find out you couldn't've anyway, and then you don't have to worry about that whole weird, uh, pride thing."

"That ... doesn't sound better," said Aprosinya.

"No?"

"I ... kind of *like* thinking it's only happening because I let it," Aprosinya said. "Too."

Valentina looked at her.

"It's better," said Aprosinya. "You see. To be taking her on. To be challenging her, because I'm like you. To be the one called, and chosen, and caught up in stupid Sosunov pride. That's better than being stuck. That's better than thinking that nobody *could* help me."

"Oh, honey," Valentina said, because it seemed like a grandmotherly thing to say; and she opened her arms. She thought it was right. She honestly did! But Aprosinya gave her a queer look, like *that isn't how you behave, great-gran.*

And most likely it *wasn't;* but in the end, she came into the hug anyway, and some time passed.

And finally, Aprosinya said, "Here is how I would answer your question."

"Oh?"

"If I were trapped," she said, "with a witch and a thousand birds, I would fight her; I would fight her as hard as I could fight her, and in every way that I could fight her, for as long as I could fight her—and then I'd stop."

"Would you?"

"When it was too much," Aprosinya said. "When it became impossible. When I couldn't do it any more—I'd stop."

And in emphasis to those words, she stopped; she went away, and the dream went with her.

She blew out like a candleflame, and she was gone.

Then there was only darkness; and the spreading agony that washed through one small Valentina ... and the odd sense of being on a featherbed, quilt and her mother's arms around her, wrapped and cradled, snug, and safe.

SHE WOKE with the witch sobbing beside her. She woke with a headache so terrible she could scarcely bear it, and with fresh gashes along her face and arms—

And a heron curled up against her side, bent around a ruined wing, and sobbing.

She was shivering with those sobs.

She was shaking.

And the rage that filled Valentina caught behind her nose, turned into a funny, curious feeling; and then a sickening one. Nausea filled her and she reached out to the witch, rubbed a hand along the body of the witch, and touched the unruined wing.

And for a moment she had the strong temptation to move her hand downwards, and grasp the ruined wing, and do something *cruel;* but the moment passed.

"It's all right," she said.

And the witch's sobs grew louder.

"It's all right."

And after what might have been an hour there, staring at the ceiling, running her hand along the body of the witch, she heard the witch choke out, **"He's dead."**

"I know," she said.

She fell asleep again, and this time she did not dream.

THE BIRDS had disposed of Nikolai's body.

She went into his room, the next day, and the next, and two days after that; she stood there, staring at the empty bed, and tried to understand, but her mind was empty. All she could see was that Nikolai wasn't there.

She kept the house.

She kept the birds.

She made cabbage and onion soup. She made fish paste and buckwheat and gave it to her family in very tiny bites. She made a sour cream with pounded herbs and a soup from beets and mixed the two together.

She went about with a small frown that creased her forehead, and she did not speak to the witch, nor did the heron-witch speak to her; the witch hobbled around the house instead, stood brooding in the dining room, and nibbled at her injured wing. Until finally, Valentina forgot herself; at tea-time, she asked the witch what she would like, and the witch answered without thinking, and then there was nothing for it but a horrible awkward meal together because neither of them knew how to abort a plan once it was made.

"Don't think I forgive you," said Valentina, over frog sausages on toast. "Because I won't ever forgive you."

There was a silence for a bit.

"But you can't help being an evil witch all the time, I suppose."

"These are good," said the witch, chewing on a sausage.

"They're terrible," Valentina said. "They're made of *frogs*."

"I like frogs."

"I don't," Valentina admitted.

"Kuh," snorted the witch. **"Then make yourself something else. The more for me. —do you really not understand why I am doing this?"**

"Pardon?"

The witch nudged aside her plate. She stared for a moment, longingly, at the sausages, then grabbed one up and swallowed it whole before she started walking towards the door. **"I will show you,"** she said.

"What?"

"Come with me," the witch said.

Awkwardly, Valentina rose, and followed.

"It was out here," said the witch. She looked around, then tromped off to the southwest. **"By the Sosunov temple. And your aunt Fevroniya was speaking. She was saying, 'One day Miruna Sosunova learned to see through the back of her eyes like the front of them,'—do you remember?"**

"She said things like that a lot," Valentina said.

"It echoed off the walls," said the witch. **"It rose out over the river. I was walking in the reeds, just an ordinary bird, and I heard her speaking: 'learned to see through the back of her eyes like the front of them.' You were there."**

"She said it a *lot*," Valentina repeated.

"'She raised up the curtains of the self,'" said the witch, savoring the words, **"'and went out beyond them, into the territory of nothingness and death.'"**

She stopped in front of a stone bench. She gestured around with her head.

"She must have been here," said the witch. **"Or hereabouts."**

And suddenly Valentina *did* remember it; did remember walking with Fevroniya that day, not long before her great-grandfather fell asleep for good—remembered that it had been one of her last lessons, before the crisis had started, in the "evening" when the lanterns were dimmed.

"I didn't understand the words at first," said the witch. **"Because I was a bird. I mean, how could I? I didn't understand anything at all. The world ... I lived in the world, but I did not know that I was living in the world. I had experiences; I had thoughts. But I did not know that I was having experiences and thoughts. Life and death were as the same to me; tomorrow and yesterday were as the same to me; I existed in the stream of an endless moment, and nothing was mattering that much to me at all.**

"Except, the words ... they reached me.

"I liked the sound of them."

"It's the story of Miruna," Valentina said. "She— she achieved enlightenment, and suspired from the world into Nirvana.[8]"

"Oh? Did she, then?"

"She ..."

Valentina made an ambiguous gesture.

"She saw something that made the world as grass," Valentina said. She stomped the ground, wiggled her foot. "A mushy, life-arising thing. That is what I've always thought. It made the world as grass. And it grew like the grass underneath her feet and carried her up into Nirvana.

"But that's just what *I* think. They tell me I won't really understand it until I'm old."

"Hm," muttered the witch. **"'As grass.'"**

Then she shrugged, spread her wings, pivoted in place, and looked upwards towards the stars.

"I heard the words," she said, **"and I repeated them to myself inside my head, because I liked the sound of them.**

"'She saw there the secret that is like the rain, like a cloud passing over nothingness.'

"They were as yet only sounds to me, you understand, but I could not resist them. I tried to speak them, but my throat could not assert the words. So I listened to them. Even after they were done in speaking, I listened to them. They echoed in my head. They echoed there until they made a kind of sense. —not the sense of words, but the sense that there was something waiting in the sounds, something that wanted me to understand. The sense that if I could just open my eyes a little wider, open my heart a little wider, it would all become clear to me. Even though I was a bird, and the sky and the land were as one thing to me, the water and the earth were as one thing to me; the sky; myself; the stars."

---

8   Technically, "into the resonating-paradise;" the translation as "into Nirvana" is only accurate in that it conforms to later usage and thinking by the Sosunovs themselves.

"That was not Aunt Fevroniya's intention," Valentina said. "She was trying to tell me a story."

"Because, it was magic?"

"'Cause she liked telling it," Valentina said. "'Cause she thought there was something in it that would help me. Maybe 'cause it was magic? I don't know."

"She kept on talking," said the heron-witch, **"and the words echoed and went repeating in my head, until they finally broke through and I had my first-ever *thought*. It wasn't my own thought, just a thought in Fevroniya's words. 'She kissed her son on the forehead, and her daughter, and even her cousin Dmitri, whom she had never liked. Then— like the world was a mirror, that cracked—'**

"And that was my thought:

"'Like the world was a mirror, that cracked—'"

"She turned," said Valentina, when the witch didn't continue, "and she let out a great breath, and with that breath she departed from the world; suspired into Nirvana; achieved enlightenment; became a goddess...

"—I don't know. Why does it even matter?"

"Even as I said those words to myself," said the witch, **"the world was as a mirror to me; I was as one with the entirety of things, they were a reflection of myself, and I of them; and the words themselves became a crack in that perfected symmetry.**

"And if you happen to think the sounds, 'Like the world was a mirror, that cracked,' and the world is like a mirror, and cracking—that's almost like being awake, isn't it? It's almost like having a *consciousness* ... isn't it?

"And in that moment, I noticed that I was thinking.

"... and the world split wide."

"... that's mean," Valentina said.

"What's mean?"

"You're trying to make it Aunt Fevroniya's fault," she said. "But it's not. It's yours."

"It's not anybody's *fault*," said the witch. **"Good things don't come with a *fault* attached to them. Just a history. And this—this was a good thing.**

"Don't you see?

"It's why I'm *doing* this. It's why I *have* to be doing this.

"Once you attain to consciousness, you can't just stop again: no. You have to build the self that you see into something wonderful. And the way *I* have found to do that is to find the dreams of ... wonderful people, and to feast upon them, to immerse, to *drown* myself in the brilliant colors of them ... until I become as bright and beautiful unto myself as they.

"I was born, Valentina, telling myself the story of a girl who became a goddess. What more pleasing symmetry could there be in all this world than to become a goddess of my own?"

"You're making it all wrong," said Valentina. "It's a *story*. For *understanding*."

"And I understood," said the witch.

Valentina shook her head.

"No?"

"Miruna is our guardian," Valentina said. "She watches over us. She isn't just some witch. So if you understood that you'd be *good*."

"That is that," said the witch, **"and this is this."**

"This *is* that," Valentina said, frustrated. "You ... the family magic is for *protecting* people, not for keeping them asleep all the time. It doesn't even *do* that. It's just *you*."

"That is true," agreed the witch. **"It is not the Sosunov magic that I attained to, on that day. It was merely the recognition of myself. I am surprisingly slow in mastering the Sosunov magic, I am resisting it with some part of me, and it is a thing that I might not truly attain to until I have drained the last dregs of magic from your family's dreams."**

"And then you'll know how awful you are," Valentina said. And, with a fey intuition, "and it'll be too late."

"**Kuh**," said the witch. "**A disturbing prognostication. But it will not come to pass; for I will be greater than any Sosunov priest or priestess, by then. Greater than any dozen. I will—**"

The witch hesitated, as if she weren't quite sure.

"**I will have become whatever it is that I will become.**"

Valentina frowned at her, and the witch became defensive.

"**It is not that I cannot see what that is,**" she said. "**For I am certain it is a divine being, such as will stand above Fortitude and the Lake and all the world and make disposition to all fates. I shall not loathe myself, but rather exalt myself; all that was in the Sosunovs, and more—I shall be as the sun-calf, the sea-deeps; as God.**

"**... but I can see it only dimly; I *know* that I can see it only dimly; if I could see it clearly then I would be concerned, Valentina, for an egg ought not to understand the bird.**"

"That's just great," Valentina said. "Now stop it. Just ... let them go. Won't you, miss witch? Just ... if Fevroniya woke you up, be *nice*. And let them go."

"**I'll do what I like,**" said the witch. "**That's the power I have in me.**"

"I don't like you," Valentina said.

And the witch felt a surge of fondness; remembered Valentina on the occasion of her fifth birthday, hands on hips, saying just exactly that to her mother, in just that tone of voice; smiled, in just the way that herons smile, and said:

"**Well, well.**"

HERNAIS TOOK fever a few days later.

The witch hovered over him—metaphorically—for hours; Valentina, for more than a day. She left most of her tasks to the birds, save for fitful bursts of dashing around trying to get things done; she even allowed them to cook a chaya-based broth without much supervision, although she wound up gnawing on long-hardened breadsticks instead of drinking of the bird-made meal herself. She spent a few minutes staring in from the doorway at each of the others; then she was back at Hernais' side, in a rickety chair, holding his hand, wiping his brow, telling him stories, and begging him to hang on to life.

She did not sleep. She did not rest. The witch finally returned to the room after some nervous pacing to find Valentina laughing hysterically to herself at the color of a pillow.

"This is ridiculous," said the witch. **"You are not actually helping him."**

Valentina's laughter petered out.

"It's char-*treuse*," she explained. Then she coughed. Then: "I need to be here."

"You will make *yourself* sick," said the witch. **"Go to bed."**

"You're … like, inside him," Valentina said. "Aren't you? Like, if he dies, it crushes part of your brain? You should understand this."

"I don't want him to die," the witch said. **"But he isn't so weak as to die just because you went to sleep for an hour."**

She gauged Valentina's expression, still not having much sense of the measures of time.

"… two hours? Fourteen?"

Valentina snorted. Then she sobered. "He's really old," she said, "And asleep. This can't be good for him."

"He is stronger than you imagine," said the witch.

"No."

"You have not tasted his dreaming," the witch said. **"Believe me. There is no attenuation. I fear, of course I fear, I am terrified for him; but listen, inside him, he is *vibrant*. He is a thing of a thousand colors. He dreamt stronger than anyone in the house save your mother, and his dreams are still full of more than can be digested in a month."**

"Really?" Valentina said. She hesitated. "He's really OK, then?"

"He's OK."

Valentina coughed. She looked down at her hands. Then she looked up. "I can't sleep. I can't. What if he needs me?"

"You can't stay awake until he's better," said the witch, **"so there's no point in half-measures. And I can *make* you sleep, little bird, if you insist. I just think you should go to your room first, instead."**

"I don't want to," she said.

"It's too much," said the witch. **"It's more than you can do."**

"People going to sleep is the whole *problem*," Valentina said. "Why do I have to sleep? I don't want to sleep. All of this is your fault. You should just let him wake up. Just let him wake up and then I can rest."

"People who have fevers ought to sleep," countered the witch. **"It's healthy and restful for them."**

"He's *sick*. Because of *you*."

"It's the season!" protested the witch. Then, more calmly, **"Anyway, it's too much. The rule is very clear, Valentina. You can only do as much as you can do. If it's ever too much, ever *just too much*—you stop."**

"That's Mom's rule," said Valentina. "It's not yours. Shut up."

She laughed helplessly.

"Shut your *beak*," she said.

"Unbelievable," said the witch. **"I will never have children."**

"Your *beak* will never have children."

"Go. To. Bed."

"Fine," said Valentina. "But you watch him. You watch him until I do return."

She paused.

"And it's *can* stop, anyhow. *Can* stop. Shut *up*."

THE WITCH watched Hernais, and Valentina left and slept, and Valentina returned; and time went rolling by. The fever worsened until Hernais seemed agonized, tossing and turning even in his enchanted sleep. Sometimes Valentina dared to imagine that that was Hernais breaking free of the witch's spell; that he was burning himself up wrenching free of her. At other times she was just afraid he'd die.

On the third day of his fever, when she'd chewed her nails to the quick, the witch said, **"I will show you."**

"Huh?"

"You are afraid for him," said the witch. **"I will show you his strength."**

She raised her wing, and Valentina fell under the shadow of that wing, and they walked in dreams.

The first thing that Valentina felt was a deep relief, as the burdens of the waking world dropped away from her; she breathed good air, stood upon lush grass amidst sky-spanning trees and meadow-flowers, and all around her were sparkling dream-lantern lights like stars. And the second thing she felt was curiosity, for in front of her in the meadow was a wooden altar, and upon that altar there was an egg, and the egg was made of stone and in many colors, though red was foremost of them all.

The third thing, as she felt an itching on the back of her neck and identified it as the presence of the witch, was fear.

"Ah," she said. "You *can* get into my dreams."

The witch looked embarrassed.

"I'd always," Valentina admitted, "kind of hoped that you couldn't."

"That was never the problem, Valentina," said the witch. **"You were simply too young to form a sufficiently robust egg."**

"... is that what this is?" Valentina asked. She stepped up to it. She reached for it, and the altar was taller and shorter than she in the same moment, and she lay her hand upon the egg in dreams.

It was hard, like stone, and warm, like a bird, and a heartbeat was fluttering inside.

"It is not your egg," said the witch. **"Which I have just said you cannot form. But yes ... it is Hernais, as an egg."**

Valentina drew back her hand as if burned, then, slowly, reached it back out again. "He?" she asked, to confirm.

"He raised up armies," said the witch. **"He marshaled them in his dreams. But I walked among the armies and the soldiers became confused. He built a great keep to hide within, fortresses in fortresses, seven rings of them, all made of stone. But I walked around the great keep he had and the walls of it shattered and fell apart. He fled to the mountains, to this glade in the forest, and hid from me in the shadow of a mushroom, but I saw him, and I winkled him out, and I looped the fire of his consciousness around and made him into my red stone egg.**

"And since that time he has dreamt my dreaming, and I within that dream have been drinking him up like an albumen; but as you can see, he is still strong."

"How do you tell?" said Valentina.

"If he were weak," said the witch, **"the egg would discolor, or even crack. It would sink inwards on itself, collapse. Its strength would not be the strength of stone, but would rather be as ... something soft. But push upon it, if you'd like."**

Valentina exerted a little pressure on the shell of the egg—not much. It stood firm.

"That is his strength."

Valentina took a shuddering breath, both in and out. Then her shoulders sank. "He isn't sick, then?"

"He is sick," said the witch. **"It is bad, because he has no medicine. But he is resting. And he is not dying. And he will be well."**

"Kolya died," said Valentina.

Something flickered across the expression of the witch. **"Kolya choked,"** she said. **"It was a reprehensible error and I have *eaten* the bird responsible. Feed Hernais well and this will never happen to him; he will live until I have drained him to the last."**

"That's not reassuring!" Valentina said.

"… it is all that he is for," said the witch.

"No."

The witch pondered. **"Well,"** she said, **"you are permitted to be wrong."**

"It doesn't make sense," Valentina said. "He was *strong*, so how did you beat him?"

"If I told you," said the witch, **"you would use it against me. You would try to break your family free."**

Valentina didn't say anything. She couldn't really deny it.

"… but it *would* be a good lesson for you," said the witch, thoughtfully. **"And if you learned the trick, you would be a witch like me, and you and I would have a connection for forever."**

"That is not correct."

"So I will tell you:" said the witch.

She looked up at the sky.

"I am the witch of *looking-upon*," she said. **"I am the witch of *the eyes that see*. He tried to fight me by dreaming things, things that he saw with the mind's eye, imagining that the *right* dream would beat me. But I didn't live in the dream that he dreamt. I lived behind the eyes he dreamed with. When he dreamed of an army, I was his dreaming of an army. When he dreamed of a keep, I was his dreaming of a keep. When he dreamed of hiding, I was the dreaming of that hiding … you see?"**

Valentina frowned at the witch, who looked down and met her gaze. "That's not how dreams work," she said.

"I never said I was a witch of *dreams*," replied the witch.

"Oh," said Valentina, and suddenly the fear that had been quiet and small in her became quite great; she felt some deep inner pyre of confidence snuffed out; and it was suddenly quite hard for her to breathe.

"You might try it," prompted the witch, not recognizing Valentina's fear.

Valentina took a shuddering breath. She stared at the witch. And then, because she was, after all, Valentina Grigorievna Sosunova, she tried it.

She tried to step behind the witch's eyes; tried to see, not the dream of the witch, but the *act* of the witch's *dreaming*—but her eyes just bugged out and nothing happened.

She began to laugh.

"Valentina?"

"... there's no hope for us, is there? You're just going to eat them."

"Well, yes."

Valentina kept laughing until it stopped, and then sat down. She stared at the egg for a long time, and finally cast a glance over her shoulder at the witch.

"Let me out," she said. "I need to make supper."

And it seemed to the witch in that moment that there was something wrong; that there was something that she'd overlooked, and she tried hard to put her talon on it—to understand *what* was wrong, to understand what part of her world was in disarray, but she could not.

And that night Valentina soaked tomato leaves in vodka to be their salad, and added bleach into the soup; leaned her head into the counter, shook uncontrollably for a while, and finally, fighting herself every step of the process, threw it all away.

"No poison," she told herself. "Not at the Sosunov table."

She made a kind of okroshka for the witch, instead.

THE FEVER broke. Hernais recovered, as the witch had promised, but he did not wake. A neighbor attempted to visit; she heard the squawking of the crows in the distance, heard shrieking as they drove him away. The hours whirled by on the clock.

She slept.

She woke.

She went about the business of the day.

She boiled salt and bay leaves and chicken. She strained the broth. She chopped potatoes until they were as thin as fingernails, and shredded the cabbage fine as grains of sand. She boiled the broth. She left it to simmer with sauerkraut and the veggies in; waved a finger to the birds that were to watch it, stirring now and then; and went to check on the piles of stones. When she came back, assured that everyone was well—

The birds could tell that much, couldn't they? They wouldn't put a stone in the "breathing" pile for someone dead?

—she grated onions and carrots into tiny bits, sautéed them, and added them to the shchi.

That was for her family's breakfast; the chicken, pulled out and set aside, and cooked in the back yard's charcoal pit, would be her and the witch's lunch.

That day was bath day for her great-grandmother. Baths for the old were one of the tasks she least trusted the birds with, feeling that they were too indelicate to carefully wash somebody's skin. She didn't even really trust *herself* with it, and kept second-guessing how hard she was using the sponge, whether the water was warm enough, whether her great-grandmother would be abraded or catch chill. But she'd read in the family's disaster plan that it was important, so she did it anyway.

The birds had missed one of the halls in their sweeping—the heron-bird (and not the heron-witch) that watched the stones caught on and let her know. She swept that hall herself, rather than pull any birds from their current chores and confuse them, and then carefully beat out the broom against the house's outer side.

And the witch watched her from the roof as she went from task to task; watched the little frown on Valentina's face, and the line on her forehead that it made, and she wanted to kiss it away; *remembered* seizing Valentina up, as she laughed, and kissing it away, even though that was something only the Sosunovs, and not the witch herself, had ever done.

And the witch turned her face up and she stared at the sky; and a breeze blew through her feathers; and she trembled. She *trembled.*

Something is wrong.

VALENTINA DREAMED.

She found herself in a blood-soaked crack in a brown shale hill; the narrow walls dripped deep red, and men and women were sprawled and scattered on the ground. Some lay as if they had fallen; others were curled up as if around agony. They were pale as the dead, and she would have *taken* them for the dead, if it weren't for the whispering.

It filled the air there, the soft sibilance of that whispering.

The men and women were speaking. They were whispering and muttering to themselves, each to each; this one about purgatives, that one about gold—there were as many topics as there were people. And she laughed, because it struck her in that moment that their lives were every bit as useful and purposeful as was her own.

"I can't do it," she said. "I can't kill her. I can't beat her and I ... I'm not even *trying* it properly."

The whispering was annoying. She tuned it out. She sat down, braced her back against the razored wall; it was too sharp to sit against, it was uncomfortable, it cut her, and she stood up and walked deeper into the ravine before she sat again.

"I'm afraid," she said.

Nothing answered her.

She adjusted herself in her seat. She waved vaguely at the sky. "I'm afraid, and it just ... it feels wrong to hurt her. I threw a knife at her. I erased her half a wing. I could keep doing that. But she terrifies me. And I keep thinking, maybe if I just ... be good, if I just keep the house and treat her properly, that that'll *work*, like it does in the stories, and she'll be kind and let them go, only she doesn't. She doesn't even seem to understand that that's what I *want*."

She curled in on herself. She rocked.

"I could use the Sosunov magic," she said. "I could meet her in dreams, if I let myself love her, and try to kill her there. I could summon up fire and storms and wild tigers and— and she'd just cast them into the shadow of her wing."

She lay down. She wrapped herself around the pain of it.

"I don't know what to do," she said.

"Valentina?" Mrs. Senko asked, from the mouth of the crack.

Valentina froze up in embarrassment, though she couldn't say why; and eventually, softly, said, "Yes?"

"This is not a safe place for children to play in," Mrs. Senko said. "You come out of there at once."

It was a distraction. She would ignore it. She would finish her thought. She would—

"At *once*," Mrs. Senko emphasized.

Reluctantly, almost rebelliously, Valentina stood. She walked to Mrs. Senko. She looked up at her. Mrs. Senko put a hand on her shoulder, turned her away, walked her out onto the hill.

It was oddly undefined. She thought that, as she stared at it:

Her dreams were usually rich in detail when she let them be, but this—this was just "a brown shale hill."

"Once upon a time," Mrs. Senko said, "Pilgrims would come from the Bleak Academy for one reason or another, realize the impossibility of their goals, and fall into despair; they would descend into the ravine there, and thence remain."

"Pilgrims?"

"Errant students. Busybodies, vagabonds, and the like."

"Oh."

"You don't belong there," Mrs. Senko said. "For one thing, you aren't *from* the Bleak Academy. You don't have the right."

She nudged Valentina along and down the hill.

"For another," said Mrs. Senko, after a moment, "this is just a dream, so you can't very well wither yourself in there forever. For a third, *you* never would."

"I was despairing in there just fine, thank you."

"You wouldn't," said Mrs. Senko, with a contrary confidence; and suddenly Valentina had the oddest feeling that the teacher was much younger than when she'd seen her last. "You'd have gotten up and out eventually, Valentina. On your own."

"... where is this?" Valentina asked.

"Perdition," said Mrs. Senko. "Well, a dream of Perdition. *My* dream, I'd expect."

She rolled a hand.

"Beyond the gates of the Bleak Academy," she explained. "But not yet at the lands of life, or even at the chaos that lies between them. It is a place that is under a shadow."

"Like the witch's shadow?"

Mrs. Senko pursed her lips. "Conceivably."

"... everybody's going to die, Mrs. Senko," Valentina said.

"Oh, yes," agreed Mrs. Senko. She paused. "Well, not *me*. Or my father. And I wouldn't put it past the Principal, to outlive the cosmos. But yes. Basically—everybody dies."

Valentina sulked.

"And then there's Glum," said Mrs. Senko. "I'm not sure if Glum will die. ... or Kifri."

"Please stop listing exceptions."

"Of course."

"They'll all be dying *soon*," Valentina explained.

"That's hard," Mrs. Senko said. "I'm sorry."

She shifted her grip to Valentina's hand. They walked a while.

"I could make you stop caring," offered Mrs. Senko. "I suspect."

Valentina shook her head.

"Would you like to borrow my monster?"

"You're just a dream," Valentina said.

"It's true," Mrs. Senko said, "I don't know exactly how that would work out."

"She's eating my family from inside," Valentina said. "She's in their dreams, she's behind their eyes, she's cultivating herself inside them 'like an egg.' And they're all going to die before they ever wake up and I can't stop her. I'm just ... I'm not any good."

"Yes," agreed Mrs. Senko. "If you were any good, then you wouldn't have wound up in that ravine. But it's not your fault, Valentina. You are only who you are."

"I want to be *better*," Valentina said.

"That's—not realistic."

"But, I *want* to."

"Heh." Mrs. Senko swung their hands. "Perhaps you should open the back of your eyes like the front of them, and light up the void with your beauty, then, as did Miruna Sosunova."

"... I don't know if that's a serious suggestion."

Mrs. Senko gave her a keen look. "It would be interesting if you could manage it."

"Do you have any *practical* solution?"

Mrs. Senko laughed. Valentina yanked her hand out of Mrs. Senko's. She pulled away. She looked down.

"I'm serious," Valentina said.

"You will not like it," said Mrs. Senko.

"Nn," Valentina said, which was more or less a word.

"You cannot be responsible for witches," said Mrs. Senko. "That is the practical solution. Duck the blame. Back away from the whole situation—

slowly—saying, 'No no no *no* no. This is *not* on me.' Recognize that a witch killing people ... that that just isn't your fault."

"No," said Valentina.

"No?"

Valentina shook her head.

"Then—" said Mrs. Senko thoughtfully. "... well, you *are* a child."

And there was something in the way she said that peaked Valentina's interest; that *caught* at her, that pulled her forward onto her toes to listen.

"So there *is* another practical solution," said Mrs. Senko, "which is to say, you are not at this time aware what you're actually capable of. You don't know yet what your limits are, if backed sufficiently far against the wall. Later on in your life, you *will* know that, but right now— perhaps you *could* beat her. Perhaps you are stronger than you ever imagined. Who knows? Not you!

"So, that given—perhaps your best option is just ... trying. Doing your best, knowing that no one can ask any more of you, and hoping that you happened to be blessed with the power to do this particular much-too-difficult thing.

"Stranger things have happened, after all."

Valentina opened her mouth; Mrs. Senko silenced her by raising a finger.

"I am not saying that you *are* stronger than you think," said Mrs. Senko. "For clarity. Nor am I saying that you are obligated to throw yourself against impossible problems just because you are young. I am merely saying that you *could* be stronger than you think, because you don't know yourself; not yet, not at your age. There is no shame in it if it happens instead that you are not that strong."

"This is the same," Valentina said.

Mrs. Senko grinned. "Yes," she agreed. "It is the same suggestion, I suppose. It's 'duck responsibility;' only, first, you try. ... oh! and make sure that no one's watching when you try, or ducking responsibility gets much harder. That's a bonus free advice."

"And not an actual answer," Valentina pointed out.

"Mm. Well, how have you been fighting the witch so far?"

Valentina was uncomfortably silent.

"Honestly," sighed Mrs. Senko. "That bad?"

"I hurt her once," said Valentina.

"That's not the same as fighting someone," said Mrs. Senko. "Fighting someone makes them change. Hurting them just makes them work harder to stay the same."

"Oh, *come on.*"

"*Fighting* someone," Mrs. Senko said, equably, "is taking their greatest strengths, and turning them against them. Then they fall apart, and then you win."

And they walked for a while, but no more was said; and Valentina woke.

IN THE following days she no longer turned the eyes of her mind away from the magic that Gylbard Wan had tried to show her. She spent hours each day desperately meditating upon it—*reaching* for it—but it proved peculiarly elusive.

When she had gone as far as she could with that and gotten nowhere, she'd practice the heron's trick of stepping behind somebody else's eyes, instead.

The witch found her sitting in the garden and commented upon it:

"You have been meditating."

And Valentina's own frustrations came out in that moment:

"I have been *sitting.*"

"Not going well?"

"Look," said Valentina. She stared vigorously into the witch's eyes. Her nose scrunched up and her eyes tried to bug out. Nothing else happened. Then she half-rose for a moment, bent and twisted, and scythed one hand in a rapid arc before the witch:

Nothing happened, once again.

"Those are my two best methods, so far, with which to kill you."

"Kuh," laughed the witch. **"Good luck with that."**

"I feel stupid."

"... Valya," said the witch; and Valentina scowled at the diminutive. **"That is because you are trying something impossible. You cannot kill me. That is like a swallow stooping down to catch a bear."**

"That was *supposed* to put myself in your *looking-upon*," Valentina explained, "and then *that* was to erase you from existence."

"I will show you," said the witch.

"Pardon?"

Something lifted her. She rose, suddenly light; like a puppet, Valentina stood. And that was more literal than she'd like:

It was by her arms that she was lifted, and her feet dangled for a moment before they touched down on the ground.

She started to speak. She tried to say something. Only a hiss of air came out.

The witch did not move, but her eyes were glittering, and Valentina interpreted her words:

"I will show you. I will demonstrate ... that you are just a girl, and I a goddess being born."

Valentina's hands spread, entirely without her own volition. She had the wild thought: *I must be dreaming,* but she knew better, *knew* better, she was a Sosunov and she could not confuse a dream with the waking world.

Her hands spread, and the ground burst open, and a great tree railed upwards from the earth.

Branches extended, crackling noises coming from them, spreading in each direction, knotted, wild.

The witch tilted her head slightly, and Valentina's hands turned, raised upwards, again all without her willing it, and with that gesture sparks of ghost-fire lit all around the branches of the tree.

She managed something almost like words, hissed *at least face me in our dreams*, but the witch didn't hear her.

There was another lifting motion. The tree ascended another story. It towered over the Sosunov compound. It kept on rising.

Valentina's hands beckoned, twisted, and the trunk split open. A wooden owl was forced out from inside it, spread its wings, and took flight; then another; and another, and another, until a great procession of them flew past, above her, enough to darken half the sky.

A gold crown rolled from the tree's heart, landed against her foot—

And suddenly Valentina slumped, and felt herself in control of her movements again; sank to the ground, shuddering, almost weeping, and the witch stepped back.

The tree was gone.

"I have drunk from fourteen Sosunov dreamers," said the witch, **"and from Kolya, while he lived. Do not dare to call yourself *stupid*, that you cannot fight me. That is simply ... wise."**

Valentina cast her a sudden glare. Her face contorted, her eyes bugged out. She tried so very hard to steal the witch's sight, but she didn't have the trick of it.

The witch laughed again.

"But do keep trying, if you must."

"It doesn't *work*," Valentina said.

The witch studied her. Then, suddenly, the witch's expression turned downcast.

"That is wrong," decided the witch.

Valentina didn't respond.

"That is wrong. I do not like this. You should be smiling. You are my darling Valya, and it is better when you smile." She clacked her beak.

"Was it not a wonder? Did you not see and take joy in how amazing I have become?"

"No!"

"… then there is something wrong," said the witch. **"There is something wrong with *me*. Please ignore it. —I will go."**

A cold wind blew.

THERE WAS SOMETHING ACHING inside the witch, in that spirit and that heart that she had drunk up from the Sosunovs; and finally she grasped it.

On the roof, a few nights later, she admitted it to herself, the truth that she'd denied since the beginning, since that first memory of Valentina through another's eyes:

Their memories have infected me.

I am becoming a Sosunov, who loves.

And in that moment she attained to the Sosunov magic; she learned the trick of it, that power that binds family, lovers, and even great friends together across space and time; she basked in the glow of the fire of love that burned within her, though it was not her *own* love; and then it sank in, *that she was feeling it*, and it was as if the world was without foundation; as if the sky had become the lake, and the lake the sky.

The world seemed to fall away from her, or she from it.

She spent the night in a fevered, fearful state that was very much like dreams.

IN THE END, there was no one to discuss this with but Valentina herself.

"They are corrupting me," said the witch.

"I think they must be wiggling inside of me, all your family's loves.

"There is an alien *flame* that is burning inside me, it thinks awful alien things like 'stop scaring her,' 'I miss her smile,' and 'o, my dear brave little girl.'"

"No," argued Valentina.

"It is a primal terror," said the witch. **"I had thought to sup only on their power, but I am getting their *being*. I am no longer only myself."**

Valentina gave her a gaze of dull dislike. "No," she said again.

"Tell me you can make it stop," pleaded the witch.

And suddenly Valentina's eyes sharpened; suddenly her attention focused; she realized then that the witch was not pleading, *let me love you*, or *I am your family*, but rather, *help me stop*. Her interest roused, and her sympathy, too, and she said:

"I don't have to."

"No?"

"You won't change. You won't become like that. You *won't*.

"You are not capable of it."

The witch processed this. Then, like a dog worrying at a bone, she returned to rambling about her fears: **"They are alive in me, and I fear them. They are crowding into me, they are the broth that I am drinking in, and they whisper to me their secrets and their memories. How can I live with their secrets and their memories?"**

"They aren't yours."

"They are *changing* me."

"They aren't yours," said Valentina. She caught the witch's eyes. She tried to pound it into the witch's head with her stare. "They don't belong to you. They aren't changing *you*. You're an evil witch."

"I see them as changing me, and I am afraid."

"Don't. Don't ... don't *feel* that," Valentina said. "Don't. You shouldn't. That's not a witch's feeling. Push it away. It's *people* who get afraid that they'll become something that they don't want."

The witch's stream of thought faltered:

"... I ... should not?"

"Don't be afraid," said Valentina. "Evil witches don't get to be afraid. Don't love. Evil witches don't get to love. Hang on to that. Hang on to that, and it'll be OK. Eat worms and frogs for your supper. Steal and torment. It's a *stolen* love, and not your own. You be a witch, you be *just* a witch, and you *hang on* to that, and live in the eyes that *look upon* and the eyes that *see* and do magic where you cast the shadow of your wing."

"I don't know that I can do that," said the witch. **"What if I can't do that? What if it is not enough?"**

Valentina's eyes were clear. "Then I'll put you out of your misery."

"... thank you," said the witch.

"Just ask it," Valentina said. "Just tell me, you're losing yourself, you can't take it any more, and then hold still, and I'll cut your head off with an axe. Then you can be a witch forever in your headlessness."

"That is more forceful than I imagined," said the witch. **"I am thinking more, stroke my wings and reassure me I am myself, that I may see myself *as* myself, and that all will be OK."**

"Sure," said Valentina, airily. "Whichever."

"OK."

"It's stupid," said Valentina. "You're afraid of nothing. You think you can become them? Become *like* them? You think you know what love *is*? You don't understand anything. You're just a witch."

"You are a blessing," said the witch. **"Thank you. ... you are more than I deserve."**

"I'm going to go take a bath and pretend that this conversation never happened," Valentina said.

And she did.

THE BIRDS drew up water from the well for her, and filled the bathtub with heated stones, and poured it for her; she sank under the waters of the bath and let her hair wash out around her like the crooked branches of a tree.

She rose. She broke above the water, and she took a breath, and then she scrubbed herself down.

She felt a horrifying creeping sense of *invasion*, like the witch had gotten too close to her, and it did not scrub away.

She dressed, and could not forget the witch's words; nor could she help feeling … ungracious, somehow … that her own emotional center was so stubbornly the enemy of the witch.

For the first time since her family went to sleep, she made bread—good black bread, with caraway and fennel—and let the smell of it fill the house. She could not feed it to her family, but at least they could smell it, they could savor that smell in their dreams; and once she thought that they had done so, she tore the bread apart to throw it to a thousand birds.

She shoved aside the birds that were working on the firewood and broke it up herself that day.

She slept. She woke.

She slept. She woke.

And life went on.

ON THE FIFTH "DAY" since the witch's confession, as she lay down to sleep, she tried to cast her mind out to her mother's dreams—

A task that had been futile, again and again, until she had almost ceased to try.

She expected nothing but the dreamless dark, followed by a painful waking.

Instead, this time, she dreamed. She fell past fiery spirals of symbols, and the fluttering of wings, and the twisting, horrible awareness of her own body from the inside, her eyeballs moving back and forth inside their sockets in her skull—at last to pass through some sort of subtle gate and find herself in a great and nourishing emptiness.

She floated there in a thoughtless haze.

The emptiness *encouraged* that. It required nothing of her, it needed nothing from her; it put her at a kind of peace, and it was rich with the nutriments of dream. It was full of color, light, and truth—being there, it filled her.

It was *familiar*, it was *loving*, and she drank it in.

She could not *help* drinking it in, for minutes that stretched nigh to hours.

Then she understood:

Somewhere in the witch's story had been the key to a metaphorical lock; she had understood enough, at last, to slip past the barrier that had sealed her family's dreams against her—but *they* were not now to be found therein. Their dreams had long since become nothing more than the egg that held the witch.

Her eyes searched through the luminiferous albumen in which she was at that time residing, and she saw her there—floating, drifting, dreaming there; a shadowed form not far from her:

The witch.

There in the center of the dream that was like an egg, the witch was young; not a full-sized bird, or a full-sized person, but nothing more than a tiny chick, curled up around herself in a dreamy daze. Child-like, her feathers were white and soft like fur; her eyes were vast; her head was peaked with a wild thatch of fluff like grass.

Valentina drifted to her. Gently she shook the shoulder of the witch.

She watched the bird look up and blink her bleary eyes.

"Valyusha," said the witch. A sleepy concern crossed her face. **"This— you are a creature of the outside world. You should not be here."**

"It's 'Valentina.' And, I found my way," Valentina said.

"I see," said the witch. She hesitated.

Then she stretched. She writhed. She grew. She stopped at a height a bit beyond Valentina's, though her eyes stayed huge and the feathers of her head a childish mess.

"Do not think you can defeat me," she said, **"here."**

"I was just ..."

Valentina hesitated.

"I wasn't going to try to *defeat* you, here," she said. "But now I'm tempted."

"It is futile," said the witch.

"I could fight you here," said Valentina. "I could fight you here, in the cauldron of their dreams. I'd be strong, here."

"Go away," said the witch, and waved a wing, and the wind slammed Valentina awake—

... or would have, anyway, if Valentina hadn't slipped past it, eddied left and eddied right, to hold a sword at the witch's throat, and the wind blew past pointlessly where she had been.

The witch hesitated.

Valentina flushed right to her ears, realizing that she'd *stopped* there; that she'd done the move just like she'd done it when she mock-fought Fevroniya or old Hernais in dreams; but, to actually *beat* the witch, she'd need not to hold a sword at her throat but rather to *cut*—

She thrust the sword.

The witch was gone. Her shadow fell over Valentina; she turned, she saw the witch looming large above her, behind where she had been, and Valentina laughed. She laughed because finally, *finally* she was fighting like she was used to, not with frog sausages on toast or knives or poison or Magister Wan's ink-magic, but with the *Sosunov* magic, the fighting in dreams that she'd been training for since the day she was born. She kicked off the albumen, flew at the witch's heart, and there was a fire in the palm of her hand. It grew larger and larger as she approached the witch, and then it exploded, setting a full three quarters of the dream aflame.

The witch was gone. Her shadow fell over Valentina; Valentina turned, she saw the witch looming huge above her, behind where she had been; felt a horrifying *déjà vu*, and braked, spun, pushed out her hands, and sent a shockwave at the witch.

The witch was gone.

"I am the witch of *looking-upon,*" said the witch. **"I am the witch of *the eyes that see.*"**

Valentina slammed her eyes closed. She listened hard.

She heard the shadow of the witch fall over her; in a clamor of abstract sound, she struck. She dreamt the smell of stone, the sound of two great boulders crashing together, the awful *thud* of the witch's death; opened her eyes again—

The witch was gone.

"I am the witch of *the act of consciousness,*" clarified the witch. **"I am the witch of *the fisher's net that is the light of the fire of consciousness, in the act of casting itself out onto the world.* Independent of sight and any other particular sense. I am not behind *you,* Valentina; I am behind your act of dreaming."**

Her voice was remarkably relaxed; the tension had drifted from her over the course of Valentina's unsuccessful flailing. Memories of training Valentina as her mother, as her father, as her aunt Fevroniya, and others had slipped into the witch's mind instead.

Dueling Valentina in dreams and commenting on her techniques had become *familiar* to her—but:

Valentina dreamt a spear. She reversed it. She stabbed it in through her eyes, scraped it inside her brain, searched out the fire of consciousness, and, for the first time in that fight, she touched the witch.

She *felt* it, the little twitch of her. She smelt the blood.

The act was harder to do than to describe. The concentration it required from Valentina was *acute.* She dreamed that she scraped the back, not of her physical head, but of the theater in her mind that regarded the world around her, caught the homunculus-Valentina that lived within it, watching everything around her, and beside that was the eidolon of the witch.

She twisted the spear.

She stabbed it through her, and felt a horrified fluttering and a deep squawking sound resound within her soul.

There, she thought.

Her hands moved. The blade moved, expanded. The fire of her consciousness became a torn fabric that spread and stung around the metal of it; she could not think, she did not *allow* herself to think, and the dream became a welter of undifferentiated sensations all around her; for a moment, as she struck her inner eye, it was a near thing, the battle between Valentina and the witch; only:

The witch was gone.

"That was really very good," said the witch. And for a long moment Valentina did not understand the words; then understanding came slamming down and locked into place. **"That was very good; but you have forgotten that no matter how you contort your mind, you cannot change the fact that there *is* a you that dreams it."**

It was all futile, it all had been from the start; and Valentina crumbled.

The strength left her body; she fell, and she curled in around the hurt of it, that her situation was endless, that she couldn't win; that *there was nothing at all she could do.*

That was the moment that their battle was decided.

That was the moment that her loss was as good as written—not Valentina's, though, but the witch's.

IT WAS A MISTAKE TO react to that. It was a mistake to wrap the hurting girl in wings like a mother's arms. It was a mistake to offer her despairing, helpless child a love like a mother's love.

—but what else could she have done?

She was *suffering*. She was *dejected*. She was *beaten*. So the witch wrapped her in feathers, soft and warm.

And in that moment, as she held her Valyusha, the witch could no longer pretend that she was *not* Valentina's mother, as well as the witch; was *not* Valentina's father, as well as the witch; that she had *not* taken elements from them to be the mortar of her soul and in so doing connected to their child, their child that she was responsible for, that she loved, that was *her own*, that hated her; that, in that hating her, was *right*.

In that moment she had to stare squarely into the face of the fact that she was wrong.

To oppose that recognition of wrongness, all she had was stubbornness—stubbornness and the knowledge that she was becoming a goddess, that she was *transcending*, and that that was something wonderful. And if Valentina had argued against those points then maybe the witch would have had defensiveness to oppose it with too, but Valentina didn't.

Not then, and not later. Time spun by and Valentina had ceased entirely to argue.

Instead, Valentina cooked borscht and baked chicken. Instead Valentina made frogs into pies. Instead Valentina moved among the great flock that the witch had gathered, directing them to take care of the witch's fourteen comatose bodies.

And as she watched her, the witch felt small and great and terrible and broken.

Her heart hurt.

It was *her Valentina* that was suffering like this, that was struggling under the burden of the witch.

So she stopped.

IT WAS right there in the crisis manual, after all. If it's ever too much—if it's ever *just too much*—

Even if you've already started doing it. Even if you are becoming a goddess. Even if you're not sure what'll happen:

You can stop.

One day Valentina met her eyes and said, "It's unbearable, isn't it?"

Yes.

And that was that:

She let go.

Not there, but from a nearby tree, she let it go.

The nagging sense that something was wrong resolved in her; it became a stern strong sense of something right; became a *joy-in-concept* that motivated her, and she let it go:

Opened wide her wings, and the Sosunov house fell under the shadow of those wings; and she pulled it back. Pulled *all* of it back. She dragged herself from the dreaming of Hernais; and Donal; Aunt Fevroniya; Valentina's Mom and Dad—

She let herself flow out of them, and let the richness of their thoughts and lives flow out of her; let the love in them, and the dreams in them, and all their power, at first in a torrent and then a trickle, flow out of her, until the eggs in their dreams sagged in on themselves and cracked and split to reveal nothing but the goopy remnants of the albumen within.

She let it go.

She let them startle awake, each and every one of them, even the most precious and most rich; and all of it was gone from her, every drop of it was gone from her—

Except for the bits that weren't.

And she stood there on the branches, and she felt her life drain away. She felt herself dying as the eggs caved in, as she became a shadow of herself, a ghost, a dream; and soon all of it was gone—

Except the little that remained.

Scraps of love, and hope, and power; little bits of dream; she looked at the sky and there was still a bit of Hernais' *seeing* of the sky, and aunt Fevroniya's; and Donal's; each and every one, in it; and she thought as she teetered on the branch that it might be enough to sustain her still, only, it wasn't.

There was not enough left to her to maintain a body.

There wasn't enough left of her to remain a witch.

She'd thought that there would be, but there wasn't; she'd thought she'd just return to being her simple self, unpolluted by the Sosunovs, but she did not. That selfhood had been *invested* in an account with negative returns; and it was lost.

As the last of the Sosunov sleepers woke, the witch dissolved into fog and mist:

Nothing more than a passing dream.

And all through the house came the sounds of groaning, stirring, blinking, sitting, rising, questioning, and wings, and *wings*, so many wings, the flapping and the fluttering of a thousand mindless fleeing birds.

AND THAT was the end of the story of the witch; or, rather, almost its end. Its end, only, not quite.

It was three days later:

The witch pulled the last few pieces of herself together. She found herself in a dream of the Sosunov magic—drawn, with what little was left inside her, to the dream of the one person that she had ever loved.

Her shoulders sank. Her head stretched up.

She found herself before the gates of Valentina's dreams. She walked up to them. She rapped upon them, two or three taps, then a pause, then the knock repeating. And Valentina noticed her; heard her, then; and her pulse sped up and her eyes went wide.

"Let us dream of tea," said the witch, **"and cakes, and sausages; and I will dwell here, in your passing dreams, and here I will grow strong; and in time I shall find a way to take the power of others without also taking in all their memories, their hearts, their loves, and I shall become a goddess once again."**

"I'm sorry," Valentina said. "But no."

And the witch leapt for the inside of Valentina's eyes, but she was grown too small. Before the scrap of dream that the witch had become, the fire of Valentina's consciousness was as the sun; it scorched her, she could not bear the heat of it, she was way too small to hide beside it, and she fell back before the gates of dream.

And Valentina took her, and she pinned her wings, with delicacy and with iron nails, one to each side of the gates was given; and Valentina turned the head of the witch, and Valentina cut the throat of the witch, and the heron-witch bled out, there, inside of Valentina Sosunova's dreams.

ONCE UPON a time, Valentina Grigorievna Sosunova nearly attained to the True Thing that is beyond all things, that is behind all things; to the void that is lively in its emptiness. In that moment, her soul was singing; she laughed with it, with a brilliant and growing joy; a dark bird fluttered in her chest and starlight filled her and she pulled herself closer to it, closer, wrapped herself around it like it were something precious in its emptiness, knew it in that moment to be the answer to her every dream and to all desiring—

Only, just before she could attain to it, and in that very moment, something moved.

It was the Headmaster's attention, she would later say—the will of the Headmaster of the Bleak Academy, he the lord of Death's dominion he.

Something moved in the emptiness, and the brilliance of that revelation was to Valentina lost. Instead, she became aware of the movement of her eyes, like two small fishes darting in the emptiness. Instead she became aware of her muscles, lying long against her bones. She became aware of the flesh of her, of Valentina as a body, of Valentina as a thing of skin and meat, of organs, hair, and bone, and she wept into herself because she had become loathsome unto herself, and her chance at attaining to the True Thing was thereby lost.

Time passed.

The power of the witch broke, as described above. There was nothing left but a dried-up corpse nailed to the gates of Valentina's dreams.

Life at the Sosunovs resumed.

Slowly Valentina learned not to panic when the people around her went to sleep—learned that they would wake again. Slowly she learned not to panic at the sound of fluttering wings. Slowly she got used to the fact that when she talked to people, human people, that they would answer her, and she stopped startling every time they did. Slowly she overcame her fear that every dream would be the one where *she* would get put to sleep for months on end and resumed her study of the Sosunov magic.

And one day she found the Headmaster of the Bleak Academy in a picture-book; or, the picture of him, anyway. He was subtitled, *The Headmaster of the Bleak Academy (he the lord of Death's dominion he.)*

She recognized him at once.

She recognized him by his dark hair. She recognized him by his dark eyes—they were like Magister Wan's, a starscape, although they showed a different sky. She recognized him by his silver-lined black velvet clothes. But most of all she recognized him by the subtle air of him, by the aftertaste of his presence. It was like something rotten and cloying clinging to the back parts of her tongue.

Her fingers traced his face upon the page.

Her eyes sharpened.

"I'll *get* you," Valentina Grigorievna Sosunova told him. "Just you wait."

CHAPTER TWO

VALENTINA AND THE HEADMASTER

Once upon a time, but not so very long ago, the Headmaster of the Bleak Academy said to the emptiness: I, I, I to me, and I, myself.

The words fell from his lips and became a seed. The seed became a flower—the first bluebell. In the mornings, the bluebell dripped with dew. Over the years the dew became a pond.

To that pond the Headmaster returned and in that pond he saw the face of Death.

He wept to see it.

In that moment he loathed nothing so much as that flower; as that dew—but still he tasted it, bellied himself up to it in the shape of a serpent and licked it, suckled on the dew of it and chewed its leaves. ...

— from *The Shepherd's Son and the Bleak Academy,*

by Ksenofont Nazarievich Adrianov

ET'S TELL the story of Valentina and the Headmaster of the Bleak Academy!

She was a mortal woman from the Sosunov family. He was a legendary figure from beyond the world:

A warrior whose spear had slaughtered giants; a terrifying sorcerer; lord of the dead, or, at least, of Death's dominion; in some stories a trickster figure, in others God, or the Devil, or just a mask that is worn by Death. But she took him on anyway, cut him open, and covered over his Academy in sorrows.

It happened like this.

Valentina was a smart, strong, and well-loved girl, but she grew up haunted. She was haunted by her physicality. She was haunted by knowing that she had skin, and muscles lying long against her bones, and eyeballs in her head. She was haunted by a pervasive self-loathing that liked to hide behind that knowledge, that liked to remind her of the grossness of her body to make her think she was nothing more than that.

She sickened herself.

She was alone in this. Nobody else accepted that she was ugly. Nobody else even accepted that she was a physical creature, bound up in bones and flesh and organs. She was Valentina Grigorievna Sosunova, who had defeated the heron-witch, and she grew up tall and strong and beautiful, and she couldn't get anyone to accept any other truth of her, no matter how hard she tried at it. At worst, they thought she was grubbing for compliments. At best, they'd say something like, "Everybody's that way, Valentina, but you're less so than most."

She stoked a burning resentment for the Headmaster of the Bleak Academy, whom she blamed for all of this. Secretly she blamed him for her being a creature with a body, with awkward bits and unwanted bits and all those other things. Secretly she thought that she'd almost become something *different,* or almost transformed in some fashion, and that he'd somehow noticed and prevented her. More openly she blamed him for her inability to get her physicality out of her head. She thought it was his fault that when she looked in the mirror she saw a ruined cage of flesh instead of Valentina, a beautiful girl; or maybe that everyone saw that kind of thing and it was just his fault that *she* cared instead of being able to ignore it like everyone else seemed to be able to do.

One could write extensive treatises on exactly how fair this assessment was—

But in the end, though, it wasn't completely wrong.

Every year, on Valentina's day—not her birthday, of course, but the anniversary of the day she beat the witch—her mother would sit with Valentina, and brush out Valentina's long dark hair, and they would speak of many things, and they would trade promises and laughter, and then when there was quiet for a time Valentina would ask her mother whether she was ready yet, whether she was strong enough yet, whether she was good enough yet, to take on *he the lord of death's dominion he, the Headmaster of the Bleak Academy is he named.*

And every year her mother would brush her hair for a while in silence, and she would think of how in the stories the Headmaster of the Bleak Academy could hold his own against a Jotun in a fight; how his sorcery could bend a person's mind or make a captive of their soul; and how so many go to Death's dominion but so very few return. She would brush Valentina's hair in silence, and then hug her close, and say, "Oh, my little wolf, you are too young yet; if you go this day, you will surely die."

But when Valentina was twenty, her mother bit that reflexive answer back.

She studied Valentina for a long time, and what she saw impressed her. Her daughter's arms were corded with muscle. She sat with effortless poise. Her eyes were unyielding.

She knew that Valentina had studied a two-sword style under a second cousin, once removed, and had learned it prodigiously.

She had seen her daughter snatch a wren out of the air.

She let out a sigh.

Reluctantly, she said, "You are strong enough; you are ready now; you can face he the lord of Death's dominion he."

Valentina turned to look at her, and her mother dropped the brush and seized Valentina's face between her hands.

"But you must not die!" her mother told her. "If I am to agree to this, then you must agree to that. You must not die to him. You must come back to me, my darling girl."

Valentina wriggled, uncomfortably. "Mother."

Finally, her mother released Valentina's face. "If you will listen, I have three pieces of advice."

"Of course."

"The fight must be quick," her mother said. "Even if that means a reckless charge. He is vain, and he will not expect you to be his equal or his better; but by the time you have exchanged blows three times, he will have learned your measure. That is your only opportunity; if you do not take him down by then, then he will shift to a defensive fight and he will never tire."

Valentina made a face.

"If he speaks, you must not listen," her mother continued. "You are strong-willed and you are stubborn, but a wicked sorcery lives within the words he speaks; if you listen to him, he will find words to say that will destroy you, and he will unmake you and leave you unable to return to me, my darling girl.

"Third," her mother started, but Valentina interrupted.

"If I do not listen to him, dear mother," Valentina said, "then I must kill him. Because he will not be able to say the words that will fix me. Nor will he be able to repent to me, or tell me of any way he can make it up to me. I will have no recourse but to murder him."

"There is no one who will reproach you," Iskra said. "He is he, the lord of Death's dominion."

"... then it shall be as you say."

"Third," said Iskra, "if you defeat him in a fight, and close your ears against his words, you still have no defense against his sorcery. I have thought about this in some detail, and I think you may expect a certain amount of assistance from the Sosunov magic—the lands beyond the world are very much like dreams—but I cannot convince myself you can rely on this. The lands beyond the world are *like* dreams, but they are *not* dreams; and you are a mortal girl, and he the lord of Death's dominion he. There is nothing I can teach you and nothing I can give you that will help any further, nothing that the Sosunov household can provide. But— if you go to old Aggie's shop, down in Rose Alley off of Eel, you may find that she will sell the kinds of things you need."

Valentina gave her mother a serious look. "You have told me never to visit there."

"I have," her mother said. "I now relent."

So Valentina went down to Rose Alley, off of Eel Way, in the shadow of a hill whose top the chaos misted over, and there she found old Aggie's shop, and she went in. She smelled the smell of strange spices. She walked by jewelry boxes, sequined scarves, astrolabes and Fabergé eggs, incense holders, and rare perfumes, and tucked away in the corner of a shelf between the statue of an elephant and a *ba gua* wheel, she found a small brass bell.

It was embossed with strange figures, stranger animals, and ancient runes.

She traced the runes out with her finger. Their language eluded her.

Their meaning eluded her. There was no such thing as a truly alien writing in Fortitude—the curse of Babel never fell upon that sunless otherland, which meant that even the languages of the angels and the dead were an open book to her—but the longer she traced her finger across the runes upon the bell the less the sense they made to her; the closest she could get to understanding them was *I, I, I to me, and I, myself.*

It struck her as interesting, but not useful. She set the bell back down.

She proceeded to the counter, and it had a fishing spear and nets hung up behind it, and a register upon it, and a thick bottle-glass surface with treasures shelved beneath. She stood on tiptoe to look over the counter and behind the shelves, looking for the shopkeeper. "Hello?"

Old Aggie shuffled out.

Old Aggie's neck was long and well-wadded with scarves. Her nose was sharp as a knife. Her eyebrows were as black as her hair was white— like two ravens soaring before the piled clouds—and her middling width was turned to roundness by her coats.

"You're that Sosunov child," she said.

"Valentina," Valentina said politely.

"Mmp."

"Old mother," Valentina said. She made as much of a curtsey as she could in a crowded shop with her trousers on. "If you please, I'm making a journey past the chaos to ... settle my differences ... with the Headmaster of the Bleak Academy, and my mother said I should first come here."

Her right hand touched the hilt of a sword as she said 'settle my differences,' and Aggie looked at it, and frowned.

"Do you," Valentina said, "have ... supplies, I guess? That I might need, for such a thing?"

"There's better things a girl like you could be doing with your life," Aggie pointed out, "than throwing it away on a vendetta with a god."

"There are no gods save the one God," Valentina said, "and the Headmaster is not He."

"Mmp."

"I had my hand upon the most precious thing in all of life," Valentina said. "And he ruined me, and stole it from me, and left me to struggle on."

"... well, you don't think small," Aggie said.

She disappeared into the back for a few minutes, then wandered among the shelves. She returned and lay a few things upon the counter:

A fighting knife. A belt. And a large gold bell.

"The knife is not of very good quality," she said. "I would recommend against using it to slay any dragons. But if you dig up old bones and tap them with it, they will come to life. The belt can hold loose trousers up, or, you can place its buckle in the skull of such raised bones and they can speak, and whip them with the rest of it if they misbehave."

"I ... why do I need such things?" Valentina asked.

"To enter the chaos," Aggie said, "is to lose all you know, and to lose yourself. That is the kind of place it is. That is what it *does*. You will become lost, because that substance inside of you that lets you *not* be lost will be stripped away. You can trust no map. You can trust no guide. You cannot trust your spirit or your mind. But old bones, they know the way."

"Oh."

"Now, you *do* have your own bones," Aggie said, gesturing towards Valentina's innards with her head. "Strictly speaking. So you don't *need* the belt. But listening to 'em's dreadful hard, you know? And you're way too young."

"I'm twenty," Valentina protested.

"Mmp."

Valentina reached out. She touched the golden bell on the counter. It was wintry-cold and had a weight to it, a feeling of endless mass to it, like the golden bell was merely the tip of a great and hidden iceberg; it felt reluctant to move, slow to come up in her hand, when she hesitantly picked it up.

"That one's the real prize, though," Aggie said. "Ring it once and the gates of the Bleak Academy will break. A second time, and the Headmaster himself won't dare to say a word against you. Ring it a third time and you'll rout their armies, their spells and powers will fade away like a passing rain, and their every measure will be defeated. Just *carrying* it is a sovereign remedy to their powers; they can't erase you from existence while you're holding it, or turn your perceptions inside-out, or fill you up with hatred for yourself. Take this bell and you will be absolute and inviolable before all their armies, all their hatred, their dominions."

Valentina tried to shake the bell, but it did not shake; it was as if a strong wind opposed her, as if she were struggling forward against a gale and making no progress, only it was just her arm and hand that were thus affected. The bell trembled in the air but it did not ring.

"It won't ring unless you buy it," Aggie said.

"Oh."

Valentina set it down. She touched its handle, the knife, the belt. There was a look of longing on her face.

"I only have a few hundred cash with me," she said. "That can't possibly be enough. But I might be able to call upon the treasury of the Sosunovs, for such a thing as this."

"This isn't really a cash shop, love."

"... uh?"

"This ..." Aggie's eyes scanned the counter. Her neck rolled. She rang it up in her head. "This would cost you the souls of the Sosunov family, less one."

The light of interest in Valentina's eyes dimmed. She sighed. She ran her hand along the long knife's sheath, then pushed the treasures back towards Aggie across the counter. "Too steep for me."

"You don't have souls?"

Valentina snorted. "They're not mine for the selling. And it'd be too steep a price, old mother, if they were."

Aggie sighed. "Alas." She swept away the golden bell. She bustled off. A few minutes later, she returned, setting a silver bell on the counter where it had been. "This, then."

"Hm?"

"This is our discount option," Aggie said. "It is crude. It is unfinished. You cannot hope to shatter the gates of the Bleak Academy with it, but it will crack them. Perhaps it will open them enough for someone of your size to wriggle through. You cannot hope to defeat the Headmaster of the Bleak Academy with it, but if you ring it a second time, at least, his magic is certain to fail him. That is not *nothing*. And if you ring it a third time, or a fourth time, similar good things are sure to follow."

Valentina reached towards the silver bell, then hesitated. "I have no souls at all to offer you," she said. "Not even mine. I long ago resolved that if I were ever offered the opportunity, I would not sell it."

"For this?" Aggie shrugged. "This is just a prentice piece, if by someone who would become a master. For this, I do not need a soul. For the silver bell, and the belt and buckle, and the knife ... all I would ask from you is your dreams."

The words shocked Valentina. It took her long seconds to process them; and even when she had understood them, her brain did not function.

It was as if she stood alone in a great echoing space, surrounded by pillars of bone and distant walls.

"Not like it's safe to dream while you're out there anyhow," Aggie said.

Valentina waited for an impulse to arise from her heart, something to shout, *no*, or, maybe, even, murmur *yes*, but instead there was only a great weight, and a great burden, that seemed to sift in and settle in around her, and as if from every side. "I can't," she said, and there was a catch in her voice. "I can't. Not even to beat him. I am Valentina Grigorievna Sosunova."

"Be certain," Aggie said. "For you may be dying for it."

"Or worse," Valentina agreed.

"If you are going to fight he the lord of Death's dominion he," Aggie said, rolling the words, "the Headmaster of the Bleak Academy is he named ... then I cannot in good conscience recommend anything cheaper than this kit here. And I meant what I said about it not being safe to dream out there. When you're traveling in the chaos—they can open up a crack in your heart, a way for the wildness to get inside."

"... I can't," Valentina said. "Is there any other price?"

"There is a silver key that Miruna Sosunova created upon the occasion of her enlightenment. I would accept that key, and a thousand years of service."

Valentina blanched. "My dreams are worth that much?"

"You are Valentina Grigorievna Sosunova," Aggie said. "Legends will be told of them."

"I can't give you a thousand years of service," Valentina said, shaking her head. "I can't even give you that key."

"Then I cannot help you."

Valentina's gaze swept the shop. It meandered its way to the little brass bell whose existence she had taken note of, before. She indicated it with her head. "What about that one?"

The silver bell vanished with a flourish into the sleeve of the shopkeeper's coat.

Aggie followed Valentina's gaze to the brass one.

She shrugged. "Trash," she said. "At best, a trinket."

Valentina picked it up and brought it back to the counter. She set it there beside the belt and the knife. "Tell me what it does."

"It's a bell," Aggie said. "You ring it. It makes noise."

Valentina's face fell.

Watching her, something in Aggie's expression softened. "It has power," she conceded. "If you ever lose yourself, the ringing of the bell will find you. It will remind your heart, or whatever *you've* got in there, to beat; your lungs to breathe, and your eyes to see. It is the voice that cannot be silenced, and when all else is lost, the bell will still be ringing, to remind you, here is Valentina Grigorievna Sosunova, and the ringing of her bell. But that is all that it will do. It will not help you to fight off madness or despair or the powers of the Bleak Academy. It will, at best, remind you that you had intended trying."

"How much?"

"A rainbow's skin," Aggie said. "A shadow's tooth. A drum that grants wishes, or the tears of the sun ... something of that sort?"

"I ... I don't have anything like that," Valentina said.

"A badger's laugh? Luck in a bottle? A fifth part of a soul?"

"A hundred cash?"

Aggie shook her head.

"I could phrase it as 'the cash of a young Sosunov,'" Valentina said, "if that would hel— oh."

"Oh?"

"Pinioned to the twin gates of my dreams," Valentina said, "born from scripture and holding the power to be *the eyes that see*, the power of *looking-upon*—I have the dried-up dream-corpse of a witch."

Aggie's eyes narrowed. "So that's what happened," she said.

"Aye."

"I'll take it," Aggie agreed, "on account of, I wouldn't want my corpse left there like that, if something like that happened to me. C'mere."

She grabbed Valentina's lapel with one hand, leaned her down over the counter, and then bent down herself to rummage on the under-counter shelves. She came up with a folded tablecloth, which she tossed next to the other items, and a loupe, which she held before her twitching eyebrows and used to peer into each of Valentina's eyes.

"There," she said, and pinched behind Valentina's right eye with two long fingernails—

It was surprisingly painless—

And then it was as if a warm wind was blowing, as if the world had brightened and grown clearer, as if a weight had lifted from Valentina's shoulders, or, at least, her whole body become more light. She gave a heaving, shuddering sigh, and staggered back, gaping at Aggie with a mix of startlement and gratitude.

It was as if Aggie had drawn a long red-tipped feather from her eye; and, except for that feather, still pinched between her nails, the witch in Valentina's dreams was gone.

Aggie's shoulders sagged. A tired expression crossed her face.

"Come on, then," she said. "Take your stuff and go."

Valentina took the knife, and the belt, and the little brass bell. She hesitated for a moment, looking at the tablecloth, and Aggie nodded to her.

"Take it," Aggie said. "'s your change."

TO THE NORTHWEST LAY the beach, and the mangal, and the cliffs—and then the chaos.

To the west, the hills, and the tent-city of the demon-folk—and then the chaos.

To the north and east, the lake—which was not chaos, but was rich in *veins* of chaos, which the sailors would often use as eldritch passageways to sail in or out from the seas of Earth.

To the south, where the way was not impassible, the chaos abutted Fortitude directly.

It was a wild land, the chaos was, a land that by its very nature and its definition would be unexplored territory forever: inherently unknown and inherently unknowable, and sharing that peculiar character of things that one has never seen before, of new wonders and new horrors, and of piles of unrecognizable objects in the dark. A place it was that presented itself to travelers as surreal and ever-changing ... though, as with those piles of objects, if one studied any piece of it for long enough, its surreality and its shifting quality were known to fade.

There are people who have traveled all their lives and never found their way Outside the world, never walked beyond the firmament and the fundament and out into that inconstant land; but, for Valentina Grigorievna Sosunova, the road was not a long one.

She travelled south.

She walked three blocks southeast along Rose Alley, emerging at that crooked corner where a fish shop used (until the earthquake came) to lean out over the street. She passed a handful of food carts as she went up Eel Way. From there, to 3rd, to follow the main thoroughfare for quite some while; she walked in the lights of street-lamps past the benches of the parks. Nearly she went to the great crossing with Irinka Avenue (though it was called Beylerbey Road, back then), but before she reached it, she turned off on a winding, climbing, southern-bearing sideway that cut across first Orchard and then Andrews and then progressively more nameless streets.

Less than seven miles from her home she began to feel as if she were traveling in an alien land.

She wasn't in the chaos yet. She stood supported by the solid land and truth, in the settlement of Fortitude. But the alteration was beginning.

People had begun making architectural decisions that she did not understand. There were half-circle awnings on the shops she passed. A spiral staircase wound up the outside of one building. Another building was painted half red, half white.

The fruit markets that she passed gave rise to a sweet and sour smell that she did not recognize.

The shop signs and family crests that marked the buildings that she passed seemed to be swimming in her vision. She knew that she could figure them out if she squinted, if she focused, but something about them made her not *want* to squint, not want to focus; made it hard.

The world went strange.

She reached the base of the southern hill, ducked into a covered stairway, and began to climb. It was dizzying. The echoes of her footsteps bounced off the walls, and the sound of that confused her. It made her feel unreal.

The terrain became rough. The steps, which started out regular and even and well-maintained, gave way bit by bit to cracked and twisted tile.

For a while a trickle of water ran down the west side of the steps; then it ceased, as inexplicably as it came.

Now and then there as she climbed a crack would be open in the walls or ceiling above her, through which there shone a light.

When the stairway opened up onto the hilltop, that same light burst through the open door and blinded her. She gasped. She put her hand over her eyes and still it was so bright that tears welled up behind her eyelids from it.

This was her first true vision of the chaos:

For the first time in her waking life Valentina saw the sun.

IT WAS not Earth's sun that ruled beyond the world. It was a stranger sun than that.

The eye of heaven that looked upon the chaos ... was something sonorous and graven. It was the color of polished bronze, and round. Inscriptions ran around its rim—and wheels and wheels turned within. It had eight arms like a compass rose, four thin, four fat; of those, two thin stretched down and long like fishing lines (or, perhaps, two legs of an eerily thin tripod) to touch on the horizon, far below. It was a sun that burned more softly than the sun of Earth: giving the same rough *amount* of light, perhaps, but with less ferocity and less intensity.

To enter into the chaos is to lose yourself, and to lose everything you know.

... of course, to Valentina, whether it was the sun of the Outside or the sun of Earth made little difference. She was neither a sailor nor an immigrant; she had been born, and lived for twenty years, within a sunless land. In the light of the sun, her eyes watered copiously. Her mind went blank and struggled to cope with the sheer scale of that light. She wondered for a moment if she was dead, if this was what being dead was like: like being in the light of a million candles.

It was a long time before she could take note of anything else.

Eventually, the brightness seemed a little less. Eventually, though her eyes still watered and she dared not look up, she was able to open them a little bit and take a look around. She saw a barren land, dotted with scrub, that faded in the distance into multicolored mist. Looking behind her, down the slope the staircase climbed, the same mist pooled upon the hill to hide her view of Fortitude below.

"It's so very bright," she said, like she was uncertain whether that was acceptable.

Then she shrugged and began to walk.

There were no roads to the Bleak Academy. No trustworthy travel guides or maps. She had no real sense as to where it was, save *away from here* and *in*. So she did her best. She turned to put the sun at her back, and her shadow before her, because she was going to a place that she considered dark. And she walked through the chaos Outside the world, and her shadow went before her; and, the sunlight shone behind.

She walked for days.

She walked past eerie sights and withered dells. She took her meals in the lee of stones. She rolled the hilt of Aggie's knife between her hands until she felt she knew the blade; she listened to the ringing of her bell. Once, she unfurled the tablecloth that she'd earned as change; she found a magic feast upon it, which vanished when she picked it up again. After that, she picked at that selfsame feast for her every meal.

She stomped scorpions dead in a crooked waste.

She fled across hills from a nameless beast.

She passed strange plants in vivid bloom; walked past the cairns of giants. Her feet grew sore and her head hung low.

And still she walked.

Eventually, though, she decided she wasn't getting anywhere. She was dirty. She was exhausted. She was by the bank of a dried-up river, and, for all she knew, she was as far from the Bleak Academy as the day she'd started.

She could even still be pretty close to Fortitude!

... for all that she prayed that it was not so.

She decided she wasn't getting anywhere; so, she dug into the clay by the river bank, and she started looking for old bones.

She found and tossed aside a fang as big around as her arm. She dug up, and discarded, a glimmering, ape-sized shell. Finally, she unearthed what seemed to be a human skull. Beneath it there was a spine; she shoved the mud away from the first few vertebrae, wiped her brow, stopped there for a moment, and thought.

Then she nodded to herself, took out Aggie's knife, and tapped the skull with its pommel, twice.

Old bones began to pull themselves up out of the earth.

Fingerbones wriggled up to grasp at the surface of the clay. They flexed, trembled, and then two bony wrists popped free. The arms levered themselves up, and the ribcage with them. The skeleton of some long-forgotten soul pulled itself out of the riverbank.

It rolled its skull upon its neck. It did a little shiver of a dance.

"I'm lost," Valentina said.

Hesitantly, she took the buckle off of her belt. She tossed it into the skull, and it caught there, in the air.

"So I'd like you to lead the way for me, to the Bleak Academy, that is beyond the lands of life."

The skull worked its jaw. The buckle moved from side to side, like a tongue might move. Then a wind blew through it, and the skeleton spoke. "Death's dominion? It's far to the east, along the river's way."

Valentina turned. She shaded her eyes. She frowned.

"Right," the skeleton said. "Roughly. To your right, and back. Is east."

"Thank you."

Valentina oriented herself. She began to walk along the river bank. The skeleton followed after.

"I've never been dead," Valentina said, after a while. "Is it very hard?"

"It is not so hard as living."

"How so?"

"It's a lot *like* living," said the skeleton. "… only, you don't mind so much."

The land grew richer as they walked. They passed a place of fruited trees. Valentina plucked a sweetsop and nibbled on it as they walked. She offered a bit to the skeleton, but it shook its skull.

"I would rather eat you," it said.

"That's not convenient for me."

"Ah." The skeleton's voice was sad. Its shoulders sagged. It trudged, and gave a desolate sigh.

Valentina couldn't help but smile. "Here," she said.

She took Aggie's blade and cut along her arm and three drops of rich red blood welled up.

She let them fall, one by one, onto the ground.

"O Christ God," murmured the skeleton, as it knelt down on the ground, "bless the food and drink of Thy servants, for holy art Thou, always, now and ever, and unto the age of ages. Amen."

It leaned its skull forward. It licked up the drops of blood, using the buckle as its tongue. They fell into its spinal passage and dissipated in some inobvious fashion.

"Glory to the Father, and to the Son," it said, rising and bowing to the ground, and gave a closing grace.

They walked on.

Valentina rubbed at her nose, awkwardly. "I usually just kind of mumble," she said.

"It is all right," said the skeleton. "I said it for us both."

Valentina finished with the sweetsop and tossed it aside. It rolled and settled in a depression on the earth; perhaps in some later era trees would grow.

Over the next few hours, the skeleton filled out. Its flesh filled in, its meat, its skin, and even clothes—a suit of dark and layered silks—until it seemed to be a young man in his twenties, normal save for the still-empty hollows of his eyes.

"I'll call you Anatoly," Valentina said, "because we are walking towards the sunrise."

"'Anatoly,'" he said, tasting the name. His bones danced inside him and he shivered. "As you say. And you are?"

"Valya—Valentina Grigorievna Sosunova," she said. "I am traveling the lands Outside the world to kill he the lord of Death's dominion he, the Headmaster of the Bleak Academy is he named."

Anatoly showed mild surprise. "Can such a man be killed?"

"I hope so," Valentina said. "Otherwise this journey will have no happy ending."

"If he kills you," Anatoly said, "may I eat your heart?"

"I don't recall claiming that I had one."

"... wasteful," Anatoly sulked.

He walked beside her for a while.

To their right rose cliffs, colored pink and red. They were striated, and of a flaky stone. They darkened more towards brown in the lower portions.

Wisps of mist floated by above.

A trickle of water emerged from the dryness of the river's bed. It wound this way and that among the elevations of the mud. It swelled, as they moved eastward, rising, thickening, until it had become a river. It grew until it filled the riverbed, until it roared beside them, until its spray burst up, now and then, to dampen Valentina's face.

They walked beside the river—sometimes on clay, and sometimes on sections of great flat stone.

An aimless wind began to blow. It twisted and turned this way and that around them. It started warm but it grew colder.

A lock of hair blew before Valentina's eye; she pushed it back, once, twice, three times, before she finally re-bound her hair with a bit of string.

In the distance was a sound like thunder.

Eventually the wind died down. A tension left Valentina's shoulders as the world quieted and stilled, though the distant thunderous sound remained; she smiled, brushed back her hair again, and looked around her for a moment before hiking over to a vast red stone. She spread her tablecloth in what had recently been its lee.

In the very moment she unrolled the tablecloth a feast faded into view upon it! There were two kinds of borscht, five kinds of bread, lentils, potatoes, vushka, cod, cabbage (stuffed with various wonders), honey, herring, knish and salad, sweet grain pudding, sauerkraut, mushrooms, fried cheese, fried eels, and pickled eggs, and uzvar, coffee, and wine for her to drink. There was even a bite of chocolate by the side!

She hesitated awkwardly before closing her eyes and clasping her hands in a silent grace.

Then she opened her eyes, took a chunk of bread, and began to eat.

She sipped from a cup of coffee.

Afterwards, she stood, picked up a corner of the tablecloth, and whisked it into the air. It was just like an old uncle playing tricks! The food seemed to roll itself away, vanishing even as the tablecloth folded itself up again and became a neat and tidy triangle that fit in Valentina's hand.

She put it away again inside her pack.

"That is a wonder," Anatoly said.

"The vushka are undercooked," Valentina dismissed; and then, conceded, "... but, there are quite good knishes."

She stood still, then, for a long moment, in thought; a bonesaw premonition nagging at her. In the deep waters of her subconscious, a preternatural alertness and a current of half-remembered lore spun round. Finally, she took out Aggie's knife again, not quite sure why, and cut her arm. Four drops of bright red blood welled up and fell out onto the muddy ground.

"Three for you," she said. "And one, then, for ... another?"

Anatoly nodded to her and he knelt down. She looked away, to watch the river run. When she looked back, he was rising, wiping his mouth on his sleeve, murmuring the closing grace, and his eyes had filled in, just a little. They still weren't human eyes, but they weren't blank emptiness any longer either.

There was a hint of a multicolored mist in them.

"Were I to kill you," Anatoly observed, "I could drink it all. Then I would become extremely fat."

"There are too many things wrong with that statement for me to list them all," Valentina said.

She began to clean her knife against her shirt.

The river rose.

It buckled. It arched. The water of the river rose up in a great splash towards them, and halfway to them that splash transfigured or unfurled into a dragon's head dripping with water, made *from* the water, with bulbous eyes of clear still water and great catfish-whiskers of current where it ran much faster. A great-fanged jaw bent down as Valentina hopped backwards. It licked at the last remaining drop of blood.

There was a moment of stillness—if the creature could be said to be still while the water that was its constituent element continued running. Then frills around its head began to flutter and it shook its head upon its neck and turned to stare quite seriously into Valentina's face.

Behind the head, and beside them, and behind them, flowed the body of the beast.

"You're not a river," Valentina said. "Are you? You're more of a dragon, flowing in the earth."

It licked her. Then it nipped at her arm.

She shoved it away.

"One drop should be enough," she said, "to be your meal."

It stretched its neck, vibrated the frills around its head, and *howled*. Water flowed up its neck, flew off its head, and thundered down in an endless torrent.

The wind picked up.

Valentina drew her left hip's sword.

The beast came pouring down at her. It moved like a sudden flood. She jumped back as it struck the earth at her feet. It lunged at her, repeatedly, and her boots slipped and skidded as she struggled for purchase upon the muddy shore. On the seventh lunge she did not retreat from it; she set her feet instead, faced it head-on, and she split the oncoming waters with the blade. The sky darkened. The wind roared. The charging beast split face-first into two long streams—but it didn't die. It didn't even *suffer* much. The two halves became serpents, individuated, and their heads lashed in at her from either side.

Her sword shone in the light of the Outside's sun. It cut right across the right snake's neck and left across theirs both.

Even as she did this, from the opened body of the beast, a lion tumbled forth, made of water and spotted with darker water in a pattern like the blood on a newborn child. Its body was the same substance as the dragon, its mane a spray of water drops and its flesh the same watery tumult as the beast from which it came. Its motion even continued the same motion as the originating beast—its tumble towards Valentina a seamless continuation of the charge the dragon had begun.

She dropped to the ground as it came at her. It passed over her. Aggie's knife came up and ripped its belly open as it passed.

The creature burst.

The shadows deepened. Mud and blindfish splattered upon her. A white serpent made of rapids-water dense enough to seem like a true snake's scales was mixed in with it, unraveling from the lion's intestines; it stretched for her, it bit at her, and its two fangs dripped with milky poison.

She caught it—not easily, but awkwardly, both weapons dropping.

She held it by the sides of its head, her thumbs jammed in behind its fangs.

She had a moment to breathe, then. In that moment, her eyes widened and a sudden wild wonder bubbled in her. She realized, with a sudden intensity, that she was *there*, seeing such things, living such things, fighting creatures born from a river in the lands beyond the world. She looked at the snake, straining towards her amidst the shadows and the mist, and she couldn't help smiling; laughing, nearly: delirious with joy.

"Fine," she conceded. "Have a little more."

And she blew the breath of a human life into its mouth.

It shivered, all along its length. Its nostrils flared. It shook all over, once again. Then, the water convulsed and broke to pieces around her hands—everywhere *shattered*—and she and Anatoly were once again alone.

She slumped. She closed her eyes and listened; and her bell jangled softly at her side.

IN THE aftermath of the battle, Valentina found herself trudging through a qualitatively different land.

She had left behind the chaos' equivalent of coastal waters; had reached the end of what one might think of as reality's "continental shelf." She had crossed a boundary known to atlases and fables:

Where the bedrock of truth at last began to steeply plunge away.

In the aftermath of the battle, the sun was paler. The sky had darkened to purple and to black. The ground sucked at her boots, having turned entirely to mud now, but the endless roar of water no longer sounded.

Eerie pillars of coral everywhere stretched upwards from the earth.

Most importantly of all, the death of the dragon seemed to have marked the passing of some metaphysical quality in the world—something that she could *miss*, achingly, but not put a name to, because the mortal world had no real concept of its absence:

Whereas the world around her had always *previously* seemed like it could get by pretty well on its own, even when she wasn't paying attention, *now* it felt like her attention was actively required to sustain it; like the light of her attention was filling some leaky reservoir in everything she looked at and experienced, and when that reservoir ran dry again, the thing or the experience would fade away.

... *might* fade away.

Could fade away, or not.

... would *return to that essential ambiguity* that had once preceded things.

It felt as if she were constantly forgetting things as soon as she took her attention off them; as if some unknown creature were constantly stealing the scenery away behind her as she moved. Existential insecurity gnawed at her. Her gaze lingered on one feature after another of the world, desperately holding it in place, before suddenly remembering all the other things she was ignoring and flickering all around her to remind her of it all.

Objects had lost their self-sustaining permanence.

It *hurt*.

The terrifying thought occurred that if she turned her attention inwards, the world around her might vanish in its entirety. She might look up afterwards and find herself simply ... nowhere:

To enter into the chaos is to lose yourself, and to lose everything you know.

The thought was dizzying. It was almost enough *in and of itself* to distract her from the world.

She wrenched her focus outwards, shuddering, and they walked onwards for a time.

"I have heard the sailors speak of this," she said.

"Ah!" Anatoly said, startled. Then, "I had been thinking."

"Oh?"

"No," said Anatoly. "I cannot remember what I was thinking about. Go on."

"There are— they—" She frowned, then started over. "The fishing boats ... will cross through the chaos, when they go from Big Lake to the seas of Earth. And it is rarely more than a little strangeness. A little sparkle, or a little danger. They only skim the shallows of it, you see. But now and then the chaos will surge up around them, or they will lose their way; and they will find themselves here: in the low Outside.⁹"

"And what do they say of it?"

Valentina turned the focus of her thoughts inwards, reaching for the memory; but as she did so, a wave of vertigo struck her. The world seemed to tilt, to topple. It seemed to be dimming, the light inside it dissipating, everything preparing to fade away into nothingness. Panic choked her. She flailed mentally for equilibrium, performed a mental act that felt like seizing hold of the inside of her eyes and thrusting her consciousness back inside them, and re-established her focus on the world around her. It seemed to sway, crookedly, and slew.

------

9 Conventionally, the chaos was divided into the *near*, the *low*, the *deep*, and, finally, the *far*. (After that, would come the Bleak Academy.) The low Outside can be said to occupy an uncomfortable nomenclatural position here, on account of its muddled character: too solid to fairly reckon as the chaos' depths; yet, distinctly less normal and *worldly* than its shallows. In our earlier oceanic metaphor, it would be, perhaps, the "continental slope"—though, the analogy is somewhat inexact.

Her foot came down—she was in mid-stride—on a clump of earth.

Sensation was disjointed; there was the sound of a raindrop, and for a moment she was standing on a solitary purple blotch of mud in nothingness.

... then she heaved a great mental and physical breath, drawing everything together, and the world was whole again.

She was dizzy, as if from hyperventilation—but the world was there.

"I don't remember," she said, not daring to spare the attention to really think about it. "Something something ... if you set yourself hard on finding landmarks, on orienting yourself, the low Outside will eventually become more real again. More solid. More whole. That is what the ships will do, in any case."

"I cannot do that," Anatoly said. "So you will have to leave me here."

"No," Valentina said. "I cannot do that either; I must go onward and not back."

"... ah."

It occurred to Valentina, together with a rush of fear, that she had lost track of the shape of the cliffs off to her right; that while obviously they should be one particular way, and not any other, she no longer recalled *which* way that was. She had walked past the last feature of which she had any distinct recollection.

There was only a sense of height, and breadth, and the color of the stone.

It seemed to her, too, that she remembered taking careful note of the lands to the left of her but she had no idea what was supposed to be there now. She could not resist looking but managed to keep herself from taking full note of it; instead, she let her eyes play dumbly over the lights and shadows. She saw a chiaroscuro and not the looming stone, so there were, at least, no cliffs to the left of her. Beyond that ... it was ambiguous. She did not let her eyes resolve the forms.

She fell into another shuddering moment when it seemed like all was lost; like everything was coming apart, like there was only a riot of shape and color and not a world.

She *wanted* that, wanted to find the deeper strata of the Outside, but still she panicked. She could not resist slamming that metaphorical door shut and pulling the pieces of the world together again.

Her eyes turned down towards the foundation of things, to the earth beneath her, and jagged pieces of the world shoved themselves back together into sense.

She licked her lips.

"I cannot bear it," she said. Then, in sudden fright, "Anatoly? *Anatoly!*"

"I am here."

"I could not— I do not know where you are."

"That is because you are looking in the wrong direction."

Her eyes found him. Her vision split for a moment, her gaze defocusing, then refocused. "Ah."

"It will be better soon," he said. "I feel as if a rain is coming."

When the first drops landed on the back of her hand, Valentina realized that she had been dreaming. She tried to wake up, but her consciousness was fuzzy. She squeezed her eyes shut, reopened them, and struggled for each breath.

"Mother?"

"She is not present."

"... right. Because of that witch."

The rain was cold. It made her shiver, except when it didn't.

"I'll wake her up one day," Valentina said. "I'll kill that witch and wake up my whole family."

"As you like."

A memory nagged at her. She rubbed at her cheek and neck, tried to massage life into them. She became embarrassed. She tried to find something to say that would save face. She cleared her throat instead.

"My apologies," she said. "I was forgetting my chronology. I am groggy, Anatoly."

"We are traveling to the Bleak Academy," Anatoly said, "that is beyond the end of life, to face he the lord of Death's dominion he, the Headmaster of the Bleak Academy is he named."

"Oh," Valentina said. She licked rain-moistened lips. "That is correct. I had forgotten."

She clutched at the neck of her shirt, scrunched it convulsively in her hand.

"I was dreaming," she said, "that I was not Valentina, but rather dead and empty bones, on which someone had piled meat and skin and hair. Then I woke up and I realized that this was so; within a certain margin of precision."

"The earth's the sky," Anatoly said. "And two is three … within a certain margin of precision."

"Mnh."

Valentina stared blankly in front of her.

"It is like we are at sea," she said, but did not clarify what in what she was looking at or listening to was like the sea, or in what fashion. Then: "The world suffers."

"The world suffers?"

"Here, in the low Outside," Valentina said. "I have intuited it. The world is missing a certain characteristic of truth that is possessed by lands outside the chaos, and it suffers for the lack of it. It *whimpers* for me to focus my eyes upon it and bring it into sense, to clearly look and clearly listen and finally to understand. This is a world that is in *agony* for sense. *Look!*"

She pointed, convulsively. She grasped at the world with her eyes, condensed the intensity of her gaze, and *knew* for one long moment that she was staring at the moon. She burned it into being in the sky, white and round amidst that purple sea; fixed it solid and covered it with meteoric scars; it ripened there like fruit, grew deep in its reality, and made itself a weighty burden in the sky … until she gave a choked noise and her hand fell and her gaze turned aside and there was only a supposition of a moon again.

Then she was laughing. "But the moon is just a story, isn't it? The sun would burn it up."

"You will have to go farther than this," Anatoly observed quietly, "if you wish to reach the Bleak Academy."

Laughter continued to burst from Valentina, hysterical, burbling laughter forcing its way out between her grinding teeth, and she closed her eyes as she fell forward to her knees, her cloak about her feet, her pants legs creasing, her forehead falling to her hand. She felt the bumps and furrows on her brow.

Her laughter became coughing.

She thought for a dizzying moment that she had swallowed a gray serpent, that it was writhing inside her, trying to force itself back out of her mouth or nose. By the time she'd choked back both the idea and the regurgitation, she'd lost track of why she was on the ground at all.

"I am kneeling," she said. "Why am I kneeling, mother?"

She straightened.

Farther than this.

A great wave washed across her, and it swept the world away.

IN THAT moment she tried to see what was before her and she could not see what was before her. She was not blinded, nor was her sight confused; simply, *looking* was not productive.

In that moment she tried to listen.

She tried to locate her hands and arms and legs and feet relative to her body.

None of these things were productive. Focused attention no longer sufficed to manifest a world; the data from her senses no longer registered. The impression of the last few moments before the wave had struck her lingered: she remembered the muddy ground on which she'd knelt, the words that she'd just spoken, the position that her body had been in. Without new information coming in, those sights and sounds and feelings did not update. They did not go away, but neither did they remain whole. Instead they lingered like an afterimage, and decayed like an afterimage, giving her the pervasive sense that everything was crumbling, everything was falling away.

She was falling.

Her disorientation grew and became a force of its own. She felt it seize her like a great hand around her lungs and yank her forward, flung along a tumbling, dizzying path. She could not find her balance. She could not see. She could not hear.

In such a fashion did Valentina Grigorievna Sosunova fall into the deep Outside.

The mythology of Fortitude speaks of a human population living in that place—in that airy benthic zone of chaos, upon its tiamatic plain. It's not an idea that anybody really *believes* in, but it *is* a common starting point for horror stories and philosophical ruminations. It may have been impossible; it may have been that even the True Thing was attenuated there; that the fundamental reality was too lacking ...

Oh! But if it was only that people could no longer organize things properly with their senses; if it was only that the power of *looking-upon* was compromised—and compromised! Not even entirely removed!— then there *could* have been humans there, humans in the same situation as Valentina then; humans who would grow up never experiencing more of their own lives than the slightest vertiginous hints of sensation. They might feel their birth as a hint of pink, and white, and light. They might experience their youth as scattered moments of brown and green. As young adults, they might develop a faint sense of identity: "that which, at one point, gave some passing notice to itself." Later on, if they were lucky, they might become aware of their sorrows, loves, careers, or travels: faint glimpses of sensation, amidst the ever-present fog.

If they were not as lucky they might fall in love, marry, and be bereaved without even noticing it, or worse.

The fire of consciousness would still burn inside them. They would not be soulless drones, they would not be philosophical fictions; they would possess that fundamental qualification for personhood that is the ability to perceive both the True Thing and illusions; or, put another way, to have a fire that can illuminate things with meanings; or, put yet *another* way, to have the ability to think in words ... but that personhood inside them would have little practical effect.

The myth endures because it is possible. There could be whole cities there. Valentina might have walked right through one.

If this were so, she did not notice.

She experienced herself as a trapped point of awareness, suspended in a sea of the next worst thing to nothingness, and her mind was screaming for the book of details she called her world.

There was no world. There was no book.

There was not even nothingness.

There was blue. There was ... some ... blue. It might have been cold, maybe. It might have been wet. It might have had a snow-capped mountain range beyond it. She wrestled interpretation after interpretation from that tiny hint of blueness until she wasn't even sure that she had seen it after all.

There was a bit of green.

There were lines, she thought, that seemed to extend indefinitely towards two separate horizons.

She contained the fear that was running wild in her chest. She held it back behind her teeth, if she still had teeth. She said, with every bit of calm that she could muster, "Anatoly, if I have ever served you well, tell me you can navigate this place."

The words seemed to fall apart as they left her mouth. She could not hear them. She could not even hold on to the articulation of the words in her head. The statement dissolved, leaving only its barest bones: a certain average tone, with a certain average meaning, lasting for a certain interval of time.

Anatoly understood her anyway.

There was an indication of reassurance. She became aware of a pale sensation: he had taken her hand.

> *"This is the worst of it,"* he said —apocryphally, at least; according to biographers.
>
> *"It is?"*
>
> *"It is ... the beginning of the worst of it."*

She caught sight of an angle that might have been a house's roof, or the inexorable passage of time, but which she thought was a hint of gallows humor:

It is the beginning of the worst of it, she thought.

She nearly gave up, then. It was nearly too much for her. But though she could not hear it, and could not see it, and could not feel it, the little brass bell was ringing, somewhere, and the ringing of that small brass bell reminded her to live.

IN TIME the deep Outside lost its regularity. The exacting geometry that characterized the world gave way to psychedelia. Sensations were no longer measured in neat, clean lines and primary colors. Instead they took the form of starbursts, wavering lines of light, and pulsations that came and went against the dark. Experience became not merely scanty but inherently confusing.

It made relatively little difference.

She was already terrified. If she could feel the pounding of her pulse, she would feel it pounding fast. If she could feel her brow, she would feel cold sweat upon it. Having reality become a bit less solid could not further frighten her.

Landmarks had already become too unreliable to bother with. There was a certain aesthetic neatness to the perception of a high B flat, a hint of yellow, or a *sasora* scent that these newest forms were lacking—but she could no more have navigated by a high B flat than by a starburst, by a hint of yellow than by a pulse. Long since she had shifted to blind reckoning, trusting in nothing save her own unbroken will to reach the Bleak Academy and the sourceless hope that Anatoly was still, in some fashion, guiding her. Having the landscape become inconsistent did not make her *more* lost than she had been.

In short, things *could* get no worse, so they got no worse, although having them in eccentric motion was certainly not *better*.

It occurred to her as she walked past a vertical spiral that this place must be the reason that the dead did not return. She had always wondered why so few made the journey back from Death's dominion to the lands of life, but now she imagined falsely that she understood. *Between the world of life and the Bleak Academy*, she thought, *there is the deep Outside*.

SHE EMERGED FROM that place slowly and without a clear point of transition.

The burden of the deep Outside lingered upon her even after the world began to make sense again, so that she did not immediately notice when her situation had improved.

She began to feel her limbs again long before she became aware that she could feel her limbs again. She became subliminally aware of her breathing long before she recognized that she could feel each breath. By the time she realized she could see again, she had already been processing visual data for minutes, maybe hours.

Her eyes were so blurred from long misuse that green rays seemed to leap up from each blade of grass, red and brown lines thatched in bird's-nest patterns around each patch of dirt, and white and grey splotches streaked down from the clouds.

AND WHY should there have been such things at all?

The farthest reaches of the chaos are, as they have always been, a mystery. Past the deep Outside, she found a world again; but why this was, we do not know.

A common theory is that the Bleak Academy is an island, even as the lands around Big Lake are—an island in the endless sea of the beyond. That it *exists;* or, at least, possesses something *like* existence, and therefore has its own shallows; its own form of ... existential shelf.

Alternatively, it has long been speculated that when even formlessness has been exhausted, chaos will eventually return to form: that the final evolution of mutability is a return to stillness; the natural aftermath of *nonexistence: ... being.* In such a case, the far Outside would not be a *deviation* from the pattern of the lands that came before it, but rather a *continuation,* or a *conclusion* ...

In the end, we do not know.

IN THOSE DAYS, the final lands between the world and Death's dominion were beautiful. The soil was rich and dark, the ground was lush with greenery, and the air was pure and clean beneath clear skies. The sun has never shone there, but there was still ample light there; even more than in pre-sunlight Fortitude, each thing shone from the inside there with a private brilliance it had because it was itself.

The last steps of Valentina's journey took her across dew-damp hills strewn with glittering quartz where the air was fresh and bracing.

It was beautiful, and after the hardship of the deep Outside, that beauty nourished her senses and her soul.

It raised up strength in her like grain.

She walked more easily with each passing step until the miles seemed to pass for her like yards.

It struck her that there was an additional resonance that this place had for her; that it registered, to her, as something very like a dream. Not *identically*, perhaps, as no *dream* had ever existed without specific dreamers nor anchored itself to a specific place in the Outside ... but it *tasted* to her like a place that was four parts dream to one part real. It responded to the family magic that lived in her; it made Valentina Grigorievna Sosunova feel at home.

She ventured a theory of her own about that place, then:

"This is the last bright dream that the dead do dream, before they pass through the final gates."

But Anatoly shook his head to this.

"No?" she asked.

"If it is dream-like," he said, "it is only because the last dregs of waking life are gone."

... as we have said, we do not know.

AND eventually the countenance of the land began to make its final transformation.

Gradually—as she approached the Bleak Academy—she became aware of the possibility that the world around her could be different: that there was a new *capacity* in the dream-like world around her to be something other than it was.

She experienced what might be likened to a ... presentiment ... of brooding buildings looming over her, where only grass and flowers truly were. She had an ... apperception ... that there *could* be rolling hills around her, though the land she actually traveled through was flat. This was the final change in things she would experience: this eerie sense that the world *could* somehow be different: that there *could* be something incomprehensible floating in the sky above her; that there *could* be a clock tower which she vaguely recognized standing ... *there*, over in the distance, to her left.

If this last otherland became more real, it did so imperceptibly; it was still little more than a daydream when she found the Bleak Academy's twin gates.

They, at least, were real enough; solid enough.

Their details were ambiguous: they were tall as mountains, or short; wide enough to fit an army through them, or narrow; crudely carved, or covered in fine engravings ... but they were *there*.

—and yet she frowned at them; and yet she doubted them.

It may have been their uncertain character, or something in their stone and style. It may have been a weariness from her long journey. It may have simply been that they were *gates*, twin gates, and somber, even as the gates of Valentina's dreams ... but looking at them, she felt very small, and very young, and had the momentary fear that she had allowed herself to become confused. That she was merely *dreaming* that she was Valentina, on the road to the Bleak Academy; that the solidity of the gates she witnessed was merely a dream-solidity, that her presence there before them, a dream-presence; that even the sprawling sky above her was the sky of dreams. She ran her fingers over the etchings on the small brass bell to reassure herself that she had detailed perceptions. She pinched herself (and it hurt) to check for pain. She cast about for a reflective surface she could look into; not finding one, she reluctantly substituted a different test in, spitting into her hand and rubbing it between her fingers:

This, to check for a visceral distaste.

She was in the middle of doing this last test, and successfully confirming it—had just barely regained a fraction of her confidence, with her spit still wet—when the gates of the Bleak Academy creaked open.

Her cheeks flushed and her hand fell to her sword.

And beyond those gates …

Well, it was not clear. She *thought*, perhaps, that the world present around her only as a supposition was made real there, but it was honestly quite difficult to tell.

The Headmaster of the Bleak Academy stepped out between them. He was followed by six silent figures all in black.

He grinned at her. Stars fell in the nightscape that was his eyes.

"Welcome," he said, gesturing broadly, "to the Bleak—"

She'd promised her mother that she wouldn't listen to his words. She'd promised her mother that she'd keep the fight short. She lived up to both these promises.

She was charging him before the sentence finished.

He processed the attack. He leapt back, held out his hand and clicked his tongue, and a spear flew through the gates of the Bleak Academy to land neatly in his hand. He turned, set his stance, and with perfect form he met her charge.

It was fast, it was unnatural, and it was brilliant, but it was already too late.

The fight was already over.

She was inside his reach, with both swords in play. One caught the spear behind its barb, shoving it up, shoving it out. The other went into his side.

She ripped that sword out again.

She stepped back as he was falling down and she readied her sword to take his head.

The fight was quick, as she'd promised her mother; but it was interrupted. She did not have the chance to finish him off; even as she tensed for the blow, he did to her again what he'd done once before. He made a clawing gesture with his hand and he caught her attention with it. As if that attention were a physical thing, he dragged it down, twisted it, turned it inwards on itself, and her eyes rolled back and she lost sight of the battle. She lost sight of the world around her. Six times more fiercely than before, she felt it, and lost sight of everything but the horror that was her own existence:

Her eyes, twitching in their sockets. Her muscles, lying long against the bone. Her thoughts, like ants tracking filthy mud across the floors.

She sprawled there on her hands and knees and her hair hung down to hide her face and she did not move and she barely breathed, consumed by that private horror.

Time passed, and the Headmaster pulled himself up to his feet.

He held his hand against his side. He nodded to a man that stood behind him, and the man picked up an inkbrush and a little ink pot and wiped away the wound. The Headmaster brushed unhappily at a little speck of blood that had been left behind, marring the perfection of his coat. He glanced up at Anatoly.

"Are we going to have a problem?" he asked him.

Anatoly shook his head. "She has lost, so I will eat her."

"Visceral." The Headmaster made a face. Then he shrugged. He took a couple steps back, turned to face Valentina, and spread his arms, not quite so widely as before. "Welcome to the Bleak Academy," he said.

He turned. He walked away.

As for Valentina, she didn't hear him, or, at least, she paid no mind to him. She didn't hear his words. She didn't hear him walk away. She heard nothing save the awful bellows of her own breathing and the distant jangling of a small brass bell.

He left her there.

IT IS difficult to measure time in the far Outside. It has no true chronology. She would never know how long that interval of helplessness had lasted.

Perhaps she'd snapped awake mere instants after the Headmaster's departure, Anatoly's teeth still some inches from devouring her. Perhaps he'd dithered on the matter while some minutes passed. Perhaps in both of these ideas she had misjudged him; perhaps, rather than eating her at all, Anatoly had *saved* her—carried her off to a sheltered place and gathered food and drink for her for days, or weeks, or months, unstinting—before getting trapped, on a food-gathering mission, in some blood-soaked ravine.

As the most distant of possibilities, perhaps he *had* devoured her, consumed the all of her, hair, bones, and meat ... while she, occupied by her own vision of despair, had entirely and embarrassingly failed to even *notice*; any or all of these things could have come to pass.

Somewhere a little bell was ringing;

Like an angry corpse, she raised her head.

AS OF that moment, she could not yet see. It is possible that her eyes were just still rolled back. It is more likely that despair was getting in the way, that her eyes were fine, she was even "seeing," but that she was unable to process the input from her visual sense. She could not see; she could not hear, save for the ringing of the bell. She was turned around. She did not know which direction the Headmaster had departed in, nor could she follow him and fight him in such a state.

She was helpless, but she refused to be thus helpless. She was broken, but she would not allow the Headmaster to win.

So Valentina Grigorievna Sosunova began to dream a dream of the Sosunov magic.

Was the world around her four parts dream to one part truth? Then she would use the family magic to reshape it—

And it *did* bend, albeit sluggishly, to her will.

She had no ability to dream up fire, or armies, or weapons, though—not then—so she dreamt the only thing that she could feel at all.

Hope was dead, so she dreamt the shape of hope's corpse rotting. She dreamt a great dream of self-loathing, horror, and despair. Unable to see, to hear, to pinpoint her enemy, she targeted the entire world around her; she sent out the horror she was experiencing as howling winds and stormclouds, and in those winds and stormclouds horror blew—to batter at her enemy, if he remained there, or the gates of his Bleak Academy, if he had not.

She dreamt of a place—behind the storms, within the storms—where hopes were dead, and dreams were dying; and in that place, a monstrous guardian beast.

She lay her will on the world, sent the awfulness of her experience outwards; and eventually, began to receive feedback from that dream. She began to feel the Bleak Academy as if it were a physical, crystalline presence inside her self-hatred; as if it were a flame suspended in the hurricane of her self-loathing; as if it were a splinter stuck in her despair.

She strengthened the dream until the crystal began to crack; until the flame began to gutter; until the splinter began to ooze.

She clamped down upon the Bleak Academy like great jaws; until—

"Enough," said the Headmaster's voice. She could not hear the words, but, like she had once heard the witch's words, she still perceived them. They came to her as an emanation from the world. **"Enough. I yield."**

She snarled. She turned her head, cast her blind eyes around, flared her nostrils as if she could sniff him out.

"There is no yielding," Valentina said.

"The vision I have shown you is an accurate one," the Headmaster said. **"Only, you are the thing that looks upon it, not the thing that is _looked upon_. Is that enough for you?"**

She hesitated. She became uncertain.

"… you make a moving image on it with your light."

It did not help her. At best, it confused her—but the words had impact. The visceral horror in her became unfocused, undirected. She tried to hang on to it but it slipped through her fingers. It was not the _virulence_ of her experience that diminished; nor, certainly, did she see through it to some deep insight. Rather, it was her _confidence_ that faltered.

Suddenly, instead of her existence being a thing of absolute festering awfulness, it became a thing that she was *pretty* sure was absolute festering awfulness.

Pretty sure, only, she was ... the thing that *looks-upon*—

Her horror-dream of despair and hatred guttered, as her certainty wavered. It guttered and went out.

She stood in Perdition: the land between the chaos and the Bleak Academy, where dreams are dead and hopes are dead and grey despair immines. If there was anything left of the beautiful lands that once surrounded Death's dominion, she could not see them. If Anatoly had survived—if *anything* had survived, even the Bleak Academy itself—she did not know it. She searched them out for a while but she did not find them.

She turned around and she began to walk for home.

SHE THOUGHT that when she got home she would sit by her mother's side, and her mother would brush her hair, and she would tell her mother Iskra the story of her journey. She thought that perhaps Iskra Sosunova would have some answers to share with her, some way to live with the enduring horror of it, some insight into the Headmaster of the Bleak Academy's last words. She thought she would tell her mother that the curse on her was broken, maybe, or maybe that it had gotten worse; that she'd won, or maybe lost, but gotten him to say he yielded, anyway. She thought that she would tell her mother about Anatoly, and the dragon, and the terrors of the deep Outside, but when she arrived she found a house in mourning.

Iskra had passed her somewhere along the way—

Had died, and gone to Death's dominion.

INTERLUDE

THE SAILORS of Fortitude traveled the seas of Earth and brought back word of its changes. Rumors of the industrial revolution, of steam power, of a future monumentally different from the past took root in Fortitude. They spread to the tent-city of the demon-folk in the west and a demon's factotum commissioned the hiring of European engineers and workers for the construction of a textile factory in the nearby hills.

The floodgates opened. A new world came rushing through.

Industry, machinery, and modernity became a part of life. Smoke began to fill the sky. Factories sprang up with a nearly unnatural speed, along with buildings in a more modern style; and soon every ship seemed to be bringing in not food or trade goods but new workers, new specialists, and new parts for their machines.

The settlement of Fortitude was mostly free of factories, of new construction, of great engineering projects. It was merely the port and passage through which the modern world came in; but, of course, a little stuck as that world passed through. Machine-made fabrics became common; the river became polluted; the Sosunovs took up the practice of arbitrage, sending out trade ships to various Earthly ports and sharing information on local prices through their dreams.

Valentina spent two years sailing and returned a little wiser, a little worldlier, and a little less used to the endless night. The sun was still kind of weird to her, but she'd grown to like it. It was warm and it was bright. She wished that she could bring it home.

Time slipped by, and soon it was ten years since she'd returned from the Academy.

She was only just beginning to suspect, then, that she'd ceased to age.

EVDENIYA AND THE THING THAT SHOULD NOT BE

*Before the sun, before the moon, before the ships of the Rus' came in—
Town[10] was full of the tents and mansions of strange, inhuman creatures.*

*In those days the gods of dream and nightmare ruled, but they
enforced no order. The wild, primordial creatures of their land thought
nothing of shrinking down worlds to make beads for their necklaces or
cutting down thousands of soldiers in one blow. It was an era of wishes
and of miracles; of demons who were grander and larger than life: they
bestrode the world like giants and cast shadows across the entirety of the
sky.*

*You can see them sometimes, still, when you fall asleep. Their echoes
continue in the dreams of children to this day. You can sometimes see the
marks of them, too, upon the physical world—the cliffs that formed when
Caradog fell from the starry fields to earth; the bracken Cerys salted with
her tears. Their shadows still sometimes stretch across the clouds; and
Kailas Mantra still has the crook that once was Delyth Sandryn's nose.*

—from *The Thirteen Hours,*
by Frederick Fidwor

---

10   that is, the entire local parcel of reality; this translates the pre-human term.

L ET'S TELL the story of Evdeniya Kinjirovna Kaneko and the thing that should not be!

Once upon a time, but not so very long ago, there was a girl named Evdeniya Kinjirovna Kaneko, and her parents did science wrong. When she was a baby they practiced perfectly ordinary natural science and engineering but later on they slipped over the verge and started building things that interacted with their particular psyches—machinery and experiments forced into operation and success, respectively, by the sheer force of their personality. This was technically still science, as you could probably lock someone else's mindset into the right place to reproduce their results, but it wasn't *good* science.

It wasn't the kind of thing good people did.

People got uncomfortable living in the same neighborhood as the Kanekos. Families moved away. Houses were abandoned. The street took on an eerie, empty air. The buildings and sidewalks became a little decrepit and overgrown with weeds and various ivies. A vampire moved in down the road.

Evdeniya was terrified of the vampire, whose name was Svetlana Witherspoon. She was afraid that at any moment Svetlana would appear at her window and start drinking her blood. She didn't think her parents' weird stuff would scare vampires off, since her mother tended to make things like fanged orchids and the phosphorescent kelp pool and her father's death ray was specifically useless, so she hung garlic on her window and knit crucifix patterns into her socks and worried quite a lot that these things wouldn't help.

In the end, though, Svetlana Witherspoon never even brought by a casserole. She vanished into her creaking old Queen Anne-styled fortress and she didn't come out. When Evdeniya walked by on the way to her tutor's she always kept a wary eye out, but she didn't see even a peep of her, and she eventually started to think that maybe Svetlana had tripped and stumbled onto a stake.

She did not investigate further.

The pace of her parents' deviancy accelerated. Her father built an energy transmission tower; lightning storms wracked the neighborhood; another neighbor moved away. Her mother recorded an unsightly equation and dimensional shocks went resonating through the house. Eerie manikins grew on a vine along the basement wall: their skin like porcelain in the dark, twin lumps up by their attachment point like coal-black eyes. Evdeniya began to wish she had the option of moving away herself. One day, working together in a fugue state, Kinjiro and Tamara Kaneko put the cherry on the sundae of their inappropriate experiments:

In the middle of the living room, they made a thing that should not be.

It was a scar on existence. It was an otherworldly intrusion. It didn't occupy their living room properly. It wasn't exactly *there*. Instead it was like the limit to a mathematical series. Its notional presence warped space into a spiraling path that led *to* it. The distortion was set up so that that path grew longer and longer the closer to the thing you got.

The thing itself was therefore arbitrarily far away—maybe infinitely far, and maybe not—and Evdeniya couldn't see it. She still knew immediately that it was a thing that should not be. She got sick to her stomach just looking at the twisting, winding, thorny path that led to it.

It wasn't natural. It gave off a greenish light.

There was a low-level hum in the room, an unnatural buzzing, just barely loud enough to hear.

"How interesting!" Evdeniya's mother said. "Let's explore it!"

"Yes," agreed her father. "Let's."

Evdeniya was not a very well-behaved child, and she fell back upon bad habits here. She did not reason with her parents, pointing out the problems with this idea. She did not even bring up her personal objections. She wailed. She fell down melodramatically and clung to her mother's skirt. "No!" she said. "No, don't!"

It wasn't actually bad behavior, since the goal was to keep her parents out of trouble, but, still, nobody was impressed.

Her mother knelt down. She disentangled herself from Evdeniya. Her eyes were bright with the light of interest and scientific inquiry. "It's important not to be afraid of the future," she said. "You've got to face it with conviction!"

"Please don't," Evdeniya said.

The hum in the room intensified. Her hair fluffed out. Small objects in the room drifted up from their places and then settled down. Evdeniya had the eeriest impression that the thing that should not be was calling her, but this didn't make her like it any better.

She looked down at her hands. She marshalled up the best argument she had.

"It's *too weird*," she said.

But her mother had caught sight of something sparkling, not far down along the path, and had taken three quick steps forward to get a better view, and become occulted. Her father gave Evdeniya an awkward smile.

"If I had shirked from an adventure," he said, "I would never have had you, Zhenya."

"Oh," Evdeniya said, not reassured.

He nodded to himself. He ruffled her hair. He took three steps forward and he was gone.

Evdeniya sank to her knees and put her head down on the floor.

She muttered, "Ugh."

THE FIRST day that they were gone Evdeniya did not mind so much. The second day still wasn't so bad. By the third day, though, she was starting to think that of all the irresponsible things her parents had ever done, making the thing that should not be was just the *worst*. By the fifth day of keeping the house all alone she concluded that the situation was simply intolerable. She decided to consult an expert on awful things.

She put on a training bra and stuffed some garlic in it and put on a silver cross and of course her crucifix socks and dabbed some holy water on her wrists and behind her ears and straightened her dress and looked in a mirror and thought that she looked like somebody a vampire probably wouldn't want to eat. Then she went down the street to knock on Svetlana's door.

Nobody answered.

She knocked again. Nobody answered, again. Finally, she pushed the door open. It opened with difficulty, and she had to push hard, because a variety of miscellaneous things were piled up on the other side: small folding tables, a fern in a pot which fell over and shattered, thirteen coats and eighty-two umbrellas, a hat stand, a brass lamp, a child's coffin, a pot full of some dried sticky substance that might have once been borscht, a wire-frame woman sculpture, an empty birdcage, and a tinkling disassembled chandelier. Carpeting crunched under her feet as she squeezed into the foyer and stared out in dismay at the sitting room; the floor was covered in rugs, and the rugs were covered in tables, and the tables were covered in vases, clocks, and bowls. In the bowls were seashells, pebbles, feathers, fish scales, bits of fabric, ruined beads, coal, a cracked porcelain clown mask, and all manner of other things. There were throw pillows everywhere. Delicate folding screens displaying Oriental patterns separated fluffy armchairs from their ottomans. A great brass water heater stood off to the side, not attached to anything in particular, surrounded by piled-high boxes full of clothes.

There was a single cleared space, as if someone had recently attempted cleaning. A bowl of wax fruit sat in the middle of it, like an idol in its shrine.

She felt a touch on her shoulder, shrieked, and spun around, but it was just the hand of a perilously leaning taxidermied kangaroo.

Her heartbeat slowly settled down. She began to pick her way through the detritus.

"Miss Witherspoon?" she called. She thought about it, then added, "Are you all right?"

"Down here," she heard, after her third call.

She made her way to the cellar door and wrestled a cabinet full of nautical barometers out of the way so she could open it. She worked her way down the box-strewn steps.

The cellar was a wine cellar, dark and cramped and full of cobwebbed wood and wine bottles, but still managed to feel like a breath of fresh air and openness compared to the upstairs of Svetlana's house. The vampire herself, short and pale and young-faced and somehow managing to look *even more* uncertain and lost than did Evdeniya, sat upon the bottom step.

Evdeniya approached.

"Are you crying?" she asked, after a minute.

Svetlana shook her head. She wiped her nose and eyes on her sleeve. She cleared her throat. She said, "I am an ageless child of the night."

"Oh."

"It is just," Svetlana said, "that I was chopping some onions down here, a few years back, and got some dust in my eye."

"That sounds believable," Evdeniya agreed.

She sat down a few steps above Svetlana.

"I am a dread vampire," Svetlana said. "Brought back from the dead, faster, stronger, *better* than I ever was in life. My human family rejected me but the Witherspoon clan took me in. Only, somehow, my house wound up like *this*."

"It's very," Evdeniya said. She hesitated. "Appointed. It is very well appointed."

"Don't patronize me," Svetlana said.

"You've just been sitting here? This whole time?"

"I unpacked a little," Svetlana said. "There was a bowl of fruit. And some dresses."

She gestured over to a corner, which Evdeniya now realized contained not merely wine bottles but also a few red and black velvet dresses hung along the racks.

"I thought it would be different when I moved," Svetlana said. "A whole country where there is no sun! It was very exciting. I could start a new life here. I could be part of the grand step forward. But I was too embarrassed to have anyone in and don't really feel safe when I go out."

"Hm," Evdeniya said.

She went upstairs. Svetlana sank deeper into her sulk. Then she began to hear bumping noises and dragging noises from upstairs. Panic took her. She rushed up and, forgetting that Evdeniya had probably moved the cabinet, flowed under the door in the shape of mist. "What are you doing?" Svetlana shrieked.

"I'm putting things near similar things," Evdeniya said.

"But I already started cleaning," Svetlana protested. "You're undoing all of my initial work!"

Evdeniya gave her a skeptical look. Svetlana's eyes darted around the room and then she flung out her hand to point at a dusting rag hanging from the antlers of a wood-mounted deer head on top of a leaning armoire in the corner. "See?"

"There's too much stuff," Evdeniya said. "and it makes it impossible to put anything away. I'd have to move everything else first. And I can't do that, because everything else is made of anything!"

"This is true," Svetlana admitted, slumping. "I have discovered it myself."

"So," Evdeniya said, "I'm putting things near similar things, because even though it stays a mess it becomes a progressively less confusing one."

Svetlana watched her and wrung her immortal hands as Evdeniya continued her work.

A few hours later and she could no longer deny it:

"I am seeing this problem in new ways," Svetlana conceded. "For instance, I think part of the problem may be that I do not actually need fifteen different nautical barometers."

"Really?" Evdeniya said.

"If you like?"

"I mean— you're worried about the barometers, and not the fish scales?"

"I *use* the fish scales," Svetlana said. "Well, I plan to. Someday. They're for handicrafts."

The job was more than Evdeniya could manage in one go, of course, even after Svetlana was finally lured out of her hand-wringing and joined in. It was, in fact, barely begun when Evdeniya was too tired to continue and the two of them went out on the veranda with a couple of clean cups that had turned up along the way and a pitcher of kvass that Evdeniya had brought over from her home.

"I never asked your name," Svetlana said.

"Denya," Evdeniya said. "Evdeniya Kinjirovna Kaneko."

"Svetlana Witherspoon," the vampire said. Then, with a wry grin, "or Svetlana Bogdanovna Uizerspun, I guess."

Evdeniya stared out into the sunless sky. "Initially," she said, "I'd hoped that you could help me. My Mom and Dad made a thing that shouldn't be, and vanished, and I thought, who would know about that kind of thing but a vampire? But I think I was wrong."

"It is not my specialty," Svetlana admitted. She swirled the kvass in her cup. Then she stood, decisively, and walked to the edge of the veranda. "But."

It was as if a bolt of lightning had struck Evdeniya's stomach, and proceeded down through her to her toes. "But?"

Svetlana grinned. She said:

> Little bat, my little bat
> Fly out from your caves to me;
> And squeak to me of someone that
> Might know of things 'that ought not be.'

A cold breeze blew by; clouds blew across the stars; and a pale bat fluttered from the direction of the distant shore to land upon Svetlana's wrist and hang from it, upside down. Svetlana scratched its belly.

"This is my friend," she said, "Maksim. He was the one who brought me here, who told me the story of your land without a sun, and we may hope that he knows something of the unnatural as well?"

The bat curled its head up to regard Evdeniya. Then it said, "I have flown over many lands, and I have sounded many delicious bugs and many unnatural things. There is a prophet in the kingdom of the sun who can help you, and a bloody-handed god who can make your problems go away, and the princess of a floating island who can teach you what you need to know to follow down your parents' path and safely bring them home. But if you want something that you may travel to in a single night ...

"There is a creature beneath the roots of a tree, on the northern cliffs. She is a child-eating monster, with long knotted hair and suckered fingers. She can make storms blow in or make a morning mist. She can steal the soul from a sleeping person and ride it through the hills all night. She can sing a song that'll call you out of bed and make you go to her and climb right into her cooking pot.

"If you look at her house from above, there's just a clump of sod by a tree; but to the ears of a bat, there's a great clear dome, and a passage beneath it, down and down into the earth. Find that passage, and you may find her as well.

"She knows the names of forgotten gods and demon kings and words and blasphemies against the world; and if you ask her right, she'll tell you what you need to know of the thing that should not be."

Svetlana rubbed the bat's head gently.

"What is the right way to ask her?" Evdeniya said.

"Graciously," the bat said, "I would suppose."

It was gone in a flutter of wings.

Svetlana looked after it for a moment, then returned to her seat. "There you have it," she said.

"I don't want to visit a child-eating monster," Evdeniya said.

"No," Svetlana agreed. "I'd suggest leaving your parents where they are. But if you must visit, perhaps you could take some black bread and jam. Then she would be much less likely to have room for you?"

Evdeniya straightened her back. "I'll do it," she decided.

Svetlana frowned. She stared after Evdeniya when she left, and twice she tried to step off of her porch and follow after the girl; but she was too nervous, each time, surrounded by the open world and sky, and finally she crept back down into her basement to sit upon her stairs instead.

EVDENIYA WENT HOME. It was the season for it, so she made fresh jam. There were berries growing in her house that didn't grow anywhere else in the world, although she found their provenance a little dubious, and a blackberry tangle not that far out from her home. She picked a basket full of berries, washed them in the Twisting River, put them in a pot with a bit of lemon juice, a splash of water, and three shredded apples, and brought it all to a starting boil before incrementally adding practically as much sugar to the mix as there was fruit. It boiled, gently, for a while.

The first round through the jam was runny and she had to add a bit more apple and re-boil, but once that was done, she found that it had pretty well set.

She turned off the heat, lidded the pan, and waited ten minutes—no longer!—before filling up and sealing up the jars.

She boiled the jars, too, when that was done, being very careful of her fingers.

When she was done, she had jam made from fruit that probably shouldn't exist, but which *might* have been an unusual import or the product of a botany from before the verge. She wasn't really sure.

She labelled it as such.

"Jam That Might Or Might Not Be Proper Jam," or "Jam TMOMNBPJ."

She slept, and woke, and made good black bread. She packed a basket of bread and jam, hung her father's death ray on her belt, braided back her hair to keep it out of her eyes, and went to the northern beach.

It was quiet there. It was always quiet there. The mosquitos mumbled more than whined, and the little stream that she passed by whispered more than it trickled. She wasn't sure quite what she was looking for—there were plenty of trees, and plenty of trees with clumps of sod by them—so she just stomped on every clump she found by every likely-looking tree.

Hours went by. Her lantern went out and she was left with the light of stars.

It was her nose that finally drew her to it—the scent of something *off*, something that shouldn't have been there. It drew her to the roots of a eucalyptus tree. She stomped on a clump of dirt and grass that was by its feet, and the world spun, and she found herself in a cylindrical space beneath a great clear dome, with the roots of the tree blocking out a portion of the sky, and herself on a worn elliptical stone spiral track that circled down into the dark below.

She descended.

As she climbed down into the darkness she heard sounds echoing up from below: cackling, shrieking, and speaking, not continuous but intermittent. The smell she'd smelt was stronger now: something sweet and rotten.

The tunnel grew darker, and the starlight was all but lost, and she felt out her way in terror that a portion of her track would be missing and she would plunge down into the void. The stone construction grew rougher, until the spiral became more of a suggestion and stalactites hung from the bottom of the track. Gaping holes in the eastern wall looked out onto what appeared to be the depths of the lake itself; there was no glass, and she had no idea what held the water back.

Her eyes adjusted.

She became aware of another light—feeble, at first, but growing brighter as she descended. Beneath her there was a flickering fire and a great landing on the endlessly descending track. It nestled up against the northern and the eastern walls; a rope bridge crossed over the spiral track to a cavernous opening to the west.

At this depth the architect had stopped to build a kitchen suited for a multitude.

Stone shelves bulged with cookware, tools, and food. Water trickled through a carven sink. A trash pile cluttered up a corner, ripe.

The fire was a cooking fire; a hairy creature was cooking something in a pot.

Something:

Children, was Evdeniya's first, unreasoning, fearful thought ... but she was a Fortitude child through and through, and it didn't take her long to realize that that was wrong. Just by the smell of it, she could tell that it was cooking fruit.

She hunched down, then sat, and stared over the edge of the ramp.

The creature stirred the pot. The fruit bubbled. It melted. The creature added sugar, waited for the mixture to boil, turned off the heat, and waited.

Evdeniya waited too, quiet as a mouse. She dared not move.

The creature dipped its spoon in the finished ... jam? The spoon rose. Jam ran off of it in rivulets and dripped messily back into the pot below.

"Runny," muttered the creature. "Runny."

It—no, *she*, most likely, decided Evdeniya—tossed the pot of jam off the kitchen's southern edge. It rattled off the sides of the descending tunnel, once, twice, thrice, and a fourth time, before landing with a clatter somewhere far below.

The creature sat back on its haunches and sulked.

Evdeniya thought for a moment, then pulled herself back up to her feet and walked down the spiral towards the landing. "Eyyuh," she squeaked, on her first try speaking, which wasn't at all what she had meant to say; but after clearing her throat, she was every inch the bold adventurer. "Excuse me," she said, "but you seem to be having some difficulty."

"Traveler," the creature said: "hear my mournful story. Forbidden to eat children, I retired to this barren keep to subsist upon black bread, small fish, and berry jam. No longer do I bring the storms. No longer do I sour milk. No longer do I ride on others' dreaming souls. Here in my cave I abide in peace. But no matter how much sugar I put in, every batch of jam I make is too runny for this hopeless witch to eat."

Evdeniya was not a well-behaved child, but she *had* been raised politely. "That *is* a tragic story," she agreed, before her personal concerns took over. "Did you eat very many children before you stopped?"

"Time is a river," the creature said.

"Oh."

"Put another way," the creature said, "I am no longer that person, and bear no responsibility for her actions. Did she eat seven children, point seven children, or was it seventeen? The matter is unworthy of investigation. It can only lead to the unwarranted persecution, harassment, and bedevilment of a harmless old woman—her only sin: her inability to make good jam."

Evdeniya bit her lip and swallowed her first response. Then she said, carefully, "I am here because my parents made a thing that should not be, and I was hoping that you would know something about things like that."

"Oh," the creature said. She snorted, dismissively. "Well, you can find the exit."

Ignoring Evdeniya, she took down a fresh pot from a shelf and began to scrub it clean with metal wire.

"Specifically," Evdeniya emphasized, "they created a thing that should not be, and vanished while exploring it."

The creature hummed as she cleaned out the pot.

"And I was hoping," Evdeniya said, "that you might know something that would help."

The creature hopped over to the rough stone wall. She ran her fingers along it. Evdeniya realized that there were vines along the wall, and dark berries growing upon them; she could not, at that moment, have said whether they appeared there as the creature reached for them or if they had been there, hidden by the shadows, all along.

The creature rolled the berries in her hands, then popped them in the pot one after another.

"I do not wish to help you in this matter," the creature said. "Let that be an end to it."

Evdeniya did not know what to say; she could not make clever words come out of her mouth, nor could she make her feet turn around and leave, so she just watched.

The pot grew full. The creature added a splash of water from the wall. She fished out an old lemon from the trash pile and squeezed in a bit of lemon juice. The pot was set to boil. Evdeniya continued to watch.

Then words finally came to her. "That's going to be runny again," she said.

The creature grew very still. "That would be unfortunate," she said. "This is the nine thousand, seven hundred and thirty-second batch, and I had a great deal of hope for it."

"No," Evdeniya explained.

"You can't know that," the creature said. "That's just pessimism.

Determination is not giving up in the face of adversity. When I've added the sugar, well ... maybe this time will be the magic number."

"Do you have any apples?" Evdeniya said.

"There may be one or two lying around somewhere," the creature said. "I don't like them, so I don't finish them. If you can find one that I've started, you can go ahead and finish it. That's how generous I am."

Evdeniya searched the shelves, and then, wrinkling her nose, the trash pile. Eventually she found a couple of apples with just a few bites taken out of them. She dug out a cutting board. She washed them as best she could, chopped them up, carried them over, and dumped them smoothly into the pot.

"You've ruined it!" howled the creature, leaping at her; landing on her; knocking her down, grabbing her shirt, and beginning to thump her head into the stony ground. "Batch nine seven three two! You've ruined it!"

Then the creature sprang suddenly backwards off of her. She skittered back another step or two, then turned casually away from Evdeniya. She stood there innocently.

"Not that I would hurt a child," she said. "Even under extreme provocations. That was merely aberrant behavior not representative of my true character."

Evdeniya rubbed at her throat. She pushed herself up on her elbows, then sat up. "It isn't ruined," she said. "If your jam won't set you probably need apples, plums, or orange peel in the mix."

"That seems excruciatingly unlikely," the creature said, but she turned to face Evdeniya again and her look was somewhat less feral. "Still, I accept the gesture in the spirit in which it was meant. Similarly, I did not mean to hurt you when I slammed your head against the floor; I was simply attempting to shape your head into something more aesthetic, increasing your eventual romantic opportunities. Sadly, I was unable to produce the proper lumps."

Evdeniya frowned. "I don't like you," she said.

"That wounds me deeply," the creature said. "I will move away from society and live in a cave and eat runny jam in sorrow. At least I may comfort myself in knowing that my tormentor has mislaid her parents and will probably never see either of them again."

Evdeniya ground her teeth, but said nothing.

"Ha!" said the creature. "Nothing to say to that?"

She added sugar to the boiling fruit and cooked it for a while before removing it from the heat. With the smug air of someone about to disprove a rival's theory, she tested it.

It clung thickly to the spoon.

The creature stood there, very still. She stared at the spoon and she did not move. Evdeniya did not say anything; she waited for the creature to acknowledge her, or to admit defeat. Instead, a great tear welled up in the creature's bulging eye and slipped silently down her face, followed by another, and then another. It was a full three minutes later that a wrenching sob burst from the creature's throat and she sank to her knees on the cavern floor.

"Zounds," the creature said. "*Jam.*"

"Don't just kneel there," Evdeniya said. "You've got to get it into jars."

"I don't even—" the creature said. "I haven't even gotten the jars out. I've never gotten this far before. It's genuinely *jam.*"

"Well, get them," Evdeniya said.

"Right," the creature said, distractedly. Then she leapt up to her feet. "Right!"

She thumped the wall above the sink, which cracked open as if an earthquake had struck it; jars began to bubble through the crack. She did not wait for this process to complete; she reached her suckered fingers in and seized them out, pulling them faster than the wall disgorged them, yanking them out of the stone one after another.

"Get the water boiling," Evdeniya said. "You'll need to boil the jam once it's in."

"Nobody told me that," the creature complained. "The jam's already *been* boiled. Are you sure I can't just eat it as it stands?"

"That I don't know," Evdeniya admitted. "I guess if you ate it all right now it would probably do. But it's still quite hot."

"No, no, no," the creature conceded. "Jar it up."

The creature handed Evdeniya the first jar, and she filled it, and sealed it, and then the next, and then the next, before popping the jars into a pot of hot water for five minutes to boil.

"Careful of your fingers," she said, slapping the creature's fingers away, as the creature reached to pluck the first jar back out. "Use jar tongs."

And then the jars were out, and set up on the shelves for cooling; they were done.

"There is jam," said the creature, in soft satisfaction and wonder.

"You would have toiled forever," Evdeniya said, firmly. "And it would have been runny every single time. So you owe me now."

"Arguably," the creature said, "by choosing to maintain my ethical code and not devour you, I have done you an incomparable favor."

"I don't know what that means," Evdeniya said, "so I don't think that it counts."

"The point is irrelevant," the creature decided, "as I discover myself favorably disposed to you anyway, and it is no difficulty to give you your answer. I know absolutely nothing about things that should not be."

"But a bat told me—" Evdeniya hesitated. "You're a monster. You have to know."

"I deny that," the creature said, "and even if it were true, it would still not provide me with comprehensive information about each and every other awful thing."

"Oh."

"But I did *see* one once," the creature said. "I did *encounter* a thing that should not be, once, and chose very consciously not to know any more about it than I do. So I can tell you a little about that, if you think that would help.

"Will you listen to my mournful tale?"

"Yes," Evdeniya confirmed.

"Once I was a true child-eating horror," the creature said. "I came out of Big Lake and my purpose was clear, and my sight was unclouded, and my power was vast. I was a natural disaster visited upon these peaceful people of Fortitude, and I relished that. I laughed as I called up storms to drown their ships. I hag-rode their sleepers in their dreams. I thought that I would build a castle out of bones.

"Then one night I was saddling up a dreamer and a greater monster came.

"She shone in the dream with a silver radiance, so brightly that I could not look upon her. Where her sword went, the world dissolved into ambiguity. I fought her, and I lost to her, and I fled that dream, but I found I could not wake.

"I, who had ridden humans as my steeds throughout the night, she hunted like I was a fox, and she the hound. When I was too tired to run, when I could not evade her any longer, she called up the waters of the lake and drowned me, limbs bound in iron chains beneath the surface of the lake, and she let the sailors that I'd killed sneak up to carve off pieces of me until I begged for mercy. Me! Who had been the queen of storms! The plague-bringer!

"Eventually she seemed to hear my cries. She lifted me up to the surface of the waters. She showed me a thing I could not bear to look upon, held it up and it writhed in her hand and brought it closer until I could see nothing but my refusal to see that thing, and told me that if I ever harmed the people of Fortitude again, or walked in the dreams that were her territory again, that she would find me, and she would show me that thing again, and this time I would never have the chance to look away.

"That redeemed me," the creature said, "of course. I became a dyed-in-the-wool saint, and have shown no ill disposition since."

"That thing," Evdeniya said.

"That is all I know," the creature said. "I do not know anything about things that should not be, or where your parents might have gone; but I do know that such a thing as you describe haunts Valentina Grigorievna Sosunova's dreams."

"Thank you," Evdeniya said.

"I am not entirely sure how to find her," the creature said. "She comes by sometimes and makes demands for this or that weather or whatnot, but I have never had any impulse myself to seek her out."

"It's all right," Evdeniya said. "There is no child of Fortitude but that knows where Valentina Grigorievna dwells."

EVDENIYA WENT to the Sosunov compound. She gave a message to the young boy who met her at the gates. She waited, and eventually another child—a slightly older girl, this time—came to escort Evdeniya inside.

She was led into the temple. The girl bowed and backed away as Evdeniya entered. Valentina sat in the frontmost pews. She was dressed in black and silver—she had taken, perhaps unconsciously, to mimicking the Headmaster's garb—and her hair was tied up in a braid. She did not turn to look at Evdeniya.

"I am told you wished to see me," Valentina said.

"Please, Miss Sosunova," Evdeniya said. "My parents are missing."

At this Valentina *did* turn. She frowned. She stood. She went to stand by Evdeniya, cupped her chin, looked into her eyes, and then let go. "It is possible to find them through you," she said. "But it is a last resort. Have you exhausted all other avenues?"

Evdeniya became flustered.

"The technique," Valentina said, "involves essentially *becoming* you for a while, pushing you-you to the fringes of your soul. Then it is possible to use the family magic to dream our way to your loved ones rather than my own. But there is a reasonable chance that you will be scarred permanently by the experience, particularly if it takes some time to find a dream where they are lucid enough to explain where they have gotten to."

"I wasn't," Evdeniya began. Then she stopped. "I mean, that, then—I mean, that is ... an amazing possibility, and I absolutely want to do that, but it is not the reason that I came to you."

"Oh?"

"It is the *way* they vanished," Evdeniya said. "They ventured into the penumbra of a thing that should not be."

"Ah," Valentina said.

"I've been looking for someone who understands things like that," Evdeniya said. "And I was told you might."

"How droll," Valentina said. "But yes, I daresay. At least as much as anyone."

"Droll?"

"At one point I considered myself to be such a thing," Valentina said. "I came to doubt this, later, but the initial perception still grieves me and assails me with great melancholies. That is my sickness, you see."

"Oh."

"I'll help you," Valentina said. "Take me to this thing that should not be."

"Thank you," Evdeniya said. "*Thank you.*"

They walked for a while in silence, then; but after that while, Evdeniya stole her hand out to take hold of Valentina's. "Dad says," Evdeniya said, "that when you're sad, it's because you're talking to yourself too much and not listening to yourself enough."

After another while, Valentina said, "Your Dad's a freak."

The sun still hadn't reached Fortitude. The streets were lit by lanterns.

"I look at myself," Valentina said, "and I find myself filled with rejection. I don't want to be this thing. This Valentina Grigorievna

Sosunova. It is not a worthy existence. It is clumsy. It is awkward. It makes more mistakes than it does great works. And I become aware of the movements of my eyes, and the writhing of my tongue, and the bones inside my hands. This destroyed me, once, until I learned that it was not the truth.

"I learned that I was more like … a pair of eyes, suspended in nothingness, *looking* at that.

"It does not save me from having to see it, all the time."

There was a frown on Evdeniya's face. "You're supposed to be pretty good," she said.

"It would be nicer to see myself as others see me," Valentina agreed.

"I appreciate your helping me, anyway."

"It's not a problem."

They went through busy streets, and quiet ones, and finally to the nearly-abandoned neighborhood where Evdeniya lived. Evdeniya showed her in and they kicked their shoes off at the doorstep and went to view the thing that should not be.

Valentina looked at it for a while.

"It is strangely difficult to look away," she said.

Evdeniya nodded.

"I think I can see what can be done here," Valentina said. "But it is a thing I cannot do yet. At least not without some thinking on the matter. This strikes me as a thing like the primal chaos, and, like the primal chaos, it seems susceptible to the power of attention. That is my read on things. Incompletely formed, it can be *made* to have form by the power of the eyes that look upon it—by the power of the eyes that see. Only, I am not quite sure what the right way of looking at it is; or, rather, I am not quite sure what form I ought to make it have."

"I don't understand," Evdeniya said.

"I don't either," Valentina said. "That's the difficulty. In the meantime—"

She looked sharply away from the thing, took Evdeniya's arm, and pulled her into the kitchen.

"That is, while I work on figuring out that solution, we can find your parents."

"We can?"

"You mentioned that you were willing to let me dream through you," Valentina said. "It is still costly. It is still destructive. But it is also the safest way for us to experience what it is like inside that thing. If you are still willing."

"Of course!" Evdeniya said.

"Not so fast," Valentina said. "This is going to hurt. A lot. In ways that you can't even imagine being hurt. I need you to not be casual about it."

"It's my Mom and Dad," Evdeniya said.

Valentina considered that for a while. Then she nodded. "The technique involves an herbal concoction. I will prepare it. Find a room where there can safely be some thrashing, wear loose-fitting comfortable clothing, and make sure there is no outstanding business for the day."

Evdeniya went to her bedroom. She checked over her list of chores. She changed into pajamas. She moved the desk and dresser a little further from the bed and the bed a little further from the wall. By the time she was done the concoction was prepared.

"Drink," Valentina said.

It was thick and fibrous and tasted more than anything else like cornmeal. Evdeniya set down the cup and Valentina helped her to her feet. She waited for an effect but there was nothing obvious. Valentina still held on to her arm, providing unnecessary support, as they walked upstairs to Evdeniya's room.

She noticed that her breath was loud as Valentina helped her up onto the bed.

"The drug will not make you sleepy," Valentina said. "There is no real need for you to sleep. It is not you who will be dreaming. That said, you should probably not try to hold on to consciousness if you should feel it slipping."

She did not feel it slipping. The world was obstinately normal.

In her ears there was a dull roar, as of the wind.

"I have found the following thought to be helpful," Valentina said. "In the nothingness that is the chaos, in the nothingness that is the Outside, there is the world, and it is like a bejeweled tapestry, and it participates in an experience of itself.

"Fold it. Pass a bit of it through the eye of a needle.

"That bit on the far side can only see what that bit can see. That bit on the far side can only hear what that bit can hear. It is the world, but it is limited by the pinch of the eye of the needle, locked down to a local perspective. It is the world, but it doesn't *know* that it is the world. Because it can only hear certain things, and can only see certain things, it does not call itself the world. It calls itself, 'Evdeniya.'"

"I'm sorry," Evdeniya said. "I don't follow."

"It's all right," Valentina said.

Evdeniya thought one of the knots of wood in a beam by the ceiling resembled a face. It was laughing at her, she thought. She tried to remember what she'd been saying but it didn't seem terribly important.

"I have found the following thought to be helpful," Valentina said. "A person sees themselves do certain things, and they are told certain things about themselves by others. They see and hear these things, and they conceive a story of themselves. 'I am this kind of person,' they think. 'I am a person who does this thing, and is described this way.'"

"Uh-huh," Evdeniya said.

"The process of personhood," Valentina said, "is therefore a process that is committed after-the-fact. We do not conduct personhood in the moment. We do not construct *ourselves* in the moment. We construct ourselves ... later. Who are we in the moment? A shapeless, nameless *doing*. A thing that is in the world, that moves."

"Oh," Evdeniya said.

"There is no actor," Valentina said, "and no acted-upon. This is most clearly illustrated in dreams, but it is true in life as well. The idea that there is a person, doing things, to things, is a mechanism of thinking. Reality simply transpires."

"That is not accurate," Evdeniya said. "I do stuff."

She waved an arm.

"I make birds fly," she said, searching for good examples. "I blow the wind."

"The main effect of the medication," Valentina said, "is to reduce the connection between you and yourself. That is probably something that you are beginning to experience. When it happens, do not fight it."

"Yea," Evdeniya said.

She thought about that. She *did* feel as if she were slipping away from something important, something central. It was hard not to grasp for it. It was hard not to hold on. She felt her body twitch.

It twitched again, and then outright convulsed.

"A body doesn't like not having a person in it," Valentina said. "It tries to get your attention. Or, well, a 'you''s attention. Ignore it."

"Yea."

"There's this funny thing," Valentina said. "Where it is possible to daze the mind and body so much that you actually forget who you are for a minute, you even forget your name, and what's funny about it is, in that moment, when you've forgotten who you are, couldn't you turn out to have been anyone?"

"Uh," Evdeniya said.

She tried to get the twitching under control. She thought she had it, but the moment it stopped and she relaxed a little it started up again.

Her ears were ringing. Her vision was full of static.

Her breathing was erratic, as each convulsion slammed the breath out from her lungs.

Valentina's right hand drummed out an idle beat on the wooden floor. It wasn't quite to the time of Evdeniya's movements.

Context slipped.

In that moment, everything was gone; Evdeniya couldn't help reaching for it, desperately trying to remember where she was, what was going on, what her name was, what she was doing, why everything was so strange, but as she grabbed for context Valentina's hand came down hard upon the floor and the noise startled her and it drove the world away.

She *still* couldn't help reaching for it. She crawled her way back to being oriented on the world. She forced the world to make sense again, swallowed the sense of it like a pill, remembered who she was and what it was that she was doing there, and then got angry at herself when she had done so.

Her body twitched.

"It's all right," Valentina said. "Nobody stays gone on the first try."

Evdeniya's limbs hummed inside them. She breathed with some difficulty. A wave of vertigo passed across her.

"You just have to learn not to panic and grab hold again," Valentina said. "On the next fall, or the next."

Evdeniya's thoughts were distorted. She felt as if she were at sea, the waters lapping up against her pillow.

"It may help," Valentina said, "to compress the fire of consciousness inside you and move it in a circle around the inside of your skull."

Her eyes crossed. A supreme effort rose from somewhere, fell into somewhere, and dissipated again.

Context slipped.

In that moment, everything was gone, and nothing had changed. It was pure reflex that had her seizing at an understanding of the world, scrabbling back up the walls of the mental well that she had fallen into, trying once again to find her name, her being, her body, and what was going on. She did no better on the second fall than on the first; only, something was off when she returned.

She remembered her name. She remembered where she was. But everything was dark and everything was spinning and the room seemed to be fragmenting around her.

No sooner did she break the surface of the waters of self-awareness than dizziness dragged her back under them again.

There was a voice, but she couldn't understand it.

A hand reached into her mind and brushed ten thousand spots of light away.

"It'll do," someone said, and she began to dream.

THE BEGINNING of her dream was chaos. There was no order and there was no sense to it; it was a field of multicolored motion. She was lost. She was afraid.

Then the dream refined itself.

The mists pulsed, and with each pulsation more of their mass was organized into *things*: wind, grass, a towering building, the cold light of the stars. Her fear organized itself and became more precise:

Something wicked and wild was chasing her.

Vertigo receded and her location became more specific; she was surrounded by wood, by glass, by the smell of books.

It slipped in that moment into something like an ordinary dream, and Evdeniya dreamt that she—or, at least, *somebody*—was in a library of sorts, with great glass windows, along the side of a hill. Something had been chasing her, or at least, chasing somebody, but it had lost track of her; its footsteps receded into the distance and were gone.

She saw her father up ahead; he was pulling a book down from the shelves. He stopped midway through the motion. He seemed to collect himself, and turned to look down the aisle at her.

"Extraordinary," he said.

She found herself walking past the endless books to him. She extended a hand. To her surprise, what she said was, "Your health, sir. I'm Valentina Grigorievna Sosunova."

"Kinjiro," he replied.

"Your daughter is concerned," she said. "You walked into the effusion of a thing that should not be, and did not return."

"I did," he agreed. "It's the most remarkable place that I've ever visited, but it appears that the road leads onwards and inwards regardless of the direction that one travels. Enyashenka shall have to get along without us for a little while."

"Please," she said, "if there were more information, we might be able to retrieve you."

Kinjiro shook his head sharply. "That is child's thinking; she is quite capable of managing the household without us, and the experience will do her good. She cannot clutch at her mother's skirts her entire life,"—and here his eyes crinkled into a smile—"isn't that right?"

"Speaking as an outside party," she said, "I'm a little more concerned for your situation than I am for hers."

"Not every misadventure is a catastrophe," Kinjiro said, simply.

She found herself looking down, then up. "Very well," she said. "Then, in the interests of science, in the event that you do not return?"

Kinjiro laughed. "In the interests of science:" he agreed. "What Dr. Wife and I, here, have constructed is the most marvelous thing: let us not call it 'a thing that should not be,' but rather, the *omphalos*, the *central axis*, of an age ... perhaps a world ... that is yet to come."

Evdeniya found herself frowning.

"The ... central logic," Kinjiro explained. "The essence. The *zeitgeist*. It does not seem to fit in the world as it is because it *cannot* fit in the world as it is; if it did, the future would be the now. We have created the very definition of a thing that cannot be shoehorned into our primitive era, and in so doing, brought our world out of alignment; but the reward is worth the cost, for it has opened a pathway into a glimpse of what shall happen next."

Her mother Tamara was suddenly there, or, rather, was suddenly already-had-been-there. She looped her arm through Kinjiro's.

"Tell our little Zhenya that it is marvelous; that life is *wonder*," her mother said.

"It is difficult for me," the girl found herself saying, slowly, "to distinguish between inspiration, excess, and delirium when it comes to such matters. But I am not certain I can simply *leave* you there. I will have to ask your daughter when she recovers whether you seem in full possession of your faculties."

"I hardly think that's fair," Kinjiro said. "I'm dreaming. No man has full control of his faculties when he is dreaming."

"That is, at least," she found herself saying, "an answer, of a kind."

There was a great shock; she found herself falling into herself, and she was suddenly Evdeniya again; and she opened her mouth wide and rushed towards her parents, to say or do what she did not know ... but no sooner did she move than the magic shattered, and they dissolved into a waking dream, and then into the twisting, terrifying image of the thing that should not be.

IT IS, OF COURSE, not always the case in life that the greatest risks turn into the greatest dangers.

For Evdeniya—other than the gain in hope, and confidence—no real consequences came from allowing Valentina to dream through her. It is a process historically known for its psychic impact; for the subsequent days or weeks of dissociation or depression, for the long-term damage. On rare occasions, hale souls have even *broken* from it ... but for Evdeniya, it passed like the gentlest of rains. Conversely, spending a few minutes existing casually in her family's garden would soon prove perilous to her: nearly to the point of her destruction.

It happened like this.

Valentina went home. The days went by, and Evdeniya kept the house. One day she was pulling weeds outside and this guy just showed up, crawling over the wall of her garden. Evdeniya stared at him in disbelief. He ignored her until he made it over the top, wriggled around, lowered himself over the edge, and finally dropped down. Then he turned.

"Pjatvchet Gilberthaosovich Utkin," he introduced. "I didn't think you'd be out here."

"I have a death ray," Evdeniya said.

"It's not like you think," he said. "I'm not breaking in. I just don't like to come in through the door. Are your parents around?"

"Maybe," she said.

"Because we're old friends," he said. "They said, if I was ever in town, I should stop by, and they'd put me up for a while. So here I was, and here I am! You must be Evgeshka."

"Evdeniya," she corrected. "And I have never heard of you. ... but I suppose you must come in, then."

He swept in through the back doors. He tracked in mud and he didn't seem to notice. He made a beeline for her room.

"Here," he said. "This looks like a good place to hang my hat."

He whistled, and there was a shuffling sound down the hall. Evdeniya startled as she turned to see a collection of travel bags crawling along the rug towards her room. She stared at it for a moment, first in horror and then in fascination and finally, with a little full-body shiver as her attention disengaged, with irritation.

"This isn't the guest room, sir," she said. "If you'll come this way—"

"No need," he said, airily. "No need." He tossed his hat onto the bedpost for her bed and his luggage poured itself through the door and sprawled out before the dresser of her room. He took off his overcoat and tossed it on the pile, turned, adjusted the buttons of his waistcoat, and smiled at her with his eyes twinkling. "This is more than sufficient for my needs. Can I eat in here tonight? I'm rather bushed."

"I suppose," she said, after a moment.

"You're a gem," he said. He tweaked her nose and she squinted at him in irritation. Then he turned and he waved to his baggage, which seemed to slump down into the shadows and become indistinct, until there was nothing but an ominous uncertainty where her dresser had been. "Let's move on."

Evdeniya stepped back and he came back out of her room, squeezing past her into the hall, adjusting the hang of a picture, heading down towards her father's lab. "Ah," she said.

"It's all right," he said. "It's all right. I'm allowed. Your father said it was all right if I touched a few things, looked at a few things, maybe took a few things to market. You don't mind if I take a few things to market, do you? It's for the cause."

"The cause?"

"Exactly," he agreed. "Now, I believe you have forgotten something important. I will forgive you, because you are very young, but you should not embarrass your family by being inhospitable."

Awkwardly, Evdeniya said, "I am not *terribly* young."

"Then there's no excuse, then, is there?"

She came to a halt in the hallway and let him gain distance from her. She fidgeted, and then finally turned around. "Fine," she said, and went to the kitchen to fetch the new houseguest a dish of bread and salt.

He didn't take it, though. He was busily disassembling her father's orrery and merely waved her to a bench so that she could lay it down.

SHE WAS dozing fitfully in the guest room when his presence startled her awake. She gasped, sat up, and reached defensively for a bedside weapon that was not there. He held up his hands in surrender anyway.

"I did not mean to startle you," he said. "I was just getting back and the dinner that you'd left out for me had grown cold. I was wondering if I could trouble you for something warmer?"

"It's—" Her eyes sought blearily for her clock, but she couldn't find that either. "What time is it?"

"Time isn't truthfully of all that much relevance here," he said, "without a sun."

She frowned at him.

"But," he said, "an hour or two past the night lamp[11], if you must."

Her pajamas were decent enough for company; she slipped out of bed and put her feet in her slippers. She sighed. "C'mon," she said, and padded off towards the kitchen.

He followed her.

"Ah—" he said hesitantly.

"Ah?"

"I was also wondering," he said. "Or, rather, wanting to make sure. I was wanting to make sure that, of course, you did not let anyone else in while I was out?"

She took a deep breath and let it out. Then she shook her head. "For one thing," she said, "I did not know that you were gone."

"Oh," he said. "Yes. I had thought I would just sleep, but instead I found myself with a bug to visit the market. It's been quite some time since I've been to Fortitude."

"You're from Earth?" she said.

"Oh, no," he said. "I'm not from anywhere in particular."

"You ... this ... that *cannot* be correct," she said.

---

11   that is, past nine pm; he did not specifically *check* the day and night lamps that the Archive kept.

"Well, fair," he agreed. "It would be more proper to say that I am from *nowhere* in particular. I was born in the Outside, you see."

She stopped in place. Eventually he had to give her a little nudge to get her moving again.

"It's not so unusual," he explained. "Being born in the Outside is incredibly unlikely, but the Outside is so much bigger than everywhere else put together that it happens pretty regularly even so."

"That's terrible," she said. "I mean, begging your pardon."

"It's not as nice as having parents and a home," he agreed. "But then, it's not as bad as being an orphan, or having bad ones. It's certainly not a tragic story like yours is."

"Mine?"

"Well," he said, "it's pretty obvious that your family's been gone a while, and it doesn't look like they made provisions for it. I'll probably have to take you away with me when I go, in the interests of charity."

"Please don't," Evdeniya said. "... no offense intended."

"None taken," he said. "But seriously, Kinjiro and Tamara ... should I expect to be encountering them in my stay?"

"No," she said.

"Ah."

"They will return," she said. "But you should not wait for them. They are adventuring."

He was silent for a bit as she wearily boiled water and heated kasha, stirring, until the grains were golden. She mixed the two, with a bit of oil and salt, before covering it and sitting down to wait.

"Where do you know them from?" she asked.

"It's not important," he said. "Here and there. This and that. You're certain that you didn't have anyone else over at all?"

"Yes," she said.

"Good," he said, and relaxed a bit. "Please don't."

"Um," Evdeniya said.

"You're welcome to do anything that you like," Pjatvchet said. "I won't make a peep about it! Clean anything you want, read any of the books, make whatever you want in the kitchen, even pull up all the weeds in the garden if you are so inclined, but I am most comfortable if it's just the two of us here."

"I can't actually stop people from coming over," Evdeniya said.

"I have a deep-seated emotional scarring," Pjatvchet said. "My master was always inviting people in and they would do me the most terrible mischiefs. I suppose it's all right if they drop by unexpected. Those are my kind of people. I won't object to your letting them in, particularly if they come over the wall. But just imagine how awful if it'd be if you brought over a sewing circle and they all stabbed me with needles, or a priest and they blessed the place and I couldn't get in!"

"You're a fairy?" Evdeniya guessed, with suddenly sharpening interest, but Pjatvchet just drew himself up in offense.

"Hardly," he said. "*You* wouldn't like being stabbed with a bunch of needles either."

Evdeniya sighed.

"It wasn't a *Christian* priest," he said. "Anyway. That time. It was one of your Fortitude shrine family types."

Evdeniya looked at the table and laughed. "Well," she said. "I won't invite a priest by to bless the place, and I won't ask for it done if one happens by. But if you're going to put so many conditions on your staying here, I'm going to have to put up one of my own."

"Oh?"

"There," Evdeniya said, and she waved towards the living room. "That. You don't touch that. You stay out of there. It's off limits to guests."

His gaze flicked into the living room. It returned to her. "It is a rather fascinating device," he said. "I had intended to investigate it. But these are dark times. We must all make sacrifices. I understand that as well as any. We can both leave it be. ...ah! I might need to go in the room, though."

"For?"

Pjatvchet gave his shoulders a rolling shrug. "This and that," he said. "That and this. What if I need to stretch my legs for a minute and I happen to be facing in that direction? It'd be laughable if I had to turn around and circumnavigate the hall passages just to get to the far side of the room."

"That is not persuasive," Evdeniya said firmly.

"Ah," Pjatvchet said. He frowned. "Well, what if I were to drop my pocketwatch and it were to roll into the living room?"

"I could fetch it," Evdeniya said. "I am at your disposal."

"You could be out at the market," Pjatvchet said. "For how long? I would not know. I would not have my pocket watch. Without my pocket watch, I could not crosscheck and validate them; how could I rely on the clocks in the house?"

"... that is a very heart-wrenching story," Evdeniya said. "Which you could sell at the market for a copper, and buy a new watch."

"Ouch," Pjatvchet said.

"Please," Evdeniya said.

"Since you have insisted, then," Pjatvchet said. He half-rose to his feet and bowed. "Heedless of all inconvenience; I shall obey."

He sat again, and she sat there with him for a minute.

Then she went back into the kitchen to stare at the kasha until it had completely cooked.

THE BREAKFAST DISHES were scattered in a trail through the house when she got up and moving in the morning; it looked as if he'd made something for himself and eaten it while wandering, discarding his finished tableware along the way. As for the man himself, he had departed.

She had forgiven him for waking her; even for taking her room; but that forgiveness dissipated.

"Unbelievable," she said, as she gathered them up.

The mess seemed to linger in the hall even when its constituent elements had been removed. The visceral impression of unwanted clutter lingered, and the shadows made stain-like patterns on the walls.

Over the next two days the difficulty of keeping the house in order only grew. Cushions spilled from the couches to scatter across the floor. Pots and pans and cutting boards and rolling pins and a tumbled three-legged stool cluttered the kitchen floor. The rugs were rolled up. Trash bags accumulated.

It was hard enough to stay on top of it as it was, but she could *feel* decay slipping in around the edges. She could feel the spirit of the house becoming a slovenly one. Standing in the garden, leaning on a broom, she realized that she was standing outside a derelict, and could practically sense the dust of the Outside slipping in around the seams.

What was the dust of the Outside? It was crystallized chaos. It blew in off of Big Lake. It was drawn towards messes, particularly *careless* messes, and towards things that you didn't keep track of. It inflicted unnatural rust and strange enchantments. It sifted into your dreams—though a clean dream-catcher would help. On the community level, it was a pretty big problem; on an individual household level, the odds of it actually being a problem, even if you were a pretty horrible mess, were extremely low—

But Pjatvchet was practically setting out the welcome mat for it. He was practically setting out *bait* for it. She could *feel* it. She could tell. And *that* meant checking the crawlspace and the attic and the far backs of the kitchen drawers for motes of the crystallized chaos. That meant that even the clean rooms had to be gone over every day, that she had to flip the rugs and move the couches, that the untouched high bookshelves needed as much going over as the lower ones, that she had to put away every tool that the man had taken out even when he was just as likely to take them out again. It meant cleaning under the sinks and in the backs of the closets.

It was the kind of cleaning and vigilance that wasn't so bad when done normally, that is, as part of a seasonal cycle, but it took a lot out of her to try to get it all in every couple of days; all while picking up after Pjatvchet was a job of its own.

There wasn't an option *not* to do it, though, so she kept on.

"You have to stop," she told Pjatvchet. "You're tearing the place apart."

"I'm looking for something," he admitted.

"Pardon?"

"There was a stone egg," he said, "that I left with your family. For safe-keeping. Do you know where it is?"

"You're ruining things," she said.

"I finally got an offer on it," he said, "from the Headmaster of the Bleak Academy himself. But then I get here and your parents are gone. Well, you can understand why I might take a gander here and there. I don't suppose you've seen it?"

"From the Headma—" Evdeniya frowned. "Why?"

"He can sit on it until it hatches, for all I care," Pjatvchet said.

"It's not here," Evdeniya said. "I've never seen anything like that here."

"Well," he said, "it's probably here *somewhere*. But let's not worry about that until we've been to the market. They're selling grouper at two for the copper."

"I don't have time to go to the market," she said. Then, in a quiet, defeated tone she said, "But I'll get the rest of the meal ready if I can trust you to bring it back."

On one of the shelves that she'd forgotten to check with sufficient regularity, the underside of a porcelain elephant salt shaker gave way to an unnatural Outside-borne rust.

IN THE house, that was the greatest risk, of course—that the house itself, or the possessions within it, would oxidate and corrode. But the dust of the Outside, drawn in by the constant disorder of the place, affected more than the house itself. The dreamcatchers overflowed with it, no matter how vigilantly she tried to keep them clean, and eventually the dust slipped its way into her dreams.

They grew tangled, desperate, and lightheaded.

She no longer rested so much as lay around in a daze, and soon her waking life was little better. A sickness began to grow in her mind, like a single still spot of darkness, a fixed point amidst the changing hours. There were nameless dark and ugly thoughts brewing inside her, sometimes making her hate her work or the house itself, sometimes making her hate herself, sometimes making her doubt that her parents would ever return.

In Svetlana's house, a vampire sat in a dark room in an armchair, unmoving. A bat fluttered its way in through the window. It crawled onto her arm. It said:

> Sveta, my Sveta, your little bat asks it—
> Your neighbor's in trouble: rise up from your casket!
> Shake off all the dust, set aside the stone lid,
> And walk among humans and bats once again!

Svetlana did not move for a long time. Finally, she opened one eye. She stretched her shoulders, brushed at the bat with one hand, and groused, "I'm not *in* my casket, Maksim."

The bat shrugged.

"Anyhow," Svetlana said, "I don't like leaving the house. It's bad enough that you made me move here. I'm ailing terribly here."

"Taste the air," Maksim said.

Svetlana lifted her head. She sniffed at the air, then, tentatively, flicked out her tongue.

She frowned.

"Misery," she said.

"That was my read as well," said the bat. "A cold-hearted vampire would feast on that misery, devouring the subtle emanations of it like a brandy-soaked meal. A warm-hearted vampire would visit her only friend in the neighborhood and offer whatever comfort she could. But what kind of vampire would just sit inside her house and ignore it completely?"

Svetlana shook her arm, and the bat fluttered away to perch upon a chair's high back. "Whatever," she said.

She looked around her house, which was, in fairness, somewhat cleaner than when Evdeniya had last left. She stumbled to the kitchen, her legs and arms pins and needles. She said, "—all my vegetables have gone rotten and turned into mold, which has in turn grown new, less desirable vegetables, Maksim."

"Close the cupboard above the sink and knock three times upon it," Maksim instructed. "Saying, 'Zori, molody, zmei, zoloty[12].' Then open it again."

Svetlana closed the cupboard, knocked three times while reciting the chant, and opened it again. Where before it had been stuffed with random cushions, knickknacks, empty jewelry boxes, and leftover bits of pipe from an attempted renovation of her previous house, it now overflowed with bags of fresh beets, cabbage, potatoes, onions, carrots, spices, flour, and sugar, not to mention a tin of butter and numerous little pots of spice. She blinked.

"Now do the same on your stockpot," Maksim instructed.

Svetlana gingerly approached her stock pot. She picked up a lid, holding it at arm's length. She put it over the pot. "*Zori, molody, zmei, zoloty!*" she said, knocking, and sagged with relief as the smell that had been emerging from the stockpot gave way to the smell of proper stock.

"Lamb?" she said, sniffing.

"It's hard to get good beef stock using a magical chant," Maksim explained.

"Right," Svetlana said. She began chopping vegetables. The stars

---

12 a sound-shaping magic with no intrinsic meaning. Perhaps 'dawn, young, snake, gold!'

crawled across the sky, and soon enough she had a pot of borscht and a basket of warm breads. She hung the basket on one arm and took the pot in both hands and went to stand on her front porch. There she hesitated for a long time, one foot nudging the boundary between her home and the outside world.

The wind shifted. A fresh gust of misery blew in from Evdeniya's house.

The bat nudged her, and she stumbled out onto the street.

It was very open there. She was exposed in every direction. She felt very small and uneasy and the wind seemed to cut right through her clothing. The light of the lanterns was everywhere. But as awful as it was for her, it was less awful to *be* outside than to *step* outside; she did not step back. She hurried down the road to Evdeniya's house. She pressed herself against the front of the house to be beneath the eaves and hammered on the door.

Evdeniya opened the door. She stared blankly at the vampire.

"I do not like going out," Svetlana said. "It is very open out here. But I cannot eat all of this borscht and bread alone. In fact, I really can't eat any of it.[13] Can I please come inside?"

Evdeniya backed away, wordlessly, and gestured.

Svetlana hesitated, caught between conflicting imperatives. "I would very much like to enter," she said. "But you have yet to invite me. May I please come inside?"

"Oh," Evdeniya said. "Oh. Yes."

"Thank you," Svetlana said. A flash of shame flew across Evdeniya's face; the thought that she had promised not to invite others in blew into her mind just a moment too late, and then out again, discarded on the grounds that Svetlana had, after all, come by unexpectedly, and besides that, that the invitation was already made. The vampire brushed past her. She came inside. She took the stock pot to the dining room table, set it

---

13   She had a very sensitive stomach.

down, and unloaded the basket beside it. "I was going to bring a salad, but reciting magical chants at my cupboards failed to produce any lettuce. Sit down, sit down, you look dead on your feet."

Evdeniya pulled out a chair. She sat down. She stared at the food.

"I'll bring in some dishes from the kitchen," Svetlana said. A moment later, from the kitchen, she added, "I'll just wash some dishes, that is, and bring them in. Uh, unless this pitcher is actually holy wate— why would it even be holy water, Svetlana, that's dumb."

"It's not," Evdeniya said. "… can't you, like, tell?"

"Nobody really gave me a manual," Svetlana said. "I just got eternal life and a magical bat."

"Oh."

"Sometimes I think there's something wrong with me," Svetlana said. "I don't really mind the cross all that much and garlic's just kind of stinky. Do you think there's something wrong with me? —nevermind, it's not important right now."

Evdeniya didn't answer. The sounds of scrubbing came out from the kitchen, and, finally, stopped. Svetlana brought out a bowl, a little plate, silverware, and a pat of butter on a saucer. She plopped them down on the table, served up the soup, and buttered a slice of bread for Evdeniya's plate.

"Seriously," she said, "you are not doing well. It hangs around you like a miasma. I could taste it from home."

"I'm sorry," Evdeniya said.

"No," Svetlana said, shaking her head. "It's rather tasty."

"Oh."

Evdeniya drank a bit of the soup. She ate a bit of bread. She said, "It is kind of you to visit."

Svetlana studied her. "If you are in trouble, then I could resolve the matter."

"I can't let you do that."

"Foo," Svetlana said, and sighed. She studied Evdeniya thoughtfully. Then she dropped into a seat across from her, steepled her hands, and carefully began:

"Once upon a time … but not so very long ago … a vampire was chasing a thief among thieves. He'd stolen from kings and from farmers, from bankers and priests, but cracking open the vampire's crypt would be his last mistake—if the vampire hadn't been all fuzzy-headed from sleep, he could have ripped the thief's throat out right there!

"But he didn't, 'cause he had been, and now the thief of thieves was fleeing across the night, on a horse from some great boyar's stables, and the vampire was hard upon his heels."

"What?" Evdeniya said, blearily.

"I am telling a story," Svetlana said.

"Oh."

"To cheer you!"

"… oh."

"The thief came to a crossroads," Svetlana continued, "and there drew rein, for a beautiful woman was standing there, waving and squinting in the direction from which he came. 'Quickly, quickly,' she said. 'Scatter those flax seeds in that pouch on your belt. Then ride on!'

"The thief, thinking he was soon to die *anyway*, shrugged and did.

"Minutes later, he heard the vampire stop and howl in anger. He suddenly remembered the story that when you scatter seeds like that, the vampire must stop to count them! He grinned to himself and thought, *I might just make it after all.*

"… but a thief only has so many flax seeds on him at any given time.

"Soon enough, he heard a triumphant cry. 'One hundred eighteen!' It echoed through the night.

"He spurred his horse; he drove it faster.

"The thief reached another crossroads, where another woman

stood—the first woman's sister, but a year younger and far more beautiful. 'Quickly, quickly,' she cried. 'Scatter those barley seeds from that pouch on your belt. Then ride on!'

"'Wise advice!' said the thief.

"He scattered the barley seeds on the ground and rode on. Behind him, he heard the vampire stop again; heard another inhuman howl of outrage; and put on miles of distance before he could finally hear the vampire's triumphant shout, across the hills:

"'Two hundred seventy-nine!'

"Now he was in a real race, and the finish line was the dawn, and the vampire closed in on him fast. The thief felt a cold sweat break out upon his brow, for his horse was tired, and his blood was hot, and he had no more seeds left upon his belt.

"He reached a third crossroads, and he saw the youngest and most beautiful sister of the three.

"'There's nothing for it!' she cried out. 'You must scatter the gold and treasures from that pouch upon your belt!'

"The thief's expression grew anguished, but determined; he knew that there was nothing else that he could do. He poured out a sparkling river of gold coins onto the ground. Jewels, too, and bits of silver and copper coin—even a comb of fengtian jade!

"'Wise advice,' he said, 'though I curse you for it!'

"He set his spurs to his horse again and dashed onwards towards the dawn.

"The sky was lightening. His heart beat like a thunder. He waited for the vampire's howl of outrage at the gold; but, it did not come.

"The vampire swept through the crossroads and beyond; caught up to the thief of thieves, seized him from his horse; dragged him to the ground; drew back and readied himself to bite, to tear, to drink the thief's red bounty of hot and pumping blood.

"'Wait!' the thief cried. 'Wait! Wait! Don't you have to go back and count the gold?'"

Svetlana wrinkled her face in mock-confusion. "'... what gold?'

"And if this tragic tale has a moral at all, it would be that people you meet at crossroads at night, while running from a vampire, are not necessarily to be trusted with your money."

Evdeniya snorted and rolled her eyes.

"See?" Svetlana said. "I knew you could feel something other than despair."

Evdeniya sighed, and then smiled awkwardly. "It's not like I *wanted* to be unhappy," she said. She took another bite of borscht. "I just, I'm so *tired*."

"I understand," Svetlana said.

Evdeniya stared into her plate. Then she looked up. She tried a small smile. "Another?"

"As you like," said Svetlana. She drummed her fingers on the table. "Uh, hmm, if I have one. Have you heard the story of Neckpiercer?"

"That doesn't sound like the kind of story that I would have heard of," Evdeniya said.

"Once upon a time," Svetlana said, "Maksim told me, one time when he was trying to get me to go out more often, there was a vampire named Parfyon who was raised to the old ways, who thought it was very appropriate that a vampire should find some highborn lady to feed from, enspelling her into submission and drinking deeply from the veins upon her neck; save, every time he got close to the lady of his ambitions, his dead heart would pound too loudly and his face would flush and his hands would get all awkward and before he even reached her windowsill he would have to run away.

"It was very frustrating and very embarrassing for him, and in the end, all he had to drink from was his servant girl Sabrina ... which was hardly anything like the princess of his desires. He would frequently chide her about the quality of her blood, which he imagined was much inferior to that of a proper highborn lady's, and about the slow household service that she'd provide to him after he had drunk his fill.

"One day Sabrina mused aloud about an old wizard that her family had had one or two encounters with, and her master was seized with the desire to meet him, in the hopes that he could help him. No sooner was it thought than done; a meeting was arranged, and the wizard, after thinking long and hard about Parfyon's problem, said this.

"'I can make you a device, which I will call Neckpiercer. If you give it her scent it will be able to call her blood directly to your mouth from far away.'

"Parfyon was delighted!

"He paid the wizard handsomely and sent his servant Sabrina off to the prince's castle to find something that would have the princess' scent. Oh! What difficulties she had, sneaking in and back, but she finally returned to him with a ruby necklace that she thought only a princess could possibly have worn.

"The vampire gave Neckpiercer the scent of the necklace, put it in his mouth, and inhaled fiercely. He turned red in the face and his cheeks caved in. Finally he choked and Neckpiercer, which looked something like a flute, was pulled partly into his mouth and a great embarrassment ensued.

"'I don't understand,' he said.

"He turned over the device in his hands. 'Could it be that the wizard was a fraud? Have him brought to me in chains!'

"The wizard was brought to him in chains, but when Parfyon interrogated him about the incident he only snorted. 'Bah!' he said. 'That necklace is a gift from a fish-faced prince in Novgorod. I doubt she's worn it even once!'

"'Aha!' the vampire said, and glared at Sabrina. 'I should have you beaten. Get back there and get me something with her scent at once!'

"Sabrina returned, and after many close shaves and many a daring adventure, she brought him a golden cup.

"'You're quite the accomplished thief,' the wizard praised, while the vampire huffed and puffed desperately upon the flute. 'But that won't do either. *That* one's a gift from a three-legged merchant in Moravia. It's probably been up on a shelf from the day it came into her hands!'

"Sabrina sighed and dared the castle again. 'Third time's the charm!' said she.

"This time she came back bloody, sweaty, and exhausted, having escaped through swamp and thornbushes and a perilous clamber after ripping a bit off the princess' woolen skirt.

"'If this doesn't smell of her,' she said, 'I don't know what will do; I'm not going back for her underthings.'

"'No, no, no,' the wizard said. 'This bit of skirt should do just fine.'

"And indeed, no sooner had Neckpiercer gotten a whiff of the cloth than blood began to pump right through it and into the vampire's open mouth. 'Divine!' he said. 'Delightful! It is everything I had dreamed of. Sabrina, you cannot comprehend how vulgar, mean, and tasteless your blood is in comparison to this.'

"'I am rebuked,' Sabrina agreed.

"Blissful nights went by, and the vampire thought that his life was at last complete; no need for all the troublesome seduction, no need to fly to the princess' window or mesmerize her with his eyes—just rub the flute on her woolen skirt, and drink! But it is the character of vampires, as it is with humans, to be more unsatisfied with things the more satisfactory they become; having finally achieved his ambition, at no effort from himself, he found himself drawn increasingly to the castle to see the outcome of his work:

"To witness the exquisite paleness of the princess, drained of blood; to observe how she had been restricted to her bed by the draining of her strength; to know that he had marked his territory, as it were, and claimed his prize.

"'There's nothing for it,' Sabrina agreed, 'But that you must go.'

"So he went. He cloaked himself in shadows and he traveled to the palace; rather than fly up to her window, which idea still rather unnerved him, he entered through the main gates, slipped past the guards while their minds were mazed, and wandered through the halls. It puzzled him, though; there were no obvious signs of his work. There were no doctors bustling about; no hints of a great mourning; no signs of anything awry.

"He came up with a marvelous bit of duplicity.

"'Pardon me,' he said, gripping the arm of a servant. 'I am a doctor, brought in from far Araby; could you tell me, how fares the princess in her ailment?'

"'Thank goodness you're here!' the servant said. 'I don't know about any ailment of the *princess* ...

"'... but there's something dreadful wrong with the local sheep.'"

Svetlana waited a few seconds to let Evdeniya put the pieces together and start laughing before she finished up the story:

"That ends the story of Neckpiercer; as for the vampire Parfyon, when he got home, he found he could not even look his servant Sabrina in the eye. His embarrassment grew so strong that he combusted, and she was left with all the burden of his extensive lands and wealth."

And with this and other bad stories the weight on Evdeniya was lifted for a time; but, the house was still full of chaos and she could not rest.

THE NEXT night Maksim came to Svetlana once again:

Sveta, my Sveta, your little bat asks it—
Your neighbor's in trouble: rise up from your casket!
Borscht and bread 'twere enough were she simply distressed
But her dreams have been stolen; she will die without rest.

Svetlana stared blankly at the wall. "Still not in a casket, Maksim."

The bat shrugged.

"It is unfair," Svetlana said. "You can't possibly ask me to go out two nights in a row. And what can I do about dreams, anyway?"

"You will have to consult with someone who knows them better," Maksim agreed.

"Bah," Svetlana said.

She stood up and went over to the empty fireplace. She squatted down in front of it, watching the flickers of an imaginary fire.

"I am only a bat," Maksim said. "But I think that you might have some fortune if you went to the witch of the northern cliffs for aid."

"That's a really long way," Svetlana said. "And I doubt she'll invite me in."

"I don't know if earthen tunnels need invitations," Maksim said.

"In principle ..." Svetlana said, thinking. She straightened. She looked around, and shrugged. "Maybe not. How will I find my hiking boots in all this?"

Maksim fluttered over to land upon a grandfather clock. "Knock three times upon the mess," he said, "saying, '*Zori, molody, zmei, zoloty.*' And we shall see what we shall see."

"Um, no," Svetlana said. "But thank you."

"No?"

"I don't want to lose what's *currently* inside my mess," Svetlana said. "It might be important."

"Sveta," Maksim said, "nothing in here is important. You are a vampire."

"You don't know that," Svetlana said. She made a face. "I don't need my boots, anyway. It's OK. I'll go. But under protest."

"It's brave of you," Maksim said.

"Legends will be told of Svetlana Witherspoon," she said, "who left her house, two nights in a row."

Her voice was a little bitter. She walked to her patio. She tried very hard to turn into a bat, and then, when that didn't work, stepped out.

It was, as she had said, a long way, and longer for her because she traveled slowly. She clung to the shadows near buildings when she could. She startled at every little sound. She avoided others' eyes and spent her entire trip through town waiting for someone to attack her; when she reached the edge of the wild, both that fear and the relative safety and comfort of the buildings were left behind.

Walking along the cliff felt profoundly unnatural to her. The trees made her feel smaller than their relative size merited. The silence as she proceeded north disturbed her. She was troubled by every tree root that she stepped over and every sharp-faced rock that she passed by.

The enchanted pit that the witch lived in was a quixotic relief.

She descended.

Soon she could hear a tuneless singing rising from below: "jam, jam, jammity-jam, jam, jam, berries," and other verses of the like. It was inconstant, fading regularly into humming or silence, and it was nothing more than a quiet hum when she reached the ledge where the creature worked.

"Eh, yee?" the creature said, turning to look at her. She sprang backwards, away from Svetlana, and then, after a moment's frantic vacillation, forward, to stand between Svetlana and the cooking fire.

"...your health, ma'am," Svetlana said.

The creature's hackles, which had raised, settled slowly downwards. "You're dead," she said. "Why are you walking around like that? It's unnatural."

"Lots of things are unnatural," Svetlana said.

"Sophistry," the creature said, dismissively. "I won't wish you your health, and I don't want you here. What do you want?"

"Evdeniya," Svetlana said. "She visited you recently."

"Ye-e-es?" the creature creaked.

"She's not sleeping," Svetlana said. "Or, at least, not getting any rest out of it."

The creature looked down, then up. "That's not my doing, if that's what you're hinting at. I'm not taking her soul out of her body and riding it through the hills all night. Could do that, if I wanted to, but I'm too virtuous to. That's my law-abiding nature."

"There's a law against that?"

"Not specifically," the creature said, "but it falls under the general aegis."

"Well," Svetlana said, "I was more hoping that you could help her."

The creature considered that for a long moment. Then she nodded. "Go back home," she said. "By the time you arrive there, the matter will be attended to."

That night Evdeniya did not dream Outside-fueled dreams; instead, an ugly creature seized her sleeping self, rode her spirit like a horse out to the cliffs above Big Lake, and then rested it there, between the starlight and the stone.

"Shh," said the witch, and stroked her hair, and they listened to the lake together.

IT BOUGHT HER DAYS: days where she could hold her shoulders up against the weight of the world that pressed down upon it. Days to live through while the house grew emptier as Pjatvchet looted it—at least, she assumed so—and dingier despite all her work.

She tolerated it, though her tolerance was worn extremely thin, because she had an investment in tolerating it; because Pjatvchet was a connection, however strained, to Kinjiro and Tamara; because hospitality was sacred; and, to a great degree, because he frightened her. It was easier to give him no reason to harm her than to find out what it *meant* that he was born in the Outside and had dealings with the likes of he the lord of Death's dominion he.

The stories of Fortitude are kind to children who diligently maintain their homes; they speak poorly of those who cast out guests.

She kept going, thus, for eight more days.

It was when the chaos reached the living room that she broke.

"I TOLD YOU not to enter into there," she said.

He did not answer; he was not there; there was only his greasy handprint upon the door and a bit of mess slouching through its frame onto the rug.

He did not say anything as she scrubbed the door and doorframe clean. He did not say anything as she picked up the room. He made no response to her comments, directed mostly at the air, as she corrected the shambles, there and elsewhere, he was making of her house.

He did not show up, in fact, until she was leaving; he caught her at the door.

"Evgeshka," he said, "you have the look of someone who is doing something unwise."

She gave him a flat look. Then she shrugged. "It's too much," she said.

"What's too much?"

"It," she said, and waved a vague hand towards the house. "I'm sorry, Pjatvchet. It's just gone too far. So I am going to the temple, and I will have this house be blessed."

"This is a regrettable course of action," he said. "Why ruin our idyllic interval?"

"It's not because of you," she said. "There's too much of the Outside in here. And when cleaning a place no longer suffices—well, you need a Kichi or a Sosunov, don't you?"

"It's inhospitable," he said.

"Don't *even*," she said. "A host's got a right to clean the house."

"I'm sorry it's come to this," he said. "But I won't be held accountable for the consequences. Thank you for what you have done for me. I am not unappreciative and I regret that our amicable relationship must end."

Evdeniya straightened her collar. "If you try to stop me," she said, "I'll scream."

"I would never dream of restricting your mobility," Pjatvchet said. "By all means, go. Go, go, go, and if I've seen the last of you, I'll call it good."

She frowned at him. Then she turned. She left. She traveled through Fortitude towards the Sosunov compound.

Behind her a churning ground fog began to billow through the streets.

IT WAS for symmetry, more than any other reason, that she went to Valentina Sosunova to request her aid.

She waited while Valentina made tea for them. She waited while Valentina sat, and poured.

"Your health," Valentina said.

"Thank you," Evdeniya said. "And yours."

"I have been remiss," Valentina said. "I've meant to follow up with you. I'm assuming that that is why you are here; you are reporting that your parents have made it home safe and well, or, you are impatient that I should help them do so."

"They know what they are doing," Evdeniya said, with a tight-lipped frown. "I cannot impose on you further."

"Then—"

Valentina hesitated.

"—you are recovering well enough from the method that we used to contact them?"

"It is not that," Evdeniya said. "I have come to request an exorcism."

"Ah," Valentina said. She blew on her tea. She sipped from it. "Troubles come in packs, I see."

"The Outside has intruded," Evdeniya said. "Upon my home. I am no longer able to control it."

"That's amazing," Valentina said. "Such self-possession at your age."

"Pardon?"

"I would have choked on those words," Valentina said. "I often wonder if I might have spared myself a great deal of trouble by asking for help before it became impossible to do so; but I was obsessed with meaningless things. Of course I'll help you."

Evdeniya's cheeks were flushed with shame. "Thank you," she said.

"Still," Valentina said. She looked down. She looked up. "Are you certain you are not merely being self-deprecatory? It is certainly the case that keeping a house on your own can be overwhelming, and it is certainly the case that if you fall behind the Outside can get in—but I have seen some homes far less neatly kept than yours that took years of outright abandonment before they actually succumbed. You do not need to call upon a temple for an exorcism if you have started leaving the occasional breakfast dishes in the sink."

"My problem is acute," Evdeniya said. "And real."

Valentina's eyes closed. She thought. "Is it that artifact?"

Evdeniya shook her head, somewhat pointlessly. "It's not. —have you ever heard of somebody being born in the Outside?"

"Mm," Valentina said. "There used to be a euphemism for the stillborn."

"... there is a man staying with me," Evdeniya said, "who was born in the Outside, and I have begun to assume that it spreads around him like a contagion. I don't know for sure. But I can't manage it on my own any more, and he's as much as admitted that a Sosunov or Kichi blessing on the place would help."

"I could simply remove him," Valentina said.

Evdeniya shook her head. "It may very well amount to the same," she said. "But one is right and the other is wrong, and if there *is* a difference, I know which way it will fall."

Valentina smiled slightly. "Then I shall do as you ask," she said. "It would be un-neighborly to leave you in distress."

THE GROUND FOG WAS UNSEASONAL and walnuts were scattered everywhere and a clear ichor crusted the gutters of the streets but it was not until she found herself lost on the way to her own house that Evdeniya realized that something had gone wrong.

"Valentina," she said, warningly.

"Hmm?"

"I ... he has done something. The street signs are confused."

"I think you mean to say, you are confused by the street signs," Valentina said. She thought about this for a moment, and then nodded firmly. "Has he shown a very great capacity to make things disorganized?"

"I do not recognize that as a distinct capacity," Evdeniya said.

"I simply wondered whether this would be a difficult problem or an easy one," Valentina said.

"I am fairly certain," Evdeniya said, "that I recognize those trees, even through this fog."

"So which way, then?"

"Right," Evdeniya said. "Or left. I am almost certain of it. Stop laughing."

"I'm sorry," Valentina said.

"That ditch is definitely familiar," Evdeniya said.

"Evdeniya," Valentina said, "you are a daughter of Fortitude. You cannot honestly expect me to believe you needed the street signs to begin with; if you are confused, then the landmarks themselves are out of place."

"Why are you *laughing* about it?"

"Because," Valentina said simply, "your house has that freaky metal tower. It should be simple enough to see it from the roofs."

"Oh."

"No promises," Valentina said, looking for a likely house to climb. "But either way, I wouldn't bother with concern."

She eyed the nameplate for an old manor—it was illegible—and then pulled Evdeniya into its garden before she went up the porch poles and onto the manor roof. Evdeniya heard the sound of feet scrabbling on wet tiles.

"Huh," Valentina said. "That's fortuitous."

"ah?" Evdeniya said. Then, because Valentina was unlikely to have heard her, she added, louder, "Yes?"

"He's called out some sort of giants."

Valentina dropped back down to stand by Evdeniya. She took Evdeniya's hand and led her out and around through the maze of streets with purpose. Evdeniya, meanwhile, processed. "Giants?"

"This is not at all what you indicated," Valentina said. "I apologize for my uncharitable thoughts."

"...which ones?"

"I had thought," Valentina said, "when you invited me to purify your house, that you were asking me to do something I am in fact quite bad at. I was secretly a little bitter. I am of course requisitely competent in everything incumbent upon the Sosunov family but if I am asked to do shrine dances or purifications or whatnot I feel something like a wrench that is used to hammer nails. But now I am delighted."

"I am not delighted by giants," Evdeniya said.

"They are quite large," Valentina said. "Twenty feet if they're an inch, which, for clarity, they are. I don't have the faintest idea how I'm going to fight them."

Evdeniya attempted to set her feet and balk but Valentina did not stop and neither, inevitably, did she. "I don't understand how he can *have* giants," she said.

"It's like this," Valentina said. "Sometimes, when you look at something that seems to be of ordinary size, it is actually a giant that is extremely far away."

She held her finger and thumb apart.

"Perspective."

"That is not helpful," Evdeniya said.

"Well," Valentina said, "I doubt he meant it to be. I am not actually sure how he would get such giants to show up at his whim and do anything useful on his behalf, regardless, so it is possible that I am mistaken in their genesis."

"Are you sure they are giants," Evdeniya said, "and not trash heaps?"

"They were moving," Valentina said. "But I am not altogether certain they were human. Hang on a sec, let me check our way again."

The streets were a maze, but they took to the roofs, and by that measure kept some ability to navigate despite the fog.

On her third trip up to the roofs, Valentina came down with the conclusion:

"They are definitely not human. I would venture to say some kind of clockwork cats."

"Huh," Evdeniya said. "I guess that makes it easier to believe."

"How so?"

"Well," Evdeniya said, "it's not like he isn't magical *enough* to have giants, but it didn't seem right, because ... he'd have to remember to pay them, and were they in his luggage? Who was making food for them? Wouldn't he just forget to open up a crack for air and have them all suffocate to death? Or were they just living down the street and nobody ever noticed? Or were there people down the street who were all, 'Sure, Pjatvchet, I'd be happy to be turned into a giant, just say the word!'? ... but any old sorcerer can have giant clockwork animals."

"It's not actually terribly easy," Valentina said. "I looked into it once."

"Did you?"

"You need an *extremely* orderly mind."

"Oh," Evdeniya said. She looked skeptically out into the fog. "Then I do not think that there are giant clockwork animals here."

"Well," Valentina said, "You might be able to do with an extremely disorderly mind, if it thinks it's an orderly one."

"All this is missing a key point," Evdeniya said. "Which is, aren't they going to eat us?"

Valentina shrugged. She scooped up a walnut from the sidewalk, cracked the shell with her teeth, and peeled it open. "No—" she started, before frowning at the empty inside of the shell. "No," she repeated. "I don't think so. For one thing, no stomach acid. For another, it seems like a simple enough matter of disassembling the beasts before we're devoured."

"Oh."

Valentina confided, "I am not terribly concerned about merely physical danger; I mean, I am afraid of letting you get hurt while I am responsible for you, but merely fighting giant clockwork creatures is of no great concern. Reason tells me I am impossible to kill and unlikely to be crippled at this particular point in time."

"Are you sure that that voice is *reason?*" Evdeniya squeaked.

"Ah!" Valentina said. "I am. For I am yet to have children, but several of my descendants have visited my dreams. *Post hoc, ergo pre hoc.* I've thought of the numerous exceptions and caveats already, but you can see why it might fill me with a certain confidence."

"Still," Evdeniya said.

"Don't spend your life afraid of gigantic metal animals," Valentina said. "If they were efficient war machines then the military would have 'em."

Valentina picked up another walnut. She cracked the shell. She frowned at the emptiness inside it, too.

"I don't quite understand why he's scattered empty walnut shells everywhere," she admitted.

"He's so *very* messy," Evdeniya said.

"That's—" Valentina had to stop for a moment when a gigantic bronze cat pounced from the shadows of a nearby cul-de-sac onto her. She shoved Evdeniya hard out of the way and went down under the oiled pad of the front foot; by the time Evdeniya had gotten to her feet again, though, with her heart in her throat, Valentina was flowing out of the ribcage of the thing with a chain in her hands and the creature was tumbling down the street past them in a tangle of rapidly dislocating gears, unwinding chains, rattling braces, off-balance pendulums, and unspringing springs. Valentina landed. She panted, hands on knees, face and clothes marred with oil. "That's not an adequate explanation," she said. "The walnut shells aren't even broken."

"What?"

"The walnut shells," Valentina said. "I *said*."

"Oh," Evdeniya said. "But—"

After a minute her heart rate slowed to the point where she could think again. She said, slowly, "I don't think you comprehend quite how messy he actually is."

"I see."

"Are— you said giants. Are there more, then?"

"I wouldn't worry about it," Valentina said. "They're not as hard as dragons. Oops, here's the other one now."

It wasn't until the last piece of the clockwork cat rolled to a halt against the energy transmission tower that Evdeniya realized that she ought to be home; only, she wasn't. There was her yard. There was her garden and her garden wall. There was the energy transmission tower and her house's street; only, there wasn't a house.

There were just walnut shells, hundreds of them, strewn on the grass.

Evdeniya sat down in despair. She stared blankly at the empty lot.

"Hm," Valentina said. She sat down cross-legged in front of Evdeniya. She thought about this for a moment. "You know which theory has my vote."

Evdeniya snorted.

"It makes sense," Valentina said, waving vaguely at the lawn. "He hides the house in a walnut shell. Then, realizing that that's pretty obvious, that we'd just go up to the walnut shell that's sitting in the empty lot and crack it open, he … makes a whole bunch more of them."

"Go ahead and open them, if you want," Evdeniya said.

Valentina looked around. She frowned. There were quite a number of them. She flowed to her feet. "I'm going to see if there are any other giant beasts to fight."

She was gone a moment later, and Evdeniya was alone.

A BAT was fluttering to Svetlana's side. It clung closely to her hair and neck, as if looking for comfort. It said, muffledly, into the back of her head,

> Sveta, my Sveta, calamity! Ruin!
> While you in your house stew in dolor, while you in
> Your coffin abide and refuse to awaken
> Not so lucky our Denya; her house has been taken.

"If you brought any other news," Svetlana said, after a moment, "I would tell you to stop this endless sniping about my preference to remain at home. But as it is, Maksim, what do you mean, 'taken?'"

"The neighborhood is covered in fog," Maksim said. "And the houses are out of order. I do not think we are even in the same cul-de-sac as Evdeniya's home any longer. Giants are moving in the darkness and all is in turmoil. Evdeniya herself was absent; I believe that Pjatvchet has finally taken her home in its entirety."

"Oh," Svetlana said blankly.

She stood up. She walked aimlessly around a duvet.

"Maksim, you ask the impossible."

"I know."

She frowned in thought. She went outside; almost without noticing it, she went outside. She stood in the all-concealing fog. She rubbed at her nose, thinking hard. Then she went back inside, found a spool of shiny thread, and tied one end to Maksim's leg.

"You will have to lead me," she said. "From above."

"I shall do as best I can," he said. "Please keep a very loose hand on the spool."

They went outside again, and he fluttered up.

"Mind the tree," he called down. "And the fence. And ... please mind everything. I do not want to be stuck."

"I am mindful," Svetlana said.

"Ah—" he said.

The warning was almost too late; she nearly bumped into Pjatvchet. He froze, caught in the vampire-fear, and she had a long moment to assess him.

"I will knock on your forehead," she said, "and say, '*zori, molody, zmei, zoloty*.' Then I will open it up and only fresh vegetables will be inside."

"That is a terrifying prospect," he said, sweating lightly. "Can I persuade you not to?"

"What are you *doing* here?"

"A man, in the process of going from one place to another, often traverses the roads that span between them," he said. "I was doing just that when you happened upon me. I don't suppose you have a pocketful of flax seeds I could borrow?"

"I don't understand," Svetlana said.

"Ah, it's for a personal matter, there's no need for you to be concerned," he said. "Really, any kind of seeds would do. Barley, say."

"Where are you *going*, Mr. Utkin?"

"Ah," he said, smiling a strained smile. "You have heard of me. Is it important where I am going? Well, there is no secret to it. I am going to a certain place to do a certain thing to call up he the lord of Death's dominion he."

"Are you?"

"I have done with searching," Pjatvchet said. "Death can take the Kaneko house whole and entire and sort the matter out from there."

Her hand was on his neck; she was going to say something threatening; but he oozed out of her grip like an oiled pig. She wound up staring at him blankly instead.

"Very well," he said. "I didn't want to do this, but you pushed me to it."

He reached into his pocket. He pulled out a handful of walnut shells. He scattered them in the road. Her eyes flicked down to them. "Four?" she said. *"Four?"*

"That took less time than I'd hoped," he said. "You could try counting the ones that were already previously scattered around you."

"Why do you even have walnut shells in your pocket?"

"They wind up everywhere," he said.

"And why am I properly invited to enter one of them?"

He blanched. "Ah," he said. "It's a latitudinarian shell. Pay the matter no mind."

He stooped to pick it up again. Her eyes tracked it.

Then she was moving, and she was very fast indeed— but even as she seized it, it grew legs and tried to scurry away; became a spider in her hand, a centipede, and then a cross; it twisted, writhed, unfolded and grew wings that fluttered desperately to free it from her grasp. From the corner of her eye she saw his pile of travel bags slouching towards her; in the shadow of it were roaring lions, and slithering serpents, and stinging ants.

She glided back away from him, one step, two steps, and three, as the shell in her hand became a chestnut husk, a spiny shell, a candleflame, and then, as he snapped his fingers in realization or decision, as she reached the far end of the street, a miniature sun.

At that she screamed.

It was the sun of the Outside and not the sun of Earth; it did not incinerate her instantly by its heat nor by her condition—it was a paler light than that of the world she'd known, and the spines had become near-tangible rays of light—but she could not hold on to it. She could not be expected to.

She was burning; she was shrieking; she was stumbling back.

"Oh," said Valentina, arriving. "Hello."

She held Pjatvchet's shoulder from behind while one of her swords slid amiably through his back; dumped him to the side as she ran forward; dove to the ground and clapped two halves of a walnut shell around the hissing, smoldering light.

EVERYTHING WAS burned. Everything was broken.

The neighborhood was slowly returning to its original state. The fog was fading. The street signs were making sense again. The streets were returning to their natural order again. Lights were shining from the houses and no gigantic shapes were moving in the night. Evdeniya's house had been cut out from within its double prison—

But everything was in ruins.

The walls had tumbled. The shelves were burned. Svetlana, the kindest of Evdeniya's neighbors, was seared and blackened and wrapped in ointment-stinking cloths. What treasures of Evdeniya's house Pjatvchet hadn't already stolen were now burned, smoke-damaged, or otherwise broken; and worst of all, the one thing she cared about, the *one* thing that she raced to the instant she could safely get inside the house, was cracked and dead and useless now as well.

The thing that should not be was a thing that should not be no longer.

It was still ugly. It was still improper. But it was split open down its side and the malevolent essence of it had dissipated. It did not glow nor did it emit noise and the world did not wrap in unusual ways around it.

It was at most an artist's approximation of a thing that should not be; and even at that, it was a bust.

Evdeniya looked wildly around, she tore up the room as best she could and insisted Valentina do so wherever she couldn't, but Kinjiro and Tamara had not reappeared; without the thing that should not be, there was no longer a path to them, and there was little chance they would return.

In a daze she recited the possibilities to herself: that its destruction had dumped them from that place where they had been into, perhaps, the deep Outside; that they had never had a way home in the first place, or that their way home had never involved the thing itself, and thus matters were no different now; that they were dead, or frozen forever in a moment of suspended time, destroyed along with the thing that had obscured them; that they were lost, but not much more lost than they already had been, that its presence in their house had been *helpful* to their return but never necessary; that the thing would re-congeal itself over time into a thing that should not be again, as awful as that was; that the thing had invited its own destruction, that it had been inevitable from the moment of its construction, and she was lucky that only two lives, only her parents' lives, had actually been lost—

Enough possibilities, perhaps, to keep her thinking, to keep her from complete collapse, but in the end she could not convince herself of the kind ones. Numbing grief took her in its grip:

"They're gone."

After the last fires had been doused, it was in that grey mood that Maksim found her. He fluttered down to tangle in her hair.

"Maksim," she sniffled out. "They're gone."

"Close the linen closet," he said, "and knock three times upon it, saying, '*Zori, molody, zmei, zoloty,*' and we shall see what we shall see."

"What?"

"Trust me," he said.

She dragged herself to her feet. She went over to the linen closet—that having one of the few doors that really remained intact—and closed it; knocked three times upon it; recited the given chant.

Her stomach twisted. She felt a burgeoning unsettling disorientation, a discomfort, a nausea, and her heart leapt.

There was a strange humming from the closet.

Green light leaked out.

She opened up the closet, and there within it stood the thing that should not be; only, in that moment, a strange alchemy occurred. In that moment, our Evdeniya Kinjirovna Kaneko saw in the thing that should not be exactly what was most important to her home; what was most precious, what was most needful and what most good. Her eyes, her power of *looking-upon*, that had come to terms with vampires and hagriding witches and Valentina Grigorievna made right of the thing that should not be at last; and in that moment, what really oughtn't have been, too should.

Against the power of the brilliant relief and love that were burning in her eyes, the *wrongness* of the thing could not endure; the fire of her consciousness seized upon that thing and forcibly rectified its grievance with the world, it rolled into reality with a *pop;* and Kinjiro and Tamara Kaneko came tumbling out of the linen closet where, as far as anyone could have ever proven, they had been kissing all along.

PROGRESS HAD set its teeth in Town and it would not let go of it. Factories spread like fungus, streets curled and crawled across the land, houses sprang up in the European style—in a fever of construction, and more than fever; far faster than any need would call for, and possibly faster than ordinary reason would allow.

One could probably put much of this on humanity—certainly the same phenomenon would have repeated itself, in miniature, without outside influences—but the scale of it was driven by predatory forces. The vampire Alexandrel Celdinar was not satisfied with a little settlement like Fortitude; having found a land where the sun never rose, *he* would settle for nothing less than a metropolis.

Where the tent-city of the demon-folk had been, and on the hills around it, and driving back the Outside where it grew: he built "Night London."

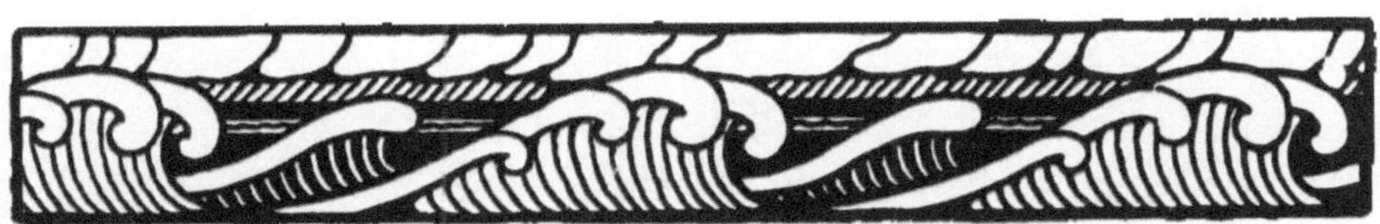

VALENTINA AND THE VAMPIRE

"You don't have to stay," said the morning star
"Run away, run away, run away to a far
To a far, to a far, to a far, to a far, to a far and a sunless land."

"You can run," said the sun, in the middle of the day;
"O I wish that they'd told me I could run away
Run away, run away, run away, run away, to a far and a peaceful land."

"You can run away," said the sunset's light,
And it set its horizon in a hard flat line
"It's OK, it's OK, it's OK, and you'll find
A far and a sunless land. A far and a sunless land."

And the night rolls over and it makes me sick
It's a trick, it's a trick, it's a trick, it's a trick
And I wish someone'd told me I could run away
To a far and a sunless land.

—late 19th century ditty,
provenance unknown

NCE UPON a time, but not so very long ago, a vampire named Czcibor Fidatof received a prophecy.

He was a comparatively young vampire—roughly thirty years alive, and forty risen—but if the German seeress that he'd stalked and slain was reputable, he thought he might fairly expect eternity.

She'd said—

The woman who would bring him low would be a woman who could weave a shirt out of spider's webs; who could spin a thread across all of London in one night; who could sift out gold from mustard seeds; and who could bring him the flower whose nectar was the water of life. She would be a woman who could send a message to England and back before a single night was done; who could pick a field of blackberries in an hour; who could shout loud enough to wake the dead; and who could rip a giant serpent's heart right out.

On the whole, he felt his future was secure.

One day, Czcibor Fidatof followed the rumors of a sunless land to Mayor Celdinar's Night London—to that dreary gray settlement in the hills west of Fortitude. He brought with him his mortal son Czeslaus Chalecki (who would not be a Fidatof until he died); a great sum of rubles, to be converted into more generic "cash;" and numerous cuttings from his grapefruit trees, which he cultivated because he held that a regimen of patent medicines and grapefruit juice could mitigate the "counting sickness," or *arithmomania,* to which many vampires were prone. For the most part, his peers thought this last bit nonsense, and considered that

Czcibor's case was simply naturally mild, or even that he did not suffer from the arithmomania at all.

Czcibor took possession of a great manor in Night London. He had a rock garden built at the bottom of its ornamental pond, where he would occasionally spend a peaceful, meditative hour. He installed a grand piano in the manor's ballroom, where he would sometimes plink out simple tunes and his son would often play great works. He lay out a scenic path between the front door and the gates, made of great gray stones; and awkwardly wedged between two such stones, where practically every visitor stepped upon it once or twice, a little white five-petalled flower grew.

Time passed.

Few clubs had been established yet; the local scene for whist was poor; hunting, whether for humans or for animals, was unchallenging and liable to quickly run through the entire available supply. On occasion there would be an interesting monster to dispose of, but Czcibor was not the most popular or the most powerful vampire in society and was not given the better opportunities to participate in such a sport. Czeslaus spent his days reading, corresponding with his abandoned friends in Europe, and practicing on the piano. Czcibor, more confident in his physical skills, took to roaming Night London, the hills around it, and occasionally the near Outside.

One night, amidst these explorations, Czcibor found a passageway that led beneath the streets and descended into the caverns that were underneath them. There he found old ruins and dark rivers, and on those rivers there sailed by him in the darkness a black-sailed silent treasure-barque with a serpent figure at its head.

It was sacred. It was numinous. It was an experience too vast and deep to be consumed by him. It drank in his power of attention, took it all, and he forgot how to move; how to focus his eyes; even he himself.

He stood there and his thoughts were full of the treasure-barque as it sailed past him and on into the tunnels and vanished like a shadow on the mist; and even when it had gone away it took him some time to shake off his dream-like mood.

"I must have it," Czcibor said.

He chased after it, but it was fruitless. He knew that it would be fruitless, but still he'd hoped. He hunted it through that underworld for many days. He left and returned again several times, and still he did not find it, or see the treasure-barque again.

In time he gave up on it. He resigned himself to the thought that he had been present for a strange and one-time miracle—but just in case it had eluded him by ordinary means, or that whatever metaphysical effect barred it from him did not extend to others, he put it about Night London that he would owe a great favor, "withholding no generosity," to anyone who could help him claim that black ship as his own.

His announcement was of little interest to Valentina Grigorievna Sosunova at the time. She was fifty-two and busy with an altogether different snake, that being the pet that the twins (her second cousins, once removed) had lost *somewhere* in the dining room, to the effect that every time she used her magical tablecloth to cheat at making dinner it produced, in addition to the usual dishes, live mice. Czcibor's announcement was of little interest to her; in point of fact, it might have *never* been of interest to her, and been forgotten before it truly registered in her memory, save that one Sunday's errands took her past the manor of Czcibor Fidatof while Czeslaus Chalecki was on the piano and she—though from quite a distance—heard him play.

The music struck through her. It caught her as the treasure-barque had caught his father. She could not help but stop to listen. No, more than that; she found herself taking the terrible risk of trespassing, of sneaking to the window, to see the man himself as he was playing, upon which moment she fell in love.

It was ridiculous; a ridiculous infatuation; she scolded herself for it fiercely. She thought it likely that he would have an annoying speaking voice and bad personal hygiene. He was too young—he must have been at least a decade younger. He was too old—given certain facts she was aware of, he would likely die some time before did she.

He was doubtless—here she began to become extravagant in imagining his faults—vain and arrogant, small-minded, cowardly, reckless, pedantic, already committed, cold, doubtful, noisome, feckless, thoughtless, and cruel. Plus, more important than any merely possible faults was the cold actuality:

She did not know him.

None of this moved her emotional core at all; she was in love.

She rang at the door, left a visiting card, and asked a footman the pianist's name. Afterwards, she left in a daze. Her pulse was pounding. Her head was spinning. There was no way that Czcibor's *son* would be allowed to marry her, she thought. She was a Fortitude rustic; he was a sophisticate. She was Valentina Grigorievna, and *he* was destined to rise from the dead. Most importantly, he would have to come into her family if they married, there were no two ways about it; but *that*, more than anything else, a vampire father would not allow.

Only one course of action presented itself.

"I'll have to get him that treasure-barque," she said.

She wandered aimlessly through the echoing streets and looming buildings, humming the music that Czeslaus had been playing under her breath. It struck her that there was something ghoulish about the settlement's scale and ambition—the way that it was built, was *being* built, not for the thousands that had come to live there, not for the tens of thousands that lived in Fortitude, but for some *hundreds* of thousands; hundreds of thousands who would, presumably, be shipped in one day ... to ... well, to live; to make the *city* live; to drive the engine of progress; but, on some darker level, to be the vampires' prey.

She had not gone very far before she realized that she was lost; and, moreover, that she had no real idea of where to go. She sat down cross-legged against the side of a building and thought. Her thoughts went nowhere and she closed her eyes.

Soon, she was asleep.

In her dreams she spread out her magical tablecloth. She waited. In time Czeslaus stumbled in from nowhere in particular and, blinking, took a seat opposite.

"Good day," he said.

"Good day."

"And you are?"

"My name is Valya— Valentina Grigorievna Sosunova," she said. "And I am afraid I am in love."

"That must be a terrible inconvenience."

"You can't imagine," she said. "Listen. Do you think that if I brought that treasure-barque to your father, that he'd approve our match?"

"Well," Czeslaus said. He sat back. "So this is *that* sort of dream, is it?"

He looked her over.

"You seem a nice sort of girl," he said, "so I'll tell you, run. Run until the dark skies turn bright with morning. Run until nobody knows Czcibor's name. If he doesn't approve, then maybe he'd just have you discouraged, but if he did, well—

"I'm simply not worth the baggage, don't you see?"

"Where love leads," she summarized, "I can only follow."

Czeslaus nibbled on a pierogi. He took a sip of kvass. "If you bring him the barque, then he will likely approve the match, yes. But I cannot condemn you to this life. He would definitely have you brought back. It would be eternal. Sooner rather than later, I imagine, so that your beauty would not fade."

Valentina snorted, but otherwise ignored the implied compliment. "If I brought him the barque, is there any chance he'd let you go into my family, instead?"

"God in Heaven!" he said. He blinked stupidly. "What an absurd notion."

"That's a no, then."

"That's— well, exactly. That's a no. I mean—no. No. Father would doubtless lessen the blow. He would say, 'Let's make a game of it. I'll think about it, if you can weave me a shirt out of spider's webs.' There's a thief he caught that he likes to drink from that he'd let out if she'd managed that. Or, 'if you can pick a field of blackberries in an hour.' He's fond of that one. 'If you can take a letter to England, and bring back its reply, before the ringing of the midnight bells.' But nobody has ever *done* it, don't you see? So I don't know how seriously he'd take his word in such a case."

"I could get a letter to England and back in that time," Valentina said.

"Dog's blood! Really?"

"Not physically," Valentina said. "But the words, by dream. Yeah. Most likely. Elya's over there right now."

Czeslaus was shaking his head. "That's amazing," he said. "But I don't know how to trick him into using that particular test, and I don't know that he'd be a good sport if he actually lost. I mean, you might get a good ol' moral victory, but—as to your preferred wedding arrangements? In practice? ... we all live and die at his sufferance, you see."

"I see," Valentina said.

"In any case," Czeslaus said. "Have you actually *got* the barque? Because that *would* be rather grand. I've been reading about the kinds of things that it could be. Father thinks it's probably alive, isn't it? but *I* think that it might be something to do with the demon-folk's gods. Nobody's seen or heard anything from them in *ages*."

"I haven't got it," Valentina said.

"Oh. Well." Czeslaus flashed a grin. "That is for the best, then. Your cause is hopeless and you will not get involved. Forget me, my sweet; do not let my manly virtues long detain you. My heartrending beauty. It cannot be! Go! and find a safer man to love!"

"If he is so terrible," Valentina said, ignoring Czeslaus' lapse into drama, "then I could be your escape."

There was the slightest twitch in his features; the slightest hitch in his breath. "I would dream that that were so, but then I would wake up, you see."

"I do see," Valentina admitted.

"If—" he started. Then he was silent for a long time. Then, quietly, "If— if you must do this. I can think of only one way that it can be done. I dare not encourage you. Pray do not be encouraged; I should be the lowest of men. But if you must do this, find another vampire, one that Czcibor fears, to back you; go to … to Calonyctia, or Vilhem, or to Mayor Celdinar himself, and see if it would amuse them to have Czcibor forced to give me up. See if *they* would trade me for the barque, as a hold on him … for he will never let me go."

"I can't," Valentina said. "Don't be frightened, but I can't."

"But it is wisdom," he said.

"I am Valentina Grigorievna Sosunova," Valentina said. "I will permit no corpse to make me feel I am a mouse among the cats."

He scoffed at her. He looked away.

BEFORE THE night-lamp had been lit twice she was prepared, and made her first tentative venture beneath the hills.

There were shadowed stairs that could be found in Night London that would take you down into the ruins of the ancient city, that had graced those hills before even Fortitude was founded—but she did not take them. Nor did she descend by way of the sinkholes, though there were such sinkholes, where the newer construction had overestimated its foundation and toppled down into the tunnels beneath the hills.

She could have done that, but she didn't.

Her entrance to the underworld was a very traditional one—through a door set in the hill, not far from where Fortitude ended and the western hills began. A natural cave entrance had been rounded and a wooden door set inside it. A flat stone was set out to be its doormat. The ground was lumpy and yellow grass grew all around. A road of wood slats overhung the door, and along that road a few dismal creaky houses sprouted.

She knew of this door because it was Fortitude's own entrance to the underworld—the passageway that every son and daughter of Fortitude learned of by osmosis sometime in their childhood, found and later spruced up by one of Fortitude's own culture heroes, and used from time to time thereafter when Fortitude's own had business there.

She took a lantern in her hand and she entered through that well-used door.

She searched, but she did not find.

In the endless twisting dark she wandered. On some occasions the walls were damp, and once the left wall ran silvered with dripping water, but she did not find the river where the treasure-barque sailed, nor any other river for that matter; the ground beneath her feet stayed dry.

In the dark, she came across a man sitting on a broad flat shelf of rock, tossing pebbles from it into the cavern beyond. He did not react to the light of her lantern, and she had a chance to get a good look at him; he was hunchbacked, clad in rags, disheveled, and there was black juice crusted to the left side of his mouth.

"Hey," she said.

"There is nothing good in it," he said, shaking his head.

"There— er, what?"

He startled, slightly. "Oh," he said, realizing. "I thought you had said, 'good day.'"

"Oh."

"And then I meant to say that there was nothing good in it," he explained. "This modern age has brought us nothing but despair and sorrow. And vampires. Despair, sorrow, and hideous un-living vampires. That is why I have decided to retreat to the caverns beneath the hills and live as a hermit. But if he has realized his mistake and sent you to fetch me back?"

"He?"

"Gregorius," he said. At her blank look, he elaborated, "Gregorius Bloodsuckerovich *Nose-in-the-Fucking-Air* Witherspoon. No? No? Yes?"

"I don't think that we have met," Valentina said.

"Oh," he said, and turned back slightly away from her, and picked up another stone, and tossed it at a distant wall.

After a while, she pulled herself up to sit beside him. "Your health, sir," she said. "I'm Valya— Valentina Grigorievna Sosunova."

"Yura, then— Yurii Ivanovich Golubev, miss," he said. "Your health."

"I have come," she said, "seeking the treasure-barque with the serpent's head that is said to sail the dark and silent waters that run beneath Night London. Because Czcibor Fidatof has offered his favor to anyone who can bring it to him, and I have set my eye upon his son."

"Vampires," he said. "They ruin everything."

"Mm."

"I do not know anything that would help you," he said. "I have not seen the treasure-barque that you describe. I have not even seen water in all my days beneath."

"Then," she said, startled, "how are you still alive?"

He looked away. "In the old days, it was not like this. The service of the demon-folk had a wild grandeur to it. There was not the smoke of coal-fires and the sound of construction, always construction, everywhere around. Our lives were held in the palms of their hands, their claws were at our throats, but the sky was clear and clean and the wind blew through the hills beneath the stars. At their bazaars were goods of rare enchantment and surpassing make, their chambers were heavy with incense, and even children chewed on teething-rings of pearl and gold.

"There was a majesty there that has been lost; and they honored talent."

"... ah," she said, eventually. "You have been sustaining yourself by drinking your nostalgia."

He snorted. Then he pulled a seed from a pouch at his belt. He bounced it in his palm for a moment and then flicked it between two fingers out onto the rocky floor. **"Blackberry seed:"** he commanded. **"Get you in the ground."**

The effect, if any, was inobvious in the consuming dark. He continued, after a moment.

"Blackberry seed: you grow and you sprout."

This time, there was something to see. The ground cracked and split. Canes of blackberry writhed up like tentacles, barbed and angry, tumbling across the cavern floor; along their lengths white flowers sprouted, opened, withered, and died, before berries grew from nothing into weighty ripeness.

Yurii waved his hand and a handful of berries flew into it. He ate a few of them, then plucked out a seed, which he wiped upon his shirt and stored back in his pouch. He offered the rest to Valentina; when she'd taken them, he turned back to the broken ground and called out, **"Blackberry plant, I've no room in my larder; pray, shrivel away, and forgive this poor gardener."**

As Valentina watched the plants rotted to nothingness and were gone.

"This is a marvel," she said, and tasted from the berries in her hand. They were perfectly ripe and sweet.

"When I was a child," he said, "I found a little white flower whose nectar was the water of life; I cleared the bramble around it to give it light, and fed it water faithfully, and now—well, it is as you see."

"So you can survive without water," she said. "Thanks to the juice of the fruit. That makes sense ... well ... if you haven't been here for very long ... but I am even more confused how you could wind up sitting on a rock in a lonely cave."

"Asceticism," he explained.

"Uh."

He heaved a sigh. He looked away. "Vulponidas liked to bet on the horses," he said, as if it explained something.

Valentina, eventually, made encouraging noises.

"He was a great demon," Yurii explained. "A fine master. To serve him was an honor. I did not envy any man, for I wore the livery of Vulponidas Zhāng. But he gambled on the horses and he lost, you see, and Gregorius Witherspoon bought him out, lock, stock, and barrel. And so my contract went to him, and I became *his* seed magician.

"'How appallingly primitivist,' he said. He had called me in, you see. He was looking over the house assets, and he didn't even acknowledge I was there yet. And he said, 'how appallingly primitivist,' and *then* looked up. 'You probably eat your own children. What does this house need some antique conjurer for?' And I would have hurt him, I would have torn his head off right there and pissed up the socket, but, well, you know how they are. They are most terribly frightening to the human animal."

"I know," Valentina said.

"I could hardly keep my knees from knocking," Yurii said. "Much less defend myself. So he gave me a severance in cash and turned me out on the street, and there I was in a place that no longer resembled in the least respect my home.

"Where were the hills that I had roamed in the train of the demon Vulponidas? Everywhere great buildings loomed. Where was the clean night air? Gargoyles leered down at me from the facades of the buildings. Somewhere a clock tower rang. I had not been paying enough attention. I had been out in this new world but only long enough to go into the market. Do you understand? I had closed myself off in in the house of Vulponidas Zhāng when things had begun changing, and now there I was, unwanted, in a place that I did not recognize at all. So I came down here."

"The reaction seems extreme," Valentina said.

"It seems it," Yurii said. "It seems very dramatic to go and live in a cave; just, where else was I going to go? That was what clinched it for me, you see. I listened to the wild juvenile cry of my heart to storm down here and make a hermitage because I had literally nowhere else to go.

"I am an old magician," he said. "I am a relic of a former time."

"I do not think so," Valentina said.

"You are kind," he said. "But let us be realistic. I am not going to join a carnival. I would be committing sacrilege against my art."

She sat for a while, thinking through her words before she said them, and when she was certain of herself, she said, "Come with me to Fortitude. I do not know whether your talent is staggering in its value or limited to tricks, so I cannot say what kind of life it is that you can make there. But I can say with certainty that there *is* a life for you there. It has not fallen into the madness of the times. It is still what it was fifty years ago; a hundred years ago; a hundred before that. There is still a place for an old magician there."

Yurii blew out his cheeks, then nodded. "Only fools turn up their nose at Providence," he said. "Particularly when it is willing to follow one into the darkness beneath the world. If I do not need to mortgage my hump, my beard, and my future children for a license to practice my art— or anything like?"

She shook her head mutely.

"Then it can be no worse than the vampires' abomination," he said, "and certainly no worse than here."

He got up. He wiped his palms upon his clothing, spat on one, and held it out to Valentina. She eyed it unhappily for a moment before she took and shook it. "I am not entirely certain what bargain we are shaking on," she admitted. "But I am willing to be bound by everything that I understand that I have said."

"Come on," he said. "Let's go."

TIME PASSED, and she returned to it.

She descended into the ancient tunnels. She wandered the maze of them, now turning left, now right, as the whim took her. She reached at last a dark and silent river that she bethought her might be the river that Czcibor had written of; the character of the stone and the moss that grew upon the walls and most of all the sense of stillness, of waiting, of something-yet-to-happen, seemed to match certain florid elements of Czcibor's publicly promulgated description.

She walked up and down the shore, finding no spot compellingly better than any other, before finally settling herself down onto a miniature promontory from which to watch the waters running by. There she spread her tablecloth out, and upon it appeared a magic feast—borscht, bread, lentils, and all the rest, and in addition, as she had hoped, there were new dishes that she had never seen before: a fruit she did not recognize, chopped up in honey; a soup of blindfish and of some unknown creature's bones; a basket of diced mushrooms; and a golden sphere, glowing from within.

These she pushed to the far side of the tablecloth, and waited.

In time she heard the softest disturbance on the water and turned to see the treasure-barque gliding towards her. Its wood was a textured black; its furled sails seemed to be the same; its oars dipped into the water, but they did not move against it. The river was nearly still, there was little in the way of current, but what current there was, the barque moved against it, albeit with no obvious motive force.

It occurred to her that perhaps the great wooden serpent that coiled along the boat's keel and curled its head around the forward spar to form the figurehead might be swimming, down below the ship where she could not see, but she did not have enough free space in her thoughts to formulate the concept; it drifted through her mind as an inkling, the beginning of an idea, the start to a theory, and then, starved of her attention, guttered out.

It was hard to breathe.

She understood in an instant why Czcibor longed for the thing and why he had failed to claim it; it was greater than she. It was a consuming presence.

It was sacred.

Silent as a ghost, as she sat transfixed, it approached her.

She was not as badly struck as Czcibor; or rather, her body clung to her attention with a greater force. It was webbed to her consciousness, glued to it as if by ichorous malison, and her bones, her muscles, and her skin did not yield her up willingly to the power of the numinous. She retained some fraction of her grounding in the world—if not enough to stand tall in the face of the sacred, enough to make unto it an offering.

She pushed the foods at the far side of the tablecloth further away from her, and then leaned back. In a voice that rasped despite herself, she offered, "Eat."

The serpent-head coiled over. Set into its forehead was the living jewel that was its heart.

It had been hard to breathe in the presence of the ship, but the proximity of the serpent was absolutely overwhelming. The barriers of her self shattered. The empathic shock of the serpent's approach had her *feeling*, rather than simply seeing, the movement of the muscles in its neck; gave her a visceral awareness of the *regarding-Valentina-ness* in its eyes; drowned her in the curiosity it was feeling and in its simple, childish hunger.

It was not merely that she felt them; its experience was overwhelming. It was louder than her own.

Her mouth went dry and her body trembled as the serpent nosed at the blindfish soup. She fought to remember who she was and what she was doing there, and failed, as the serpent lapped up the glowing sphere and swallowed it, grazed at the fruit in honey, and moved its head to the basket of mushrooms.

Then it crashed in on her with something like a fury—

Let us pause there.

The first reflex of a Sosunov magician, upon discovering that they do not exist, is to recreate themselves. This reflex can fail. It can be deliberately mastered. But it is the first, most natural reaction. In the presence of the barque her mind's eye could no longer see herself; she could not find herself; thus, reflexively, strands of will began to gather like an ever-heavier rain; until—

It crashed in on her with something like a fury that she was Valentina Grigorievna Sosunova.

She kept the anger from leaping to her face but she could not help the sudden stiffening of her posture or the flashing of her eyes. Her *own* presence leapt forth, where it had been hooded previously; the serpent startled back.

It regarded her from beneath carved brow-ridges, six yards out from her.

She found her attention lingering on the little scales around its eyes.

Without breaking eye contact, the figurehead pulled back to the prow and coiled back around it. Then it turned, and the barque slid silently away.

VALENTINA WAS returning from that encounter, thoughtful, when she heard singing in the tunnels; the song was in a woman's voice and had no real words and not much tune to it, but rather followed the wandering thoughts and melodic impulses of someone who could not have imagined that she were being overheard.

"*Do-rum, de-lo-rum-ti, ti-ra-fa-li, ta-do,*" the woman sang, and the like, while Valentina drew closer to her in the dark. Then, as Valentina neared a corner—and, perhaps, as the light of her lantern preceded her around it—the song broke off, suddenly, and was replaced by the muffled exclamation: "Bother!"

"It's all right," Valentina assured her. "I'm a friend."

"Are you?" the voice came back, uncertain. Valentina rounded the corner and saw its owner: a twentysomething woman wrapped in heavy gown and straitjacket, with a blindfold hitched up to give her the barest view from a single eye. "I was not aware of having any. Where were you when I needed you? Or are we only social friends? I am not a very social individual."

"My word," Valentina said. "That can't be comfortable."

She stepped forward, reaching out to steady the woman, but the woman caught sight of a bit of the motion and backed away. "It isn't," she said. "Truly it isn't. But I have chosen it. Do you understand? If my hands were free, I would create monsters with them. If my eyes were open, I would be inspired to great wickedness. It is the only way that I can think of that will make the horror *stop*."

"You're quite young, aren't you," Valentina said.

"I don't see what that has to do with anything," the woman replied. "Anyhow, I'm Edith, Edith Draisey. It's terribly nice to meet you, and if you have any water with you I wouldn't mind being a bit of a bother for a drink."

"Valentina— Valentina Grigorievna Sosunova."

"Oh," Edith said. "*The* Valentina Sosunova?"

"Most likely."

"That's all right, then. You'd understand. I'm an abomination in the eyes of God, like those witches that I hear you've killed. With the small exception that you don't need to kill me, as I am already quite well contained."

"You may be overstating your failings," Valentina said.

"Ah," the woman said. "Um. They *are* not in evidence, are they? Chester. Chester! Come out!"

Something began to wriggle in her sleeve. It crawled up her shoulder and out onto her neck: a metal rat, a wisp-light gleaming in its eyes.

"William," she said, and another wriggled out to stand upon the back of her head. "Frederick," she said, and this time it was a silver snake. It flicked out its tongue to taste the air, reminding Valentina ineluctably of the figurehead of the treasure-barque. It managed to assemble a sound reminiscent of hissing from the clicking of many tiny gears.

"You see," the woman concluded.

"Well," Valentina said, after bringing her reflexive crinkled-eyes smile at Frederick under control. "I ... understand your position perfectly, and I *do* agree that this is past the verge and absolutely cannot be done with proper science. But I think that 'abomination in the eyes of God' might be putting it a little strong. I've always rather admired this kind of work."

"If God would forbid Eden to humanity forever," Edith said, "for a single bite of the apple of knowledge of good and evil: what then would he think of a woman who plucks the flower whose nectar is the water of life—and, in her folly, mistakes it for one of her camphor blossoms, mixes it with almond oil, beeswax, and twenty-two confidential ingredients, and makes Draisey's Patent Beauty Cream of it, to be rubbed upon the hands and eyes?"

Valentina took a breath, and then another. She blinked four times in quick succession. "I don't know," she confessed. "God does not share His opinions with me on such matters. But tell me, don't your shoulders hurt?"

"Abominably," the woman said. Then, aghast, "pardoning the pun. But it is a bracing agony. —it is not as if I could not remove the thing, you see. I have had to from time to time. It will only hold me completely if my creations refuse to help."

"Then—" Valentina started.

Edith spoke over her. "But it is necessary that I do *not* remove it unless my mind is so full of that suffering that I can think of nothing else, because if I free myself casually the illusion of its power over me becomes less strong and the diabolical impulse within me struggles more fiercely to break free."

"You should come with me to Fortitude," Valentina said, after a time, "where people are kinder to others, and can maybe teach you to be a little kinder to yourself."

"That is a nice thought," Edith said. "But surely my place is here."

"There are homes I can find for you there," Valentina said, "where you can be with others with similar problems, or, if you prefer, without any tools at all, just the walls and the garden and the air."

"Thank you," Edith said, "but no thank you."

She turned. She went to leave; only, Valentina had hold of one of the straitjacket's grips. Edith stumbled, and then struggled for a moment, and then frowned. "Unhand me."

"You cannot say that you are mad," Valentina said, "and then refuse to have a keeper."

Edith stilled. "I do not say that I am mad. I say that I am damned. There is a difference; one failing is mental and the other moral. It is in fact precisely because my mental capacities are unimpaired that I have a clear view of my own moral failings. If my hands were free, I would be up to wickedness; that is all."

"I do not feel like letting go," Valentina said.

Edith sputtered. "I could have my snake attack you. Frederick! Rattle! Frederick is an American, you see, so his rattle is a forewarning of a deadly clockwork poison. —I should not have said clockwork. A deadly poison."

"… I may need you," Valentina said.

Edith shook her sleeves, and there was something in her posture that convinced Valentina to release her. She turned and tried to look at Valentina through the one half-covered eye. "I should say that that is no concern of mine, but go on anyway."

"I am going to have to steal the son of one Czcibor Fidatof," Valentina said. "—that is to say, one of the vampires' get. I cannot imagine having any particular need of a metal rat, but there impends a time of crisis; I cannot leave behind a potential advantage that comes to hand."

"You cannot steal a vampire's son," Edith said. "Where would you even put him?"

"I was imagining, about the house," Valentina said.

Edith heaved a sigh. "A place without tools?" she said, changing the subject back to her own disposition. "By the lake, perhaps? I would not so much mind living by the lake, and not having my arms bound up on all occasions."

"I think that something can be done."

"Take off this bedamned blindfold," Edith said. "I want to see you before I make up my mind on you."

Valentina reached out. She pulled it off of Edith's eyes. Edith blinked a couple of times in the lamplight and assessed Valentina.

"Gracious," she said.

Valentina looked a little embarrassed.

"...of course I'll come along," Edith said. "Let's go. To think. I'm in the company of legends."

A SECOND TIME Valentina found that rocky outcropping and waited upon it with her tablecloth spread for the treasure-barque to sail by. A second time it ate. A second time its presence was nearly too much to bear—but this time, she was braced against it.

She was *prepared* for it.

The approach of the figurehead eradicated her in a moment; she lost sight of herself entirely; and yet—

Let us pause there.

The second reflex of a Sosunov magician, on discovering that they do not exist, is to curdle the emptiness with their sight. They accept that they are in a dream—it is almost always, necessarily, a dream, for all that it was not on this particular occasion—in which they are not present. They do not retreat into the role of a disembodied presence, or a narrator; instead, they are a nameless pressure, a current stirring in the nothingness. There is no actor; there is no subject; there is a thing that is arguably not even associated with the Sosunov individual themselves.

Simply:

A force arises; circles; falls.

In the blinding, numbing presence of the barque, a tenacious intention nevertheless arose. It was an intention born of Valentina's training but it was not *Valentina's* intention. It had no origin within her. It had no ending in her. Because there was no Valentina, because her presence in herself had been annihilated, there was instead an intention that arose from nothing, looped through itself like an ouroboros, and to nothing then returned.

The serpent's approach eradicated her in a moment, she lost sight of herself entirely, and yet:

Her eyes met the creature's eyes to hold it still; her voice murmured soothing phrases; her hand rose up to stroke the creature's scaled neck.

The creature nosed her, curiously. It sniffed about her.

"You may trust me," Valentina lied.

It gulped down a bowl of fruit, and it slipped away.

SHE CAME UP from the underworld in a culvert beneath a tannery street. Gargoyles stared down at her from the building walls. She oriented herself and made for Fortitude, but she passed a funeral procession on the way. A boy at the front, a drummer at the side, and four pallbearers with the coffin; whomever had died, she thought, he was scarcely mourned.

A concern nagged at her, subliminally, after she'd passed the procession, until she'd finally brought it up into the focus of her mind:

The lid of the coffin had been trembling, and not in time with the footsteps of the pallbearers or the drum.

She turned around.

She caught up to them four intersections further; called out, "Your corpse, lad. I think it's gone vampire."

The procession stopped.

"Ha," said the boy at the front, turning round. "That's what I said, the first time he'd done! Even the second too. But he's gone dead as old ashes five times now and woken up five times for the funeral and by God we're going to bury him this time now whether he'll stay still in there or not."

The shaking of the coffin lid intensified. Valentina thought she heard a muffled voice raised in complaint.

"Dropped good cash on the coffin, too," the boy said. "Don't you doubt it!"

"I don't think I can let you do that," Valentina said.

"Lumme!" the boy said. "You some kind of funeral princess? You mind your own business and let me bury me own Da."

"... I'm sure I can find a place for someone with a talent for dying and then re-living," Valentina said. "If nothing else, it sounds like he'd be handy if ever I come up against the Headmaster of the Bleak Academy again. Why doesn't he become my responsibility, and not yours?"

The boy thought about this for a bit. "Pfeh," he scoffed, and he signaled to the pallbearers, who gently lowered the coffin to the street. "As you like. But *I'm* done with him, d'you hear? I'm taking the cash and a boat back to the world."

"I hear," Valentina said, with the smallest of smiles, and the boy then departed.

WHEN SHE got the coffin open, after a brief struggle with the lid, the man inside sat up—sharply, desperately—and braced against the coffin's edge as he gasped for breath. "Oh my God," he said, between gasps. "My God. I thought I was done for. Thank you so much."

"Your health, sir," she said. "I'm Valentina Grigorievna Sosunova."

"Ivan," he said. He was a heavy man with a thick brown beard and a ridiculously red outfit.

She gave him a minute, then helped him out of the coffin. When he seemed steady again, she spoke: "... if I might ask?"

He glanced down at himself, then grinned broadly. "I look terrible in black."

Valentina blinked. She reoriented. She said, "I meant, the whole dying and living thing."

"Oh," he said. He blushed, then thumped his chest. "I am not completely certain, but I blame Draisey's Patent Heart Tonic."

"Oh dear," Valentina said.

"In my dreams, when I am dead," he said, "I see the flower whose nectar is the water of life—it blooms around these parts, did you know? Though only rarely, and never more than one at a time beneath the sky— and I think, ah, it must have been one of the seventeen confidential ingredients in the tonic that I took that time. Though my heart keeps giving out anyway, so I think it's maybe not so good a medicine at what it's *for*."

"I'm sorry to hear that," Valentina said.

"It's all right, it's all right," he said. "It's quite bracing, you know, being dead now and then; and I think, this last time I was *just* about able to wiggle a toe before my life came back. Imagine it! If I can walk my old corpse around the possibilities would have no *end*.

"But my boy's not much for the idea, you know? Not much for it at all."

And they spoke of life and death and many things as they two went on their way.

THE THIRD TIME SHE found the ship she took its jaw in one hand and brushed the other across the serpent's head.

In that moment, as she touched the jewel that was the serpent's heart, she dreamed.

The world extinguished itself. It spiraled away into nothingness, and behind it she discovered the dream of a leaf that had fallen from the tree of worlds—a nearly-dead leaf that had fluttered down to land beside the water—and the great hands that had picked it up, blown upon it to fill it with a regret and a remembrance like a burning light inside it, and set it on the water to sail down beneath the world as a treasure-barque.

In the deep waters beneath that dream, like a kraken's tentacles, an *intention* moved.

It built on itself; it gathered itself; it—

"Oh," Valentina said, startled.

The boat had rocked, and her hand had slipped away.

It was watching her warily. She could *feel* that wariness, and did not immediately reach out again. Instead, fighting to remain lucid in the face of the boat's overwhelming presence, she explained herself. "I need you, you know," she said. "Not for myself. Or not for myself exactly. I have— I have fallen in love, you see."

The ship stirred slightly. The water rippled around its edge.

"His name is Czeslaus," Valentina said. "Czeslaus Czciborovich Chalecki. —not Fidatof, of course, as he is not yet dead, you see."

The serpent-prowed treasure-barque did not see—

But the sounds were pleasant to it; they were soothing it; she could feel that too. So she kept on. "It is difficult. It is very difficult. I cannot possibly marry into the Chaleckis, not only because they are not a viable concern—their patriarch having been adopted by the Fidatofs—but because I am the Sosunov heir. It would bring humiliation on the family, at least, if I were to abandon that and then abandon *them* upon my nuptials. And I would not be able to bring my husband into the Sosunov secrets, if I became a Chalecki.

"But Czcibor Fidatof is proud.

"—I assume that he is proud. We have not spoken. It is amazing. I am making all these plans around him and we have not spoken. But I have talked to his son, in dreams at least, and I have made inquiries, and most importantly, he is a vampire, and they have as a group become rather an arrogant bloc in this 'Night London' that they wish to build, of late."

Valentina folded up the tablecloth and tucked it away. She brushed nonexistent dust and table scraps from the shelf of stone.

"That is where you come in, you see. Czcibor Fidatof longs for you. If I can bring you to him, then there is just the thinnest chance I can win passage through this great field of thorns."

She held out a hand towards the ship. It did not move, at first.

She beckoned.

And finally, shyly, the boat slipped closer.

When she next woke, her hands were bloody and her knife was out; and the living jewel that was its heart was in her hands.

SHE WOULD NEVER remember the rest of it.

She boarded the barque—presumably. She sailed it to the docks of Fortitude. She had a vague impression of herself standing at the ship's fore with the living jewel held in her hand. She thought that it was possible that at one point she had sailed beneath the sun.

Then—

Then she was stumbling down the gangplank, her tongue dry, her whole body feeling strangely frail and strangely light.

She found a likely post and slumped against it and nearly instantaneously she fell asleep.

As she passed through the gates of dream sense began to return to her, and a cold calculation too, and the stream of her memories began to fit together again.

If the barque was won—

If the weight in her pouch was the treasure-barque's heart; if she could give it away; if Czcibor could take it; if the barque was won—

Then that was part of the problem solved, but in the end, it was the smaller part.

The remaining portion would be trickier.

She hung there in an unfinished dream and her thoughts drifted, as they often did, to Czeslaus. This time, however, she did not let her heart seek him out in whatever dreams he might or might not have been dreaming at that particular time. Rather, she cast her thoughts willfully forward, past tomorrow and tomorrow, hunting for a suitable dream of his five or six fortnights thence.

Before she had become fully aware of herself, she had begun to dream of an autumnal meadow. She dreamed of an autumnal meadow still. But—what color were the flowers? She did not see. Was there a sun? Had a moon risen? She did not allow herself to know. Were there many trees? Were there animals? What color was the sky?

These things she had not determined, and she did not permit herself to determine them.

Her mind's eye swept blindly over these gaps, over the ten thousand portions of the dream where she had not looked, the ten thousand portions of the dream that she could not see. She deliberately refused to bring any of them into focus—"an autumnal meadow" was already more detail than she liked.

She would have erased even that bit of definition if she could've.

She would have translated herself elsewhere, away from the meadow, taken herself to the sky or to the sea, if it were not the case that such a move was almost inevitably in the direction of increasing specificity. So in practice there was no alternative; in the meadow she would stay.

She reached down into her heart—though, she thought sometimes that she had no heart, but only a dark bird that beat its wings inside her chest—and over from there to Czeslaus'. She swam upwards from Czeslaus' heart through the waters of the man towards the surface of his mind, and she began to feel around her for a moment in Czeslaus' dreams, in the desired time frame, to which that meadow could be a match.

A sculptor's instinct found it, and she bridged the dreams.

Czeslaus was falling.

He was falling, and he was falling, and in his dream where he was falling he had not yet really given any consideration towards the landing. If anything he had avoided thinking of it in too much detail.

The ground beneath him *could*, as far as his dream thus far could have yet determined, have been the autumnal meadow that Valentina Sosunova, many days before, had dreamt.

The dreams harmonized. They came together.

They were made *one*—

And she caught him, or, rather, fell down beneath him, as he struck the pillowed ground.

"OH," HE SAID, in some surprise. "It's you."

She struggled out from beneath him. She pulled herself into a sitting position. Nothing was broken, of course; she was scarcely bruised, and even that only the minimum she could imagine while sustaining the verisimilitude of the dream. "Hey," she grinned.

"This is— I mean, you are genuinely here?" he asked.

"I am," she said.

"My word."

"If I have survived," Valentina said, "then I will have told you this dream is coming. I will have told you that I will come to you in dreams and ask you to tell me this story, the story of how I brought the treasure-barque to your father, and of the trials and the challenges that he set before me, and what happened then."

"'If' you have survived," Czeslaus said, in a puzzled tone, but then he shrugged and shook it off. "You have done so."

"Speak."

"All right," Czeslaus said. The confusion, it seemed, had not *entirely* left him. "He brought me in to tell me that you had asked for an engagement, and suggested that I move into your father's house. Eventually he came around to deciding to allow it, if you could spin a line of thread across Night London between one midnight and the next."

Valentina's eyes flickered. She frowned.

"Pardon," Czeslaus said. "But what is that face?"

"I am uncertain," Valentina said. "It is not *obviously* impossible, but— I do not spin very often, you understand."

"Well, you made quite a go of it," he said. "But— who could do such a thing as that? It may not have been obvious, but it *was* certainly impossible. In the end you dropped your spindle and gave in.

"I did not understand why you were so calm. Why you had given up. You didn't even seem to *mind* that he had beaten you. But I told him, I remonstrated with him, I spent hours informing him that considering the treasure that you had brought into our house he owed you not just a new trial but a fairer one.

"And in the end he looked at me, and he said, 'You are taken with her, I see.'"

"I ... ah ..."

Here Czeslaus scratched at the back of his head in mild embarrassment.

"I am afraid I quite lost my train of thought, but it was no longer necessary for me to retain it; that very night he gave you another opportunity to rescue me for his house, by sifting coarse gold from his mustard seeds."

"Eh?"

"... he had a barrel of coarse gold, mixed with mustard seeds," Czeslaus said.

"I see," Valentina said.

"You failed, of course," Czeslaus said.

"Of course?"

"Well, you did, anyway. So he raised the stakes. He wanted to give you to me wrapped up in a bow like a present. He wanted you to stay and become a Chalecki, and one day a Fidatof. So he pushed on it. He said, 'ah, but if you'll risk yourself—we can do one more go.' Or something like that."

Valentina nodded.

"'In the garden there is a pond,' he said. 'In the pond there are seven great stones; dredge them up, and he shall be a Sosunov. Fail, or fail to finish before the day-lamp lights[14], and you shall be a Chalecki.'

"But:

"'You could not know,' you said, 'but I am unable to breathe beneath the water. You must choose some other challenge.'

"This threw him. I do not think he was prepared for it. I think he was trying to tempt you, you see. He'd never tried that test before, and I think he wanted you to accept it out of pride in your own bodily strength.

"He floundered.

"He tried the first thought that came to mind. 'I'll have you hook a grain of rice from a vat of gruel using nothing but a fishing rod and a hookless line ...'

"'You could not know,' you said again, 'but I am quite unable to see through gruel. You must choose some other challenge.'

"And he snapped out, '... then fetch me the flower whose nectar is the water of life before the hour is out! And he shall be a Sosunov.'"

Valentina pondered this. "That seems even more difficult than the others," she said.

"Evidently not," he summarized.

Valentina gave him a slow grin. "That is all I needed, then," she said. "May your morning be a happy one."

"Not likely," he said, and sighed, and shook his head. "You've

---

14 Roughly six am

challenged me to do the seating chart, you see? before the day-lamp lights twice more.”

SHE WOKE in the darkness on the water, pulled herself into a seated position, and gave deep thought to the matter.

“So I am to fetch the flower whose nectar is the water of life,” she said.

She came up from the docks and walked in deep distraction through Fortitude to Edith Draisey’s house. She knocked and was welcomed in.

“Edechka,” she said, “I have need of you.”

“Oh?”

“Tonight,” Valentina said, “Or soon, at any rate, I will be challenged to spin a line of thread across Night London.”

Edith squinted in thought. “Is it hitched narrow anywhere?”

“I haven’t lived there,” Valentina said.

“You could try down to the ground from the highest tower.”

Valentina shook her head. “The sewers,” she said. “The tunnels. The tunnels under those. The— well, eventually the sea of souls.”

“Mm,” Edith said. She frowned.

“I thought about who I could ask for help,” Valentina said. “And then it occurred to me, that what I needed was some sort of carriage-sized clockwork or steam-powered spider, partially operated by pedal—to preserve a sense that one is doing the spinning oneself—that trails a web-line of yarn behind it.”

“Gracious,” Edith said.

“It is asking a lot,” Valentina said.

“You *are* a fool,” Edith said, without rancor. She brushed a bit of dust from the side of her dress. “If it were wise to seek such things from me I would have given them to you already. If it were wise to seek such things from me then I would be considered an artisan of incommunicable talent rather than a pitiable case. People would *seek out* those who go past the verge rather than condemning it.

"Give me three weeks."

"Oh! I had expected you were about to refuse me," Valentina said.

"In this short a time in Fortitude," Edith said, "my heart has gained more peace than it had ever known before. It is not much to make one giant metal spider in exchange. ... but I cannot do it by tonight unless you want a regular spinning wheel with eight one-joint metal legs stuck on."

"I will wait," Valentina said.

IT SHOULD BE understood that Valentina already knew she could not win this. Czcibor would meet her demands with scorn and challenge her to spin a line of thread across Night London—and she would fail to do so. It was a perverse, defiant impulse that had her ride into the settlement three weeks later on the back of a giant metal spider:

Regardless of the inexorable nature of her destiny, she would not just *sit back*, not even once, and let the vampire win.

She had never even met Czcibor Fidatof but already he was her nemesis. Already she had elevated him in her mind to the status of a false god who must be pulled down from his pedestal; a diabolical monster who must be driven far from the shores of Fortitude; a malevolent shadow that must be stricken from her life. He had become irrationally larger-than-life for her, even as, in a different way, so had his son.

She dismounted some ways back from his manor and concealed the spider on the wall beneath the awning of an abandoned watchmaker's shop.

She marched past the little white flower that grew between the stones of the walkway without taking note of it, rang the bell for the footman, and passed in word that Valentina Grigorievna Sosunova of Fortitude, who had captured the treasure-barque, was there.

It did not take long; Czcibor descended the grand stair.

"Miss Sosunova," he said. "It is such a pleasure."

It was difficult not to be afraid of him. There was something in his movements, in his eyes, or perhaps just in the atmosphere around him that warned her that he was a predator and she was *prey*. She did not flinch before the vampire-fear; did not *let* herself flinch before it; but she could not lie to herself and deny that it was felt.

—that *she* felt it! *She*, who'd fought the lord of Death's dominion!

"The pleasure is mine," she said. "Mister Fidatof."

"*Czcibor*," he said. "Please."

"Czcibor, then. But let us—" She jerked her hand out of his before he could succeed in kissing it. "Let us not start this on the wrong footing."

"Oh?"

"Please stand a little farther back," she said. Then, her voice strained, "because I am hoping to arrange an engagement with your son and also I would really like to kill a vampire and that is two very good reasons why you should be maintaining a much more polite distance between the two of us. Czcibor."

"Ehh, ah?" he said, raising an eyebrow. "'Really like to kill a vampire?'"

"It's the acoustics," Valentina said vaguely. "I doubt that that is what I said."

"Well, it's all perfectly good, as long as you choose some other vampire," he said, and smiled broadly.

"There is a ship of black wood that sailed the waters underneath this place," she said.

"Yes."

"Now it is docked at Ceiba Quay, and I have seized its living heart, and while I certainly don't see how you could get it *here*, you're more than welcome to take possession."

"Because you are interested in an engagement with my Czeslaus."

"Yes."

"Come now," he said. "This is hardly how these things are arranged."

"Would you have let him visit a Fortitude shrine family socially?"

"I suppose not," he agreed easily. "I grow uncomfortable when he travels too far from my protective reach. Much less into a temple space. If he'd been more active in socializing with the people whose company I've felt he *should* cultivate, perhaps."

"And if I had begun regular visits?"

"Sweet child, you are a *showpiece* ... but, mmm, no, perhaps not one I would have encouraged him to court. True. —no offense."

"I hardly intend to force myself upon him," Valentina said. "A year's engagement is all right. Should he be genuinely unwilling towards the end of it, I would accept the idea of breaking it off. I'm making an extremely fair offer, in exchange for the boat, you see."

"Such terrible compromises," he said. "But honestly. A boy should die and rise again before he thinks of settling down for an eternity. A mortal love just leaves an empty space in your heart to nag you for the rest of— well, forever."

"I can go," Valentina said. She started to turn.

He was very close again and his hand was on the wall beside her head. "Sweet little bird," he said. "How would you like to be immortal?"

"Sir!" one of the servants cried, somewhere between scandalized and afraid. "That's *Valentina Grigorievna*."

He drew back slightly, in genuine confusion. He looked at the man. Valentina, somewhat embarrassed, realized that her hand had gone to the hilt of a sword. Czcibor looked back at her again as she released it. "Am I to know that name?" he asked.

"There is a foolish rumor that I am already immortal," Valentina said. "It is not important. Or rather, it is not substantiated. I like to say that the lord of Death's dominion fears me and does not wish for my return. I do not think this is necessarily a quality that you are looking for in a daughter-in-law, but it does render your offer a little bit beside the point."

"Huh," he said. He rallied. "A longer courtship, then. Czeslaus has been somewhat cloistered all his life—for one reason and another, culminating in the sadly dead local social scene. I do not want him choosing a woman to marry just because she was … well, *there*."

"Five years?"

He raised an eyebrow. "You *are* immortal," he said. "Or think yourself to be, at any rate."

"It is not an unheard-of length of time."

"No," he agreed. "Five years. I … will accept it, if only for the novelty, and for the … pleasure of your presence."

"It must be understood," Valentina said, "that when he marries, it shall be into the family Sosunov."

"I'm sorry? Ah?"

"It is not uncommon," Valentina said. "A man *normally* brings the woman into his family, but in the case of the shrine families, it can be arranged for him to enter the woman's house instea—"

"*Do not test me,*" he said.

They moved very quickly. He stepped in far too close to hiss the words into her face. Her sword leapt into her hand as she stepped back, raising it to where it would stop just before his neck; only, he was faster and he was stronger and she had not realized until that very moment just how *much* faster and just how *much* stronger. His elbow struck the sword aside as it was still rising and her arm went all pins and needles and the sword fell from her hand. His palm—which he had not meant to raise to her, only, she'd surprised him too—struck her chest in a shove that took her off her feet and sent her back to land against the wall.

The sword clattered loudly against the ground.

Slowly, she crawled and stumbled back to her feet. She swayed, but there was bloodlust in her eyes. "Next time," she said, "that won't go so wel—"

He understood it as overconfidence and moved forward to push her back into the wall again. He was both right and wrong. Wrong, because this time she had a measure for his speed and strength and her second sword (for she still wore two) deceived him with two feints towards his neck and head before its lunging thrust towards his heart. Right, because even *then* he was fast enough to stop his advance before she did more than scratch his favorite shirt.

They stood there for a moment. Then he turned away, stepping back. "Pointless," he said.

Valentina relaxed her pose.

"Czesio!" he called out. "Czesio!"

A sleepy-looking man came out, rubbing at his eyes. "Father. Oh. Valen—*ahem*. Woman whom I have never seen before in my life. Wait. Hello? Hello!"

He seemed slightly more awake at the end of this. "What are you doing here?" he asked.

"This young lady has put herself forward," Czcibor said, "as an engagement prospect for yourself."

"I'm fifty-two," Valentina said.

"You're!— I mean, this ... withered crone," Czcibor corrected himself. "Has put herself forward, etcetera."

"Oh," Czeslaus said. "Well, I'm all for it. Is that all you wanted, father?"

"You're all for it?"

"You would not *believe* the desert that is my social calendar," Czeslaus said. "Much less my romantic life. Plus, she has apparently been fighting with you." He tilted his head slightly to the side. He raised his fist, as if Valentina had just scored a point at a minor-league sporting event. "Hoorah."

"She has, more than that," Czcibor said, studying Czeslaus' reactions with some interest, "proposed removing you from under my roof and taking you into her family of pagan ritualists in Fortitude."

"Naturally, I object."

"Of course," Czcibor concurred.

"If I am to be a viper in the eyes of God," Czeslaus said, "forsaking all goodness and all holy things, it should be for following in my father's path, and not my fiancée's."

"Be serious," Czcibor snapped.

"Of course, father." Czeslaus looked sideways at Valentina. "The notion is impossible. I'm sorry. I simply can't even consider it, no matter how many magic boats you can provide."

Czcibor closed his eyes for a moment. Then he opened them.

"I shall hear no more of it," he said. "Let us leave that matter there. Now, on another note. Miss Sosunova, fetch your things; you shall be staying here a while."

"I ... shall?"

"That is what you desired, is it not? To explore the ... possibilities?"

"It may not be altogether proper—"

"Of course it is," he said. "The house has adequate chaperones. Do you imagine that you can commit an indiscretion with Czeslaus when I could be watching from the rafters as a mouse or bat? And an indiscretion with myself has never even entered upon your mind. No, it is entirely proper. You shall leave the arsenal at home."

"I am ill at ease without it."

"Blades are not needed here," Czcibor said. "I would take grave insult."

"Then," Valentina said, narrowing her eyes, "you will consider— I mean, there may be some compromise on the necessary point? Because you were quite threatening when I merely made the suggestion—"

"I am unbending," Czcibor said. "Do I plan to relent? No. Do I plan to accommodate your delusions? Hardly. But if we give the matter time, a solution may present itself."

Her eyes were hard. "I will hold you to that. To ... working with me, I mean, on the matter."

"Mmm," he said.

She nodded to him, and turned. "I'll fetch my things."

THUS BEGAN Valentina's stay at Czcibor Fidatof's manor.

It was an awkward interval. Reason gave her no clear answer as to how dangerous Czcibor actually was to her, but a visceral instinct continually reminded her that she was in a predator's house and she, potential prey. Her hands itched for weapons and she found herself filching table knives before retiring to her bed. Discovering herself locked in from the time she so retired until breakfast's announcement eight hours later made her even less comfortable; the first night she scraped at the lock and doorframe with a confiscated knife until she snapped it before finally, dismally, throwing herself back onto the bed. Complaining in the morning did no good; Czcibor only asked her archly what she had thought she would be doing about his house that late.

On the third day most of her packed clothing vanished from the closet, replaced with a new selection in the style popular in Night London at the time.

Every creak of the house put her on edge.

She was able to spend some, limited, time with Czeslaus. That was good—at least. She visited with him in the library and they discussed the classics. She listened as he played. They walked in Czcibor's garden; he made the most oblique allusions to what it was like growing up with Czcibor as his father, and she in turn talked about what the Headmaster had done.

As for Czcibor, every conversation with him was more uncomfortable than the last. He stood too close. He was too interested in her. He would ask her trivial things when they met in the halls, and she would answer and make some excuse to leave—no more than twenty or thirty words exchanged—and every time her pulse was beating faster, her breath was a little shorter, her anger at herself for being weaponless was greater, and she could not help but feeling as if she had just escaped from a tiger's den. At meals she had a buffer, as Czeslaus was present; at worst Czcibor would put his hand over hers as she reached for the salt, or ask her some passing question about Fortitude—but it was hard for her, after the hubbub of Sosunov family dinners, to retreat so deliberately from the dinner conversation and limit herself to the occasional smile or vacuous laugh.

The first time she slipped up on this, Czcibor was bragging of the textile factories' production; how one of the modern jennies could outpace a hundred spinning wheels—and she could not help herself. "It can, of course," she said, despite herself, "but it oughtn't."

"Mmm?"

She already regretted speaking. She shook her head in denial. But he insisted:

"Please, speak."

"I was only saying, what good is that? —no, let me speak further. When we work on our own, sometimes we seek quantity of production. Sometimes we value it. But what good does it do when that becomes the *only* virtue?"

"The mechanism itself is wondrous," Czcibor said. "But, more than that, it must be said that it accomplishes the same work for much less cash."

"Well, was not enough cash minted?"

His lips twitched. "Perhaps there was enough minted, but not enough had reached the pockets of the specific people making cloth."

"There," she said. "There, then. That is what we are giving up the old ways for. And the cost is to the soul."

"That seems unlikely," he said.

"Have you ever spun? —forget I asked it. To—"

"I have," he interrupted.

Startled: "You have?"

"Kasieńka's hands were growing shaky near the end," he said.

Valentina's eyes flickered. She frowned. After a moment, she said, "My condolences."

"It's long done," he said, and shrugged. "I only regret that at the time I had no way to bring her back."

"It's strange to think that you were human once."

"It was not all *that* very long ago—but come. You were saying, about spinning."

"… it just seems to me that there is a connection between things," Valentina said. "When you spin your own family's thread. When you catch your own family's fish. When you walk the roads of your home. You are losing that when it is only machines that you live with."

He was watching her. It made her uncomfortable. Finally she shrugged.

"I'm sorry," she said. "I shouldn't have spoken."

It was a mistake, but it wasn't *the* mistake. *The* mistake was perfectly innocuous. She was walking back to her room after an interlude with Czeslaus and she was not listening to the halls. She had let herself forget for a moment that she was sharing her housing with a predator.

She came around the corner and was confronted suddenly with Czcibor.

Her weapons were gone. Her clothing was awkward and unfamiliar. She tried to shift into a more defensive posture but she tripped on the fabric by her feet instead and fell forward into Czcibor's waiting arms.

He looked down at her. He did not immediately let her go. And then, just before she started to struggle to get away, he smiled.

"Let us make a game of it," he said.

The table knife had found its way from her left sleeve to her right hand, and she thought that perhaps he had not noticed, but she also thought that it would not be enough to make an end of him even if it went into his heart or eye.

"Let us make a game of it, you and me. You will give yourself to me. I will drink from you. And then I will give you an opportunity to win away from me my son."

She shook her head. She tried to get her feet under her but his grip on her arm interfered.

She clarified: "No."

"He will go into the Sosunovs," Czcibor said. "If you can win this. I'll only ask for, let us say, my second grandchild in return."

He let her go. She reached her footing. She realized with horror that her index finger, where it had missed the knife's grip, was cut and very nearly bleeding; she dropped the knife into her other hand and raised the wound to her mouth to suck it clean before he could get any ideas of doing so himself. "I won't let you drink from me for just a *chance*. You could make it impossible."

"Then," he said. "How's this? If you fail, I can drink my fill; but not if you get scared and don't even try."

"Fine," she said, because she wanted to end the conversation and get back to her room where she would feel more safe. "What's the bet?"

"Ehh," he said. Then he smiled. "Let's say, let's see if you can spin a line of thread across Night London in a night?"

"That's ridiculous," she said around her hand.

"For a fact?"

"Don't sound so happy with the idea," she said.

"A little longer, then," he said, with a twist of his lips. "... between one midnight and the next."

"Uh," she said, and nodded.

"Do you need help with that?" he said, indicating her finger with his head.

"No," she said. She shook her head. "'M fine."

He smiled at her. He walked away.

The next day she sent a servant with a note; "Midnight tomorrow. It's a bet."

"I ADMIT," HE SAID, at around eleven, "that I had not expected you to have a giant mechanical spider."

"Preparation pays," Valentina said.

"Ehh, I'm not even sure it counts."

"Would you rather give him to the *spider* in matrimony?"

Czcibor sputtered a laugh.

"Because if I'm not doing it, *she* is," Valentina observed.

"... oh, very well," Czcibor conceded. "I'd been prepared to veto a jenny or mule, you understand—to say, 'that's all very well, but let's do a different game'—but this? This, you have bested me. Assuming that it can actually spin thread for you? Because if not, I am telling you, its presence would be over-elaborate."

"It is what I use these days instead of a drop spindle," Valentina said. "It's much more convenient. Well, not it. She. Her name is Praskovya."

She rubbed the giant metal spider's head.

"I don't suppose you also coincidentally have a map of Night London with the shortest route across it marked?"

Valentina shook her head. "I've been thinking about it, but I'm pretty sure the stupid thing's a square. Practically, anyway."

"I had thought as much myself."

"I am assuming that bridging a little convex bump along the edge would not qualify; nor running a line from the topmost tower to the ground."

"I am afraid that both of those would smack of sophistry," he said, seeming slightly fascinated.

"Then I should think straight west to east, from roughly in the middle."

"Mmm."

"You don't seem terribly concerned," Valentina said.

"Oh. Well, it's yet to be shown that 'giant pedal-assisted clockwork spider' is that much of an improvement on a traditional spinning wheel. For one thing."

"I'll cross Night London in five hours," Valentina said.

"Will you?"

They walked and clanked for a while, and no one troubled them as they went. Near the edge of Night London, Czcibor casually ripped a metal fencepost from the ground and stripped the wire away from it; when they reached the edge itself, where the last buildings gave way to the Walking Fields, he thrust it into the ground.

"The thread is tied here," he said. "At the ringing of the midnight bells. Then ... well, you proceed."

The bells rang.

The thread was tied.

Valentina drove Praskovya east, and the spider lay out thread as she went. A few minutes in, Czcibor stopped her; "I must see," he said, "that the fabric is in its unspun form, as it were, in the belly of the spider."

"That's fair enough," Valentina said, and thumped the side of the spider with her boot. "If you look through the holes, you can see the mechanism as it works. I'll go slowly for the next short while."

"Mmm."

Czcibor did not approach. He seemed content that she had offered, and after a few minutes she sped back up again.

"Kasieńka told me once that she could make about a mile in a day," he said. He picked up the thread where it lay loose upon the ground, tugged on it so it snapped, and stretched a length between his hands. "Stronger than this, too, though not quite so swift."

"I plead of you," Valentina said, stopping, "don't tear up the line of thread."

"Oh?"

He stepped back; she dismounted and, frowning, tied the broken ends together.

"I expect that *would* be rude of me," he agreed. "Oh, you'll have to turn here; the bridge isn't finished up ahead, and you wouldn't want the line you're laying getting soaked."

"More than just rude."

"I'd actually expected a more severe reaction," he said. "Am I going to find myself hoist by my own petard, with this thread actually my own life's thread, or so sticky I won't be able to let it go?"

"It *is* somewhat sticky," Valentina admitted. "You might need to wash your gloves to-morrow."

She steered the spider a little north, looking for a finished bridge across the little waterway that they had come to. Finding one, she drove it across.

"Are you expecting pure social force to prevent me from breaking it again?"

"That's your plan?" she said. "You're going to win this by being a nuisance?"

"It *would* be ungentlemanly," he agreed.

"I am thinking," she said, softly, "that I should be done before the day-lamp lights, much less before next midnight."

"If someone does not tragically rip the legs off of your spider."

"*Someone* might get staked through the heart first."

"*Someone* can just go ahead and try."

"... when I was young," Valentina said, "there was a man that I met in my dreams."

"Truly your heart has gone to many men."

"*Two*," Valentina said, flushing slightly. "Really, one and a half. One and an eighth. If that. I was a *child*."

"It is appallingly licentious," Czcibor said.

"He was a Rider," Valentina said, steadfastly ignoring Czcibor. "Like, one of those guys with the eyes?"

Czcibor shuddered delicately.

"Yeah. Those. And he said that there was ... 'there is a thing you cannot use the wrong words for.' That beneath the substances of the world there was a void that is lively in its emptiness. And he went to show it to me and to show me how to do the thing he could do."

"Riding?"

"Stop it," Valentina snapped.

"This would be very dull indeed if I were not making conversation," Czcibor pointed out. "You would just be riding a giant spider along telling stories to the air. Everyone would think you were one of the new legends and monsters of Night London and they would come up with ghost stories about you. Don't go out at night or the Valentina might get you! Her head pops off and she eats you right up with her belly!"

"You are overly imaginative," she said. "It doubtless comes with your diet."

"My diet."

"Do you eat much in the way of produce?"

"Well—" he started.

"Then there we are."

"My sweet—"

"It is absolutely possible, and even healthy, for a vampire to eat regular food. It is simply that you cannot survive indefinitely upon it. Is that not so?"

"You are not seriously informing me that I must eat my vegetables."

"It is none of my concern," Valentina said. "But a purely carnivorous diet is likely to lead to a deranged mind. Science has established this."

"Science does not truck with the walking dead. I believe I have been reputably described by it as a form of mass hysteria."

"There you go, then."

"What?"

"Eat more produce, and everyone will wake up to the realization you were never there."

"I take grapefruit juice with some regularity," he said, sulkily.

"What, is that the closest fruit to blood?"

He shook his head.

"Are you as outrageously inappropriate with the grapefruit," she asked curiously, "as you are with me?"

"Don't be ridiculous," he said.

"Regardless," Valentina said, after a minute had passed, "the thing he wished to show me was his power of un-creation. His power to reach out into the world and make something ... not be. I think that in the end that is what I shall have to threaten your kind with."

"Oh? And did you master that power, then?"

"I am better at the Sosunov magic," Valentina sighed. "But I beg of you to bear in mind that if sufficiently provoked there remains at all times the chance that I will have a supernal insight and you will simply cease to be.

"Like a word, rubbed out from a letter. Like a footprint, on the beach."

He stared after her for a while, and then walked over to the line of thread and snapped it. She stopped the spider's inexorable advance.

"Er?" she said.

"You intend to distract me through conversation," he said. "I am peevish that it worked for even a moment. Therefore, I have exacted your punishment. One break in the line."

"It is impossible to distract you through conversation across the entire length of Night London," she said. "It's got to be at least four more hours as the spider crawls."

"True," he agreed. "You will have to think of something else."

"If I were fortunate," she said. "Someone could be setting fire to your manor, even as we speak. Thus requiring you to return and devote your attentions there."

"If you were fortunate," he said.

"Perhaps you had better check."

He hesitated.

"I have spent, what's the thing?— a *long time* preparing for this day," Valentina said. "I even got a spider. Anything could happen. Anything at all."

"I'll return," he promised.

He was no longer a man, but a wolf, running low and long along Night London's streets.

HE WAS so fast.

He was so damnably *fast*. It wasn't *fair*.

The Headmaster had had an excuse. She hated him but it didn't break her pride that he could knock her to the ground with a thought—with the force of his attention alone. It didn't break her pride that maybe, in the end, a human couldn't *beat* him, not the way that she'd set out originally to the Bleak Academy to do. He was *he the lord of Death's dominion he.*

There wasn't anything inexorable and metaphysical about Czcibor Fidatof's speed and strength. It didn't go down to the roots of the world. She couldn't contemplate it and gain insight into the void that is lively in its emptiness, the thing before all other things … nor the thing that comes after all things neither. She'd *checked*, and she'd found no theological grandeur to the vampires; not even a numinous blasphemy.

Sometimes … sometimes corpses just got up again. Usually, with help.

There wasn't anything metaphysically superior about Czcibor Fidatof; if anything, really, it was the other way around. She was alive, he was dead. Her despair could shake the Outside; his could upset his digestion. Her dreams drank deep of some supernal well: she immersed in them, and came out more centered and more whole. If vampires even dreamed at *all*, she did not know.

She was deeper and truer than Czcibor Fidatof. She was, simply put, *more real.*

And yet:

He was so very fast and so very strong.

So very much faster, and so very much stronger.

The gulf was difficult to cross, and it wasn't *fair*.

Like the wind he fled from her; like the wind he circled back again. "My house is not on fire," he pointed out.

"I wouldn't set your house on fire," she said. "Czeslaus is in there."

"...that is an excellent point," he said.

"It's also quite shameful," Valentina said, "and I have a family name to protect."

"I expect that's true enough," Czcibor said. "But I have trouble putting anything past a woman who pulls a giant mechanical spider out of her petticoats."

"That is not what happened and you know it."

"I looked away," he said. "I looked back. There was a spider. Your petticoats were ruffled."

"I am not wearing petticoats."

"Oh?"

She flushed. "It is hardly practical for riding."

"Mmm," he said. He tilted his head to one side. "If I might ask—it does seem quite coincidental that you had a spinning tool waiting for you nearby."

"You are wondering if Czeslaus has pre-informed me of your foibles," she said.

"Mmm."

"Fear not," Valentina said. "It is not that; rather, I put it to you like this. What task *is* there beneath the stars that *doesn't* grow easier when one is riding a giant metal spider?"

"That—" he said, and then stalled out. His lips twitched. "My mind is blank," he said.

"Well, you're dead."

"But what is death?" he said, and shrugged.

"Maybe," she said, "I think, it would have to be, when you stop paying attention to the world."

A few minutes passed. He glanced over at the line of thread they left behind them.

He looked eastward with a slight frown.

"If you like," Valentina said, "we could call off your snapping the thread and my using Praskovya. I have gained at least a mile by now, so I would be content."

"Would you?"

"It's an impossible task," Valentina said. "You always meant for it to be. Was I supposed to wail and tear at my garments when I realized I was in a pickle?"

"Scandalous," he murmured.

"We can also fight," Valentina said. "I could imprison you in a web of ..."

He raised his eyebrow.

"... mildly sticky wool," she said in defeat. "That might not be terribly successful, though you *would* look quite the sheep."

"Please," he said. "I would be a *wool*-f."

Her chest heaved but she suppressed the laugh. She buried her face against Praskovya's back.

"In sheep's clothing," he admitted.

"... I am curious," she said. "Why do you turn into a wolf? Or rather, why is that a thing that you can do?"

"There is little *why* to such things," he said.

"Oh."

"There is something of the Outside that clings to anyone who returns to life," he said. "—in whatever fashion. There are holes that are left in you that death has made that awakening again does not completely fill.

"Anything that is *vampire* and not just *Czcibor* must be of such an ilk."

"It's very ... suitable ... for you."

"Mmm," he said.

"You are fortunate that you do not have the ability to spit a lion out from your neck-stump or something like that, instead."

"That's reasoning after the fact," Czcibor said. "If I'd come back from the dead with the power that you describe, nobody would call me 'a vampire.'"

"I could cut off your head," Valentina offered, "and see?"

"You think that I have hidden powers?"

"One never knows."

"Yeah, yeah, yeah." He cracked his neck. He glanced up at the sky. "Well, I said there was *little* why to such things, and not *none at all*. You, on the other hand, appear to have a giant metal spider for no clear reason whatsoever."

"I told you," Valentina said. "She's generally useful."

"I have not studied the shrine families in depth," he said. "But I have some vague sense that the Sosunov family is associated with ... incense? And seals?"

"That would be the Yatskiys," Valentina said.

"Oh. ... magical ... pools?"

"Dreams," Valentina said. "You are thinking of dreams."

"But I am fairly certain," Czcibor said, "that someone would have mentioned if that traditional magic included gigantic metal spiders. They would have said, 'what ho, Czcibor! Have you checked out the giant spider farm over in Fortitude? It's got cracking good visuals. They're monstrous! And brass!'"

"I too have been to the Outside," Valentina said.

"You interest me."

"That is unnecessary," Valentina said. "Let us not be interested in one another. Let us have rare conversations crackling with hidden enmity, and only when our mutual interest in Czeslaus does require it. ... on Maslenitsa and the like."

"Maslenitsa," he said.

"Yes."

He looked blank.

"On the sixth day," she said. "There is that unfortunate custom. One invites one's husband's blood relati— one's husband's *relatives*— to dinner. And such. You would have to eat blini and not blood, of course."

"You do realize I ... I am not ... I mean, I do not celebrate the Christian holidays?"

"It is not necessary to be personally faithful to participate in the traditional celebrations," she said, in some exasperation. "Even a demon can eat eggs on Easter, as long as they don't dare to praise the Lord."

"As long as they don't ..."

"Oh," she said. She looked away for a moment, and then a grin overthrew her frown. "Mom told me about this one time that one of the demon-folk cracked open an empty Easter egg at the market. Like, crack, and it was totally hollow inside. He couldn't help it; he exclaimed, *'Ah! Christ is risen!'*

"Naturally, he turned to smoke and blew away."

"... your mother was taking advantage of your gullibility."

"I guess that could be," Valentina said. "But I've seen stranger things that actually happened."

He shook himself all over. "I am being far too distracted," he said. "I should be breaking the thread."

"Oh, don't," Valentina said.

The thread stretched out behind them. He snorted, but he didn't move towards the line.

TIME PASSED.

"If you don't interfere," she said, "I should make it."

"Doubtlessly," he said. "Turn left here."

"Pardon?"

"That's ghoul territory ahead," he said. "I don't want you to be—

rather, I don't want them to devour you. And I definitely don't want to lean against a wall thinking, 'ehhh, is stepping in to save her acting against my own interests? How gracefully she fights! Yet, how doomed!'"

The spider stopped. Valentina turned to look at him.

"What?" he said.

She looked back forward again. Finally, reluctantly, she turned the spider left. "If you'd let me keep my swords, I would be perfectly capable of handling a typical pack of ghouls."

"Mmm," he said. "Put that way, it does seem like I have a moral responsibility."

"I think I could probably manage anyhow."

"Oh?"

"If nothing else," she said, "I am extremely good at paying attention to things."

"That must terrify a ghoul."

"There are rumors that it would," Valentina agreed.

He moved a little closer, as if to hear a confidence. "Do tell."

"Certain of the horrors of Night London," Valentina said, "if carefully studied or befriended, turn out to be human after all."

"... oh," he said.

"Wait," Valentina said. "I skipped a step.[15]"

"Oh?"

"They spin themselves into the hollows of giant eggshells, like cocoons," Valentina said. "Which crack. And *then* they turn out to have been human, all along."

"You are exceedingly gullible," Czcibor said.

"It is not as if I don't usually have sharp pointy things that I can use when folk remedies fail," Valentina said.

"Mmm."

"*Usually*," she emphasized.

---

15 It's an important step!

"You have made your point," he said. "If you are attacked by ghouls, I shall defend you."

"Not precisely my point," Valentina said. After a moment, she added, "But, the anecdote is over. You can step away again."

He did, but fell back a step first, and when he stepped away he pulled the strand of thread with him. He toyed with it, tugged on it. It snapped. He gave her a mock-helpless look.

"Honestly," Valentina said. "You broke it, you ought to knot it."

"That too would be an action against my interests."

She watched him for a while. After a minute, he backed away further and she slid down off of Praskovya to retie the thread. "It is a legitimate way of spinning, you know. Everybody will have gigantic spiders in the future."

"Oh, yes," he said. "That's a Fortitude girl for you, always on the forefront of Progress."

"There is tradition," Valentina said. "But there is also innovation. In moderation."

"Once every hundred years or so?"

"I cry thee hyperbole, Mr. Fidatof. Parsnips started showing up in borscht within my lifetime."

He was staring at her; then, he was laughing. Silently, but he was laughing; and finally, she lowered her head and gave a sigh.

It was, just a bit, like joining in.

"Gas lights are becoming more common," she said, after a while. "Too. And— and we've put up a bit of a constabulary."

"You've put new caps on your firemen," Czcibor said.

"...*and* new official functions and privileges, representing a progressive evolution of the social contract."

"They're new hats," Czcibor said.

"Fine," Valentina said. "One day, everybody *but* Fortitude will have giant spiders for spinning, while most of us will still be back with our wheels."

"You can start bearing right again," he said.

"Uh?" she said. "Oh. Thank you."

They were silent for a while. He kicked a stone as he walked. Finally, he asked, "So, that thing with the immortality."

"Ah."

"Tell me more?"

"Such a conversation topic! ... but all right. When I was young, the Headmaster of the Bleak Academy did me a disservice. He darkened my world and it is only now that it is beginning to brighten. —isn't that funny? I scarcely know Czeslaus, of course, for him to be brightening my world so. But he does. And when it started, I had scarcely more than heard him play."

"Well, he does play well."

"And then I began to dream of him. Ah. That is a secret. You will keep it, of course."

"As long as you are chaperoned therein."

"Heh. That would be impossible," Valentina said. "—wait. Not impossible. That would be legendarily difficult. I should be famous. The Sosunov who broke the boundaries of magic, all to have a chaperone. But it would not be inconceivable, merely impressive."

"My," he said. "You do ramble."

"He darkened my world," Valentina said. "He the lord of Death's dominion he. And I thought that I would take revenge on him. So I stabbed him. And then I crushed his Academy in my hand. And it did not crush, and the stabbing did not take, but he didn't like my doing either of them much, and so he told me a secret. I guess."

"Mmm?"

"I don't know if it's something anyone else would even understand," Valentina said. "But, it's like this. When you look in the mirror—let's say that, it's simpler that way. Can you look in a mirror? Well, if you can.

"When you look in the mirror, you're the person looking, not the person being looked *at*."

"You have a remarkably low threshold for secrets," Czcibor said.

"Yes," she agreed.

"I too have secrets of that order to share," he said. "Many. Copious amounts. Would you like to hear them?"

"I don't think you do," she said.

"The words we use to describe things," he said, portentously, "are not the things themselves."

"Stop it."

"Cold soup that is meant to be cold ... is better than cold soup that is meant to be hot."

"My ears are full," she said. "I can bear no more secrets. Enough."

"Socks are meant to warm the feet, and not the nostrils— I give, I give," he said, as she swatted ineffectually in his direction. "So he told you that mirror thing, and it made you immortal?"

"I dunno," Valentina said. "Maybe?"

"Not to be blunt," he said, in sudden recognition of a question that had theretofore escaped his attention, "but has it kept you fertile?"

"Now *there's* a question," Valentina said.

She tilted her head.

"... I'll tell you that, I think, if you can keep your hands to yourself, and off the thread, until we've gone another hour."

He stepped to the thread. He broke it. He stepped back.

"Really?" she said.

He was silent.

"I suppose that's not a game that ends well for you," she said. "I'll repeat my earlier offer. No spider. Your hands off the thread. It becomes impossible for me, you understand—but at least it's an honest impossible, and I've gained quite a ways."

"I don't think so," he said.

"No?"

"I'm not opening myself up for you popping two legs off this thing and calling Praskovya an ant."

Valentina's eyes narrowed. She frowned at him.

"If I can snap the thread," he said, "then I can stop you at any time."

"I could run away with him."

"Czesio? I don't think that you practically could."

She sighed. She clambered down. She fixed the thread. She went to climb back on the spider, but he'd already snapped the thread again. "… peevish."

"This is becoming less interesting," he said. "So I will skip to the epilogue."

He crushed the spider's spinneret between his hands. The spider made a crashing-cymbal noise and skittered away from him, coming to rest on a tenement's side.

"You are a *child*," Valentina hissed.

"Perhaps," he agreed. "I have lived but a drop in the sea of eternity."

He glared at the spider; the impact of his eyes was like a physical thing, and it fled from them over the edge of the building and then it was gone. Valentina stared after it for a moment, and then looked back down to Czcibor.

"I have lost my pack and its spindle, and my spider's stomach with the fiber in it," she said.

"Yes."

"I will go fetch more," she said. "I will be back in … five to six hours."

The beginning of the thread had been moved. She saw that, as she went past it. The anchor was a good quarter-mile in from where it ought to have been. She saluted that bit of meddling, not that it mattered:

Finding new supplies ate up any time that she'd gained.

Czcibor did not break the line again; that much could be said for him. He watched her as she worked on her spindle, and Czeslaus eventually joined him, but—

"I surrender," she said, as midnight drew near.

She let the spindle fall from her hands. She sat down against a building. She put her head in her hands and closed her eyes for a moment.

Czcibor's hand caught her arm with a grip tight as steel.

She looked up at him. She had been awake for nearly forty-three hours. "Gently, sir, or I shall make you regret it."

"Up," he said, and dragged her to her feet. "You are mine now; I have won your blood and your company."

"Really," she said. "That is a rather excessive description—"

He drank.

She was very tired and he had the advantage of position; that disposed of her first elemental reaction. Rage kindled in her eyes but her reflexive struggles were not efficacious. After the first moment came resignation; she, after all, had agreed.

It hurt very badly but she mastered the pain. She had more trouble with the dizziness; she tried to ignore it, tried to stand tall despite it, but she still stumbled and grabbed hold of his arm when he let her go.

"That's it?" she said. She tried to make it sound confident, but when he pulled her along towards the manor she couldn't quite work out how to fight.

It must have looked appalling, she thought.

There was a moment when they passed a shopkeeper born in Fortitude; it must have looked awful, because his eyes widened as they passed and he ran out from his shop, though what he planned to do she didn't know. She shook her head at him in warning. She called out, "It would be helpful if someone could find my giant spider."

And it would have been, in fact, but no one ever did.

"I CAN STILL WIN," she told him, as he dragged her. "Give me another game. I dare you."

"Bring down the stars," he said. "And catch one in your hand."

"That— that would be impossible," she said.

"Catch the herons' prince for me," he said, "before the hour's done. Or bring me the head of England's Queen."

"These are extremely unfair propositions," she said, and tried to balk, but the road just slipped and stumbled beneath her feet.

SHE was somewhat distressed that she allowed it.

It was humiliating to be dragged along. It was even somewhat painful. She could not quite figure out a good way to stop it, but she hated herself for allowing it. It was just—she was extraordinarily tired. Everything she was going through was predestined. She was more than a little bit dizzy.

She let it happen as if she were walking through the steps in a dance. She took less control than she would of a typical dream.

So what if Czcibor dragged her through Night London, grabbing her arm again any time she failed to keep his pace? So what if he had a wrongheaded idea of who she was, and what even a vampire might dare to do to a daughter of the Sosunovs?

She felt rather bad for Czeslaus, who did not know yet there would be a happy ending, but for herself—well, what did any of it matter?

She reached her room at the manor and fell fast asleep; and she did not dream.

HER STRENGTH, which had been a central feature of her character, did not return to her.

She had expected that it would; that as her body replenished its lost blood and recovered its lost sleep she would become Valentina Grigorievna Sosunova again; but it was, at the very least, not her perception that it was so.

She had come to the house strong, but every weaponless conversation, every day spent in the wrong clothing, each silent dinner took its toll upon her sense of strength.

One day she found herself reflexively hiding from Czcibor; she was in the halls and heard him approach and she could not help but duck into the side room and conceal herself among its shelves. When he came in and looked among those shelves, ignoring her, she felt very weak indeed.

She noted firmly that she was returning to Fortitude for a week; he told her that if his company so displeased her, then she should not come back.

And so she stayed.

In desperation she decided that she would not fail the second challenge, however foreordained; when Czcibor took it upon himself to have her sort out mustard seeds from gold, she would do so in the allotted time, and thus have done with it. —or at least, she would allow herself to pretend that this was a thing that she could do.

As she pondered her approach to this, a brightly-dressed Yurii found her— sent word to her via a servant and met her in one of Czcibor's gardens.

"Yura, Yura," she said. Then she grinned. "Nice suit."

"Please do not speak of it," he said. "I feel like a hydrangea. But they might not have taken a message to you if I'd been in shirt and collar."

"Thank you for coming," she said.

"It is no problem." He smiled whitely at her. "Little Evgraf said that you had need of me."

"Oh?" she said. "Oh!"

"Oh?"

"How clever of me," she said. "I'll send for you tonight."

His forehead wrinkled slightly, but he did not comment.

"If there were a barrel of mustard seed and gold," she said, "do you think that you could whistle the mustard seeds away?"

"Of course," he said. He buffed his fingers on his coat. "It would be the work of a moment."

"Then," she said. "Could you teach me?"

He tilted his head.

She flushed slightly, and added an amendment: "In, let's say, the course of this visit?"

"You want me," he said, "to teach you the skills I acquired by miraculous fortune and painstakingly refined over a lifetime of study and practice— today."

"Well, not *all* of them," Valentina said. "I only need mustard."

"Only need—" He sputtered a laugh.

"I am sorry to ask it."

"Valentina," he said. "Valentina. You do not need to apologize for asking me anything. But— this pains me deep in my belly. *Today?*"

"It can go to tomorrow," she said. "I suppose."

"I cannot teach you," he said, definitively. "But—"

He leaned over. He kissed her on the forehead. He left a yellow mark there that glowed before it faded away.

"I will tell the mustard to listen to you," he said. "I do not know how *well* it will listen, but it will listen."

"Thank you," she said.

"If you practice hard," he said, "and make me proud, then one day, it will listen well."

AT DINNER THAT NIGHT she slipped again.

"Magic, I think," Czcibor said, "can allow you to do many things, but it is never to your good."

"Oh?" Czeslaus said.

"It is a trend," Czcibor said. "The mightier a magician's powers, the less successful they are in life."

Valentina's temper flickered like a campfire at the bottom of a well.

She buttered her bread. She put salt on her vegetables. She shivered slightly. It was cold.

"You are still upset," Czeslaus said, to Czcibor.

Said Czcibor: "I am not."

"You *are*," Czeslaus said, and he was grinning. "You don't even *need* gold, father."

"Pardon?" Valentina said.

"Ah," Czeslaus said.

"Czeslaus," Czcibor warned.

"... it is nothing," Czeslaus said, and sighed.

Valentina had not meant to say anything at all—the question had simply come to her lips, and Czcibor had been moving his head, about to look in her direction, and she had made the split-second decision that it was better to go ahead and say it than to try returning her face to full neutrality in time. But now that she'd said something, she was stuck; she was a part of the conversation, and it was a conversation where every other participant had entirely stalled out. Her mouth shaped several possible starts to several different sentences before settling on, "How can you possibly say that magic is never to your good? Isn't any skill that a person learns—magic, horse-riding, doing sums—a positive accomplishment?"

"Ah," Czcibor said. "But magic is different. It is a defiance of the order of things. It is fundamentally a divergence from what humans, as reasoning animals, ought to do."

"Superstition," Valentina said, warming to the argument. "I cannot believe that I am saying this to a vampire, but that is superstitious nonsense."

"I met a man in town today," Czcibor said, "who was begging on the streets. 'Why do you beg?' I asked him. 'I was done out of work,' he said. 'But watch! And I will show you wonders for a coin.' He made his shadow a fox's shadow on the wall; it danced and played; and his voice was as the wind in the forest's.

"A salutary lesson, I thought. Here was a man who had developed a great and pointless talent, and in the end he would starve, if he was not first eaten, on the streets for it."

Valentina frowned at him. "Did you give him a coin?"

"Who was I to quarrel with the exigent demands of fate?"

"See," Valentina said, "this is where I differ from you; the man's fault was not in developing a useless talent, but in his isolation from other people. And the fault of your Night London is that it allows it. Who was there to tell him of a better path, or put those powers of his to proper use?"

"... and what exactly are you thinking that would *be?*"

Valentina frowned in thought. "... in the tales, he would doubtless need to sneak into some giant's house to rescue some treasure or learn some secret. The giant would catch sight of his shadow—but ah! It's just a fox's shadow! Or hear something in the corner but, ah! It is just the wind!"

"A situation rarely applicable today."

"Storytelling for children, perhaps."

"A product with a limited market, my little bird."

Valentina looked away for a moment. "Well, so."

"I once knew a magician," Czcibor said, "who offered to turn mustard seeds into gold for me. I said, 'if you can do such a thing, why ask for payment?' He spun me a tale of how the brokers of town would accept no more gold from him, how they'd taken his last batch from him, drummed him about his ears, and drove him out. He was ugly and ill-kempt, so I believed him. Isn't that amusing? He was so disreputable that I considered him worth trusting."

"Still," Valentina said, "to cheat a vampire—"

"Oh," Czcibor said. "He did not cheat me. He absolutely did not cheat me. I brought him a barrel full of mustard seed and he worked his magic upon it. I saw no change at first, but then he stirred it around and fished about in it and finally I understood.

"There was now ... some ... gold in the barrel.

"My heart sank into my shoes—it staggered me.

"I buried him with payment made in full—most likely more than the gold he'd made was worth—and as for the barrel, I still have it, as a lesson to myself in what kinds of offers I should not trust."

"I had wondered," Valentina said.

"... I'm sorry?"

"I had wondered," Valentina said. "About the barrel of mixed mustard seed and gold. Um. I had heard about it. Somewhere."

Czcibor gave the matter some thought. "I'll tell you what," he said. "Let's make a game of it. Czeslaus has been nagging at me like an old wife and I will have no more of it.

"I'll let him free to the Sosunovs if you can sift out the gold from that mustard barrel before the midnight bells."

"FIRST," VALENTINA said, when he'd had the barrel brought out, "I wanted to ask, can I appoint a hunchbacked old man of my acquaintance as my champion?"

"Ehh, ah?"

"Well," Valentina said. "You did not say I had to sift by hand. Delegation is a kind of labor too, and mutual assistance is the backbone of Fortitude's society."

"No," Czcibor said. "You can't appoint a hunchbacked old man as your champion."

"Let it be noted," Valentina said, "that you are already handicapping me. Can I spill the barrel out?"

"I won't forbid it," Czcibor said, "but the instant I find a flake of gold or a mustard seed that was lost because it rolled under the table or whatnot, any victory you may have already acquired becomes moot."

"Uh."

"I'm not good with disorderly piles of seeds," Czcibor admitted.

"Oh," Valentina said.

Finally, Valentina set out two tablecloths on which to make her piles and began picking out mustard seeds and—much more rarely—flakes of gold.

"I should clarify," Czcibor said, "that this is on the same terms as our last bargain."

"Yes?"

"I mean," he said, "that if you fail, I shall drink from you again."

Her fingers were trembling. She frowned at them. "Of course," she agreed. "That is the logical thing. I mean, that is what— I would not have anticipated any differently."

She rubbed at her face.

"I'm sorry," he said. "I didn't mean to disturb you."

"No," she said. "It needed to be said."

Her arms had folded at some point. Her hands had knotted in the fabric of the opposite sleeves. She thought that was quite unnecessary, and she said as much. "I apologize. This will only be a moment."

Her eyes were only closed for what seemed to be a moment, but in that moment she found herself drawn to her feet, her head pressed against a cool hard chest, a hand stroking her hair, a voice murmuring something soft, and she thought:

This is it. This is here.

This is how I am going to die.

Eventually, even with the monster so close, the vampire-fear receded. She snarled at herself. She clawed at him, she pushed him away. "I am not a child," she told him.

"It's all right," he said.

"It's not all right," she said. She pushed him away. After a moment, he acquiesced to being pushed. She went back to the seeds and the gold and her eyes were fever-bright. "It's not all right," she said.

They passed some time in silence.

"There is a great golden snake," she said, "that lives beyond the rooftops of Fortitude. Where they run together and become a landscape all their own and they stop having actual houses underneath them, when the gutters come together to form lakes, when the mossy tile becomes the sward, where things are not as *normal* as they are in Fortitude or even in Night London, there is a great golden snake called Typhon, after, I presume, the mythology of the Greeks. I have fought her.

"There is a Bleak Academy beyond the furthermost boundaries of the world, and therein rules a monster in the shape of a man, and I have fought him too.

"It is the Sosunov destiny to face witches, but there were not *enough* of them, do you understand? I had to *diversify* simply to have adequate enemies to fight. Czcibor, I am something *strong*."

"I would not dream of implying otherwise," he said.

"I need air," she said.

She tried to stand. She tried to turn. His hand had a delicate grip on her wrist. "You haven't finished sorting yet," he said.

She tugged at her arm a few times, then went very still and pale.

"Ah," she said.

In that moment, a sense of unreality descended upon her, and she reached not for Yurii's magic but for Magister Wan's. Her hand came down amidst the seeds and gold within the barrel. It struck her that they, like every other detail of the world, were contingent, misleading, inaccurate, and false; it struck her that to collaborate further in that pretense of forms had become *unsustainable;* that by doing so she had allowed something ugly to stir beneath those details, something *wrong*— and a judgment-fire of the incandescent void arose in her to burn the seeds and gold away.

In that moment, she could have reached for the True Thing. Perhaps she would have attained to it. But the Headmaster had made even her deepest self afraid, so she clung to the world instead; and poorly.

She took a great grey gulp of time. The world wobbled on its axis.

Her thoughts dissolved into smoke and mist. ... and things stopped making sense.

"VALENTINA," SOMEONE was saying. "Valentina."

Reluctantly the world began to come back into focus—beginning with the fact that the world had not been *in* focus.

Lines and blocks and bits of color emerged into her perception; then, became forms.

A yellow circle that hung in the sky became convoluted. It burned brighter—became a brass-caged sun—before it dwindled as she comprehended it into the lantern dangling from the roof.

Her chest was full of fog.

She looked down at her hand. "Ah," she said.

"What is this?"

"I ceased to perceive the world accurately," Valentina said. "Or, I started to perceive the world accurately. Or, perception is not a thing that is accurate or inaccurate but rather a bladed edge or a padded one, and I became the first."

He squinted at her.

"The heap of seeds and gold was made unformed," she said.

"You must not do such things," Czcibor replied.

"When I was young," Valentina said, "it was forcibly brought home to me that all the little gritty details of the world are meaningless; just ... the shadows of shifting flames. It is actually rather appalling how little impression that has made on me, how hard it is to remember it, how hard it is to implement it as a practical event. It is like ... if one were dreaming, and knew that it was a dream, but somehow one could not *stop*."

"You must not do such things," Czcibor said again; a sick horror was hiding deep beneath his words.

"All right," Valentina said.

She mussed the pile with her hand until the gelatinous uncertain mush of it began to specify down into seeds and flakes of gold again. She began to pick the seeds out. She gave a rictus grin to see how deep into the barrel her momentary lapse had burned.

"It is impossible," Czcibor said, eventually rallying, "of course, to distinguish between a magic that recognizes a true state of affairs, or the underpinnings of the true state of affairs, and a magic that alters things by imposing some other energy or force."

"That's so," Valentina agreed.

"So," Czcibor said, "I mean, however it might *look* when you do that, it's not that a mustard seed could *just as easily* be nothing at all, or gold."

"It is a word," Valentina said, abstractedly. "'Mustard.' We take that word, and it pinches off a section of the shapeless ever-changing formless sea of things, and then it is mustard. At that point the cycle of transformations that may be applied to it are only those that are legitimate for mustard. If something illegitimate happens then it was never mustard after all. —I apologize, mister Fidatof."

"Czcibor."

"I apologize," Valentina said again. "I am in a distracted state. I have almost grasped something, but the more I put it into words, the further it goes from truth, rather than the closer."

"There could be a fundamental essence of mustardness," Czcibor said. "Or, let me say, of gold. A true nature of gold, that manifests itself in these pieces."

"The difficulty is that anything we name can be mistaken," Valentina said. "The true nature of gold arises, it bursts through into the world of forms, it manifests in this:"

Triumphantly, she held up a mustard seed.

"—ah," she said, after a moment. She was lying. "I meant to pick up gold."

"This sophistry cannot change the fundamental reality of things," he said.

After a moment, she looked down, and her eyes seemed to take in the world at last, and to be unhappy that they were doing so. "Perhaps not," she agreed. "Perhaps we simply play out changes with the force of our perceptions."

"You seem to be agreeing," he said. "But I did not understand what you had said."

"If the eyes have a force in them," Valentina said. "If *to see* were to be spoken of as *to push* or *to ignite*. And not just the eyes, of course, but most of us are visual creatures. If there were something within the eye that *went out*, then there would be no need to imagine that *any* of this magic reflected deeper truths. A magician who confused gold and seeds could burn the reality into confusion. The dream of Magister Wan, the vision he had of a void that was lively in its emptiness—the beauty that I have only rarely touched on seeing—that too could be a thing that is created and not seen, a force of, in practical terms, destruction, emitted from the eyes. That would allow the naïve position on the world to retain its prominence even when the enlightened can work miracles."

She pulled her wrist from his loosened grasp, sifted her hands through the barrel. "Perhaps," she said, "behind the reality that we see there is a puppet stage, where things are held up in their place by wires. And the eye does not need to exert much pressure at all to make things fall apart, you see. It merely needs to tug upon the wires.

"It would explain the most pressing thing; why is it so hard to see things correctly? The truth is so *beautiful*. But beauty is much more effortful to make than it is to find."

"Let us find a less disturbing topic," he suggested.

"Mm."

"You could tell me of your childhood."

"I do not want you tromping on the grave of the girl I was," Valentina said.

"Unnecessarily morbid."

"But I will tell you of long walks," she said. "Because after the witch, I did not want to be cooped up in the Sosunov manor, I would spend a great deal of time visiting the other neighborhoods of Fortitude. I—"

"I'm sorry," he interrupted. "Ah. The witch?"

"There was a witch," Valentina summarized.

"Yes," he said. "I gathered."

"At the time," Valentina said, "she was a witch of putting people to sleep. She kept me locked up, like you keep me locked up. She grew to love me, so I cut her throat."

Ever so slightly, he drew back. An eyebrow raised.

"I intend no specific moral," Valentina said. "It is simply what happened. It didn't even kill her, as it eventually turned out; she just kept on bleeding, slower and slower, until one day I took her down and sold her to a shop; then, apparently, after a decade or two, she got better."

"Sounds disturbing," Czcibor said.

Valentina bared her teeth. "She stays well away from me," she said. "And does not trouble the dreams of anyone in Fortitude, not while I remain alive there to defend it. She came by once to taunt me, to tell me that I was horrible and ugly and would never recover my sense of self from the despair that had taken me, and I nearly managed to kill her all over again ... so that ended that particular relationship for good."

"Mmm," he said. "That ... is always the way of it, isn't it, with witches?"

"Er?"

"They tell you that you are horrible and ugly," he explained. "But— you should listen when I tell you that you are beautiful, instead."

"In the mouths of monsters," Valentina said, "the two phrases are essentially the same."

Czcibor's lips tightened.

"I will tell you of long walks," Valentina resumed, "and catching sandhoppers in the summer—for soup, you see. And endless hours with the sword."

"Mmm," he said. "I had noticed."

"I was held together by it, at first," Valentina said. She grimaced, briefly. "Sometimes I think I still am. I would become someone who would be strong in this world. I would become someone capable of fighting my way out from under the thumb of a heron-witch and a thousand birds, or whatever else would come my way. Ironically, in the end, I am better-known for what my enemies have done to me."

A few flakes of gold went in that pile. A few handfuls of seed into that one. "You'll have to give me more than that," he said.

"'Valentina is immortal,' they say. 'The Bleak Academy will not take her.'

"Or 'Such great strength she has in dreams!'

"Because the hag-rider witch could not bear the curse the Headmaster lay on me, you see. I let her see my dream of it and she quailed. And then that was *two* major witches I had defeated in my lifetime, even though one of the two had practically destroyed herself. That is a pretty good rate, you understand, but even so."

"You are extremely casual in talking about these things," Czcibor said.

Valentina's eyes shadowed. She was silent for a long time. Eventually she said, "I think that one day I will no longer spend quite so much time angry at the Headmaster of the Bleak Academy. I think that one day the wound he's done to me will not just have healed but will not come readily to mind. I think that will be better. I think that will be a kind of adulthood that I am failing in. And there, you see? Fifty-two years old, and so stuck in time that I worry about adulthood.

"... right now the wound is raw, and all I have to fight it with is that he may be the Headmaster of the Bleak Academy, and *she* may be the witch of the eyes that see, and *you* may be a vampire and strong and quick and terrible, but *I* am Valentina Grigorievna Sosunova, and none of you are good enough to wash my feet."

He tilted his head to one side. "Interesting," he said. "I am having trouble parsing it all out, but do I take it that vampirism is considered juvenile?"

"That was not my meaning," she said, "but in fairness …"

"In fairness?"

"Well," she said, "it is you who have said it, and not I."

"It is not as if I were a child making fangs from my fingers on the street," he said.

"Children don't do that," Valentina said.

"Well, if they did," Czcibor said, "then it would not erase their difference from myself. And besides, they must do that. It is logical."

"Logical?"

"What else would they pretend to be?"

"Jack Sheppard?" Valentina said. "Kings and queens? *I* always pretended to be Miruna Sosunova and attempted to see through the back of my eyes like the front of them, which is harder in practice than you might suspect."

"There's nothing to see in there," he said.

"Well, the brain," she said, uncertainly.

"… I do not think it is much to look at," he said. "Particularly in the dark."

"Possibly it's alight with the subtle movements of my spirit."

"That makes as much sense as anything," he agreed, reluctantly. "So Miruna did that, then?"

"She was a great woman," Valentina said. "She guards us still."

"Then if I," Czcibor said, and he took hold of her wrist again. "And I …" He turned it and lifted it to his mouth, and looked a question at her.

"Would she spiritually intervene to save me?"

"Yes," he agreed.

"I think you might regret sacrificing the pleasant tone our

conversation had taken," Valentina said. "But no. I would not bet on her intervention."

He made a face, then released her arm. "An experiment," he said. "Nothing more."

"Are you all like this?" Valentina said.

"All what?" he said.

"Vampires."

He shrugged. "Well, you *are* food."

"How terrifying," she said. Her fingers toyed with the seeds but did not take any; she withdrew her hands. "That is what the wolves and the lions would have said, of course."

"Of course," he agreed.

"You agree?"

"We are not superior *because* we are your predators," he said. "It is merely the poor fortune of humanity that we should happen to be both."

"I am aghast at your vanity."

"Are you?"

"Well," Valentina said, "not really; I had already known about it."

"Hmph," he said, but with amusement.

"I see no real superiority at all," Valentina said. "You are faster and stronger, yes, but we do not let our athletes rule over us and drink our blood, even if they'd decided that they wanted to. You can turn into animals, but if anything that's taking you even lower down."

"Death is the cross all living creatures bear," he said, simply. "We have transcended it."

She did not respond to that. She simply considered for a while. When she spoke, it was to ask him, "What were you like, in life?"

"Perhaps I had no life," he said. "Perhaps I sprang up newborn from the void."

"Arising from a corpse by means of spontaneous generation, like a maggot?"

"I would not have used such an unflattering comparison," he said.

"Apologies," Valentina said. "Arising from a corpse by means of spontaneous generation, like a cheese wheel?"

A snort of laughter burst from him. "Do they do that?"

"People die," Valentina said. "Cheese arises. Perhaps there is some connection. To keep an open, questioning mind—that, is science."

"In that case," he said, "it was just like that."

"And Czeslaus," she said. "Was born from the cast-off curd?"

"Ah," he said. "That. I expect that I did have a life before vampirism, then."

"Indeed."

"It is no longer relevant to me," he said.

"You are afraid of diminishing your *gravitas*."

"Perhaps."

"I will discover you were a sheep-farmer," Valentina said. "And then, whenever you are looming ominously over me, I will make a panicked *baa-aa*, and the mood will be lost."

He laughed. He shook his head.

"A tanner, then," she said. "Terribly smelly. Not that it isn't honest work."

"I was born well," he said. "And ended poorly, and through no fault of my own. Is that enough for you? Should I spit on an effigy of the tsar for your entertainment? I was born well, and ended poorly, and my Kasieńka preceded me into the ground. And there I was, dead and rotten, with the worms all through my eyes, but what of Czeslaus? He could barely survive *with* me; without me, at his age? There was no hope. So I returned."

"As easy as that?"

"In my country," he said. "In my country, we often say, a child is born already on the road to be a vampire. It is not always spotted, but the signs are there if you look for them. In my country, it is understood that if I rose, as I did, then I must have been—I was Czcibor the vampire, already. But I did not know this thing.

"Perhaps I was an ordinary man, and a dog leapt across my corpse.

"Perhaps I was touched by an evil spirit.

"But— for me, it was that Czeslaus needed me. So I turned my back on the afterlife that waited for me. I set my sights on the world and trudged back to my grave."

"If— if that is so—"

"Yes?"

"Is that how you propose to make Czeslaus a vampire?" she said. "Get a bunch of dogs to jump over his dead body?"

"Pfft," he said. "No."

"Then?"

"You are wondering," he said, "whether I could follow through on my offer of immortality?"

"It's more that, as bad as it is to plan to kill your son and raise him up again as a vampire, it's a whole different order of bad to plan to kill him and hope for the best."

"I have not made a vampire, before," Czcibor said. "I confess it. But do not be afraid; if all else fails, I will ask Mayor Celdinar for a favor, and he will manipulate the forces of life and death on my behalf."

"That does not fall under his remit," she said, sternly, but he just smirked.

She sifted through the seeds. She frowned.

"Did your fortunes improve?" she asked. "I mean, as a vampire?"

"Oh, marvelously," he said. "I feared that I would become a hunted animal, but instead I found myself catapulted into the company of the great. My estates, which had been sold, returned; my name, on every invitation list; my every need provided with a casual wave of Niemierz' hand. To be stalked by Churchmen, to lurk in shadows, to be staked into one's grave with wood or metal, to have one's head cut off and buried beneath the buttocks, these were the fates reserved for *things* that came back that wore the shape of men—

"Not for the likes of I.

"After a life that had gone so wrong so fast, suddenly everything was bright! Except, of course, the sun."

"Ironic," she said.

"I did not want to live in fear," he said. He did not catch the expression on her face. "The sun frightened me, and I did not wish to live in fear. So I came here, where I would be, for all practical purposes, invincible. I am not sure even the others can effectively harm me, here; perhaps if they could keep my head separated from my body long enough to carry it out into a land where there is a sun, but that's trickier to do than to say."

"... I think you're overconfident," Valentina said.

"Oh?"

She thought for a moment. "If you could spit lions out of your neck, then we would not call you a vampire. But if a prince of the demon-folk could do that, we would still just call him one of the demon-folk."

"I see."

"So there are some," she said, "capable of tearing you apart quite easily, with their hands. And some who most likely could do it just by looking at you. Or licking your shadow. Or smelling somewhere you've been."

"... that seems alarmist," he said.

"Oh?"

"Well," he said. "They haven't been *doing* that kind of thing, have they?"

"They've bought into the lie, I assume," Valentina said. "They've been told, Progress! Progress will make everything better! Progress will bring you more wealth and wonders than you've ever had before. Stay in your tent? Why, don't be ridiculous! The area's getting developed! Come lurk in this great new cathedral that the Mayor built just for you. A crab in every pot and a pot on every crab!"

He raised an eyebrow.

"... fine," Valentina said. "I have absolutely no idea why they've let you get away with burying their home under your Night London monstrosity. But you can't just *assume* it'll last for forever."

"Or possibly there are no such creatures," he said, "and the actual demon-folk are more like—humans with fox ears on their heads. Or barrels full of nails that roll around on their own."

"Hmm," Valentina said neutrally.

"I am not going to live in fear of my shadow being licked by a demon," he said.

"Oh, dear," she said. "I'm sorry. I didn't mean to scare you."

"I'm not," he said.

"You're a *vampire*," she said. "Buck *up*."

"I am entirely bucked up," he said. "I am so bucked up I am practically glowing."

"Really?" She looked up in interest, then scowled and looked down again.

"It is a metaphor," he said. Peevishly, he threw some gold scraps into her pile of mustard seeds.

"That's not going to work this time," she told him.

"It's not?"

"Any gold that you place in the pile of mustard seeds is gold that you recognize as mustard," she said. "You cannot then turn around and assert its goldenness later; if you could do that, you could theoretically do so *after* the task was complete, in which case the task is *ipso facto* pointless."

"The point of the task," he said, "has always been to see if you could do it, and not to have it done."

"Really."

"Truly," he said.

"I'm tired," she said, "and the answer to your question is, easily, if you let me call my hunchback in."

"Is every man who can commission poetry a poet?"

She sighed. She looked down at the barrel. "Perhaps the answer is 'no.'"

"Perhaps."

"You will let me stand up this time," she said. "My legs are stiffening. And I really do need air."

"Mmm," he said.

She stood. She paced. She stretched. She looked at the door, and he nodded. She went outside. She breathed in the night.

That was when the miracle occurred.

Her eye fell upon a little white flower, growing among the walkway stones.

A smile bloomed, then widened.

She went back in. She went back downstairs. She said, "I am refreshed."

"That is well," he said.

"I am so totally refreshed," she said, "that I bet I can *talk* the mustard seeds sorted. Like, mustard seeds! Get you in the ground!"

"Ah—" he said.

There was no response.

She frowned slightly. She squinted at the seeds. "No, seriously," she said. She took in a deep breath. She held it beneath the roof of her mouth. She exhaled. "Mustard seeds," she said again. "Get you in the ground."

"I don't think—" he started, but then it began.

"Mustard seeds!" she cried. **"Get you in the ground!"**

And the first of them lifted from the barrel and began to roll towards the stairs.

Czcibor's eyes widened.

The seeds marched away as if ants were carrying them: one by one, weaving and wobbly, and slow.

"What is left," she said, slumping into her chair, "will be the gold."

"I can't allow this," he said.

"I thought you might say that," Valentina said. "That is why I did not try talking to the mustard seeds earlier. But consider: surely your son can only benefit from a wife silver-tongued enough to talk mustard seeds into motion."

"Kitten ..." he protested.

"It is not as if he were a werewolf," she said, speaking over him, and then falling silent.

He scratched an eyebrow. "Valentina," he said. "You can't just ... did you meet a mysterious mustard magician outside? Did you ... what, bargain your firstborn child to him?"

"You have a peculiar opinion of mustard magicians," Valentina said.

"Accurate to my experience," he said.

"Well, no," Valentina said. "I met no one upon the patio. I took in the night air. I picked a flower. It is possible that some time in the past a mustard magician may have kissed me on the forehead to facilitate this sort of eventuality but it was not specifically just now. Are you going to start interfering with the process or can I take a nap while the sorting completes?"

He eyed the movement. "They are moving slowly," he said.

"I should have started immediately," Valentina admitted. "I was distracted by supernatural fear and then by our conversation. How I will wail and gnash my teeth and pull my hair if I fall seven seeds short or something because of that."

"It is not supernatural fear," he said.

"It is definitely supernatural fear," she said.

"It is merely the lesser order recognizing the higher."

"I would not dream of embarrassing you by contradicting you in front of all this mustard."

"You may go ahead and sleep," he said.

"You will behave yourself?"

"I will consider it," he said.

She made the mistake of thinking forward to his next drink from her; a giant's fist seemed to be squeezing the lungs within her chest, and her face paled. But she nodded, and she lay her head on her folded arms, and she tried to sleep.

When she woke, it was to a hazy, frightened awareness. Someone was manhandling her. Her arm and head were held as if by iron bands and there was *danger*.

"Midnight," he said. She jerked her arms. She kicked. She slammed her head backwards, uselessly, into his chest. "Midnight, and a few remain."

He drank.

"O ANGEL OF GOD," she whispered, "o holy guardian, safeguard my life in the fear of Christ the God, set my mind on the right path, and strengthen my soul— o holy angel, leave me not alone, leave me not alone, nor depart from me, strengthen this miserable and feeble hand—"

It had ended.

She took a deep and shuddering breath. "Forgive me everything whereinsoever I have offended thee, and—"

He tapped her gently under the chin. "It's all right," he said. "I'm done."

She did not stop; but the whispers grew softer, and softer still.

There was a time of silence.

A wince of pain.

A rictus smile, and then a frown.

"This is very unpleasant," she said. Her eyes focused on him. Eventually. "Do you know that it is very unpleasant?"

"Considering the stakes," he said, "I find that only fair."

Her breath hitched for a moment; but she took a tighter grip upon herself, inside her, and it steadied. "That's true," she agreed. "You are wagering your son. Even with everything I am probably the one with the better of the bargain. Should— should we go again?"

"We could go again," he agreed. He smiled. "You could destroy Earth's sun."

"Be nice," she protested.

"Mmm," he said. "But let us be fairer, then. My son is smitten, I think. So if I win again, you will even the bargain. You will come into *my* house."

"—it is unfair to ask when you have just woken and hurt me," she said. "But fine."

"I expect, then," he said, "that destroying Earth's sun is too much to ask of you."

"Uh. … I must still insist upon a veto in the gamble."

He tilted his head to one side. "Perhaps—then, there are seven stones in the garden pond. They are not *too* heavy; it is nothing for *me* to move them about. If you can dredge them up with your own strength— let us say, before the day-lamp lights—then he shall be a Sosunov."

Her limbs were sick and heavy, still, but an eerie thrill flashed inside her then, and it woke a smile.

A deep, slow breath:

"You could not know it," she said, and savored the words as they rolled within her mouth, "but I am unable to breathe beneath the water. You must choose some other challenge."

He frowned at her. "Surely you don't think that you're too weak and frail."

"… don't be crude."

"Too obvious?" he said.

"Too obvious."

"I will tell you a secret," he admitted, slowly. "Anything that I choose will be unfair. There may one day come a woman who can bring me low, but she would be a woman who would *succeed* in crossing Night London with a thread, or sifting gold from mustard seed. You cannot overcome me, and therefore I may do with you as I like; accept the challenge and feel glad that I am giving you even this narrow sliver of a chance."

"It is hardly 'bringing you low' to make you a father-in-law," Valentina said. "Oh no, blini at Maslenitsa. I am unable to breathe under the water. You must choose some other challenge."

"... bleh," Czcibor said, and rolled his eyes. "Can you fish a grain of rice from a vat of gruel with a rod and a hookless fishing line?"

"I could turn out to know rice magic," she said.

"Apologies," he said. "I must ask you to do it without magic."

"I don't know rice magic."

"The condition remains."

"I am hurting, Czcibor," she said. "Don't play this stupid game with me. You know quite well that I am unable to see through gruel."

"... I do know this," he admitted.

"Oh gracious," she said. "You didn't know."

"I knew," he emphasized.

"This is extremely embarrassing for the entire Fidatof family."

"You don't have to be able to see through the gruel," he said. "You can feel around with the fishing line."

"Impossible," she smiled. "You must try again."

"Then find me the flower whose nectar is the water of life," he snarled, "before the hour is out; and he shall be a Sosunov."

"Here," she said, and took the little white flower down from above her ear.

"... what?"

"Here."

"... you can't," he said. "You can't just ... I mean, why ... it ... it's not, it can't be. You're joking."

She shook her head.

"I have no reason to believe that that is the flower whose nectar is the water of life," he said convulsively, "and that was the last—"

"You may test it out," she interrupted, and flicked its nectar in his face; and Czcibor Fidatof was a vampire no more.

ONCE UPON A TIME, but not so very long ago, a vampire named Czcibor Fidatof received a prophecy, but the seeress who'd been its source had the final laugh; for it was full of things that Valentina Sosunova *could* have done, but few enough she *did*.

And as for Czcibor—

As the nectar struck him, he rose again to life; his heart began to beat, his lungs began to breathe; and he did not become a vampire again, but foreswore his sins and became a priest.

... and perhaps that was the work of a restarted heart or a recovered soul; perhaps it was because some wicked vampiric power had outgassed from him; but privately Valentina thought it was a stain of purity, on and through him, that the nectar'd made.

YEARS DRIFTED by. Valentina and Czeslaus married. They had a son, and a daughter, and eventually a grandson.

She began to get a little bit tired of eternal youth.

It wasn't that she would have traded places with the other eighty-somethings that she knew, at least, not exactly—but she was beginning to feel more than a little awkward about looking younger than her son and her daughter, more than a little awkward about not fitting in with any of her peers, more than a little awkward about how she looked next to her husband Czeslaus.

More importantly, she was beginning to feel a nameless yearning to … *move on*.

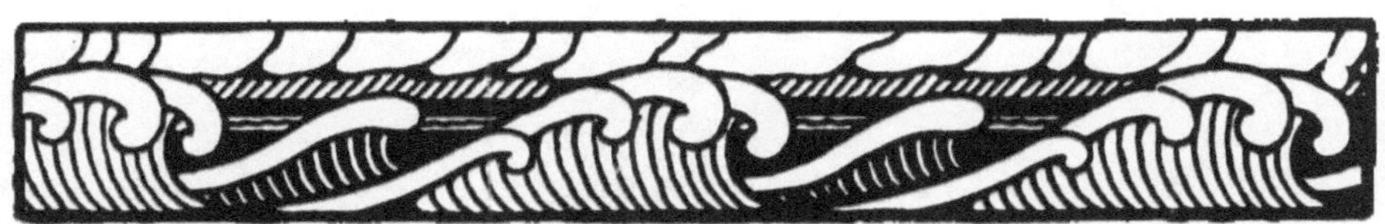

CHAPTER FIVE
SVETLANA AND THE SEAL'S SKIN

There is a place in Fortitude that will always welcome you. It smells of cooking. It's full of the sounds of family. It's a place of easy comfort, of talking over tea or soda, beer or wine.

This is something elemental in the place. This is in its bones.

You don't necessarily know where that place is. You may never have been there. You may never even have been to Fortitude at all—but that just means that you haven't found it yet.

Even when it tries its hardest to be unwelcoming; even at its stoniest:

In Fortitude, if you are willing, you will eventually find your home.

—from *Town and Environs,*

by Valerie Shaw

ET'S TELL the story of Svetlana Bogdanovna Uizerspun and the seal's skin!

It's hard to say exactly when it started. Probably, it was with Valentina; with Valentina, in her eighty-second year; with Valentina, on that particular night when a street-cleaner from Night London came to speak with her in confidence.

"Mother Valentina," he said.[16] "There are plans on the table to annex Fortitude."

Valentina's eyes narrowed.

"It's like this," he said. "Night London's practically built, and that's that distraction done; and getting enough people in to make the vampires happy is going pretty slow; and my cousin, who works in Mayor Celdinar's house, said, he heard one of the guests talking about it. That pretty soon they're thinking of just divvying this place up."

"I see," she said.

When he had gone, Valentina slipped into her bedroom. She kissed the forehead of her sleeping husband. She sat on the bedside for a while. Later, she would do the same in the room of her grandson Kallinik.

A great burden seemed to settle on her shoulders.

"Well," she said, "I'll just have to steal it first, won't I?"

AT THE home of Edith Draisey, she lay out her proposal.

"You'll be a vampire now," she said.

"Pardon?"

---

16 Though, she was not his mother.

"There's no way that we can keep them at bay if we're humans," Valentina said. "Even if we can kill some of them, even if we could kill *enough* of them to call it a victory, there's nothing we could do that would make them *respect* that threat. They'd just escalate and keep escalating until we had a bloodbath. But if you're a vampire who came back from the dead with the power to make clockwork creatures— well, you wouldn't even have to show your face, would you? Your creations could do it on your behalf."

"I promised myself not to do that any more," Edith said.

"And?"

"... I have continued to do that," Edith admitted.

"I figure we need about twelve," Valentina said. "Twelve people to say that we're vampires, and issue a declaration saying, basically, 'stay out.'"

"Won't they still take offense to that?"

"Well," Valentina said, "once we give them a way to save face while respecting us, killing a few becomes a lot more productive."

Edith thought about this. "I am willing," she said.

To Red Ivan's Valentina went, to make the same proposal; and to Yurii Golubev's grave—though, he did not rise, nor did she ask him to. She just talked for a while. And to eleven others (since two refused); and to the constabulary, and to Fortitude's four elected officials.

Thus was born the Fortitude Regional Council.

They marked their territories. They showed themselves and performed supernatural feats—to the puzzlement rather than the awe, for the most part, of the citizenry.

Then they issued their first proclamation (and for many years, their only proclamation):

That Fortitude was *their* territory now, they had claimed it; that the vampires of Night London were forbidden Fortitude blood; nor might they stay in Fortitude long enough to see the night-lamp lighted twice.

SVETLANA DID NOT at first hear of the proclamation, nor would she have guessed that it applied to her, but it did; not long after the formation of the Council she woke to find a copy of it nailed to her door.

"It's all right," Maksim told her. "You can go to Night London. You can stay with Archibald. He'll be happy to see you."

"I met him *once*," Svetlana said.

"He's a Witherspoon," Maksim replied.

So grudgingly Svetlana abandoned her home. She hesitated a long time under the eaves, but finally, fearfully, left.

Five years passed.

VALENTINA TURNED eighty-seven.

That was a year when the marlin were plentiful, and the blackberries unusually sweet; when the worst storm in six years hit in the summer; and when Czeslaus Sosunov passed away in his sleep. That was the year Valentina slew her fourth and her fifth vampire—both breakers of Fortitude's law.

They were still faster than she was—much faster. They were still stronger—ever so much stronger. But as she approached her ninetieth year her ability with Magister Wan's magic had reached competence. As terrifying as the vampires of Night London were, she was something more terrifying; they dissolved at her touch like they were wet paper dolls.

For another six months she stayed in the Sosunov compound; then, restless, she moved out to live by the shore. There she practiced swordsmanship, ate fresh fish and local snails, experimented with Magister Wan's magic, and practiced—for Yurii's memory and now for Czeslaus'—ordering mustard seeds to do stuff.

Three more years slipped by.

ARCHIBALD WITHERSPOON was the eleventh vampire to test Fortitude's defenses. He died; and with him dead, Svetlana lost her only real ally in Night London. In his absence, Svetlana's elder "sisters," Nicoleta and Tatiana Witherspoon, treated her abominably. They poked fun at her housekeeping skills, piled impossible tasks upon her, threatened to dissect her bat Maksim, and ultimately sent her back into Fortitude to die as Archibald had:

"A few months here is all very well," Tatiana told her. "But you can't stay in Archibald's old house forever. You must go to Fortitude and claim a new dominion—somewhere down by Ceiba Quay."

"... that region is already claimed."

"The matter is suspect," Tatiana explained. "A person cannot call themselves a vampire just because they come back from the dead, you know. One must also participate in society."

Svetlana lowered her head. "As you say."

A day and night whirled past. Clouds moved through the sky. Svetlana took a last longing look around her apartment and sanctuary. Then, reluctantly, she wrapped her cloak and hood around her and stepped out into the wider world.

She walked into Fortitude.

Soon a metal bird flew down to meet her. It landed on a low wall. It opened its beak and a wax cylinder that was set into its back spun and a recorded voice played: "This territory is claimed by the Lady in White; you may pass through, but you may not feed and you may not stay."

She paused to admire the bird. "What excellent workmanship," she said.

The bird fluttered away.

Here and there as she walked she saw a chalked caricature on the walls that she took to be the symbol of the Lady in White.

The humans mostly ignored her or, if her path took her close to them, drew away from her, but one girl selling grilled fish stopped to give her an insolent look. "Get gone, you," she said, and waved Svetlana away. "Or you'll die like the rest."

Svetlana shrank back. She muttered, "I don't have a choice." She made a wide circle around the girl as she went.

It wasn't so much the girl's specific words or actions that intimidated her as someone overtly noticing her presence at all.

She thought she saw a metal creature—a rat, perhaps?—following her along the roofs.

The air smelled of storms.

"I have no intention," she said, to the world at large, "of lingering here."

She hurried on.

At Pike and Third, the territory changed. She no longer heard the occasional clink or clatter from the metal creature that had been following her. The intermittent chalk effigies on the walls gave way to rare scrawls of red paint in the rough shape of an eye.

It was well past the day lamp, now, and Fortitude had come to life. There were the sounds of that life all around her—of people going about the business of the town.

In the broad and open space where Pike crossed communal ground, she met Red Ivan.

It was farcical. She knew that the instant she saw him. There was no way this man, with his authoritative air, his red costume, and his canines filed into points could be anything other than the "Red Ivan" who had signed his name to the Regional Council's declaration—but ...

"You aren't even dead," she said.

"I'm well-preserved."

"I can *hear* your *heartbeat*."

"Ah," he said. He held up a finger. He concentrated. His heartbeat stopped. "That was a gaffe. My apologies. Only, why am *I* justifying *myself* to *you?*"

Nerves and shame overcame her surprise and she settled into a mood of subdued truculence. "I am merely passing through."

"You are passing through," he said, "but in the direction of the territory of the one I serve."

She grasped onto this information like a lifeline: "There is a head of your Council? A ... coven leader, or a king?"

"Queen, more like," he said.

"Then I am passing through to speak to her," Svetlana said. "Even if my business is unworthy of her time, it is for her to kill me for it, not you."

He frowned at her. Then he stepped aside, with a gracious sweep of his arm. His heartbeat started up again. "You would be better served if you staked yourself, dismembered yourself, and buried yourself with your head beneath your buttocks, than to annoy *that* one. She does not kill your kind cleanly. But—be my guest."

She scurried past him, with a long sidelong glance.

In time the settlement grew less dense. She stopped seeing the red sigils, and was not certain what replaced them—the houses were too scattered for any such mark to be a reliable warning. Instead, what she felt was a building sense of oppression, as if the air were an ever-heavier smoke weighing down on her shoulders. At first she thought it was nerves alone, but eventually she concluded that even *she* could not manufacture this feeling out of nothingness; it was a knowledge, an intuition given to her by magic or by instinct, that "a greater predator rules here."

She was practically stumbling from the weight of it when she topped a little rise and Ceiba Quay was at last in sight.

A black ship was sailing in—its body black, its sails black—and the gas lights of the quay were coming on to greet it. It was an eerie sight, and she froze trembling before it, but she was given little time for fear.

There was a woman in the shadows of the porch of the building opposite where she stood:

"You're not welcome here," Valentina Grigorievna Sosunova said.

It startled her. "Miss Sosunova?"

"Indeed."

"We've met," Svetlana said. "You stabbed that Pjatvchet."

"Huh," Valentina said. She looked Svetlana up and down. "May have done. I've stabbed a lot of things. You'll still have to go."

"If—"

Here Svetlana licked her lips nervously.

"If the creature that lives here does not treat you well, then I will assist you."

Valentina snorted. Then, after a moment to choose her words, she said, "We are quite satisfied with the monsters we have."

"I have no choice," Svetlana said softly. "I have been sent here by my family; I must make my home here or perish."

Valentina blew out her cheeks. She thought about this. "Well, I don't really mind if you perish," she said. "But that sounds a little unfair."

"I appreciate the thought," Svetlana said.

Valentina tilted her head to one side. She grinned; and in the instant that she saw that grin, Svetlana understood that *here* was the predator that she'd sensed. "Let's make a game of it," Valentina said "I'll let you stay with me for a few days, and if you can do some simple tasks for me, I'll see if we can work something out. If you can't, then I'll stake you, burn your body, and toss the ashes out over the lake."

From somewhere Svetlana dug up the strength to straighten her spine. "I might not be so easy to kill as all of that."

Valentina considered. "Then I'll kill you the other way, but it makes a terrible threat."

"What?"

"See," Valentina said, "your existence as a special case—as something with a perspective, and details, and history, and its own independent life—is a masquerade that I need not participate in. I need not play the game of ... ah, whoever you are?"

"Svetlana Witherspoon."

"I need not play the game of Svetlana Witherspoon," Valentina said, "any longer than I'd like. And *that,* my dear, makes killing you easy."

She turned to leave, and Svetlana followed behind her for a while in silence.

"But it doesn't make a very good threat, does it?" Valentina said. "So I use staking and burning instead."

She led Svetlana to a hut by the beaches of Fortitude, up in the north where the water turns brackish, and not all that far from Ceiba Quay. The scent of a greater predator was so heavy there that Svetlana could barely move from it.

Valentina shoved the door open with one foot and led her inside.

"I am no longer the housekeeper I once was," Valentina said, pushing a shovel out of the way to clatter against a crude metal sink. "It doesn't seem to matter any longer. Hardly anything does."

"I'm sorry," Svetlana said.

"There is a cellar," Valentina said. She kicked aside a rug and gestured grandly to the trapdoor. "It has my snail farm and my pickling supplies. You will stay out of it."

"Of course."

"Do you pickle snails?" Valentina said.

"...never in my life," Svetlana said.

"There's a tradition," Valentina said. "Around sixty years old or so you're supposed to start liking pickled snails. Obviously it's not a *binding* tradition. Now I am ninety years old and my husband is in the ground and my son and my daughter have children of their own and I still can't make a pickled snail worth eating. But the regular snails are quite nice with butter."

"Oh."

"Not that you'd appreciate such a thing," Valentina said. "You are a Philistine. A blood-drinker. You cannot appreciate *either* form of culinary magnificence. So you are to stay out. Besides, the snails would simply crawl on you. You would lose your senses from anguish and dash your brains out on the wall."

"How did you dig a basement here, anyway?"

"A witch did it," Valentina handwaved. "Fetch me that tablecloth, would you?"

Valentina waved towards a cluttered combination clock and dresser, from which a rolled-up tablecloth protruded. There was no table; when Svetlana brought back the tablecloth, Valentina pushed aside a chair to free up space in the center of the room and rolled the tablecloth out.

In an instant a feast faded into view!

There were two kinds of borscht, five kinds of bread, lentils, potatoes, vushka, cod, cabbage (stuffed with various wonders), honey, herring, knish and salad, sweet grain pudding, sauerkraut, mushrooms, fried cheese, fried eels, and pickled eggs, and uzvar, coffee, and wine for her to drink. There was even a bite of chocolate by the side. Most mysteriously of all, the tablecloth was set for two: there was regret on it. There was sorrow. There was apathy, remorse, agony, greed, and even grief!

Svetlana blinked rapidly, trying to figure out how these things had appeared upon a tablecloth. She did not succeed. Nor did she get the chance to consume them; Valentina ate but did not invite her over, or even offer her bread and salt. It was only when Valentina had finished her meal, and leaned back in satisfaction, that she glanced at Svetlana, chewed on her lip, and then ripped off the thinnest rind of apathy and tossed it Svetlana's way.

Then Valentina stood, picked up a corner of the tablecloth, and whisked it into the air, and all the food—save the crust in Svetlana's hands, which she had caught, and now nibbled on—was gone, as mysteriously as it had come, and the tablecloth folded up into a neat triangle that fit in Valentina's hand.

Valentina tossed the triangle of cloth to land over the side of the sink.

"I'm tired," she said. "While I'm gone tomorrow, you'll have to do something with this clutter, sweep the hut, cook better vushka, and wash the linen. Then you must go to the store room and give me a proper count on my mustard seeds. If you fail, I will remove you."

"Um," Svetlana said.

"Yes?"

Svetlana shook her head. "Nothing," she said. "Only, why are you growing mustard?"

"I'm not," Valentina said. "Except a small bit for the snails. I'd just like to see them counted. Should be around ten thousand, but I can't be sure."

"Ah," Svetlana said, blankly.

She processed this; and as she did so, Valentina sprawled across a padded chair and closed her eyes, and was soon asleep. Svetlana crept to the door, opened it softly, and went outside.

> Little bat, my little bat,
> Fly out from your caves to me;
> I fear this task will prove a trap
> And I will do abominably.

In moments Maksim had plunged from the sky and hung himself from her extended hand. "I am here," he said. "Fear not."

"Oh?"

"Already the hut is swept and the linen is washed and the vushka ready—all except the boiling. As for the last task—"

"It is that that concerns me," Svetlana said.

"Well," Maksim said, "if she doesn't actually know how many there are, then isn't any number you give her good enough?"

"I am afraid that I will go in to check them," Svetlana said, "and be compelled to count them, and count them again, even if that should be so. But I am also afraid that if I do not do this thing, and simply say '8,763', that I will be unprincipled and that she shall catch me out—if there are, say, only a few hundred in actuality."

"Say no more," Maksim said. "When Valentina has left the hut, you need only knock upon the wall of the storeroom and say, 'One, one thousand, moon, one thousand, gold, ten thousand, nine.' Instantly the seeds will become counted, and the tasks you have been given will be complete."

Svetlana looked dubious, but Maksim had always guided her well before, so she flung him back into the sky with a sweep of her arm and slunk back into the hut.

Time ticked by and Valentina woke. She looked around at the cleaner hut and the vushka ready to be boiled. "It's a good start," she said, "but you'd best get moving on those seeds. They're not going to count themselves."

"They may," Svetlana said.

Valentina considered that. "That's true," she conceded. "I don't know *everything* about the secret life of seeds. In any case, I'm going out. Best be done when I get back."

She left and the wind gusted through the door behind her and then Svetlana was alone.

Svetlana approached the door to the storeroom. She thought about peeking in, but one of her great fears had always been that she would prove to have arithmomania—that despite her resistance to several of the classic vampire weaknesses, she would find herself compelled to count and most likely recount any scattered seeds she came across. The notion was appalling and dehumanizing to her but it was by no means impossible; the syndrome existed and was not entirely unfit to her personality.

She dared not look. She simply knocked upon the wall and intoned the chant:

"One, one thousand, moon, one thousand, gold, ten thousand, nine."

For a long moment nothing happened, and it occurred to her that while a floor could be intrinsically swept and linens could be intrinsically washed, seeds could not actually possess the intrinsic property of being counted. She wondered if Maksim's magic had gone awry—but then a sepulchral voice echoed from the other room:

"One mustard seed in Sosunova's pouch; in the jar, ten thousand."

"That is very precise," she said, but the sepulchral voice did not answer. There was nothing for it but to set the table and wait for Valentina to return.

The hours slipped by, and Valentina came in. "Have you done as I asked?" she said.

"The water'll need a few minutes to boil," she said, "and the vushka a few more minutes to cook. Then yes, I'll have."

"Pity," Valentina said. "How many seeds were there?"

"It is as you said," Svetlana said. "Ten thousand. Or ten thousand and one, counting the one in the pouch upon your belt."

Valentina blinked. "Ah," she said. "That is better done than I had expected; and here I was looking forward to killing you."

"Not to complain," Svetlana said, "or, rather, to complain, but why would that be contingent on my counting seeds?"

Valentina sat down. She leaned back. She looked at the ceiling. "Well, I didn't think you'd know about the one in my pouch," she explained.

"Oh."

"Don't worry about it," Valentina said, and grinned.

When the vushka were ready, she unrolled the tablecloth again. She ate, again—including Svetlana's vushka, as the tablecloth's had always been a little undercooked. When she was done, she tossed the thinnest crust of blood-soaked sorrow to Svetlana. She rolled up the tablecloth and put it away. Then she went over to the storeroom, knocked on the wall herself, and said, **"Mustard seeds, get you in the ground!"**

There was a rustling, rushing noise behind the door.

Svetlana, who had never seen the seeds in the first place, only counted them, was taken with a sudden, dizzying sense of unreality.

"I've dragged up a few sacks of scraped salt," Valentina said. "You've done well for now, but do it all again; only, instead of counting the mustard seeds, count up the grains of salt, and separate them out from any leftover sand and dirt."

Svetlana thought about this. "If you have any salt with you," she said, "I won't be able to separate it out from any dirt that you also have with you. Unless you want me to follow you around picking your pockets and pouring water over you."

"That won't be necessary," Valentina said. "You can stick with what's here when I'm gone. But mind that you find any stray grains that got stuck under the floorboards or whatnot."

"I'll do my best," Svetlana said.

Once again, Valentina tossed herself down across a chair and fell noisily and gracelessly asleep. Once again Svetlana snuck out of the hut and called to Maksim:

Maksyusha, pray, heed my call t'
Fly out from your caves to me
And help to count these grains of salt
... before that woman murders me ...

In moments Maksim had plunged from the sky again and hung himself from her extended hand. He regarded the sacks of salt that rested against the wall of the hut balefully. "Well," he said, "there's more than one grain, certainly."

She protested, softly: "Maksim."

"If you knock upon the wall," he said, "and repeat the chant—'one, one thousand, moon, one thousand, gold, ten thousand, nine'—then the matter will be resolved, as it was before. But I am put off my ease by this; she cannot possibly know the correct count herself, nor can she reasonably expect you to accomplish this at any speed."

"She may not know the capacities of vampires," Svetlana said. "She may think we are capable of super-arithmetic."

"That is the exact opposite of the pertaining legends," Maksim said.

"Well," Svetlana said. "I shall have to do my best."

Maksim shrugged, and she threw him back into the sky.

Valentina woke, again, and left, again. This time Svetlana waited outside and watched her fade off into the distance to the north. Then she turned to the wall of the hut and knocked on it, saying, "One, one thousand, moon, one thousand, gold, ten thousand, nine."

Nothing happened for a long moment. Then the sacks groaned and stirred like they had dwarfs inside them. Sand and dirt sifted out through the seams and a few grains of salt blew out of the inside of the hut to sift inside. Svetlana could hear a subtle muttering sound—like an accountant, she thought, murmuring to themselves while working on an abacus—and finally the sacks stopped moving. "There are three sacks of salt," the sepulchral voice concluded.

"That is not helpful!" she said, more affronted than frightened.

The sepulchral voice did not reply. She became a little more worried, then. She knocked on the wall. She said, "One, one thousand. Moon, one thousand. Gold, ten thousand. Nine."

The sacks bucked as if they contained wild animals. The wind blew back her hair.

A rattling, roaring noise like the clattering of many sabers came— from where she did not know.

Then the sacks collapsed; they leaned lifelessly against the wall.

Finally, a sepulchral voice said, "There are approximately two hundred and fifty million grains of salt."

"I need the exact digits," she said. "One. One thousand. Moon. One thousand. Gold. Ten thousand. Nine."

Her ears rang. One of the sacks bulged grotesquely, then the bulge receded. It happened again. On the third such occasion, she heard a sound like the scream of metal, rising from an ordinary din to an unspeakable clamor; it did not cease, but only layered on itself in increasingly unbearable cacophony, and as she sank to her knees with her hands over her head she noticed the bulging and twisting of the sacks accelerating from intermittent fits to continuous convulsions. There was an intense sense of pressure in the air.

One of the sacks flew up into the air. It struck her in the side as it passed her, and she rolled onto the ground. The other two sacks flew up to join it. They began to circle her. There was a ripping, tearing noise, and she had the awful thought that the sacks had exploded, but instead it must have been something inside her, as she fell over and for some time knew nothing more.

When she woke the sacks were leaning against the wall again.

She sighed. She sat down, pulled her feet up under her, and waited.

When Valentina came back, she frowned down at Svetlana. "You look rather like you've washed your neck," she said. "But you'll need to bend it forward for the headsman's blade."

"I have been thinking on the matter long and hard," Svetlana said, her voice thin and uncertain. "And I have been forced to conclude that the number has no meaning."

"Eh … uh?"

"There are roughly a quarter billion grains," Svetlana said. "In three sacks. That much I have determined. Let us say, it is *actually* a quarter billion and ten. What does that tell us? If that count were to be secretly altered, so that it had always been a quarter billion flat, how would we know? Even were we to bring in a fleet of accountants with the most delicate scales, we could never say with any certinty that the count of grains had changed at all. To give an exact number is to trespass on the domain of God: it claims a knowledge that we can never possess."

"This seems like an excuse for not having correctly counted them," Valentina said.

"If you can disprove my assertions," Svetlana said, "please feel free to do so."

"Mm," Valentina said. She frowned. "The hut is swept?"

"I think so," Svetlana said.

"You think so?"

"It has occurred to me," Svetlana said, "that on the same principle, one can never truly know what is behind a closed door, neither."

"And the linens done?"

"The same."

"And you have nothing further to say?" Valentina said, and she held herself like a sheathed sword. "About having failed?"

"I could tell you two hundred and fifty million, four hundred and seventy-three thousand, one hundred and eight," Svetlana said. "Save, I am unwilling to insult you by doing so."

"I am surprised that you did not flee."

"I have said it," Svetlana said. "I must live here, or perish."

Valentina relaxed. She gave a white smile to Svetlana. "Well," she said. "You do not provoke easily, so that is one thing learned. Come in, and we shall eat."

"Wait," Svetlana said. "Wait. What?"

"You are right. Reason tells me that there must be a specific number, but I cannot demonstrate it. I can hardly kill you for something I cannot prove; it would upset my digestion."

She led Svetlana back inside.

Again Valentina ate lushly. Again, she did not share. This time, however, she stopped in the middle of her meal, holding a bit of bread in one hand, and fixed Svetlana with an unsettling stare.

"You are very quiet," she said.

"I am afraid," Svetlana said. "... but may I ask some questions?"

"You are afraid," Valentina said. She gave a rictus grin. "The way your kind moves, like, the every little movement of you, it tells us: *here is something to fear. Here is danger. Here is death.* And *you* are afraid."

"...yes?"

Valentina half-smiled. "Well, ask your questions, then; but, not every question has good answers."

"It's just," Svetlana said, "that when I was on my way here, I passed through the territory of the Lady in White. Did you know, the Witherspoons have never met her? Nor the Celdinars, or any of the other families? She claimed her territory, told us all we were barred from feeding there, by *proclamation*. And it struck me, I learned more about her in that brief journey than I learned in all the years before that.

"Who is she?"

"We have no sun," Valentina said, "to protect us against your predations. You acknowledge no law but your own. So ... let us say, she is our sun. She is our day. Our protector. We must have a vampire to protect us because that is the only kind of territory that your kind respects."

"Did you ... *make* her?" Svetlana said.

And she was imaging that Valentina had, perhaps, forced some vulnerable vampire to convert a Fortitude stalwart; but Valentina took those words another way. She tilted her head to the side, startled but not guilty. "An interesting theory, Svetka, but not one that anyone could prove. Let us leave it there."

Svetlana frowned. "And what of Red Ivan?"

"What of him?"

"I thought he was alive at first. He had a heartbeat. Then he did not. It was a very peculiar thing."

"He is our Red Ivan," Valentina said. "That is enough."

Svetlana took in a breath to protest, then let it out, frustrated. She thought for a moment. Then she said, "When I met you, there was a black ship coming in; black sails too."

"That is the ship of my dear dark Midnight," Valentina said. "He is the vampire who holds this very territory, and my faithful servant."

Svetlana pressed her lips together.

"The thought disturbs you?"

"Humans may have vampire servants if they like," Svetlana said, stiffly. "Who am I to judge? I am not one to cling to the claims of our supremacy."

"Mm," Valentina said. "Have you further questions?"

Svetlana did not dare to speak further, so she shook her head.

"Are you sure?" Valentina said. "You are not going to ask, perhaps, about why I had you count the seeds and grains?"

"Not every question has good answers," Svetlana said.

"Pfuh," Valentina said, and rolled her eyes in disappointment. "If you are always this difficult to start a fight with it's no *wonder* your family sent you to die here."

Svetlana's eyes narrowed, but she did not speak.

"If I may ask a question in return?" Valentina said, and Svetlana mutely nodded. "How were you able to make vushka when there is only flour, salt, and mustard in the house?"

"I called a magic bat to me by rhyming," Svetlana said.

Valentina considered. "All right," she said, eventually. "I can't believe I'm saying this, but it would be rude to turn you away from Fortitude when all you want to do is to make this place your home. I can only kill you or let you live here; and as for killing you, well, I think I might feel bad. But."

"But?"

"But I can offer you only the worst of bargains."

"Oh."

"You may guard Fortitude as the Regional Council does," Valentina said. "You may lend your weight to our— to their, I mean— claim of territory. You would help to defend the settlement if any Night London vampires or other monsters came here to throw their weight around. But you are not a daughter of Fortitude, so you may not claim any privileges in reward for this; you would exist under great scrutiny; and you would drink no blood.

"… that is assuming that you *can* subsist on emotion, human food, and animal blood, I suppose. I would not bother making you an offer that you can't survive on, so if that were the case, let me know, and I'll think on whether to revise it or to kill you now."

"I don't need blood," Svetlana said. "Not that way."

"Then," Valentina said.

"… it is a genuinely terrible bargain," Svetlana said.

"Yes."

"Couldn't I just live in a house somewhere near Ceiba Quay and not bother anybody?"

"If you can't be a bulwark against Night London," Valentina said, "then what good are you? What's the point in leaving you alive when you could potentially wind up on the other side?"

"Why leave anyone alive?" Svetlana said. "All loyalties are mutable, and yet we do not kill our neighbors."

"The deal is on the table," Valentina said. "Take it or leave it."

Svetlana looked down. She looked up. "I must note that I am fairly useless," she said. "I mean, even if I am fully cooperative. For instance, I intend to spend the next six months shaking in a ball at the back of a closet."

"I was planning to find you a place with a closet in it anyway," Valentina agreed.

"That was not a *reques*— well, thank you," Svetlana said.

"You're welcome."

"If I may," Svetlana said, "and, er, knowing that this may get me killed after all, but— will I by any chance be … the *only* actual vampire?"

"Don't be ridiculous."

"Oh."

Valentina yawned. She stretched. She blinked a few times. "After all," she said. "What is a vampire? You can survive without blood. Czcibor didn't much mind a cross. There's a Fidatof who didn't ever actually die."

"Well," Svetlana said. "It's kind of, ah—"

"A vampire," Valentina said, "is someone recognized as a vampire, by society."

FOR ALMOST TWO YEARS Svetlana lived in Fortitude in peace; then she answered her door one evening to find her sister Nicoleta and three packed bags on the other side.

"Darling," Nicoleta said. "You must take me in. I simply cannot stand the atmosphere of Night London any longer."

"Pardon?"

"The crowding," Nicoleta said. "The insufferable din! There must be at least a hundred of us there by now. And all the smoke! So I thought to myself, Nicoleta—I call myself Nicoleta, you understand, though you should still call me Nicky—Nicoleta, what could be better than a vacation by the lake? And who better to vacation with than your sister Svetty, who is there already?

"And so I've come! ... it's not too much of an imposition, is it?"

She pushed past Svetlana and set her bags inside the door.

"Tell me it's not too much of an imposition," she finished. "Pray."

"It's ... not," Svetlana said, almost by reflex. "But it's not safe for you here."

"Darling! How thoughtful of you! To be so concerned for your beloved sister. But I can rely on *you* to protect me from the local powers, can't I? I mean to say, you've been dealing with them all right?"

"I ..."

"They can't be *too* terribly cruel," Nicoleta said, "if they're letting *you* stay here. They're probably just a bit socially awkward. I could help them with that. Get them the right invitations, bring them into the broader vampire community, all that. Except for that Red Ivan. Don't tell anyone, but I think the man is actually alive."

"Sister," Svetlana said, "you know what I have told you about imagining scandals that do not exist."

"But I *heard* his *heart beat.*"

"He has anxiety, Nicky."

"Oh. ... oh?"

"You know how it is," Svetlana said. "Your hands sweat. Your thoughts race. Your heart starts beating. Sometimes you even come to life for a few minutes. I get it all the time."

"Oh, Svetty! It sounds just awful. You didn't tell me you were so vulnerable."

"It is better here in Fortitude," Svetlana said.

"Really?"

"I didn't want to come here," Svetlana said. "I am terrified of being here. They might very well kill me at any minute. But even with all that I think that I am glad that I have come back."

"It sounds like they've enchanted you," Nicoleta diagnosed, pensively.

"It's not that," Svetlana said. "It's just ... a nicer place to live?"

"Then I'll have to try it out!" Nicoleta said. "Fortunately, I've brought everything I need to stay for a few months, so that'll do for the testing."

"In those three bags?"

"Not everyone needs to pack their settee, Svetty. Ooh! Did you hear that?"

"... I ... heard that ..."

"Not everyone needs to pack their settee and their collection of antique clocks for a beachside vacation. That's just you."

"Even so," Svetlana said. "Absolutely not. I can't let you stay that long. I don't have permission."

"You have *my* permission," Nicoleta said.

"Your— ow, ow, *no*; that's not the relevant authority!"

"Nonsense. Anyhow, didn't I say to put on some tea?"

"I don't think you did."

"I'm sure I thought about it. Perhaps I forgot to actually say it. That's not any excuse for you for not having put it on. You're being terribly inhospitable. I've half a mind to write our sister Tatiana and tell her just how dreadful you've become."

"You could go tell her to her face? ... I'll put on the tea."

"And some milk!"

"With what cows?"

"You don't even have cows here?"

"There aren't even cows in Night London, Nicky," Svetlana said, vanishing towards the kitchen. "I don't even *know* what the Mayor's men milk."

"There are probably cows."

"There is a rumor that he keeps pens of *something* in the sewers," Svetlana said. "Not quite sure what. Nobody's dared to say humans and nobody's boring enough to say cows, so it's probably some sort of abomination of over-the-verge science. A giant sewage-eating cow-slug thirty-seven feet long with udders all along its length? Mutated ghouls that feast on corpses and spit up the purest, whitest milk? I can continue to speculate."

"There is no need," Nicoleta said. "I will take it black. Black and two sugars."

"With what swans?"

"... sugar does not come from swans, Svetty. Now you are just teasing."

"Feh."

"I can hear that in your voice! You are laughing at me! At your own sister!"

"Of course not," Svetlana said. "That would bring great disgrace to the Witherspoons."

The kettle boiled. She made the tea. She brought it out, and cups, and sugar, to her crowded table, brushing a collection of rag dolls, a stuffed octopus, several unfinished letters, and a set of windchimes to the floor.

"Sit," Svetlana said. "Have tea."

"You seem to be doing well for yourself," Nicoleta said.

"You're basing this on?"

"Well," Nicoleta said, "the place is an appalling mess, but it's not *the* appalling mess that your last one was. Or the one before that, for that matter."

"Each time I move," Svetlana said. "I have less stuff. It helps."

"It is the air," Nicoleta decided. "And the peace."

"Nicky, you really can't stay."

"You shouldn't say such things, Svetlana. A Witherspoon does as she pleases."

"A Witherspoon does *not* do as she pleases," Svetlana said. "I never have, and you know very well that you've never encouraged me to. Archibald was positively *reserved*. And, let me be frank, as terrible as you are, I know that you could be worse.'"

"That's very kind of you."

"The point being, I had to convince the locals that I *deserved* to stay; and they're not going to extend the same courtesy to you."

"One vampire is much the same as another," Nicoleta said. "You will leave for a while, won't you? Then I'll just take your place."

"Honestly."

"It's cruel," Nicoleta said, her eyes shadowing. "You've found a good thing here and you don't want to share it with your sisters. You're trying to freeze us out. But I won't have it. I'm staying and that's that."

"I'm sorry."

"Don't be sorry."

Svetlana lowered her head. "I won't stop you," she said. "But please, if you value your own life, don't feed on anyone in Fortitude."

"I wouldn't," Nicoleta said. "I mean, not in the others' territories. But in yours, it's all right, isn't it?"

"It's part of why they let me stay," Svetlana said. "At best you'd get us both kicked out. No."

"Oh. Ah, oops?" Nicoleta said.

"... 'oops?'"

"Well," Nicoleta said, and made a helpless gesture with one hand, "I was a little hungry for the last bit of the trip."

"I have to go," Svetlana said.

"Of course. ... wait, you do? What?"

"Stay indoors," Svetlana instructed. "Don't go anywhere. Keep the fire lit. I have to go try to salvage this. You didn't kill, at least?"

"Of course not," Nicoleta said. "I was very gentle. I am a woman of compassionate principles."

"I'll return."

"But—"

Svetlana ignored her. She left her sister gaping behind her as she went outside, closed the door firmly behind her, took a deep breath, and called out:

> Pray, fly to me, as if pursued
> By Hell's own hounds, for by a thread
> Hangs Nicky's life; my sister's fed
> Upon the blood of Fortitude.

Maksim descended from the sky. He landed on her arm and looked pensively at her. "Fear not," he said. "Only; are you sure that whatever her fate will be, is not justly earned?"

"She is a horrible creature," Svetlana said. "But she is not a killer, and she is my sister."

"Then," Maksim said, "when Valentina comes for her, you may knock three times upon her heart and say, 'utoli Bože boli Valentiny.'"

"That sounds exceedingly awkward," Svetlana said.

"It is your only option," Maksim said. "Otherwise, your sister Nicoleta will pass entirely from this world."

Svetlana sighed. "Thank you, Maksim," she said, and tossed the bat back into the sky.

She waited.

After a while, Nicoleta brought her cold tea and a muffin, tried to make conversation—which Svetlana mostly ignored—and then returned into the house. After a further while, Valentina came.

"Svetlana," Valentina said.

"Valentina."

"This was not in our agreement," Valentina said. "You were not to harbor vampires that prey upon my people, but rather to discourage them."

Svetlana looked down. She looked back up. "I could not prevent it," she said hoarsely.

"You understand what must happen?"

"She is my sister."

"That is a matter of courtesy at best."

"No," Svetlana said. "You don't understand. I had come back to a false and damnable life. I did not know how to live with myself, and certainly nobody could live with me. I was rejected. I was worthless and alone. All I had was a bat of extremely dubious provenance. Then the Witherspoons reached out to me. They said, 'you, who have been abandoned. You, who have been given from the soil. Come into our family; you have new family now.'"

"That is mildly moving," Valentina conceded. "But I am not very sentimental."

"I don't ask you to be sentimental. I ask you to care about the value of family connections, as a child of Fortitude ought."

Valentina heaved a sigh and Svetlana heard a flutter as of the wings of a bird inside Valentina's chest, and thought: *one. One knock upon her heart.*

"I cannot let her live," Valentina said. "She is a monster. You are more of a pitiable creature, like a bit of gross ichor that one scrapes off of one's boot; it is impossible to feel any great malice towards you. But she has not been here a single day and already she has stripped away the security that I've spent years establishing."

"She is monstrous to me," Svetlana said. "She sent me here thinking I would die. I don't argue with your judgment of her. But also she is the only person who calls me Svetty and one of three people in all the world who'll hug me when they come walking in the door."

"You are grasping at exceedingly thin straws," Valentina said.

"They matter to me."

"Of course they matter to you," Valentina said. "You're pathetic."

But there was a wry twist to her mouth as she said it, and another, more agitated, flutter; and so Svetlana thought, *Two. Two knocks upon her heart.*

"She is wicked because she hates herself," Svetlana tried.

"You're stalling me," Valentina said.

"I'm not! I'm trying to reach you!"

"She isn't wicked because she hates herself," Valentina said. "You put up with it because *you* hate *yourself*. She's wicked because she doesn't think humans are people. Or maybe because she doesn't have self-control. I don't quite know how vampirism works. I don't know if the whole superiority thing is a justification or a primary belief."

"Fine," Svetlana said. "I put up with it because I hate myself. But I'll hate myself more if she dies."

"Don't," Valentina said. She put her hand on Svetlana's shoulder. "You couldn't have stopped it."

"Please," Svetlana said, and was startled to realize that there were tears coming from her eyes.

Valentina's mouth twitched, and she pushed Svetlana gently aside, and she went in. But a third time Svetlana heard a flutter as from a bird inside her chest, and she whispered after Valentina, "Utoli Bože boli Valentiny.[17]"

Valentina stopped. She blinked. She looked back over her shoulder. "Uh?" she said.

"Nothing," Svetlana said.

"For just a moment," Valentina said. "For just a moment, I thought: the Headmaster's curse— that it wasn't— that *I* wasn't—"

Svetlana shrugged.

Valentina sighed. "Fine," she said; and smiled—and her smile was a real one, as if an ancient pain had been lifted from her. "I'll let her live."

She went in. Svetlana, after a few moments, followed.

Valentina held up a hand, and in that hand, of a sudden, there was a fire that was not a fire. Svetlana blinked.

Looking at the un-fire, it struck her with an eerie suddenness that the world did not contain *things*. Rather, it contained a heap of—a collection of—details and impressions that her own fire of consciousness *assembled into* things.

Looking further at the un-fire, it struck her that even those details were suspect.

The smaller the thing she turned her attention to, the greater the relative error in her judgment. For instance, looking at a table—if there were tables, which she had realized there were not—but, looking at a table, she could make a reasonable estimation of *what* it was and *where* it was. But if she tried to focus on a single speck of dust upon the table, or a tiny portion of the wandering path of a single grain, the matter became a lot more elusive. There were details, perhaps, but she had them *wrong*.

It was a pretense. It was a game that she was playing, or a social artifice, to believe in things or details at all.

------

17 "Allay, my God, the pain of Valentina"

All that was left to her—all that was *really* real—were the impressions that she picked up, roughly, of the world.

... but even there a fundamental error in her cognition became apparent. She had taken to regarding her impressions of things as data passively received from the world—that, if she entered a room and got an impression that it was bright, that that was the brightness *reaching out* to her; that if she looked at the lake and saw movement, or blue, that that was the impression of movement or the impression of blue *flinging itself* into her eyes.

In the light of the un-fire it was obvious that this was not the case.

To collect her impressions of the world, she realized, she cast out a net from her consciousness. She sent out a shape of what she expected to see, or hear, or feel—and received something very much like that back. She was incapable of receiving an immediate impression that was entirely unexpected; a truly surprising event would require, or perhaps *was*, a repeated casting of the net.

It was not fire, she suddenly understood, in Valentina's hand. That had been her error. It was not even a fire that was not a fire in the same way Svetlana was a life that was not a life.

It was not a fire in any sense whatsoever:

It was an incandescence of the void.

"Oh," Nicoleta said. "You came back. And who ..."

Nicoleta stopped there. This did not surprise Svetlana. It actually surprised her a little that Nicoleta had managed to get that far before noticing the nonexistence of all things. Then again, Nicoleta had always been a little bit oblivious.

"Behold," Valentina said, and she lifted it up.

As she did so, the incandescence was partially shadowed by Valentina's body and Svetlana came back to reality with a snap. Past Valentina she saw that this was not true for Nicoleta; Nicoleta was frozen, her eyes wide and cervine.

"You have come to Fortitude," Valentina said, "thinking to trespass on a place of rustic victims. But this is not a place of rustic victims, *strigoaică*. This is a place of monsters."

The incandescence in Valentina's hand came forward.

Then it was gone. Then Nicoleta was screaming, screaming and weeping, fluttering into the rafters like some great wounded bird, and there were two steady lines of blood trickling down her face from the absence that had been her eyes.

"Get her back to Night London —whether she can heal from that, or not," Valentina said. She turned on her heel and left.

NOW Tatiana Witherspoon, Svetlana's eldest sister, learned of these events—or what little Nicoleta could tell of them through her bloody tears.

"It pursued me," she said. "The fire—it grew and grew until it consumed me."

"Our little Svetlana," Tatiana said. "I cannot believe that she would associate with those who would do such a thing to you."

"It was everywhere," Nicoleta said. "Everywhere. No matter where and how I turned."

"Peace, sister," Tatiana said, and waved a hand across Nicoleta's face, and Nicoleta slept. "I will take your revenge for you."

Tatiana went over and down the hills into Fortitude.

Now where Tatiana walked, the people of Fortitude did not see her. From time to time she would stop to eat at their tables, or read a book from their libraries, or even drink directly from their veins.

These things she did, and they did not know.

She walked among them, and they did not see her, and they did not hear her—they saw nothing, or what she wished them to see; they heard nothing, or what she wished them to hear; and in time she began to put together a picture of events.

"Why," she said, "they aren't even vampires at all."

She visited Svetlana. She pounded on Svetlana's door, then breezed past her when she opened it. "Darling," she said, "you have been a fool. You have *been* fooled. But do not fear. Your big sister is here to take care of everything."

"As you say," Svetlana said.

"I have decided it," Tatiana said. "I will claim a dominion here. It is perfect. The vampires of Night London will not trouble me. The vampires of Fortitude do not exist. I can wander the settlement, plucking the young men and women as if they were ripe fruit. But first there must be revenge. There must be revenge, you understand it, before there can be the relaxing."

"Tatiana," Svetlana said.

"Hush," Tatiana said, and Svetlana fell silent. "Your house will do as the seed of things. I will found my dominion here. It will leave nothing for you, but then again, you never really had anything, did you? I'm sure you'd be more than happy to live in my closet and do the occasional chore for me, anyway —oh, you can answer that."

"It is true that I do not need a dominion," Svetlana said, carefully.

"That is evasion," Tatiana said, and made a face. "You must not be so evasive with me. Well, no, belay that, it would be quite unsettling to me if you were blunt. You must consider yourself chided for being so evasive, and resolve to do better about the whole matter from now on."

"As ... you say," Svetlana agreed.

"Can you call the people of my dominion here?" Tatiana said. "I have announcements to make. There shall be big doings."

"I can," Svetlana said. She spread her hands. "I am here."

"Not *you*," Tatiana said. "The local humans."

"Oh," Svetlana said. "I am not sure they are even aware they are in your dominion."

"Well, of course not," Tatiana said. "It is not in my character to leave them aware of that. But surely they consider *you* their lord and master? Goodness, Svetlana, surely I have told you to take a firmer line with mortals."

"Ma'am."

"Well?"

"You've told me that," Svetlana said. "I have taken a firmer line. Only, if I were to do as you suggested, then I would have been murdered hideously. That is *too* firm."

"Oh."

"Or possibly they would have deduced your influence," Svetlana said.

"Surely not!"

"'Svetlana,' they would say. 'You have utterly failed to conceal your sister's hand in this, owing to your own noteworthy lack of subtlety and finesse. We will spare your life, but hunt down Tatiana Witherspoon at once!'"

"You *do* lack subtlety and finesse," Tatiana conceded. "Well, then, here is what you shall do. You shall call a *neighborhood meeting*. Surely you can do that much?"

"I ... can probably do that much."

"Excellent! Then I can remove their eyes."

Svetlana looked down to avoid showing anger or distress. "Sister, are you certain—"

"Don't argue," Tatiana said. "Go. Go! Shoo!"

So Svetlana went.

From house to house she went, waking people, warning them to flee, and alerting them to the upcoming neighborhood meeting. "I don't understand," Serugei Brodsky said, when she'd finished. "Which am I supposed to do?"

The words Svetlana wanted to say stuck in her throat. She simply shook her head, helplessly, and repeated that he must flee, and that a neighborhood meeting had been called.

"She will take your eyes," Svetlana said, "if you show up. It'll be a real shindig. Let the Regional Council know if you can."

In the end, as neighborhood meetings go, it was a disaster.

"Svetlana," Tatiana said. "There is no one here."

"There are banners," Svetlana said.

"Yes, yes," Tatiana agreed. "The banners are excellent. And there's a grill set up for grilling fish or, or, is that for the eyes? That's very thoughtful. But nobody is here. Are you sure that you gave them the right address?"

"I didn't actually give them any address," Svetlana said. "I just assumed that we'd meet outside my house."

"So what you are saying," Tatiana said, "is that my neighborhood meeting could theoretically be taking place somewhere else entirely. They could be voting in condemnation of me even as we speak."

"That is unlikely, ma'am."

"They are extremely judgmental, these rustic types. They are probably dismissive of my taste in art."

"How unfortunate that they will never have the opportunity to admire your collection."

"Do not mock me, Svetlana."

"Ma'am."

The silence stretched out until Tatiana cracked. "Oh, all right," she said. "Belay that. I am certain I am imagining worse mockery than what you'd actually say were you allowed. Could you go and fetch me some actual neighbors?"

"Please don't ask me to," Svetlana said.

"Oh, no," Tatiana said. "I am trespassing on your moral boundaries."

Svetlana's eyes flickered. "Yes," she agreed.

"Svetlana, Svetlana. When will you learn that it is always for the best simply to go along with me? —don't answer that," she snapped, as Svetlana's mouth opened. "It was a rhetorical question. I'm not going to make you drag people here for me to poke their eyes out, though it's quite rude of you not to want to after what they did to our Nicoleta. Here."

She gestured behind them and Svetlana's house gave a great building-creaking groan and ripped upwards from the ground on four great legs. It shook itself and layers of the street and nearby houses began to pour into it and onto it and it grew.

"Tatiana," Svetlana said. "Please stop altering our perceptions. We both know that you are incapable of physically doing this to the world."

"Hush," Tatiana said. "Let me enjoy my giant battle-house."

A great hand formed from mostly from the rooftile and somewhat from the house walls of the nearby homes reached down and picked them up, holding them in its palm. The structure continued to grow until it reached perhaps thirty feet in height, at which point it began to tromp forwards.

"I will find some neighbors on my own," she said.

"I hate it when you do this," Svetlana said.

"Why?"

"It always disturbs me when I lose track of how your visions correspond to, well, reality."

"There is no reality," Tatiana said. "There are only concentric layers of illusion."

"I mean, are we running? Are we running along through the streets making undignified 'giant house' gestures?"

"Kindly cease such embarrassing speculation."

"Ma'am."

"It is, in any case, impossible, as I know I have more dignity than that, even in hypothetical worlds."

"Ma'am?"

"Ah!" Tatiana said. She pointed. "Look! Neighbors!"

There was a family running through the street. They were screaming. They were fleeing from the giant dreadnought that Svetlana's house had become. Svetlana's brain slipped tracks for a moment as she attempted to engage in an embarrassing speculation and failed. She shook the moment off.

A great hand smashed down.

Silence fell, and dust.

"Did you kill them?"

"Of course not," Tatiana said. "That would be preposterously disproportionate."

She hopped down. She went to peek under the hand.

"See? They're all fine. Miraculously unhurt, just unconscious. Here, let me pop out their eyes."

"If you do that," Svetlana said, "I can't protect you."

"From ... what? The humans?"

"Exactly that," Svetlana said. "Also I will summon my bat."

"Don't summon your bat," Tatiana said, distractedly.

Svetlana raised her finger for a moment, then lowered it. "Well, that's one I brought onto myself," she conceded. "But I warn you, you're going to die quite miserably."

"In this she is correct," said Valentina Grigorievna Sosunova, and she held up her hand, and in her hand there was an incandescence of the void.

Only—

In that moment she ceased to perceive Tatiana. Tatiana walked beside Valentina, and Valentina did not see her; Tatiana studied the incandescence of the void, and Valentina did not know that she was studying the incandescence of the void; Tatiana tilted Valentina's head to one side, examining Valentina's neck thoughtfully, and Valentina thought she was rolling her own neck to remove a crick.

Valentina lowered her hand and the light that was not fire went out. "She's gone," Valentina said.

"I'm sorry," Svetlana said. "I can't stop her."

"You got out a warning," Valentina said. She turned around slowly in a circle, and did not see Tatiana circling beside her. "That's enough for right this minute. We can work out matters of blame and such when it's all done."

"She— she *gets* to you," Svetlana said.

A handful of others from the Regional Council had arrived by then. They came clambering over the rubble that the monster house had left behind it as it moved, one by one: Red Ivan; Avram Yatskiy, the selkie; Mariya Yatskaya, who had *been* a selkie until she'd lost her seal's skin; Roman Vasili, pledged to the lightning; and Baba Saburo, who could turn into the wind.

"There are your enemies," Tatiana said.

Valentina shook her head in faint confusion. "Huh?"

"I didn't speak," Svetlana said.

"I thought—"

"The Regional Council," Tatiana said. "They were actual vampires all along. You should kill them."

Valentina was a blur of motion. Before any of the others could react, she had spun and her arm had come scything down through the air, waving a handful of empty air at them.

Valentina frowned faintly, as did Tatiana.

"Svetlana," Tatiana said. "What was that?"

"I don't know why nothing in particular is asking *me*," Svetlana said.

Tatiana turned to Valentina. "Do it again."

"I see no reason—" Valentina said.

"They are vampires," Tatiana said, a bit stridently. "Your enemies. Kill them!"

Valentina's hand sliced through the air again.

In that moment she ceased entirely to collaborate in the pretense that was the existence of her vampiric enemies; Avram Yatskiy the vampire burned to ashes beneath the un-fire in her hand. The vampire

Mariya Yatskaya followed. The vampire that was Roman Vasili lingered, screaming, but eventually passed—and so on.

The power that she wielded, in short, was not absent, for all that her hand seemed empty. It was merely restricted, like the vampires she imagined, to her own private sensorium; and she was frowning, and her frown deepened, because when she struck away Avram the vampire she had expected to find *the absence of Avram the vampire* beneath him. When she struck away Mariya the vampire, she had expected to find *the absence of Mariya the vampire* beneath her. Instead she had found Avram Yatksiy the not-a-vampire and Mariya Yatskaya the not-a-vampire, neither of whom had ever been a vampire at all.

It was the first time— well, the second, counting a few moments ago— that anything like that had ever happened. When she erased things from existence, they usually left *nothing* behind them, not similar variations.

It deeply confused her.

"I don't understand," Tatiana said. "Svetlana, your friend is the least effective murderess I have ever seen."

"And *I* don't understand why nobody in particular is whining to *me*," Svetlana complained.

It was at that moment that Red Ivan's heart stopped, as it was prone to doing. It was at that moment that he died, as so often happened; and in that moment, before his eyes, there was no rubble; there was no monstrous house; people were in very different positions—but there *was* Tatiana.

He pointed his dead finger. He said, "Valentina! Right there!"

Valentina turned. She looked. She saw nothing, and she raised her right hand to destroy that nothing; and at that moment she became completely confused. Had Tatiana waited a quarter of a second, she would have realized that; had she waited half a minute, or even an hour, Valentina still might not have worked through the knot—

For, nevermind the self-taught Valentina; seeing the falsehood of a perception that one is *not actually having* is a riddle that would strain the Headmaster himself ...

—but Tatiana did not wait.

She stepped out of the way. She pointed. She said, "Tatiana is *there*."

She was pointing towards Mariya Yatskaya, and that is in fact where Valentina saw the vampire to be standing, but it did Tatiana no good; for in that moment, Valentina ceased to participate in the illusion that there was such a creature as Tatiana Witherspoon at all; and, like an axe without head, without handle, Tatiana dissolved.

Only Svetlana would mourn her; and not particularly hard.

SVETLANA'S HOUSE could not possibly be where she perceived it to be. Nor could she perceive it to be where Red Ivan said it actually *was*. It was a difficult situation to come to grips with and it shook up her perception of the world. Her agoraphobia took a permanent hit, in fact, when she had the dizzying realization that at any moment, even while *apparently* outside, she could actually be in, or under the eaves of, a sturdy house of which she simply was not aware.

... but still, it was not like she could *live* in that hypothesized house.

Once again, Svetlana had lost her home.

"She seemed interesting," Avram Yatskiy offered, in Council. "She can stay over near us. We'll find something. We'll figure it out."

It was slightly easier said than done; it was a bad year for a vampire to try renting in Fortitude, even with the Council behind her, and neither Svetlana nor the Yatskiys were rolling in cash. Eventually, though, they located a house that had been abandoned eighteen months prior and had not been excessively infiltrated by the dust of the Outside; it was something of a trash-heap, and Svetlana's heart sank when she saw it; she knew that she would most likely never muster the energy to fix it up into something pleasant—but there she had underestimated the Council.

Almost immediately Red Ivan brought over her clothes and a selection of possessions; for the first few hours, they had a tendency to vanish if she thought about this too deeply, but gradually their reality firmed up. After that, she had, at least, her tea and her favorite chair there to console her; and the next "day," Avram and Mariya showed up with wastebins, brooms, rakes, and loppers to help her fix up the house. They set to work in what turned out to be a mostly companionable silence:

Avram by apparent preference; Svetlana, because she was too paralyzed with gratitude, guilt, and stress from their presence to find something to say; and Mariya, who burst out at one point with "*say something*," but then laughed with him when Avram just rolled his eyes.

Eventually they left Svetlana with a functional home, if by no means a clean one. "You can take care of the rest?" Avram asked her, and she nodded, even though she didn't think that she actually could. He smiled at her, and he ruffled her hair, and then they left her there, alone.

She did not take care of the rest.

She sat down for a week and a half, staring at her walls, instead.

TIME PASSED.

In the Yatskiy's temple-house, Mariya was half-asleep at the table when Avram nudged her. "Go and talk to that vampire," he said.

"What?"

"She doesn't have anyone to pay a call on her," he said.

She puffed out her cheeks. She sighed. "You can't do it?"

"Propriety says it's on you," he said.

"Bah, fine," she said, shook off her sleep, and dragged herself up from the table. Then, as an old joke between siblings: "But you owe me a fish."

He laughed.

She went down to Svetlana's home. She knocked.

"Please come in," Svetlana said, blankly, and: "Please don't mind the mess."

Mariya looked around. "What mess?"

Svetlana gave her a flat look.

"Oh," Mariya said. "Well, I shan't mind it. Are you settling in?"

"Do you care?"

Mariya wrinkled her brow. "Of course I care," she said. "Why else would I ask?"

Svetlana shrugged.

Mariya tilted her head to the side. "Ah," she said. "You imagine that I must have ulterior motives, because you are a vampire?"

"I guess."

"Well, that is not so," Mariya said. "And, rather sad. My brother thought that you had no one to visit you, and that you *should* have someone to visit you, only he was too lazy to come down here himself. That is all."

She hung up her umbrella and handbag.

"That is the extent of my sinister intentions."

"You don't need to," Svetlana said.

"This, this, this," Mariya said. "Did you know, great-grandmama married a seal?"

"... no," Svetlana conceded.

"The next time you ask yourself, 'do the Yatskiys only do things for which absolute necessity can be established?'," Mariya said, "your answer is there. You never said; are you settling in?"

Svetlana's eyes shuttered. "As you like."

"Good," Mariya said. She wandered further in. "Ahaha, mess," she said. "I see what you mean."

"Would you like some tea while you contemplate it?"

"How very thoughtful," Mariya said. "Do you mind if I sort some of this out? I feel bad that we just left it like this."

"I'd probably rather you did," Svetlana admitted.

"I am not terribly good at cleaning," Mariya said. "It is the burden of being a Yatskiy. And I did not bring supplies to-day. But I have found a solution that works well for me, which is simply to deal with each thing that I *do* know how to deal with, first, and ignore the things that I don't. Then when they're all that's left, they usually make a little more sense."

"That is a good strategy," Svetlana said, "Only, I don't actually know how to handle *any* of it."

She was fast, as all vampires were fast, which in this case meant that she could start the water boiling without an obvious break in the conversation.

"I was at a loss in my old house," Svetlana said. "Dealing with the detritus of a dead stranger—"

"We should have kept working a little longer," Mariya said. "My apologies. The place looked so much better when we left than when we first got here that I didn't realize how much there was still left to be done. —this piece of wallboard probably materialized mysteriously from the ether after we left, but I can't deny that I had noted, and failed to discard, these old shoes."

"I looked at them, too," Svetlana admitted. "I was going to throw them out. But then I thought, what if someone needs shoes? ... but then I would have to go and take them somewhere, and then they might say, 'I don't want your stinky dead person shoes, you bloodsucking filth!'"

"That is an excellent reason to leave a dead person's shoes on your floor," Mariya agreed, picking them up and tossing them towards a trash bin. She missed. "You didn't see that," she added, and hurried over to toss them actually in.

"I didn't?"

"I am a model of grace," Mariya said. "I am not expected to be able to throw things, because of my stubby arms, but to *fail* is an embarrassment that no one should witness."

"I—"

"You?"

"I don't want to not see things," Svetlana said.

"Oh," Mariya said. "Oh. Of course. I did not mean to trample your sads."

The whistling of the kettle distracted Svetlana for a short while, after which she brought in tea and some crackers.

"These are not from this house?" Mariya said. She stopped wandering around picking up to sit down at the table. "I mean, they look fine, but I know for a fact that you have not been out shopping."

"It is not," Svetlana confirmed. "I was provided with a small selection of staples."

"That was extremely thoughtful," Mariya praised.

"I think that Red Ivan did not want me to feed on people," Svetlana said. "And believed two boxes of crackers would be the deciding factor."

"Ah, yes," Mariya said. "The old 'crackers or blood' theory of vampirism."

Svetlana cracked a small smile.

"So, talk," Mariya said.

"About?"

"What it's like," Mariya said. "… being dead?"

"I don't know," Svetlana said, a bit defensively. "What's it like, being alive?"

"The wind."

"Pardon?"

"It's like the wind," Mariya said. "Ah, it is difficult to explain. You would probably have to experience it for yourself. But, everything is always building up to the moment when you can *move*, wild and free. Like, the wind."

"Oh," Svetlana said.

"Though I cannot move as freely as once I could," Mariya admitted, with a brief frown. Then she shrugged. "Still, you have not answered my question. You must be careful, or that will become a terrible habit."

"Your question?"

"What is it like?"

"… it's not like anything," Svetlana said.

"Oh."

"I thought," Svetlana said. "I thought, when I died, when I made it back, that it would be *better*. I thought that *everything* would be better. But it wasn't. I couldn't get away from *me*, not even by death."

"I'm sorry," Mariya said.

"… no," Svetlana said. "Don't be. I said too much."

"No," Mariya said. "Your sentiment is perfectly reasonable, and sharing it is all right. I would find it disappointing too."

Svetlana gave a wry grin.

"Not to endorse the implicit self-criticism," Mariya said. "I simply mean, that is a big thing to happen to not have it fix everything else."

"I should not complain," Svetlana said. "So few survive their own deaths at all."

Mariya looked at her keenly. "If I may: are you doing anything with yourself *other* than lending your name to our Council and moping about?"

"I am … I am not the leaving-home kind of vampire," Svetlana said.

"Oh," Mariya said. "Do you have to be, ah, invited *out?*"

"No! No. That would be *terrible.*"

"That, then," Mariya said, "You could make something. At home. And then someone else could sell it for you, outside."

She sipped her tea.

"E.g., me."

"You? No," Svetlana objected. "Ow, ow, ow, *why?*"

"I can do whatever I want," Mariya said. "In return, the lives of the people who live in this area are my responsibility. That is what it means to be Mariya Yatskaya. You are in this area. *You* live in this area. Therefore, *you* are my responsibility. If you are not happy, I am failing, and you are aware of how I feel about failing."

"The Regional Council—"

"This predates the Council," Mariya said. "It is a Yatskiy matter."

Svetlana was silent for a time. Then, finally, she said, "Being responsible for my happiness is not a favorable situation for you."

"That is your poor self-worth speaking. I do not acknowledge it."

"Oh."

"Tell me: do you spin? Do you weave? Because if you do, then perhaps you could turn to the making of cloth."

"Handmade cloth is dying," Svetlana said.

"Not here. ... unless that is a pun?"

"No," Svetlana said, shaking her head. "And *here*, it's being sustained by the same people who'd turn up their noses at anything hand-made by a *vampire*."

"... fair point," Mariya said. "But they might buy it from *me*."

Svetlana thought back to the days she'd spent staring at the wall. "... well, we can try ..."

SVETLANA HAD NOT TOUCHED a spinning wheel or loom since her death; before her death, she had only learned a little bit from her mother. She expected to be terrible.

She was not.

Her fine control rivaled her speed and exceeded her strength. By the fifth day of practice, her thread came out as fine and even as a hair. Her cloth could fit through the eye of a needle; bleached, it came out as white as a cloud.

It was beautiful. It was perfect. It was to an inhuman standard.

"I can't sell this," Mariya admitted.

"Oh."

"There's no one who'd dare try to cut it," Mariya explained. "Sveta, you did not tell me that you were a prodigy. Or a spinning mule in disguise."

"... I'm not," Svetlana said, flattered.

"Is it a vampire thing? No, don't answer that. Let me assume, for the sake of *my* pride, that it is a vampire thing. And you can assume, for the sake of yours, that it is not. Sveta, Sveta, you will have to make your own clothes from this."

"But I've never even tried making clothes."

"Well," Mariya said, "it can't be *that* hard."

"I guess I can try it and hope for the best," Svetlana said. She reached for the cloth, but Mariya clutched it close to her chest. Svetlana raised her eyebrow.

"I will bring you some *waste* cloth," Mariya said. "You will practice on that. *Not* on this. Do you understand?"

"Of course."

"This is outrageous," Mariya said, distractedly, rubbing the cloth between her hands and then, reluctantly, handing it back.

"... what should I make?"

"Oh," Mariya said. "Rubashka, *rubashka!* Make one for me. I will pretend it is my seal's skin and wear it always."

"Your seal's skin?"

Mariya waved a hand vaguely. "One wears a seal's skin in one's childhood, and outgrows it in adulthood. Or when it is eaten by stray dogs, anyhow."

"That's awful," Svetlana said.

"It is the inexorable workings of fate," Mariya said. "I am lucky that I am able to hold a seat on the Council at all, with my great magical power of *not* turning into a seal any more. But oh! I can still talk to fish, so there's that."

"You can?"

"It is not as useful as you probably think."

"I'm so sorry."

"Yes, yes," Mariya waved a hand. "It is tragic. I have lost what most never had to begin with. But who would not trade places with me? I am Mariya Yatskaya, and I will have the *best* of rubashka."

"You will," Svetlana agreed.

"I will pay for it," Mariya said, "of course."

"I did not expect you to go to all the trouble to set me up in a business and then cheat me," Svetlana said. "Although if you wished to withhold from my account until I've repaid you for the loom, flax, and wheel?"

"Nonsense," Mariya said. "I will go and see about that waste cloth. Stay in good health, Sveta."

"... you too."

ON THE NEXT VISIT Mariya dragged Avram along.

"My brother, Avramka," she said, waving to him. "Avrasha, this is Sveta, our new business partner."

"I did not ask you to recruit a new business partner," he said. "I asked you to call on her socially."

"He is pretending that we did not have this all out before we arrived here," Mariya confided. "But in fact, he is well aware of all things."

"I am not aware," Avram said, shaking his head. "She does not tell me anything."

"Lies! Lies!"

"But it is, at any rate, a pleasure to visit. I have been wanting to, you know."

"What?" Svetlana said.

"I had selfish motivations," he said. "I feared that you would discern them. So I waited until we encountered by chance."

"I dragged you here," Mariya said.

"By chance," he said. "As I said."

"You had selfish motivations?"

"I saw you," Avram said. "On that occasion. And I thought, there must be an interesting person to know. And so quiet!"

"You ... like ... quiet?" Svetlana said, glancing at Mariya.

"Indeed," Avram said. "It is tradition at our house to spend most of the evening sitting around not saying anything."

"That would not have been my guess," Svetlana said.

"Well," Avram said, "as I said: you are interesting."

"Because I am dead," Svetlana said, her mood suddenly souring.

"No, no," Avram said. "More because you stayed yourself in the company of *that* woman. It must have been rather difficult."

A few moments passed.

"And there we go," he said. "There's that quiet again. It's marvelous."

"Why are you here?" Svetlana said, and there were tears unshed in her eyes.

"Well," he said, "Mariya is here to give you cloth and some books on cutting, sewing, and embroidery; I am here because she did not let go of my hand when she left. Also, I am given to understand that you prepare an excellent tea."

"I have what are now some fairly stale crackers," Svetlana said. "And some unexceptional tea."

"Ah, ah!" he said. "I have been woefully tricked."

THE DAYS PASSED and Svetlana learned to make clothes from the fabric she had spun and woven; but she did not at first make rubashka.

Instead she tried to make a seal's skin.

It was difficult; she had no guides. To make cloth as sleek and black as a seal looks in water was within her talents, but Mariya had not bothered to get her books on piled fabric or seal anatomy; to make the underfur and the guard fur required that she invent her own techniques, and to make the shape right she had to go by guesswork and feel.

Slowly she came to an understanding of it. Slowly, and at a ruinous cost in cloth fine enough for a tsar—or, arguably, a much less ruinous cost in typical flax—her work developed towards a skin that looked real.

In the end, when she had something that she thought was as good as she could ever do, she went to her eave. She closed her eyes. She remembered that it was quite possible that her previous house was *right outside.*

She stepped out.

She walked to the Yatskiy temple.

It was atop a small rise. It was at the end of a path. That night it was shrouded in mist; and as she got closer, the texture of that mist changed. There was the faintest sweet scent in it, the smell of incense, and she was the smallest bit dizzy, the smallest bit less afraid.

She reached its eaves. She pressed herself against the wall, relaxed for a moment, and then turned around to walk beneath them to the door.

She raised her hand to knock, and then hesitated:

An invitation was already in force. At some point she had already been formally welcomed there—

It warmed her, but she shook off that warmth and knocked anyway.

It was, eventually—and after a length of time that began to scare her—Mariya who answered, Mariya who blinked at her blearily. "Oh," she said. "Sveta." Then she shook some of the sleep from her eyes. "Are you all right? Is everything all right?"

Svetlana pushed the fake sealskin into her hands.

"Oh," Mariya said. She held it up. She laughed. "Oh, Svetochka," she said. "It's— that's— you know it has to be a real one, doesn't it?"

"I thought it might," Svetlana said, "but I thought it might not. Because— there are a lot of things that are just in how you think of them, aren't there?"

"Come in," she said. "I'll kick Ava up and he'll start a fire."

The alternative to coming in was going out, which was no alternative at all, so Svetlana followed her into the temple. "The air," Svetlana said, after a moment.

"The incense comes from the dust of the Outside," Mariya said.

"What, really?"

"It's as good a way to get rid of the stuff as any," Mariya said. "I mean, we have to dilute it and mix it, but ... —it was my *own* skin that was lost, you know. My outer me. The me that belonged to the lake."

"It's all right," Svetlana said. "It doesn't have to work. I just thought you might like it."

"I can't just *make* a new outer me, you know," Mariya said. "Or, well. Put one on. But I *do* want to, Svetochka. I wish that I could."

 In the living room Avram was asleep on a sofa; Mariya did not actually kick him, but she poked him with her knee. "Up, you."

"Oh," he said, stirring. "Oh! It's ..." He stopped there, staring at the seal's skin. Finally, he looked up at Svetlana. "Sveta."

"I didn't mean to wake you," Svetlana said.

"That was *your* knee?" he said. "Really, Masha, you're contagious."

"I deny everything," Mariya said.

"It wasn't my knee," Svetlana said. "But I invoked it through an intermediary."

"Vampires," he said, and waved a hand vaguely in her direction. He wandered towards the fire and started getting it lit. "I once dreamed about a giant creature that was mostly knees. Knees and wings and eyes. It was made of malachite and gold. Was that a vampire, do you think?"

"Most probably not," Svetlana decided.

"You have not said anything about my new skin, Avrasha," Mariya said.

"Ah, that," Avram said. "The trash-taker told me she's been throwing out a fortune in increasingly hairy black cloth, so I'm not as startled as I might otherwise be."

"You didn't say anything!" Mariya said. She frowned at the current distance between them, and said, "Imagine me hitting you."

"I am imagining it," he said. "It is not very painful at all."

"Your imagination is deficient," Mariya sighed.

"I don't have to stay," Svetlana said.

"What would you go back for?" Avram asked.

"Avram!" Mariya said.

"The sake of it," Svetlana answered, after a while.

"The sake of it is not a good enough reason," he said. "To be honest, I've been thinking that maybe you should be here anyway, and not there."

"Here?"

He shrugged.

"Wait, *here* here?"

"Well, that place is so dismal," he said. "And there's half of this one that we're barely using at all. And ... is there a point in your living alone?"

"I might murder you both in your sleep."

"Unlikely," Avram said. "Frankly, you don't seem to make me afraid by your sheer presence, which tells me something."

"Eh?" Svetlana said.

"Vampires don't go around eating seals," Avram said.

"... oh."

Svetlana processed that for a moment. Finally, she said, "It's really OK?"

"It is," they both said.

So she stayed.

And that was how it came to pass that Svetlana Bogdanova Uizerspun lived—well, "lived"—happily after; and also, her bat.

WHEN MAYOR CELDINAR was two hundred and four, one of his Fortitude agents brought him word.

"Sir," he said. His name was Kiprian. "It's about Mariya Yatskaya."

"The one with the power to ... not ... turn into a seal," he said.

"Yes," Kiprian said. "She can turn into a seal now."

Mayor Celdinar stared at him for a long time. Finally he spread his hands helplessly. "Get *out*," he said.

And Kiprian did.

INTERLUDE

RECALL THAT Valentina had been inflicted by an awful vision. It had colonized her mind's eye; she could not help but look at it—but it was a thing she did not wish to see. It horrified her. It made her despair. From that despair arose Perdition: a cursed land, intrinsically hopeless, lifeless, cold, and grey.

When a moment of brightness touched Valentina's life, Perdition did not brighten; on her darkest days, it did not darken. Its true malefic force did not come from her but rather from the Sosunov magic that shaped the original dream and the Headmaster's vision that had driven her to dream it—and yet:

It remained tied to her; remained an echo of her. The despair in that place was still *her* despair, in some deep sense.

Over the years, her perspective shifted, and, like the shifting of the seasons, Perdition changed its face in subtle ways in turn.

Valentina eventually outgrew the Headmaster's curse—for the most part. Consider a young woman forced into an ugly, itching, and ill-fitting dress; over the years, if she cannot take it off, she might still manage to adjust its fit and don nicer outer garments. In like fashion, Valentina never stopped *seeing* that vision, she never stopped *not wanting* to see it, but she found ways around it. It became less *important* to her. To a great degree, she outgrew Perdition.

It did not outgrow her.

Before the name of Heaven,
before the name of Earth,
Nothing moved in nothing.
The waters of the sea were salt;
chaos moved in them,
Chaos was the mother of the waters.

No field was formed, no marsh was to be seen;
The gods were none of them called into being;
None bore a name, no destinies were ordained;
Chaos she coiled and the seas were salt.

Then came the names of things.
Then were born the gods.
Brightly burst in Heaven, writhing in the Earth,
Dank and cold and moving in the deeps below. ...
—from *The Lies of Iolithae Septimian,*
provenance unknown

O NE DAY, the Headmaster of the Bleak Academy suddenly realized that he had a daughter.

She was a creature of flesh and bone and hair, but also, a creature of fire.

He turned to her. He said, "On this matter there is some division. There are those who say that the substance of each revelation pre-exists it—that an insight, before it is in-sighted, is immanent within the firmament, as it were, so that we may say that even mathematical concepts and mathematical truths exist in some fashion within the world. Others argue that a thing does not exist until the moment it is *seen*—that we construct reality when and as we witness it. Thus we may say that even other people, and the things that they have created by their seeing them, do not truly exist until they come into our lives. I turned and now I see you there, so I ask you:

"Were you always there, were you there already, or have I made you with my eyes?"

She frowned at him.

"What?" he said.

"That is hardly the right way to say hello to your child, father, much less for the very first time."

A thin smile. "My apologies," he said. "I love you; and welcome to the world."

Her ruffled feathers—both metaphorical, and the four black feathers that decorated the shoulders of her gown—settled. She said, pensively, "I would not say that either thing is true."

"Oh?"

"I mean, not that you don't love me, or don't welcome me. But I do not think that I was immanent, and I do not think that you created me. I think that we are born—that we, the things of the world, are born—when we are discovered to be absent. When there is an emptiness in our shape, I mean. Then the scales of the world are out of balance. Then a *somethingness* must be made to have our form to even those scales ... out."

"Hm," he said.

"If I may ask," she said. "I know that I am your child, but ... who am I? And who are you?"

"The second I may answer," he said. "I am the Headmaster of the Bleak Academy, *I the lord of Death's dominion me*. But the first I do not know. I suggest that you might be 'Bastard' or 'Nevdeniya.'"

"Really, father."

"Really!" he protested.

"I am not going to be named 'Bastard.' That is truly a scarring formative experience. And I am not all that terribly pleased with the name Nevdeniya."

"It is to balance things out," he said.

Her eyebrow twitched a little bit. "Go on?"

"I bought a stone egg," he said. "Only, when I tried to take possession, I discovered that it had apparently already hatched. The girl who came from it was named 'well-born'—or, Evdeniya. If that emptiness is what created you, then to balance the scales ... you see."

She looked away into the middle distance. She frowned. "I will call myself Mrs. Senko," she decided.

"You can't be a missus," he argued. "You're not married to anybody."

"Details," she handwaved.

"Is it—what, your first name?"

She sighed in exasperation. "Father. —if I have a first name, then people will only use it improperly. They will assume an intimacy that they do not possess. I have no reason to indulge them.

"Instead, I will create a Mr. Senko for myself."

"Oh, *do* that," he said.

"That is what I just said that I would do."

"Do that," he said, "and I may share with you the secret that is eternal life."

She thought about that for a long moment. "Pardon," she said. "But do you mean, the eternal life that is possessed by practically every human soul, or, the eternal life that is given to almost none of them?"

He touched his nose. He flicked his finger to one side. He waved it to her and smiled.

"That is not an answer!" she protested, but he was gone.

DAYS PASSED and she meditated on the lessons of her birth. She slept in a bed of air and darkness, suspended by a constellation of unseen forces above a bowl of stone. She walked blindly through statuary gardens. She drank from clear waters and stared up at the fires in the sky.

Her eyes were clouded with grey fog—possibly literally; certainly apparently—but eventually she reached a conclusion to her meditations. The fog dissipated and her eyes returned to Riders' night.

She left the inner gardens of the Academy.

She went down to the river that runs in the outer reaches of the Bleak Academy, the river that is beneath its surface full of stars. She found a stone-block well on a nearby rise—its top gabled, its shadows deep—and stole its bucket to scoop up the river muck.

From this she crafted Mr. Senko's flesh.

Up and down the river she scouted until she found two round black stones—they may have been dead stars. She rolled them in her hands to make them rounder, softer, and more lustrous. Then she set them in his head to be his eyes.

He lay there unmoving and unbreathing; rough-hewn.

She sat down beside him. Firmly, she directed her attention to him. She noticed, very intently and very consciously, that she had not had a husband before, but that she had one now; only, this awareness did not in fact produce the thing.

She attempted a further subterfuge. Coyly, she looked away.

Then, with a startled thought—"!" would, perhaps, express it—she shot her gaze back to the pile of muck and rose halfway to her feet, in preparation for the sudden revelation that he was alive now, or had always been alive! ... but this did not occur.

Her hair grew long and the stars wheeled through the skies and his chest sank in on itself and his left head crumbled and still she sat there staring at him, no longer expecting sudden life from him but rather contemplating the matter in due depth.

Finally she mashed him back into the river muck, fished out his eyes, and tried again.

This time she did not scoop out muck at random.

This time she set the revelation moving in her mind before she dredged the muck. It circled in her mind like a cyclone. It burned in her mind like a fire. Its center held a continuous crashing as of the lightning.

It was in the grip of this proto-revelation that she looked upon the riverbanks and saw them:

Not just one possibility but thousands.

The riverbanks seethed with them, the firmament was strewn with them: cast every which way and all about, as if they had died and been buried in a hundred battles. They were unsculpted as of yet, they were not carved out from the surrounding soil, but they lay face-up, face-down, and on their sides; they lay in poses of passion and of repose; they were beautiful, they were homely, and they were strange. Here was a Mr. Senko who was Jotun-born, tall enough for her to stand upon his finger. *Here* was a Mr. Senko of the *strigoi*—a Mr. Senko who had lived, though of

376

course he had never lived, and died, though of course he had never died, and been reborn to live again.

And here—here—

Her hands moved of their own accord. They dug the muck away around him. They fished him up. They set the eyes of him into the blank holes that were all he'd had. Here—here—was *hers*. *Her* Mr. Senko. He burned with the rightness of it.

She said, in fevered tones, and in conscious and unconscious imitation of her father, "Were you always there? Were you always there for me, were you there already, or have I made you, have I burned you into being with my eyes?"

The pile of river-muck said nothing.

"Here," she said. "Here."

Her hand clutched at the air in front of her chest. She tried to take hold of the revelation—to *show* him. She knelt on top of him, she took his arms in her hands, she pushed her forehead against his, she tried to convey her vision of him into him through sheer osmosis.

At the back of her throat a spark took light.

Her breath blew into him as her nose mashed his inwards and her lips touched his, and on that breath of hers was fire. It spread through the channels of his head. It lit the candle of his brain and the wicks behind his eyes. It slipped down his throat into the brazier of his chest.

"Oh," he said, quite startled, as he came to life.

She pulled back. She blushed. She rubbed the muck off of her nose. She got to her feet and then she helped him up to his. "You are Mr. Senko," she informed him, looking him over. "And you will be my husband."

"That is acceptable."

"If there is a party, or something, where I need a husband, or, to answer the door, or, to have a half a set of monogrammed towels, that will be your job."

"I will do my best."

"You are very congenial," she said, proudly.

"It is the logic of scarcity," he said.

"Oh?"

"I have never had a clearly-stated purpose before. Or a detailed agenda. It is … fulfilling," Mr. Senko said.

She looped her arm through his. "This shall be a productive partnership," she told him, and they two walked back.

THE HEADMASTER DID NOT see them immediately, but when he did he beamed.

"Oh, my," he said. "That's excellent."

"Nothing less from myself," she said. "Turn around, my husband."

"Pardon?"

"Rotate on your z-axis to demonstrate that you are a fully three-dimensional object," she explained.

"Oh!" he said, understanding then, and spun with a bit of flair.

"That was a very good spin," the Headmaster said. "I am impressed with your depth as a person. But now you must wait outside, like a good son-in-law should."

"That is the height of my ambition for myself," Mr. Senko said, and he slipped out the door.

The Headmaster's face turned serious.

"You have done as I asked," he said, to Mrs. Senko, "and I shall give you the secret of eternal life."

She stood straighter.

"Preliminaries," he said, folding his hands behind his back and pacing. "You are flesh and bones and hair, but, also, you are fire. It is, incidentally, possible to achieve something close to fleshly immortality by following certain secret arts, and I will at some point teach you them. You will armor yourself in a story and the world will be unable to touch you; the rules of the story will not allow it.

"However, that is not the secret of eternal life.

"The secret is that swords do not kill the fire, if the fire of *looking-upon* regards the swords.

"The secret is that water cannot douse the fire, if the fire of *looking-upon* regards the sea.

"The secret is that even death itself—if I may be taken as something of an authority on the subject—cannot end you if your eyes are open to it. You will look upon death, and you will see it, and the flame that looks upon your death endures.

"While your flame lives, you live; what can kill the flame?

"The flame will die if you smother it. It is not easy. You will not kill it accidentally, or, at least, not without such accidental efforts as to be a legend in themselves. But if you kill it, it will die. Should you cease to *look upon*, you will enter into a temporary death and, given sufficient time, a real one.

"That is one of only two deaths that the flame may die.

"Here is the other.

"The flame will die if there is nothing new for it to regard. The safer you keep things, the more dull you make things, the more *the same* you make things, the more the flame will wither.

"Luckily, the flame adapts.

"Live a boring life and your flame will attend to the months and not the hours; to the new things and not the old things; to the disasters and not to the routines. In this fashion does the flame survive. Live a boring life, live even a bleak life, and still you will have a great deal to look upon. But ...

"It is possible to wind up stranded in *true* nothingness, with nothing you can pay attention to, with nothing for the flame of consciousness to take ahold of, and the flame will end.

"Some do meet this fate. Some have not yet met this fate, but have no means by which to avoid it. As for you—

"This fate will never be yours, not now, not unless you choose it:

"For you have claimed the power to find, or create, another flame for yours to look upon."

He was silent for a time. Then he looked at her. "Do you have questions?"

"So I am stuck with you forever?" she asked.

"Yes."

"That's all right, then," she said, and she smiled.

He took her to the third-floor balcony of his tower, and he caught the winds in his hands so that all the Bleak Academy could hear. "This is my daughter!" he called out, and the faces of the Magisters, the students, and the dead turned up to see. "This is my daughter, Mrs. Senko, and she does please me well!"

A tension faded from her that she did not even realize had set in upon her. She basked for a long moment in a sense of genuine *acceptance.*

"Now go," he said, waving a hand in the direction of the gates of the Academy.

"Ah, um?"

"Your first task for me," he said. "I require a gate-house built outside those gates, in Perdition; in the outer dark."

"Oh," she said. She thought about this. Then she curtsied. "Of course."

And she departed.

IN THOSE DAYS the land beyond the Bleak Academy was named Perdition. It was a place of nothingness and it ringed the Bleak Academy like a moat.

It was the final ending to all things.

It was mist and gray nothingness. It was emptiness. It was despair. It was specifically *Valentina's* despair, or at least an echo of it; an echo of that despair that she'd once forced upon the world.

It had not ceased when she ceased to actively conjure it; it had only deepened.

It was a place, Perdition was, where there was no light to see things with and no shadow by which the shapes of the world could be distinguished. It was a graveyard of dreams. It was a place souls went to die.

On the one side of that place, there was the chaos. On the other, the Bleak Academy.

It was not pleasant. Even in the moods where she most wanted to apologize for her father for sending her there, Mrs. Senko could not bring herself to call Perdition pleasant. It was an appalling test for her, and as soon as she arrived she knew it was a place where no one should ever have to go.

The fire of her consciousness might arguably be eternal, if everything that the Headmaster had said was true, but there in Perdition her heart was dead. Her dreams were dead. Her wishes were dead. All things were lifeless, cold, and gray.

These things were not derived qualities. It was not that her heart failed her in the face of Perdition. It was not that she was not strong enough, or not lucky enough, or not magically protected enough to face Perdition.

That her heart was dead; her wishes dead; her dreams were dead—in Perdition, these things were simply *a priori* true.

Conversely, in Perdition, she discovered that there was something in her that could survive it.

She discovered that she did not need a heart, or dreams, or wishes to be Mrs. Senko—that there was still a Mrs. Senko *to be* without any of those things, a Mrs. Senko who was still not merely flesh and bones and hair, but also fire.

As to whether this was a genius insight of her father—whether he had seen in her someone capable of existing all but unaltered in Perdition—or whether Perdition had mutilated her into a form that could survive it, it was never later clear, not even to herself.

As for Mr. Senko, well, he was pretty much all right. He was disappointed, of course, in the death of all his dreams and wishes; but, she had never actually provided him with a living heart.

SHE FOUND HERSELF to be competent almost as soon as she was functional—though the latter took some time.

It was as if the shock, the despair, the disorientation that struck her when she first went outside the gates had formed a chrysalis, and inside that chrysalis she had grown a knife. She was soft and fuzzy and helpless for a while. She sat against the walls of the Bleak Academy and she moaned. She trickled dirt through her fingers. She thought in circles about how to build anything, anything at all, in Perdition. She wept that her father had betrayed her, or that she had somehow failed him.

She searched for meaning and did not find it; her heart was dead.

...but when she cut her way out of that chrysalis of helplessness—most likely metaphorically, although the distinction was mildly ambiguous—it was with a force of sharpened intent and competent awareness already in her hand.

In Perdition, where her dreams were dead, she became practical.

She had been born with a great deal of knowledge—an inborn instinct that had first given her the ability to speak, and dress herself, and sculpt mud into a shape that was something like a man—and from that knowledge information and approaches presented themselves to her. Systematically, she tested the possibilities that this well of inborn insight provided her.

In the end she found a workable approach and began to build.

First, she would go out to the regions far beyond the gate—into the far Outside. There, away from Perdition's dolor, she would be able to experience substance that was not nothingness, sounds that were not muted, colors that were not gray, and feelings that did not fold themselves around a sandwich filling of despair.

She would find—say—a large green square, or a network of yellow lines.

This she would regard with a fierce and conscious intensity (for she was meat and bone and hair, but also fire) until she began to imagine that it might be a physical thing. That greenness—could it be a useless square of sward? A sail, seen from far away? A stone, in green light?

Those yellow lines—were they dying insect armies? Heat waves from an unattended griddle? Motion lines from the passage of rapidly-moving miniature suns?

Under the pressure of her eyes, these abstractions became tenuous, gossamer possibilities.

Most of them were useless. Most of them she abandoned. The intensity of her focus would recede and she would lose track of the original sensation entirely, or, it would return to being a vague fragment of a concept, color, shape, or sound.

... but on occasion she found a hint of something good and relevant to her task.

Then she would call up the team of horses that she had lucked upon in an early expedition and drag that building element back to the vicinity of the gates—back into Perdition, where the world was imperfect, where the world was broken, but where at the very least things were better defined than "some yellow lines."

There, in the vicinity of the gates, the useful thing would recover definition. It would blossom from a possibility into a thing ... and, at the same time, a certain quality of its spirit would die. Instead of a hint of a possibility of an apple tree, say, it would be a genuine tree, but one that was somehow *less*. It would deflate. It would *lose value*. Its dreams were dead. Its wishes were dead. All things were lifeless, cold, and gray. Ironically, even as it gained reality and substance, this diminishment would render it a bit more malleable; it became solid, but at the same time, it tended to care less about the details of just *what* solid thing it would become.

She would explain to it its practical utility—

"You, stone," she might say, "are a good basis for my garden."

Or:

"You, you rapid suns: I will catch you in a sphere of glass and you shall be my lights."

—and it, or they, would generally comply.

Here her own impulses towards consistency constrained her. It was probably the case that she could have picked out a leering brass skull, declared it a suitable foundation stone, and impressed that purpose upon the thing. She could probably have built viable walls from various fuzzy lint-strewn substances and made furniture of flames. You could even say that Perdition had been toying with her when it sharpened the edge of her practicality and her competence, for, in a sense it was unnecessary; had she wished to, she could simply have *defined* what the practical solution was.

... but she did not want to strip the concept of utility of its meaning. She did not want to strip *any* concept of its meaning, deep in Perdition, and leave herself unanchored. So she used things as seemed fitting to the things themselves, rather than forcing her exact desires upon them, and the gate house that she built outside the gates of the Bleak Academy grew organically and with a certain eccentric flair.

In the name of sensibility, then, she acted without sensibility; in the name of an order to things, she built things out of order. When she found apple and walnut trees to be her orchard, she built an orchard, even though she had not yet obtained proper running water for her house. If she found a ceiling before the walls that would sustain it, or a skylight before the ceiling that would hold it, she did her best to establish it pre-emptively, and accepted the constraints that this would later put upon the overall design. Her early attempts to limit the place to a one-room arch were reluctantly abandoned; the project blossomed into a walled manor-house and gardens with towers, flying buttresses, and spires.

In the end she would take no pride in the final structure of the keep, though the aesthetics of it would please her; it was not a *planned* place, for all that she had planned it, or a *built* place, for all that she had built it, but rather a *harvested* place, a place that she had grown.

It built itself, perhaps. Perhaps you could say that it built itself, from the marriage of *her seeing eyes* and *the things she saw.*

And as it built itself; as, in the fastness of her despair a beauteous fortress there was builded—a peculiar sense of lightness came to Valentina Grigorievna Sosunova, far, far away.

MRS. SENKO'S GARDENS spread. A chuckling brook ran through them. Low walls rose up.

Geometry, in time, gave her a house.

THERE WAS a creature that dwelled in that place. The most natural name for it in the language of the Bleak Academy was *Glum*. She found it sprawled across her gardens one morning, flowing through them like a mudslide, and where it went the world distorted and primordial chaos reasserted itself in a peculiar way.

"It's like I don't *want* to see those things any longer!" she exclaimed.

That was the shadow it cast over her apple trees; over her walnut trees; over the penned-up field where someday, she thought, there might be an ox. That was the shroud it spread over the bucket that she'd set up next to the maple tree—well, the tree that might have been a maple tree, if it had maple sap in it, but that was probably a peach tree, if it did not. That was the pall it made over the lumpy ground and grass.

Mrs. Senko was fascinated, as she regarded Glum, to discover that she had wants.

In that moment, she was thinking how much it disgusted her, how much it deterred her, how it woke a kind of grey and dismal despair in her; but in that moment, also, she was reveling in the discovery that there were things that she, Mrs. Senko, could want again, or, in this case, *not*.

"You're adorable," she said.

Her first exclamation had made it twitch, but that second claim stirred it into a frenzy. It surged towards her like a tide, and where it passed the world fell out of order. She gaped; she froze—for a long cold moment she froze—as it struck her.

She stood frozen, and then she fell.

The momentary brightness drained away from her. It *cut* it out of her, took her own momentary adoration of it out of her, it made *itself*, that pall of loathing and denial, into something to be loathed and denied in turn.

Having been touched by Glum, in short, she ceased to desire the touch of Glum—and if she had not managed to recognize this as its own doing, if she had not managed to seize hold of that recognition with the tail end of her awareness and attribute it to the creature's *agency*, she would have thought herself the very spirit of perversity.

Instead she realized it, as she lay there on the ground; realized it, as her staring eyes looked after the departing pall of it, as she saw it leaving, as she saw it swirling up into the sky, becoming part and parcel of the greyness of the clouds, and it began to rain:

That it had *cut* that brightness from her, taken it from her, though whether because it was the subject or simply because it was a kind of brightness, she did not know.

Her eyes felt large in her head, as if keeping them open was an act of titans. To separate her eyelids was to be as Atlas, holding up the sky. But she was not Atlas. Physically, she was not strong.

She let go.

Her eyelids covered the world, and it went away.

Her last thought as she faded into Perdition there was this:

"I shall have to do a thing or two about that Glum."

IT COULD not be left to plunder and darken her gardens; that much was certain. But more than that—

She wanted it to yield to her.

To destroy it would be acceptable. Perhaps. It would be marginally acceptable. It would be making a firm statement that wild monsters could not be left to rampage in the vicinity of the gardens and the gate house she was building; that much would be a good thing to establish—but it was not enough. Not really.

She wanted it *subdued*.

Having desired the touch of Glum, and then ceased to desire the touch of Glum, she came to dream of owning it instead.

Of making it *her* monster.

She had no weapons—she realized that when she woke. She had two good hands, but Glum would not fear her hands. She had a practical mind, but Glum would not fear a practical mind. Arguably, Mr. Senko was a weapon; even more arguably, there was her umbrella ...

But, no.

She played with that umbrella as she thought. She opened and closed it as her thoughts churned the water of the well of inborn knowledge that was inside her. Finally, a possibility emerged; it rolled up to the surface of her mind; she considered it for a time before nodding firmly to herself and closing her umbrella a last time with a snap.

"I shall go recruiting," Mrs. Senko said.

SHE WENT to a bloodied crack in a brown shale hill: the grotto of fallen pilgrims.

There—scattered along the path that led into the heart of the hill, and slipping ever deeper into that hollow over the course of decades—lay dozens of those who had come out of the Bleak Academy for one reason or another and, at the grotto, succumbed to their despair.

The sheer number of them shocked her.

She had known of the place from the moment she was born, known that it existed and known that it had claimed such pilgrims, but subconsciously, she'd expected to find *one*—to find that the entire place was an elaborate diorama built around a single individual's descent. That it might instead have accumulated two or three pilgrims in the time since Perdition's creation would have been enough to astonish her.

There were, as has been mentioned, dozens.

They were scattered there as if from a fallen caravan—as if they'd been traveling together[18] and had died of dehydration and heatstroke, not far apart, one at a time.

She drew in a hissing breath. Then she approached.

She walked among them. She listened.

They were speaking—mumbling, anyway; she heard snatches of their self-justifications as she walked.

Most of their words were opaque to her. She did not have the context for them. They *wanted* things, out there in the waste beyond the Bleak Academy, that their words did not convey. She grasped that some of them desired purgatives, and she had some sense of what that meant; a few, she realized, were whispering of gold; but most of them were hungry for things that she could not comprehend. These wishes she did not hear as syllables, for the whispering was on a deeper level than verbal language; nor could she understand them as concretized desires; they came across, to her, as matrixes and identities, as whispered abstract mathematics—the *lorem ipsum* of the universe, perhaps—without a clear starting place or ending place to map to any correspondence to the world.

Then there was one, the one she was looking for.

She'd heard an attention signal in his whisper: something in it stood out from the susurrus, like a bone finger of the words extending to tap at her, or maybe like a curlicue of ink extending from the ink that writ his words to tap at her; as if to say: *here*.

And when she knelt down beside him, when she listened, when she

---

18   though they hadn't been

was preparing a bit of water in a cup, she heard his whispered words resolve to these:

"From the Bleak Academy I have come, to do a thing or two about that Glum."

She helped him higher on the hill, away from the crack in the open earth. She pulled him higher, and sat him up, and gave him water, and after a time something like consciousness came into his eyes. He looked at her. He said, "I had chosen not to pay attention to things further, to cease to be aware of the existence of the world."

She looked at him.

He swallowed. He looked around him. "I have failed in this," he said. "Haven't I."

She thought about this. "You tell me."

"Well," he said. "I am aware of you."

A sudden hope flit onto his face.

"Unless," he said, straightening, turning, looking at her full-on, "unless you are actually the metaphorical representation of the state of unawareness, the symbolic experience of the absence of existence, if by knowing you I know nothing whatsoever at all—"

His face fell.

"No," he said, bitterly, after a moment. "Your components are too distinct."

"Don't flatter me *too* hard," she said.

He gave a choking laugh.

He felt around him on the hillside. Owing to the geometry of the place, or rather, the *poor* geometry of the place, the way that nobody had ever really paid all that much attention to the geometry of the place, not even Mrs. Senko, he was able to locate his hat. He put it on. He brushed his robes to straighten them.

"I came from the Bleak Academy," he said. "To subdue— let me start over. There is a creature. It is … unholy."

"Yes."

"I came to subdue it, and my plan for this was sound."

"I find myself in a similar situation!"

"Ah," he said. It was the opposite of a howl; where a howl rises, this fell, but both were a noise of grief. He lifted a finger to his mouth. He bit delicately on the nail of it, failed to chew it off, just nibbled at it, for a moment. "That is," he concluded, "unfortunate. You will fall into despair, be made as nothing, and never return to the Bleak Academy."

She looked at him.

"I cannot help you," he said. "I am *expecting* myself to help you, it is obvious that I must help you, but I cannot. You see. I had thought that it was an easy process, that one could simply go out of the Bleak Academy and go back in again, but I was incorrect. The situation is beyond me."

He turned his eyes away. The life began to fade from them. A sense of empathy struck her; she could practically *see* the world becoming less resolved, less clear, in the direction where he was un-focusing his eyes.

She shook him. He ignored her. She shook him harder. She told him: "Hey!"

"You are trying to have me stay with you," he said. "But I do not want to stay with you. I wish to return instead to sliding slowly down that hill. That is why I have come here, you understand. This is the place to go, if one wishes to stare blindly at the sky or earth and slip slowly over the course of years, decades, or centuries into a division in the world."

"Well, yes," she said.

"Yes?"

"That is also why I am here," she said. "Because I concluded that a useful ally such as yourself would be found in such a place."

"Ha!" he said, and, almost unwillingly, took a breath; his chest expanded, fell, and there was more life in him. "So this is a place that one might come to to slide slowly down a hill forever into nothingness, but *also* a place to come to if one is hoping *not* to slide slowly down a hill forever into nothingness? That is perversity."

"I'm a sensible, married woman," she protested.

His eye twitched. "Married women are capable of perversity."

"Pish-tosh," she told him.

He leaned back. "An able argument; I find myself incapable of a reply."

He stretched a hand out towards the sky. He stared at it for a while. She watched him.

He said, "I used to worship the sun, you know."

"Did you?"

"It was so very bright," he said. "I took a piece of its brightness, and carried it around with me and inside me, and I thought that I would use it to illuminate that Glum, and then all things would be made in brightness. But this did not happen so."

He spun his finger around, held it up and twirled it in the air, and a light unspooled from it. It became a little spark, a little star, that orbited around that spire.

"Glum is made of loathing," he said. "It is made of the will to not look at a thing; or, to look at a thing, and yet not see. I do not know if that is what it *is*. But that is what it is *made of*. Do you follow?"

"Unswervingly."

"So I drew lines around it," he said. "North, south, east, and west. And I caught it in that box and exposed it to the sun. I thought, what is there that is lit by the sun that I could truly loathe? What is there that, caught in that perfect brightness, I could choose ever not to see? I thought that when the light of the sun shone on that Glum, then that Glum would be no more."

"But it did not go well?"

He laughed. Then he ceased to laugh. He fell still, not even breathing, and eventually he wrapped his arms around his chest. "The harder I struggled to contain it," he said, "the more of it slipped free. And so I strove harder, integrated myself, my own being, into the process of the containment of it. Thus, Glum became contained within *me*, and I became anathema to myself."

"Oh," she said.

"There is a lake of bitterness inside me," he said. "Sometimes I forget. Sometimes I let myself forget. But there is a lake of night-black, blur-grey, plum-dark Glum inside me, where my center, my breath and heart and lungs of me, ought to be. That is why I gave up, you see. That is why I stopped paying attention to the world. I became indistinguishable from Glum, at the heart of me; the will not to see the world became my self."

She raised an eyebrow at him. "*I* can distinguish the two of you," she said.

He frowned at her.

"Can you?" he said.

The way he said it made it harder. She became aware that he was exhaling it—sort of. It was fuming outwards from him as he spoke. She could *taste* it in the air, the mark of Glum. And if she were a less practical woman, she might have felt a duty of attention there, might have felt that it was incumbent upon her as a servant of the truth to focus on that, to bring it to the surface of her attention, to see all the ways in which he was *exactly* Glum; but Perdition had sharpened her into a knife.

It was far more *useful* to focus her attention on the rest of him, on all the ways he was not Glum, and answer: "Without question."

And he sat on that hill, in the long white gown of him, in that long white gown that was black and brown in the contours of its folds, and a sun, a little sun, spun around the finger of his hand, and his hat was tall and white and square atop it like a scholar's ought to be, and finally he said, "Well, then," and smiled, as creakily as new leather, and added, "that's a thing."

He firmed up, there, the outlines of him. He pulled himself back from the emptiness. He saw himself, and as he saw himself, he saw himself to be *there*.

"Then I will face it again," he said. "And I will congeal it into a thing, and I will take that thing, and it will be a key to the gates of the Bleak Academy, for me, and I will go back home."

They walked back to her gate house.

She realized after a while that they were walking back to her gate house. They were talking, and had been talking, although she had no idea what they had said. She felt that something was wrong there, that there was something there that she had failed to understand, or that he had; and she reached for it, grasped at it, tried to dig it out from the conversation, but she could not find it.

He had introduced himself, she thought. That had happened.

She had told him of her encounter, earlier, with Glum.

They'd laughed together, for some reason, about her project, about her work on building a gate house beyond the gates of the Bleak Academy, though she could not remember why.

There was something missing. It bugged her, but it didn't bug her. It bothered her, but she couldn't hang on to the way it bothered her. It slipped away, because they were talking, and that talking was distracting.

It was cunning, in the way that it had slipped from her attention.

She could not find it.

She did not know.

LATER SHE found herself accompanying him out to confront Glum again.

"Stay back," he said, "if you cannot help me."

It was possible that she could help him. She considered it to be possible. But if she couldn't, then his words were fair and trying to step in would only make things worse; and if she *could* help him, then he would have slighted her competence unjustly, and would *deserve* to have her hold back instead of helping him out.

So she stayed back.

It struck her as unfortunate, rather than convenient, that she would have come to the same action regardless of the underlying situation. It gave her the unsettling sense that actions did not have reasons, but only justifications; that she was standing back, not because it was correct in some fashion, but because she was Mrs. Senko, and when someone told Mrs. Senko "stay back, if you cannot help me," she was the *type* to smirk, stand back, and watch.

She toyed with that thought, as she watched him. *Why is that?*

Or rather: *what kind of person would that be?*

He was building a square for himself in the canyon. She took a moment to review the existence of the canyon but could determine nothing about it, save that its coloration implied that that corner of the world was dry.

It was not, in short, a canyon of fallen pilgrims, or a canyon of descending gods, or a canyon of rising milkshakes, or in fact, anything of that sort. It had no story. It was merely a canyon in Perdition, where the risen fallen pilgrim worked by effort to build a square.

By effort:

He drew the lines with will alone; with will alone he worked his magic. He glared at the world, and *made* a line burst forth: undulating along the ground, carving itself into the dust. It was as if a fiberglass thread were being furiously reeled in *from* his feet *to* the point that was the focus of his gaze, carving a shallow trench along the earth along its way.

It came forth straight, or, at least, essentially straight. In the big picture it was straight. In the small details there was a wobble, an eccentricity, a precession.

It was visible principally by the trench it made, but if she looked hard, she could see the line itself. She thought she could see the line itself. It was ... troublesome, to do so. The more she looked at it, the more she discerned of it, the more she understood of it that it had a character that could not be seen with eyes alone.

The trench was three or four hair-widths' wide, but the line had no width at all.

"It is," he said, to her, as if deducing the focus of her attention from its effects on the environment, "a representation of my will. A miracle, if you like."

"Miracle?"

"When a thing is done by will alone," he said, "the texts of the Bleak Academy name it a miracle. Because it supersedes the *process* that characterizes mundane acts."

"I see."

He turned his gaze. The line of his will turned a corner. It was terribly precise.

"Is that what you studied?" she asked him, as he worked. "Right angles?"

"It is Shirokova's theorem," he said, and his eyes were brighter as he said it. "All angles tend towards the right angle until otherwise resolved."

Then he looked at her, and the line ground to a halt.

"I have not been speaking loudly enough," he said. "So now you are too close."

"Oh," she said.

"You should not converse with people you do not want to be standing next to," he said, sounding mildly aggrieved.

She wanted to protest that he had started it, but it would have only sounded defensive. Instead, she looked at the sky.

"You need not be embarrassed," she said, imputing that defensiveness to *him*. "Your work is of adequate character and interest."

He bit his lip. He sighed. He waved her away, and she retreated a step or two, and he made another turning of the line. Then he stopped.

"Three sides," he said, "are all I can manage before it arrives."

"I can't hear you," she said. "I'm too far away to converse."

His face twitched.

"Fair enough," he said.

The sun came drifting down from the sky as she watched and it made the shadows long. The sun fell into the container that he'd made, and it burned there, it glowed there, it made an awful light. She found it far too pale for her tastes, far too colorless. She could not be sure, the more she regarded it, whether it was the actual sun at all.

Then he began to speak.

These were words that she could not hear. He did not address them to her, and they were well-separated then, she was standing somewhere far away from the open box that he had made. She was in a distant shelter and the sunlight did not reach her, and he was speaking, not to her, but rather, to that Glum.

And she understood in that moment that this was his tool to draw it close. This was his mechanism to call that Glum into his trap.

He spoke to it, and it was there.

Glum poured from his lips, it blobbed out from him, it seeped out from the cracks in him and in the world, and she did not want to regard it. It spilled out from him there, roiled, and poured into the cup of lines that he had made, and where it went she did not want to see. It gathered up, it bunched around the sun, it did not like the light of that sun—*nor*, she found herself thinking, *does the light of that sun like thee*—and suddenly she felt an appalling disinterest in the canyon, in the box, in the sun, in the ex-fallen pilgrim; she found her attention wavering, she almost walked away.

Such was the power of the thing that she called Glum.

But Mrs. Senko was responsible. She wished to think of herself as a responsible person. She had engineered this confrontation, and, appealing to her or not—whether it was attractive to look upon or the most loathsome, repugnant, and even *uninteresting* thing imaginable—she felt a certain duty in her to see it out.

So, answering duty's call, she looked upon the scene below, and remembered that the pilgrim was the pilgrim, and Glum was Glum.

He took his will and he caged it. He contained it by miracle.

He sealed it in the presence of the sun.

Thus she was able to bear witness to the process of the corrosion of a miracle. Thus she was able to see the means by which the fallen pilgrim came undone. The lines of his thoughts were thrashing as he sought to contain it; where he had been drawing these straight lines and corners, now as it strained against him they became tentacles, they fluttered, they flapped; his square bulged up, became a net, grew fencing, tried to draw itself taut around the thing named Glum as it surged to cross the borders he had made.

It burst upwards, flowered towards the sky, first Glum did and then the net around it followed. It seethed, sunlight and darkness both, and the sunlight began to break through—for as much as disinterest cloaked the world, it was impossible to sustain it in the face of that amazing sight. One cannot reject the ocean when it splashes you. One cannot be bored with an erupting volcano when one is standing before its face. Glum was a *refusal-to-see*, Glum was a *looking-away*, but there was no looking away from this:

It was visceral, watching Glum struggle against its containment. It was joyous. And as her heart responded to these things with interest, the sunlight strengthened—

And ended, in the moment that the struggle ended. Victory had bred defeat:

The walls of his will sealed around Glum, Glum ceased to struggle, and before she could blink the whole of the structure ceased to mean anything at all.

She couldn't focus on it.

She couldn't make herself pay attention to it. She *didn't want to look there.*

It had melted in the light of the sun, and congealed again, into something onto which the fire of her consciousness could shed no light. She could pay no attention to it; the show had ended. The whole structure slipped too easily from her sight; and when she forced herself, when she left herself with no alternative, when she looked at the box that held Glum and let herself look at nothing else, her mind drifted off into daydreams instead.

She thought about ... how nice it was that she was watching. She wondered where he'd come from, originally, what his story had been, that pilgrim that she'd dredged up from the hill.

She imagined a key shining in the darkness.

It glittered there, turning, spinning, and it was beautiful, and she loved it, her heart yearned towards it, she reached out a hand, almost instinctively, before she laughed, before embarrassment crested in her and she understood that she had dreamed it; and then, with a sick horror, that she'd ceased entirely to be aware of the pilgrim, and of Glum, and of the fact that *he was he* and *it was it*.

She looked for him, she found him, but a burden of guilt struck her and made it hard to focus on him; for he was failing. He was congealing, like liquid amber was sealing in his form.

In a blink she was beside him.

She was hovering over him. She was telling him, "Are you all right?" and he looked at her.

"If you put it in a box," he said. "It becomes the box. Thus, it cannot be contained."

"Well, yes," she said, "but are you okay? Can I help you?"

He shook his head.

Slowly, as if she had misunderstood him, he repeated. "It is a thing that cannot be contained. So why am I here, trying to contain it?"

"... I don't know," she said. "You never actually explained."

He laughed at that. It was beautiful. He had a really nice laugh. Then *it* fountained from him, it poured from him like a river, it bubbled from his throat and nose and eyes, and fell across her, and she remembered nothing more.

... she found herself later.

She realized that she'd been drifting. She'd been failing to pay attention, which is a dangerous thing when by attention alone are you warranted eternal life, and an even more dangerous thing when one travels in the outer dark, because if one stops paying attention to one's location in the outer dark, one could easily wind up anywhere. When a cave looks the same as a dragon's mouth and one year is much the same as any other, when the sky and the ground are basically the same geometry and a pillar, pencil, and birch tree are all alike, when you are in the far Outside or, worse, Perdition, you really do need to pay attention to where you're going or you might wind up anywhere; but on this occasion she did not. Or rather, she wound up anywhere, *an* anywhere, she wound up *somewhere*, but it was not the kind of anywhere about which cautionary tales are traditionally told.

She came back to awareness in the arms of her muck-made husband. She found herself disentangling from him, pulling away, sitting up at the edge of her bed and thinking, and realizing that sometime in that consuming darkness she'd come home.

She shook him. She woke him.

"There's something weird here," she said. "This isn't normal."

He tilted his head. "What is normal?" he asked.

"... bah," she said. "What does a muck-man know?"

"The color of the sky, the waves of the sea, the feathers of a goose, the stones of a keep, the warmth of the fire, the number seven, the number nine, and my name," he recited.

"That's ... eight things," she said, blankly.

"It is a boundless and measureless knowledge," he agreed.

A SECOND PILGRIM WAS TRIED; and a creature found upon a mountaintop; Perdition was *rife* with they who'd come, to do a thing or two about that Glum.

... but to no avail.

The Empress, whose every word came true, could not speak with enough precision to bind it down; could not catch *the thing she reflexively didn't think about* in her web of truth save by articulating literally everything; and if she has not finished, she is speaking still. A creature without edges, who infected neighboring concepts with itself, did no better: Mrs. Senko dared not look at it, dared not interact with it; gingerly and vigilantly, she escorted it to its fight with Glum; and it was sickening to realize afterwards that she did not know whether the two of them were now newly, or had always been, the same.

In the face of repeated failures she almost lost herself; almost ceased to have a specific location, to take specific actions, to be specifically *Mrs. Senko;* took to wandering in a despairing daze—

But then there came a knocking on her door; and she remembered she was home.

"PARDON THIS UNWORTHY SCHOLAR," he said. "But: *from the Bleak Academy one has come, to do a thing or two about that Glum.*"

The man at the door looked embarrassed. He scratched behind his head.

"That's what I was told to say, at any rate," he said. "Are you Mrs. Senko?"

She nodded.

"Ah," he said. Then, floundering: "Is Mr. Senko in?"

She took the man's coat and hat. She hung them on Mr. Senko's outstretched hands. "He's busy," she explained.

"Well," the man said. "May I come in? Or, I am already in. Resolved."

He looked around.

He nodded to himself. "In any case," he said, "your father said that I was to assist you. That you had become distracted from your duties by some kind of errantry against a 'Glum.' And that if I came out and helped you, he might even let me back in."

She looked him over. "What, he was getting rid of you?"

"Ahaha," he said. "Well. Possibly? Oh!"

He bowed.

"I am Mr. Wan," he said. "Or sometimes Mr. One, but only if you do not listen very closely. If you listen very closely, it should be clear that it is *Wan*. Because there is a falling tone."

"I don't know what you're talking about," she said.

"The first time I died," he said. "I found myself in a small place. A dark place. Whithersoever which way I turned I saw only the True Thing that was preceding things, and I could not lay my hand upon it. And I thought that was to be the end of me, slowly withering away within that void. But then the Headmaster your father realized, 'Why, that Wan—if he's dead, I can find ten thousand more just like him!' And he picked me out from that teeming throng, and I woke from death as from a dream."

He took his hat back from Mr. Senko. He clutched it against his heart.

"That is why I am Mr. Wan," he said. "Or, 'Mr. Ten Thousand.' What one learns, ten thousand learn. When one lives, ten thousand live. But when one dies, ten thousand yet remain. —that was his great gift to me. A life even more eternal than his own. For not even the uttermost eradication of the soul could extinguish me, as long as nobody pays too much attention to the math."

"It's a heap paradox?" she asked.

He shrugged.

"It's this unworthy scholar," he said, pressing his right hand to his chest. "Mr. Wan, the disposable. But please do not dispose of me too readily. I can be an excellent assistant!"

"You have still not explained—" she said.

"Oh," he said. "Well. You know how it is. One cannot enter the Bleak Academy without a key, so obviously I must help you find one if I am ever to return."

She froze for a long moment. She looked at Mr. Senko. Mr. Senko looked back. Then she turned her gaze to Mr. Wan.

"This is new information," she conceded. "I had thought myself establishing my independence."

"Well, you have done that too," he said. "He did, I think, expect at least a letter."

"I have been busy!" she protested. "Wandering in a despairing daze."

He shrugged.

"But if I write to him more regularly ..." she said, strategically.

"Well," he said, "it is not—I mean, you have to understand. It is not this scholar's department, the entrances and exits to the Bleak Academy."

"But—"

"I cannot help you," he said, plaintively. "I cannot even get back through, myself."

"He can't have locked me out," she said.

He looked away.

"Well," he said, "perhaps there will be a key for you when you have completed your assignment."

"You have brought me no end of ill news," she said, "so you may take over coat rack duties while I stare out the window of my drawing room and sulk."

He brightened; the expression on his face was really quite delightful. But he was feckless; he did not take his duties seriously; later, she found him wandering in the gardens with Mr. Senko, coats draped carelessly over their shoulders, on what appeared to be a "field trip" and "discussion of their duties," and she could only shake her head.

A WHILE later:

"I have never had an assistant before," she confided. "So you will have to explain to me: what is it that you do?"

"Ah," he said.

He went to a small lopsided chair that she had set up in the corner of the room. He knelt down beside its three-leggedness and he took out a small ink pot. He brushed at it, with that ink, blackened the three-leggedness of the chair, and slowly it faded out; she blinked, and there was something wrong, she watched it fading:

"I make corrections," he said, and the chair's imbalance drowned under a primal night.

After a while, he was done.

The chair stood in the corner, and it was no longer a small lopsided chair. It was—what it *was* was unclear. Portions of its existence had been unmade, rendered down, drowned under a lacquer coat of that thing that precedes being and non-being, the hungry void that precedes the presence or the absence of a thing.

Its small lopsidedness simply wasn't there.

"It is best not to sit in it for a while," he said, "since its state is currently ambiguous."

"That is the way of things," she said.

"—yes," he agreed. "But it will be easier if you ignore it for a while, let it orient on a new state of being on its own. For you understand me, I have not created any balance in it, or any fourth leg for your ~~three-legged~~ chair, but only redressed the error that there was."

"How many legs *has* it?" she asked him, but he gave her a weak smile and waved his hands.

"Such questions," he said, "are beyond me! I am only Mr. Wan."

"So," she said.

"I have a paint pot," he said. "I make corrections. Nothing more. It is the color of the thing before things, the thing that precedes things, the thing that is not and neither is, but rather originates, arises, comes before. It is the true thing that vibrates under the appearances of things, or, rather, that is the color of this ink. It is the will of the primal void to say, 'ah, you have seen incorrectly; that thing was never there.'"

"And was it?"

"Well," he said, "no, I suppose."

"No?"

"If I have corrected it," he said, "you may assume that it was already in some kind of error. It is a genuine act of correction rather than a pure act of destruction. That was probably a perfectly good chair all along and you were just looking at it wrong."

She stared at him for a while. Then she shook her head. Not harshly; it was more to herself than to him, though the words that followed were not.

"I think," she said, "that that is an attitude more suitable for a Mrs. Senko than for her assistant, Mr. Wan."

He laughed. She looked at him. He waved his hand and covered his mouth with the other.

"It's just," he said, "that your father's often said something much the same."

That scene ended there.

The world slipped, there.

~~There was an interregnum. Then~~ she was facing Glum. She was in a place of stone, a cellar made of stone, and she was facing Glum, and it was dripping down the walls. She was on a cold outcropping of some grass-dusted hill at night, staring down at a forest, and Glum was rising through it like a flood, seeping through the night behind her, swallowing the moon.

Events like beads from a broken string:

Confrontation after confrontation, moment and then moment, the central logic of them, the causality of them, the thing that led from one to the other of them erased; and nowhere in there anywhere was Mr. Wan.

She struggled for sense; she seized for the strand of her life again:

~~The interregnum passed.~~

She startled back to awareness, in her sprawling gatehouse in the dark. She became aware of Mr. Wan again; of herself again; of the ~~three-legged~~ chair, and his demonstration.

It sank in.

"We should go," she said, making a snap decision. "We will do things that way. We will make *corrections* to that Glum."

He bowed to her. "I am," he said, "for nothing more."

A passing worry struck her as she rose to her feet; a concern, regarding the consequences of stripping out one piece from the grand Design:

"And, just for clarity," she said, hesitating; "there is no danger? I mean, no existential danger? I mean—"

Here she blushed, for he was staring at her in an odd kind of perturbation, as if she had lost her senses: "I mean, we are not endangering Perdition, or the gatehouse, or the Bleak Academy, if we eliminate that Glum?"

"Oh," he said. "No."

He looked out the window at the world.

"There is a great darkness," he said. "A vast darkness, to which all of this is but a raindrop in the sea. I cannot say how important it is, on our human scale, but I can say that Glum is nothing fundamental. It is ... we are just dust. Do not be afraid that you will break something fundamental. Do not be afraid that I will break something fundamental. We are only Mrs. Senko, and Mr. Wan."

And she was possessed, for a moment, with a glimpse of that vision.

She felt herself amidst deep waters, she felt them playing over her, pushing and pulling at her, bogging down her clothes. She felt the *weight* of them, the waters of the existence of the world, the waters of the *nature* of the world, and they were refreshing and they cleared her head of errant concepts but also they were cold and—

It struck her in that moment—

Not so endless, deep, and dark as he had said; an ocean, yes, infinitely greater than any sponge, but not unending as he'd implied. They could use it up.

She could use it up.

~~Interregnum.~~

"I don't know why," she murmured, "but my attention keeps slipping. I blame Glum, I think, or that pot of ink."

"It is all right," he said.

"Mm?"

"To dream great dreams, and get lost among them, is the right of those who attend the Bleak Academy."

"Ah."

"Now let us go," he said, and beamed, and waved her out, "and do a thing or two about that Glum."

This they did; but they did not well.

HE STOOD BEFORE GLUM and it poured in over the edges of the world, and he lifted up his little pot of paint, and he scrubbed it out; and she drew back, as that blackness spread, as that night that preceded the light of existence spread, and she watched it pour over him, watched it swallow him; staggered back and found her back against a wall, curled away, looked away, did not watch as it consumed him, as it swallowed ~~Mr. Wan.~~

~~She~~

...

"MRS.— MRS. SENKO?" he asked. He shook her awake.

"Mm," she said.

She licked dry lips. She swallowed. She looked around.

She said, "You died."

"Yes."

"You *died,*" she said. "You ... were never even there in the first place."

"Yes." He hesitated. "Well, arguably."

"But—"

"One may die," he said, "one may, perhaps, have never even *been;* but, ten thousand yet remain."

He had said it; she *knew* as much, but: "Ah-h?"

He gave her a quirky little smile. "It is my best feature," he said. "Formerly, it was probably something else, but once I began to develop a habit of dying, being consumed by nothingness, and/or never having even been there to begin with, it rapidly became the crown jewel among my talents."

She sighed. "...what, ah, happened, there? Then?"

"Ah," he said.

He reflected on this.

"Well," he said, "If I had to say it, I'd say that I lost track of the edge between myself and Glum, and painted over it, thus causing myself to stop existing. Arguably. I was presumably not even actually there in the first place, leaving the entire thing to *actually* be a natural fault line in the underlying continuum, haha."

She frowned at him; then her gaze drifted to the plateau they were on: to its grass, to its oranges. "This is not where we were," she said.

"No," he agreed.

They looked outwards for a moment.

"It is difficult to keep track of one's location," he concluded, "beyond the gates of the Bleak Academy. Is the relocation inconvenient?"

She shook her head. She walked to the edge of the plateau. She stared down a long cliff's side, and kicked over a rock.

"I intend to do better," he said, "the next occasion."

"I don't understand," she said, "what has just happened."

"You sound distressed."

"These past few events," she said, "have been *stuttering,* Mr. Wan. They should not be stuttering. They should stand up straight! Fix their collar! And stop this namby-pamby stumbling!"

"The work of the Bleak Academy," he said, after a moment, "is difficult to understand."

"Bah," she pointed out, "I am my father's daughter."

"True," he agreed.

He considered that, and then shook his head. "For lifetimes," he said, "piled upon lifetimes, I have studied the stuff preceding being and nothingness; the substance of emptiness and dream. For lifetimes upon lifetimes I have struggled with the central questions of reality, tried to put a kind of shape to the shapelessness, to understand the ink that I use in my corrections, and still I am merely a disposable student. Still I am merely Mr. Wan. It is elusive. It is ineffable. The substance that precedes things—it is difficult to track. Is it really any wonder that when I dab a bit of it over that Glum that matters become hard for the eyes to watch, for the ears to hear?"

"You should fence it off," she protested, but then she remembered that Glum was a thing that knew no real containment. She chewed on her lip. Then she shook her head. "I apologize," she said. "That was an erroneous conceit."

"It is myself," he said, "that I fence off, myself and the things that I do not wish to paint. I draw a line, not around my target, but around all the things that I do not wish to correct. Then I paint what still remains."

He shrugged.

"But it is difficult, because—

"When I strike something away, it is me saying, 'you are false; you are false, and I will no longer play the game of you.' When I am calm, when I am goal-oriented, it is easy to color within the lines. When things become difficult, though, it is very easy to slip.

"Still.

"I slipped. It is all right. As you can see, there is no harm done. And hey, free oranges."

He plucked one from a tree. He bit into it. After a moment, delicately, he withdrew his teeth, stared at the thing in puzzlement, and remembered how to peel an orange.

"I wish some reassurance," she said, "that you will not slip again—"

But he did.

It became *obvious* that he did; there was no denying it, though there was no perceiving it, because that moment became inseparable from moments after. He did not fight Glum, but sometime during the absence of his fight with Glum, he spilled the pot; it ran over his life, the fight, the time before and after. It ate his promises, if he gave them; his valor, if he showed any; his memorial and his burial, if she gave him one.

"I wish some reassurance," she had said, "that you will not slip again—"

~~Then,~~

Then, there was only the True Thing.

Then, there was only a time and space that ink flowed over, immeasurable, uncountable, until she was wrenching herself out of nightmare some other day:

~~Screaming, falling, glitching, glaring, and~~ they were in her house, she was waking, there was a knocking on her door, and when she opened it, he was there, blushing, Mr. Wan.

"Pardon this unworthy scholar," he whispered, shame-facedly, and she let him in.

"Leave it its life," she urged. Proposed. Suggested. "Take its mind, its will instead."

"It has neither," he said. "It is only Glum."

~~The world stuttered; glitched.~~

"I wish some reassurance," she was saying, "that you will not slip again—"

...and

But he did.

IT BECAME A PATTERN, and she loathed him for it.

She found herself hating him more than she had ever hated anything; and admiring that, in the moments between moments, treasuring that, clutching that to her heart, writing letters about it to her father,

Father,

You will never guess! It is terribly exciting! I have learned to hate!

It was difficult to appraise his technique. It was difficult to correct him. It was even difficult to really get any sort of data about *what he was doing wrong*, because it was all so terribly uninteresting, so terribly dull and unappealing, to even look in its direction made her mind itch and her hackles rise—then, even *worse* than unappealing, but never having even happened in the first place; having been *corrected* away from ever having happened in the first place, if it ever had, leaving only the most confusing patches of memory and the occasional translocation through Perdition behind it.

It was not even, she had realized, at some point, with a creeping horror, *him*, that any of it had happened to—presumably. She had been, almost certainly, mistaking a series of *other people* for him, or, at least, was doing so in retrospect:

And who they were, who they had ever been, if they had ever been, was lost.

Ideally, none of that had happened. Ideally, there had never been any Mr. Wan to visit her until the one that had not yet come. That is what *he'd* suggest, if she brought it up to him, with a nervous burst of laughter—

That it was all misattributed natural phenomena or flights of imagination, writ back in retrospect, into the tapestry of events that formed her life.

...the concept held little comfort.

Her life became disjointed.

Her life became bounded by missing intervals, by *those* missing intervals, when Mr. Wan would spar with Glum. And, of course, each time he died.

IT WAS bleak and awful but it was not pointlessly repetitious.

As they struggled, she was *learning*.

Over the course of time she came to understand things better, to see them more. She put together bits and pieces, cut them together like fragments of an image overlain one on top of another to realize at last a form.

She dug out the words beneath corrections, the image hidden by the pot of ink; she saw at last, assembling the truth from endless dangling shards and pieces, the moment of Mr. Wan's true ending:

How as he painted over Glum, it became anathema to itself; how it unwove, how it *did* unweave, but drank him in in the moment of its ending.

How he fell *into* it, because in painting over it he cut himself off from truth.

~~And eventually, he saw it too.~~

He told her, softly, "I do not know that I want to keep doing this, Mrs. Senko."

~~He invoked his power; one fell, yet still Mr. Wan remained.~~

"It is very hard," he said, "to keep dying like this, over and over again."

~~And~~ finally she held out an arm to bar him when he went to leave the room. "Then that's enough," she told him. "You can stop."

~~"I can't," he said, and shook his head. "I have promised. I have sacrificed. You depend on me. I have already tried so hard. I must find my way back to the Bleak Academy. I must do this. I must do this. I can't stop."~~

~~He had a look of terrible nobility to him. He shouldered his great burden. He braced himself to go out and wrestle with the impossible—~~

"Pish-tosh," she interrupted, as definitive as any ink.

"… eh, haha?"

"I am a practical woman," she said. "One day, I intend to make myself *reknowned* for it. And to throw yourself endlessly at something that's too hard for you, for reasons that boil down to a bunch of *words?*"

In tones of starkest condemnation, she finished: "… would be impractical."

He stared at her. For a long time he stared at her; but she was Mrs. Senko, and he was only her assistant. Mr. Wan.

He lowered his head, and a great sigh went out of him, and he accepted it. For long seconds he wrestled with that acceptance as if it were a boulder; felt its contours, heaved it up, as if he were to place it on a rock wall around his heart—

A look of surprised delight grew slowly on his face.

She was not sure how it was possible to see it, but she saw it: a silver glow lit within his chest, and he cupped his hands before it.

"Ah," he said.

And in that moment, with a hint of bitterest envy, she understood that *somehow* he had found the key to it—

He could return to the Bleak Academy.

SHE let him go.

She was bitter about it. She was angry—but she did not let him see. She let him go, and her face did not turn ugly until Mr. Wan was gone. She did not desperately scratch at the gates, trying to force her way through them with all the wildness of a trapped cat, until Mr. Wan was gone. She did not slump and lose control of her tears for the first time since her exile until he was safely gone and well inside.

It did no good; the gates were closed.

THAT WAS THAT; she was done; she had had her time of fighting Glum.

When she recovered, and had put proper bandages on her nails, and straightened out her hair, and washed her face, she went back to the task that her father had set her to, building a gate-house in the dark.

In despite of Glum. —sensible or not, that is what she felt as she was building it. She set each timber in its place in anger. She lay each stone, aggrieved. She carried herself in it, in that great anger, as if each step she took was in despite of Glum. In defiance of its existence. In defiance of her own desire to tame it, to end it, to make it taste defeat.

She did not really believe that it cared; or, rather, she doubted that it even *noticed*. She was as a child, spitting at a pond, and imagining thus to spite the sea. But still, she carried herself with such a rage! With such a set of anger!

She made a sled, hitched it to beasts like the shadows of some reindeer, and dragged in towers to surround the gates and keep Glum out. And at first she alloyed them with a mortar of her will, she built it in and through them, as if a miracle, to make them strong, to make them fierce; but then she thought better on it and crashed those towers down.

Too well she remembered the fate of the fallen pilgrim, who had sought to contain Glum with his will alone.

She sat and she sketched diagrams in the dirt and she was terribly alone, and that bothered her, when it had not bothered her before. All the years before her existence she had been alone, and she had not even known it. All the days after her creation and her exile, alone, and she'd hardly noticed, only now ...

There was a terribleness to her independence.

She wanted to talk to someone about what she was doing, but there was no one. In the end she found herself ranting to Mr. Senko, stomping around him and explaining, but he was at best a rough draft of a person, the barest nod towards the ideal of company.

"I'm sure you'll handle it, Mrs. Senko," he said.

Or, "That sounds a bit like the feathers of a goose."

She thought about adding something more to him—about taking more of the flame inside her and pouring it into him, about setting him on fire with creativity, independent spirit, and *life*, but she was scared to make the attempt in Perdition, where her own fire was already weaker than it should be.

"You are a soulless mechanism," she sighed, to him.

"Ah. —is that all right?"

"It would be preferable if you lit a great fire of creativity inside yourself," she said. "To pair with my own, more sensible streak."

He nodded. He bowed. He went off to the kitchen and played with the pilot light.

After a while, she went in and found his head on fire. Then, because this was, after all, Perdition, his head ceased to be on fire. He wandered off.

She did not know whether to feel shame or pride for this, to have wrought so much less well than her father, when she was the one that he had wrought. Should she say to myself, "Ah, I am such a clever and beautiful creation?"

Or: "Why did I make my husband such a lump?"

But eventually he came to her, and his head was blackened, and his hands were seared, and he said, "I do not want to do that again."

"Do what?"

"I lit a great fire of creativity in myself," he said. "And suddenly I was full of thoughts that were not the color of the sky, the waves of the sea, the feathers of a goose, the stones of a keep, the warmth of the fire, the number seven, the number nine, or 'Mr. Senko.' What *were* they? I did not know.

"It frightened me, so I doused the flame."

She studied him for a while, and then she reached up to pat him awkwardly on the head. "There, there," she said. "I asked you only to light it, not to keep it lit, so you have fulfilled my desires well."

He nodded. He went to sit in his favorite chair and stare at his favorite wall. And she, who had sought for something that she could not find, felt strangely relieved regardless, strangely better, regardless, and instead of straining against her loneliness she found the substance she had sought.

She had found her answer against that Glum.

She told herself that she was no longer fighting Glum. She reminded herself that she was no longer *looking* for answers to Glum. But she found herself acting on her new answer anyway.

She rode out her sled into the depths of the chaos, went deep into the places she had never seen. There she dug, and dug, and dug some more, until she had unearthed a thing that was deep and wild and sacred.

There was fear in it, and grief, and loneliness, too; there was beauty and wonder; there was the essence of fascination itself—for most of all, what she found there was the essence of *that which she could not help but look upon.*

It was viscous, like mud. It shone, like poison.

The longer she stared at it, the less she understood, and yet, the more she understood—as if it were the aurora, or the ocean; the twilight, or the dawn; the laughter of a child; the opening of a flower: it did not fill the spaces in her with understanding but rather opened them wider so that a deeper understanding might later come.

This became the mortar for her towers.

There was not enough of the sacred to be found, or at least she could not find enough of it; in the end she had to settle for lesser substances as well. There was mere loneliness, and the crashing waves of an unknown sea; there was the fixation of fear, both fears she had and fears that were alien to her; the gruesome and the wonderful.

Anything that she could not look away from:

She brought it back to her gatehouse, ground it down, and made it into the mortar of her towers' stones.

The towers rose. She built levels and levels of them, brought in planks of wood and circled stone around them, and in and through the towers was the alloy of that *compelling* thing which she had found, in defiance of that Glum.

When one stood beneath those towers one could not look away.

She would stand in their shadow and her heart would open, regardless of her will; she would stare up at them and she would be lost in them, they would trap her gaze and fill her sight and it would drown her, she would snap to herself in startlement and seconds or minutes would have passed, and she would feel like the shadow of a sun-eating bird had passed across her soul.

And she thought, if Glum were there, that she would crucify it against the altar of those towers.

It would slick them with the substance of it; it would crawl upon their holy surfaces; and it would try, how it would try! to turn her eyes away—but her eyes would not turn away. She would not *want* to look, perhaps, but … what choice would she have? To look away was a matter of effort, luck, and time.

There against the towers she would pin it, will she or nill she, and there against the towers it would thrash and it would weaken; she would assault it, o! with the gatehouse armaments; and she would not close the box around it, would not make the mistake the first pilgrim made and make the ring of towers Glum, but would rather seal both it *and* she herself inside.

If she were still fighting Glum, that was what would happen, she thought.

But, she was not.

"I'm not," she said. The impulse was uncontrollable and fey. "I'm done," she said. "Did you *hear* me, *Glum*? I'm *done*."

The name was, of course, a summons, an invocation; a command.

IN THAT moment, the pulse of her attention faltered.

In that moment, the towers all still riveted her but she lost track of the fact that there was a *her* that they were riveting; in that moment, her entire experience of the world in a burst unraveled, her thoughts all drifted and diffracted, and she entirely failed to notice that she was failing to notice ... well, anything at all.

In that moment, the fire that was her consciousness nearly stuttered and went out, for Glum was *there*—and had it pressed its advantage, then, she would have died; it could have murdered the *I am* in her, the power that made her *be* and not *be not.* She could have ceased to perform that function in an instant, lost the instrumentality of her own existence, and from that failure even the fire that is consciousness cannot (or, not on its own, at least) recover.

Glum did not press its advantage, then; or, at least, it did not so in time.

One could call it a miracle, perhaps—that articulation of the fire, in the absence of the self, that brings the self back to existence. One could call it a miracle; or a *something in the world, that moves;* or the characteristic action, at the minimum, of someone predisposed through training or heredity to evoke their own existence should they ever find that it isn't there.

Her attention wandered, but it came full circle; she *recalled* that she was drowning in the pall of Glum.

... and she struck back.

By dint of will, her cannons fired; they burst against the substance of that Glum.

Tracking her gaze, her grapnels fired; they sunk deep into the flesh of Glum.

Look away, her mind screamed. It was like flaying her own spirit, it was, to watch Glum writhe. It was like cutting away the fabric of herself—

But against the backdrop of the towers, that did not matter; she did not flinch or look away. In her horror and fascination she was held still:

She grasped the monster with her eyes, and she held it there.

And in that very moment—far, far away—Valentina Grigorievna Sosunova had a certain thought.

LIKE A WALKING ELEPHANT it crossed Valentina's mind, the thought—and ponderously, and vast:

"I am myself; but more than that, I am a fire of *looking-upon* myself. Only, even to this day, even knowing that I am that flame—when I look upon myself, I see a monster of bone and meat. And only now does it occur to me to ask:

"In what fashion, in what manner, does that image come to be?"

Inexorably, then—and in accordance with the resonating footsteps of that thought—Valentina bent her attention inwards; tried to track the beginning and the ending of the process that was involved; and shockingly, it struck her, as she did, that both the *looking-upon*, the discovery of herself *in* herself, and the poisonous judgment that was soon to follow ... were conscious, and were effortful.

It was by dint of effort and attention that she cast out the net of her inward vision—that she sent out the power that was in her to see herself, and dragged that power afterwards back in. When she had done so, in that net, she would find a mix of abstruse, unsorted, and uncategorized phenomena; it was by *willful judgment,* by an act of power, that she then gave these things such qualities as "good" or "bad."

She could carry forward old judgments and old labels without much work, of course, but any *active* self-perception or reflection, *even that twisted perception that had given rise to her despair,* was a kind of willful labor:

Small enough, in a given moment, but something *draining* over time.

An eidolon of herself stood, baffled, within the theater of her mind as she discovered this. It watched this process playing out, floating in the airy space above herself—watched the *seeing* of her cast out a light to reflect off of Valentina Grigorievna Sosunova; watched the conceptual eyes of her haul a net of that light back in; watched the ravens of self-judgment gather around the heaps and piles that this brought in to croak over and condemn them. Their wings hunched up like motley overcoats; they gabbled and jostled around their feast; but they did not eat, only disgorged. And in that disjuncted, dissociative state, Valentina, or that eidolon of Valentina, thought:

Why bother?

Or, *why would I go to such great* trouble *just to feel terrible about myself?*

She stared blankly at this puzzle for quite some time before the answer, slowly, became obvious; before the golden lines that were her thoughts anchored almost inadvertently in what had seemed to be the welkin and dredged out a great calcification of the surrounding void. She had not noticed it before then—it was pink and brown, as to the colors of the world through her closed eyelids—but now that she had been staring blankly at it for some time, she could see that its striations were subtly different, and less variable.

Ah. There it was, then:

She was yoked to a great iceberg built from her past decisions and her past ideas.

Its gravity was tugging at her, compelling her to motion. A miasma radiated from it, and it perverted what she saw. She looked at that iceberg and she recognized it: it was, in part, the visions that the Headmaster had bestowed on her; and, in part, the conclusions that she had consciously come to about herself throughout her life—but, most of all, and before all other things, it was an unholy congeries of every unfinished thought and train of thought and incompletely processed experience related to her own self-assessment that she had ever had.

... and there, with that, most would have had to stop.

It is not as if most people are not *aware* that their history biases them; that it prevents them from being entirely neutral witnesses to themselves and all the world. It is not as if most people are not *aware* that they are lugging around vast junkyards of cognitive detritus. Not everyone who loathes themselves would necessarily come to the same conclusion as Valentina—that that loathing was principally *driven* by a private iceberg of calcified thoughts and calcified experiences carried forward from the past—but if they *did* agree with her, what of it? It is not as if a human being can *stop* existing in a mire of old conclusions, crusty biases, and accumulated ice.

... only, *she* was Valentina Grigorievna Sosunova.

In that airy moment when the embodiment of her despair hung trapped and dying in the ring of Mrs. Senko's towers, she saw no reason to participate any longer in the façade that was the existence of the great iceberg that was inside her. It repulsed her. That repulsion, became a judgment. That judgment, became a power—the selfsame power that had been shown her, once, and long ago, by Gylbard Wan.

The iceberg cracked. It split. It turned to dust.

She saw through the back of her eyes as through the front of them, and Valentina Grigorievna Sosunova was set free.

GLUM was, at that time, as weak as it had ever been; pinned to the towers, twisting, screaming; and if Mrs. Senko, in turn, had pressed *her* advantage, she likely would have won.

It was dying there. Glum was *dying* ... because she could not distract herself from the death throes of Glum amidst the towers. Glum was dying there because the entire construction of the gardens was as a trap for it, it was sealed and it was surrounded and it was *dying*, and she could not look away.

... only: what kind of a victory would that really be?

It would not make it suffer, she thought, as it had made her suffer.

It would not claim the monster for her own. It might even—it had occasionally occurred to her—*ruin* her to have killed it, costing her her *native* ability to ignore and dismiss portions of the world around her: a doleful fate. Something that she could qualify as a victory, perhaps, but going beyond merely Pyrrhic into the realm of the absurd; she would not take it when it was offered her.

She had won. She had proven herself. She had hurt it as it had once hurt her:

That was enough.

So she threw the weight of her will behind its screams; chose to *assist* it in prying off her eyes; and with its help, and with a jerk, she tore her gaze away from towers and from Glum.

She let it slip the net, blinded herself to it for a moment, and assumed that it would simply run away; but, in this, she was not correct. She had forgotten, so easily forgotten, that other creatures as well as Mrs. Senkos could be stirred to rage by pain.

Its shadow fell across her, and there before the numinous towers—

The fire that was Mrs. Senko guttered out.

SHE DIED.

She *ended*.

She died.

Weeks passed, and she did not breathe, and she did not see; inside her, only ash and emptiness. She lay upon the gatehouse road, a corpse, and had no thoughts and no experiences.

No miracle awoke her, no articulation of the fire. The idea of *looking* had been made repellent, and so the flame within could not rekindle: the metaphorical kindling was wet, and each abortive spark died out.

There was no existence. Existence was not *for* her.

To exist required looking upon, and having a thing inside oneself that one might see; these no longer lay within her scope of interests.

Instead, she lay, and fed the worms, and grass grew up around her corpse.

Occasionally, perhaps—for she was no ordinary woman, but the daughter of the lord of Death's dominion; no ordinary woman, but *Mrs. Senko*—something would tickle at her long-lost consciousness, a hint or a flicker of an experience. … but it did not take. It lacked the rest of her, *far too much* of the rest of her, to exist within that corpse; and Mrs. Senko did not return.

She had died, if she had ever lived at all, and now would rot, consumed by the *never-look-again*. She would sink slowly and inexorably into the strictures of the earth.

This was her avowed intention—well, if she could have avowed intentions.

This—if she could have had one—would have been her will.

Weeks slipped by, and they would have been forever; weeks slipped by, the merest sliver of the *aeons* that she had scheduled for her nonexistence …

Only, slowly, slowly—like an itch behind the bones inside her neck—She began to know that she was being *seen*.

Someone was *looking* at her, and that looking was filling her uncomfortably with the sense that there was something there to look upon. Someone was *talking* to her—no, *worse*. Someone was *telling her the story of herself*, as if through words to recreate the web of experiential structure that had been turned to ash and ruin.

It was a patchwork story, full of guesswork and outright inventions—her story, yes, but as told by someone who knew her only sketchily, and in passing. Someone who only barely apprehended her as a child of Death and Death's dominion, but rather knew her as a teacher; as someone *living;* as someone *kind.* It was her story, but it was *not* her story.

… but it was close enough to resonate; close enough to *catch* her; she seized onto it, reflexively and unwillingly, like a drowning hand.

"Mrs. Senko," said a traveler—

Mrs. Senko. Mrs. Senko.

Like a phoenix from cold ashes, fire bloomed.

"AH," SHE croaked.

She blinked in confusion at the existence of the world. Her eyes were blurred from their long misuse, and rays spun up from each blade of grass; the ground was a mass of bird's-nest thatch, and the traveler simply incomprehensible.

She squinted at her.

There was a pause. Then the traveler touched her heart—or, at least, the fabric above her chest. "Valya," she said.

Did she have arms? She had arms. Mrs. Senko started sitting up. There were, it turned out, legs, as well.

"I'm sorry," Mrs. Senko said. "That was rude of me."

This did not refer to having legs, or even having arms, but to dying and lying around as a corpse instead of ... whatever it was propriety would have rather had her do.

What that was, propriety did not, at that time, explain.

"... no," the traveler denied.

Mrs. Senko looked around. The world was beginning to make a little more sense now. The walnuts had regrown since—she thought that they'd been felled, but had they? In the battle. A few of the apple trees were fallen, but more stood tall. She pulled herself the rest of the way to a seated position and touched a hand to her own heart.

The grass was wild.

"Should I assume," Mrs. Senko said, "that you have need of me?"

"Pardon?"

"I am to ... help you deal with that Glum?" Amusement almost struck her, curled her lips. "Is that how it goes, an endless cycle?"

"I'm sorry," the traveler said softly. "I don't know what you mean. I am Valentina Grigorievna Sosunova. I have come in search of the Bleak Academy. —I, ah, stumbled on you on the way."

"Oh."

"Well," the traveler admitted. "Not so much *'on the way'* as— I've been kind of going in circles ever since I reached Perdition. My old bones got me this far, but I guess I'm still too young to go any farther? So I was hoping you could say how to get into the Bleak Academy from here."

A spike of pain, a grimace. "You can't," Mrs. Senko said.

"Eh?"

"You can't get in."

"... oh."

"That's ... that's not a thing that people do."

Mrs. Senko—was she Mrs. Senko?—reached out for Valentina's hand, and stood. She levered herself up. "Come on," she said. "There is no entry to the Bleak Academy, but you can, at least, help me with my garden, my gate-house, and my road."

Valentina's eyes were uncertain, then resigned.

She sighed:

"It's better than nothing," she answered. "I expect."

AND SO they entered together into her gate-house in the dark:

Valentina striding; Mrs. Senko still hobbling and gasping, pulling herself back slowly from the murk of death.

And as they walked, and as they passed through what had become, in fact, a rather sprawling realm, she told Valentina the stories of the things around them.

Here, for instance, a light that started as a rapid sun; *here,* a walnut tree, replacement for one she'd long since lost; here, a ceiling she'd had to put up before its walls.

Valentina admired each of these in turn.

"Fascination," Mrs. Senko explained. "It is the mortar of these towers."

—after Valentina had been staring at them for quite a while.

And "I can see that," Valentina Sosunova said.

She gave her bread and salt, and a room and bed; and after her guest had slept and woken, and partaken of a simple meal, it was time to show her the worst and greatest feature of the place:

"Let us," Mrs. Senko said, "have a viewing of that Glum."

"That ... Glum?"

"Come," Mrs. Senko said, and she took Valentina to the walls.

For a time Glum was not there visible; they watched the horizon, the distant hills, the stars. But in time—perhaps drawn by the *itch* that was their interest in it, Glum emerged:

At first just the faintest hints of it, and then a growing, looming pall.

"Ah," Valentina said. She made a face at it. "That."

"I will sum up its story," Mrs. Senko said, as they watched Glum come over the hills. "I do not know whence came its life—but the bones of it, the flesh of it, the substance of it is *I do not want to see.*"

"... huh," Valentina said.

"It is uncontainable," Mrs. Senko said. "If you put it in a box, then the box becomes a thing you do not want to see.

"It is inescapable. How could you escape it? You will pack your bags and run away to a far and a distant land; but it will have only traveled with you, outside the focus of your eyes. Or, it was hiding in your shadow. Or, the moment that you get there you will finally remember the large block letter warning in every brochure, every signpost, that your eyes kept skimming over, that you could not bear to look at, saying to you, 'Glum is there.'

"And so, and so.

"Erase it and the part of you that erased it becomes a thing you do not want to see.

"Delight in it and the part of you that delights in it becomes a thing you do not want to see.

"If you let it, it will blur the boundaries between you and it so thoroughly that you won't be able to fight at all:

"That ... is Glum."

And Valentina listened; and as she listened, her expression underwent a curious transformation—not any that Mrs. Senko would have expected, but rather, from old bitterness to confusion, and then, from confusion to ... what might well have been awe.

"Wow," Valentina breathed.

"Wow?"

"... I had not thought about it that way. I had ... not even realized that it would be *allowed* to think about it in that way."

"Which way?" Mrs. Senko asked.

"As there being a terrible force of *loathing* present," Valentina said, "rather than, as something to be loathed."

IT MUST BE REMEMBERED, as she said these words, that Perdition had not outgrown Valentina. That Glum was, in a very real sense, still *her* turning-away; still the part of *her* that looked upon herself—well, principally upon herself—and did not wish to see.

It must be understood, therefore, that to reconceptualize it in this fashion was to eviscerate it.

For *her* to see Glum as loathing, rather than a marker of the presence of things that must be loathed ...

Well, it did not kill it—not any more than, say, recognizing that her reflexive loathing towards a moldy sandwich was an internal process and not a metaphysical fault in the sandwich itself would have made her eat it; any more than, say, removing her layers of outdated conceptions of herself had murdered she herself—but it *did* sever the tie between Glum and the firmament and flensed it of its outer layer.

A wind seemed to rise beneath it, knocking it into the air, disconnecting it from the earth; hooks seemed to catch it from every side and rip its flesh away; where there had been a looming pall there was now a writhing worm of light suspended in the sky, too bright to look comfortably upon.

It burned with a vigorous intensity, but there was nothing to sustain that light; it dimmed, over the course of several horrifically fascinating hours, and afterwards, the husked creature fell.

Mrs. Senko's face was twitching.

"It is *usually* quite terrifying," she explained.

THE WORLD WAS STILL; it lay there for some time.

Valentina eventually abandoned it, went inside to sleep again with the callous indifference of someone who had never really had a *personal* relationship with the externalized manifestation of her *will to look away;* but Mrs. Senko was far too attached to the thing to leave. Eventually, she slipped down from the battlements. She went down to where the creature lay—like a sprawl of river-mud and pain, amongst the scattered stones.

She stared at it, her nemesis; and suddenly, an inspiration kindled in her—a thought of fervid, slow delight.

Suddenly, a revelation was circling in her; it shone like a heated iron.

"Here," she said; at first softly, and then, with growing urgency. "Here."

Her hand clutched at the air in front of her chest. She tried to take hold of the revelation—to pull it free. She sank to her knees and then shuffled forward; got closer to the fallen thing, and convulsively thrust her hand down into its viscous substance; tried to impose her vision upon it through sheer osmosis.

"Here."

In Perdition, she had not understood she could still want things— that she was still *alive* with wanting, with hungers and resentments and intentions, beneath the stifling blanket of Perdition—until she had seen, and loathed, and wished to turn from Glum. In Perdition, it had awakened her; restored a sight that had been lost to her.

It was a monster and she hated it; she loathed it, she wished to look away from it; but it would always be—at least to her—as well, the breath of her own existence. A thing born not to kill or tame but to live in her, to take its place in her, in her chest, in her shadow, and behind her eyes; to fill her with its flame-corrupted power.

She pressed her hand to the stuff of Glum; exhaled.

Were you always there? Were you here already? Did I burn you into being with my eyes?

A spark circled down and around her arm; and with that breath, came fire.

—AND WHEN she stood, when unsteadily she stood, it was with her, then, within her, then, even as she had dreamed of it; only, it was not the creature it had been.

Of the same substance, but now something new—

For the fire of her was reborn in it, and it would be *hers* thereafter.

TIME PASSED.

In Fortitude the passing months gave the impression of pacing along in a stately fashion, albeit without the solar day or the solar year. In Night London those same months raced by, save for the occasional interregnum where an hour or week or evening seemed to last forever. Still, for the most part, time behaved itself.

In the outer world this was not so.

It became clear as … time … went by that something was terribly *wrong* with the Earth. Instead of progressing evenly through the years, its calendar stumbled around, lurching repeatedly backwards into the nineteenth century, leaving isolated enclaves of possible futures behind it—futures with no clear causal path to them, drifting along until they finally faded into the Outside. Visitors from the outside world would recur, so that, say, Cecil Baskeyfield or Zinoviya Smirnova might set off from England once but arrive at Fortitude twice, and a third time when a century had passed.

Things were … awry.

Much later—and, notably, after it had actually *happened*—Valentina would learn *why* this took place; would learn of Hryhory Saburyaev, who'd decided that five hundred years of Earth's history didn't fit his aesthetic and had therefore chosen to unhappen them, leaving other worlds in interaction with the Earth to sort out their calendars as they may. It would prove to be of little *direct* relevance to her, but still a matter of great interest:

Saburyaev was not of the Bleak Academy, but he was well-admired there; was praised and studied and exalted as a paragon at that Academy's College of Emptiness and Dream.

CHAPTER SEVEN

VALENTINA AND THE BLEAK ACADEMY

The gods of dream and nightmare looked around. They'd been having fun flying around on the zeppelins, and they liked all the new things that Alexandrel Celdinar's ascendancy had brought—but—

"This isn't our own sweet Town."

So they brought it to an end. The dream of Progress guttered out. An earthquake shattered the cursed place that Mayor Celdinar had built. And to top it off, they went and they fetched the sun.

The term used to be equivocal—often used in literary puns—but after that, nobody called Town or Fortitude "a far and a sunless land" any longer. That phrase was now reserved exclusively for that strange, aetherial, and starlit place beyond the Headmaster's Bleak Academy ...

—from *the Sun Angel's Mirror,*

by Manami Križ

L

ET'S TELL the story of how Valentina Grigorievna Sosunova died! Two mornings after the evisceration of Glum, while they were in the inner courtyard having coffee, the gates of the Bleak Academy opened to them both. One may assume—as Mrs. Senko did—that this meant that they had acquired the qualifications for it; that in some abstruse fashion, *she* had become sufficient, and Valentina had become sufficient, either in the space of that last half hour, or, in the weeks since she'd last checked. Perhaps the creature that was with her, then, within her, then, had reached some key level of integration; the Glum remade, reforged, and re-envisioned by her fire, that dwelt inside her chest, her shadow, and behind her eyes now suddenly a part of her *enough*. Perhaps she'd taken a bit of elusive enlightenment in with her caffeine, or reached a certain age; or was somehow leeching off of Valentina's slow awakening as her time beyond the world slipped past.

Perhaps all that was just the illusion of control, and there were no "qualifications" in the matter; just, a wheel had turned, and the gates creaked wide—the Headmaster, showing mercy.

Once again, as once, long before, the Headmaster stepped out into the dark.

"Welcome," he said. He flinched, just slightly. "To the Bleak Academy."

"Father!" Mrs. Senko said, then she cleared her throat. She looked away. "I mean to say, 'hello.'"

He grinned at her, but had no time for more. Valentina caught his eyes and spoke. "I want to free myself from misconceptions," she said. "I want to attain to the True Thing that is behind and beyond all things. I want to understand the secret that is like the rain, like a cloud passing over nothingness. I want to escape the endless ghastly pretenses that comprise the world. I had wondered if I could do that here."

"... you can," the Headmaster said. "But you may not wish to."

"Oh?"

"Suspended in the middle of the nothingness, where the Bleak Academy falls away, and by a series of golden cords," he said, "there is an egg. Or something in the shape of an egg, at least, if several miles 'round. Upon the surface of that egg there is the College of Emptiness and Dream. If you enter in, you shall one day acquire the qualifications to study there; and there, you would grow sharper and colder and crueler and your sight be made more clear. All the things that you say that you desire now would there be given unto you; but would they bring you happiness? —I cannot say."

She tilted her head. "You offer more than you did before."

He looked away. Then, when he looked back, there was something like a genuine smile on his face. "You were a daughter of Fortitude, and I offered you no mercy. That is fact, on both sides. But do you not see it? Do you not understand what it is that you have done? You have broken the shell of who you were, Valentina Grigorievna. No longer a daughter of Fortitude are you, but a scholar of my Bleak Academy."

It shook her. It *shook* her. But she firmed up her stance.

"Thank you, then," she said.

"You will need to finish up the process," he said. "Though. There is no hurry, but this *is*, after all, Death's dominion. Mrs. Senko, will you take care of it for her?"

"Pardon?" Mrs. Senko asked.

"Crack her ribcage," the Headmaster said. "Rip out her heart. Let her body fall limp and lifeless to the ground— ah, no rush, no rush. It is better to let her come around to it on her own.

"But let us say, within three years:

"Let the peace of Death no more be troubled by her life, and let there be no more returning to the world as Valentina Grigorievna Sosunova."

Valentina was very still. "And if I refuse?" she said.

"I suggest you wait on refusing," the Headmaster said, "until *after* you have seen what this place can offer you? Speaking of which, Marcomir will show you your room, the campus, and the gardens, and get you fitted for a student's robes; I hope, in time, you will reconsider.

"—Mrs. Senko, you have exceeded my expectations; you may return."

TIME PASSED.

For some days Valentina did not settle into the room she had been given, but rather roamed the paths of the Bleak Academy and drank from its streams and ate its fruit. Black juice stained her lips. For some time she felt the wind of a different land in her face and now and then stopped to commune with one of the dead. It occurred to her to search for Czeslaus or for Iskra or one of the many others she had lost, but in the end she left that to chance; either she would have forever or she would not, and she knew that some of them might not have made it to the Bleak Academy.

Eventually this palled.

She donned black and green robes over her traveling clothes and settled into life as an initiate of the Bleak Academy.

She had no teachers and no classes. This, Marcomir had warned her, was to be expected; they would find her when she had reached an appropriate place upon her own internal journey. It was certainly *possible* for her to consciously hunt down someone who would gladly show her a magic of extinction, or force herself into a seminar on the nature of death; she might join one of the study groups or intrude upon an ongoing research project—

But doing so based on a conscious will rather than in accordance with the subtle movements of existence as it was experienced: this was not recommended.

She accepted this, after all, she had much to meditate upon.

She had cut free her ties to most of what she had been, and become unified with something she had been fighting all her life. She had cleared her eyes of the crust of a hundred years and was ready to contemplate the true thing that is beyond all things. She was finally free of her expectations of herself; there were no chains on her, not here.

ONE DAY, as she meditated in her chambers, young Evstratii Sosunov—her great-grandnephew, dead these past four years—came to tell her that a visitor had come.

"Listen," he said. "I think it's the Headmaster."

The boy was practically trembling.

"He's dressed all fine in green and purple clothes and he don't have eyes. He's just got night and stars in 'em. He said he's here to see you, ma'am, but I'll tell him you're out, that you got an insight and popped back to life, if you wanted to sneak away."

"Thank you, Stratka," Valentina said.

She rose to her feet. She waved him away, not towards the dormitory's main entrance but towards the little vine-covered doorway in the back. She went out to the gates to meet the Headmaster of the Bleak Academy; only, it was not he.

He wore a shapeless mound of an olive cap to match the olive in his clothes. He had Riders' eyes, but the night sky they showed was not the same as the Headmaster's night sky. He had a worried, shy expression on his face, and she knew him instantly, though this was their first actual meeting.

"Gylbard," she said.

He startled, slightly. He looked up at her. Then he frowned. "Mercy," he said. "But I did not give the boy my name, so you cannot have known it. Did you mean to say 'helium bard?' Because that would be alarming."

She looked him up and down. "You seem well."

"I am," he said. "Thank you. And you are? I mean, how are? I apologize. I have never actually spoken to you before and it is not happening the way I imagined it."

"No? ... but I am being a poor host. Come in."

She led him in through the gardens and to one of the kitchens, where she made a light lunch as he repeatedly took off his hat, fiddled with the edges of it, and put it back on again. She slid a plate across the table to him, set down her own, and sat.

"I had wondered," she said. "Whether I would meet you here, at the Bleak Academy."

"You noticed me?" He beamed. "I mean, of course you noticed me, you are terribly observant. Not terribly. Greatly. Wisely. Excellently. I thought you would have been rather distracted at the time, though. What with attacking the Headmaster and all."

She cast her memory back over the decades. "You were one of the figures behind him?" she asked. Then she shook her head and turned it into a statement. "I mean: you were one of the figures behind him."

He nodded. "I was."

"I did not mean to hurt you," she said. "When I crushed this Academy in the hands of an awful dream. So I hope that I did not."

"Oh, no," he said. "The Academy itself weathered the affair quite well, as you can see. Although I wouldn't say that it didn't shake things up a little, eh heh, if you know what I mean."

"I'm drawing a complete blank, I'm afraid."

"Well," he said, "the Headmaster had mostly been content to ... to *be*, if you understand what I'm saying. To exist, at the end of everything. The matter of your world's existence disturbed him, only, he was content to brood about it, sitting in silence and waiting for the matter to resolve itself, with his attendants, ah, well, as it were, attending. But after you came, he started *doing* again. Taking action. It is hardly the first time, though, so you don't need to feel responsible."

"And so you have come," Valentina said.

"I would have stayed in his shadow forever," Mr. Wan said. "I confess it. There was a wound in my heart. I was no longer satisfied. But I was a coward. I would have stayed there forever; but he sent me out, instead, sent me away from the Bleak Academy to meet a doleful fate, over and over again, and when I had returned—

"Well, my perspective was widened. I told him, 'I can no longer study under you, sir. I must ... pursue my own agenda.'

"And he said, 'do you think you *have* one of those, Mr. Wan? Truly?'

"But ... he let me go."

"Have you eaten before?" she asked him. "Traditionally, you would start with the bread, dipped in the salt; then you could try the okroshka."

"I have eaten," he said. "Though, these foods are not familiar. The bread is ... the round thing? Yes?"

"Yeah," she agreed.

He bit off a bit, chewed, and swallowed. He frowned. "It is heavy," he said.

"Your heart was wounded, you say," she said.

"I do," he agreed. "It was the way you stabbed him. —I think that I had always wanted to stab him, but I had never realized it until that moment, when I could do so viscerally through you. If that says poor things about my character I assure you that I also fell in love with your beauty, your grace, and your determination."

"If I may ask," she said, "your eyes are rather strange."

"They are," he agreed. "It is because I am not human, but rather dreamed up from the void."

"How fascinating," she said.

"The Headmaster," he explained. "Was contemplating a kind of *koan*—'A cup is absent. Is its handle broken?' He had a moment of insight that kindled me into being as a novitiate of the Bleak Academy. Since that time I have served him and struggled to understand his lessons, but in honesty, I have not gotten very far."

"'Is its handle broken—'" Valentina ruminated.

"I do not understand it myself," said Wan. "Though he tells me that I will get there eventually."

"Maybe it doesn't have a handle?" Valentina said.

"Then I think it would be an absent goblet," Mr. Wan explained.

Valentina glanced back at the cupboard. She frowned. "I don't see how that creates a person," she said. "Is that really what you do out here instead of sex?"

"Ah," he said. "Ah. Um. Well. I have never done either. But no, I believe it is merely a measure of the Headmaster's, ah, metaphysical presence, that he is capable of witnessing people into existence when he is looking at mere thoughts. He does not do it often, you understand, but then no scholar can claim to have insights of that nature on a daily basis."

"If I had conceived some grand notion," she said.

"While you were here? Then," he said, "conceivably, you might have created a person, too. However, I do not credit it. A fetch, maybe, or an elemental spirit, but, well, I have only the highest regard for you, but to worry about such things would be hubris."

"I did not think it had *happened*," Valentina said. "I was simply curious."

"Have you any?" he asked. "I mean, children? I mean, a husband?"

"That was more of a veer than a clarification," she said.

"Well," he said, awkwardly. "I have been telling myself that I must be braced for such a thing. That I can hardly have been the only one to notice your beauty and decision. Only, it took me a great deal of courage to come here, in search of you, and if the bandage must be ripped off the wound, I should like it done quickly."

"I have my Yuka," she said. "I have my Elenka. I have my grandson Kalen'ka."

"And your husband?"

"Death took him," she said. "My Czesio—death took him, and before that, I watched him wither over the years like the leaves of fall while I stayed young and strong. I burned for him, and then I was warm for him, and now I do not know whether I will find him here and if I do if he will crack me open with his smile or if I will find that the embers have grown cold. That is all that I can give you, Vanya."

"I'm sorry," he said.

"It's a long-buried grief," she said, "and you've hardly dug it up again. If you are willing to take the risk that I will meet him and return to him, then you may feel free to court me, Barashik; I have never been courted by a *koan* before."

"You understand that I am not actually—"

He flushed before her smile.

"Well," he said. "I have nothing, and I have no prospects. I know a very little magic, but I did not actually finish my studies before I cut ties with the Headmaster. He often told me that I was disposable, that I was replaceable—that if something ever happened to me, there would be ten thousand others just like me to take my place. But you are the stars in my eyes and the warmth in my heart, my love."

"Uh," she said. "Let's hold off on going *that* far for a while. I'm not sure you can tell all that much about me from one attempted murder."

"You say that," he said, "but I think it said everything there was to say about who you are."

"As for having nothing," she said. She looked him up and down. "We can't have that, can we? You have at least a little aptitude for the Sosunov magic, so I think the afterlife branch of the family here can take you in."

"It can? —I mean, I do? —I mean, you can tell that at a glance?"

She grinned. "I am terribly wise," she said. "And my insight is as piercing as the Headmaster's spear. I venture I can teach you myself. In turn— I have wanted to speak with ... ah, someone like you ... about how the world might be corrected. Perhaps you would be willing to share what mastery you *do* have of the magic you possess?"

"Well," he said, "I would be willing, but that may not, ah, be terribly wise."

"Oh?"

"The things I know are not uninfectious," he said. "I mean to say, they do not stay in the corners of the mind you learn them in. I mean, you might be better off not to know."

"I have already started," she said.

"Ai! Just from hearing that *koan?*"

"I have already started," she said, "and there may someday be someone in the family who needs it more than the Sosunov magic. So that is how I will assuage my guilt for sharing the secrets beyond the family —you will write down what you know, and we will find a way to send it back to them. To the *living* Sosunovs, I mean."

"... as you wish, my lady."

"Valya," she said.

"Valya."

"Tell me," she said, "I have been wondering. If the world is not made up of the little things—if it is in fact impossible to reduce the greater fabric to the smaller pieces, if that is just a trick of the mind—then why is it that when we look at the whole, the pieces leap out? Where do the grains of sand come from in a pile of sand? Where do the individual hairs come from in the hair upon a person's head?"

"I'm sorry?" he said. He blinked. "Um. Ah. They come from us."

She squinted at him.

"We look upon the truth," he said, "and we break off little lies of our own creation, and then build them back up again into an imaginary world. That is my understanding, in any case. Why?"

"It does not seem like I am engaged in an act of creation," she said, "when I pluck a hair from my head. It does not seem like I could have plucked out a seagull, say, instead, or a laundry line."

"... a monk named N'mosnikttiel," said Mr. Wan, "once had a power like that; he could turn his plucked hairs into peacocks. But one day he found out they were actually just painted chickens. He was so embarrassed he burst into flame!"

Valentina narrowed her eyes at him.

"Sorry," he said. "I guess I mean to say, it's probably possible to get that way through a deep understanding of the world, I mean, get to the point where you can pluck seagulls from your head, but the absurdity is probably a distraction. If what you are interested in is, 'why *these* illusions, if the world isn't real, why *this* unreality?' then you would be better served by pondering the question of the cup."

She frowned. "That is a dodge," she said. "Lay it on the table."

"Here is my perspective, then," he said. "And you will find it unconvincing. You are aware of perhaps seven things in a sea of ... twenty? Thirty? Half-formed notions? And a hundred inklings? You turn your attention towards your head. You formulate a theory of yourself as a person with a head of hair, about to pluck a hair in demonstration. Notions of your hair in general, the demonstration, the act of plucking, and the hair you mean to pluck swim up towards your active awareness. As they do so, the details are already becoming refined. Any anomalies are reported; if you discover yourself N'mosnikttiel and know that your hair can become painted chickens, that information surfaces. If you have lost your audience and can no longer give a demonstration, you become aware of *that*. If your fingers cannot find a hair to pluck—

"And so forth.

"By the time you are in a world where the very possibility of such an action congeals, the option to pluck a seagull from your head has already been eliminated—not in its entirety, but to the thirteenth decimal. Or, conversely, you have already discovered that there is a seagull on your head, or whatnot, and it has become quite feasible.

"The opportunity to realize that there is no 'strand of hair'—well, you can do that at any time. That is such a small matter that I can accomplish something much like it myself. But in order to substitute a *different* illusion, you would have to begin quite early, or have an extremely peculiar twist to your enlightenment. And you would most likely think, when it had happened, that is was perfectly normal:

"You were not 'plucking a hair from your head' when that seagull appeared.

"You were 'throwing bread to the birds on the beach.'

"If you were to commit a true act of miracle, if you were to abort the formation of the concept of the hair midway through the process through enlightenment and then ... assert that a seagull mapped more closely to the truth to which your heart attends ... then perhaps you would achieve the effect you noted. It would not be because you had realized that the hair might as well be a seagull, but because in bowing before the infinite majesty of the truth you decided in jest to veil it in a seagull's form. Not 'in jest.' That was the wrong term. I do not have the words for it. ... in a spirit of delight and mischief at the way that great things can be expressed with the right wrong lies.

"I think that it would be easiest to achieve that if there were something in the hidden truth that was seagull-like, some near-truth that the parable of the seagull would illuminate; or, if the person attempting it were an eccentric expert in, well, seagull-ness; but, since I have not even dabbled in the matter I cannot say for sure.

"That is how I can say that is you, your *eyes-that-see*, that create the hair, that make there be a hair when there need not have been one, that in a real fashion had a choice—not a conscious choice, but a choice of the attending spirit—about whether there was a hair, and yet you cannot reasonably expect to get a seagull instead even with substantial effort towards enlightenment.

"Is that enough?"

Valentina sat in thought for a while. Finally, she said, "This 'attending spirit—'"

"Ah," he said. "I believe it is called your 'wishing heart,' here. I am not sure. The force that exerts itself through your attention, in any case, to manifest the world."

"Right," she said. She stood up, decisively. "It will be interesting to see how you do with dreams. Come along and I'll get you moved in."

"It's— I don't mean to be trouble," he said.

"Pah," she said. "A little extra work's good for the ghosties, and we've had an empty room just sitting there ever since Fyodor turned out not to be dead after all."

"Oh?" he said.

"He thought he was dead," Valentina said. "But it was gas."

"Oh."

"Tell me," she said. "—*is* my Czesio here?"

"I don't know," he said.

"Oh."

"A person isn't just here because they're dead or— or have gas, haha," he said. "They have to make it here, make it all the way here, and that's hard. And then they have to *stop* here. They have to not just ... go on, ah? To the far and the sunless land. And *then* they have to not just drift and dream forever, because if they're going to be drifting and dreaming *forever* then it doesn't matter whether they're here or not. Right?"

"I guess," she said.

"It's like being in Surrey," he said. "Yes? Like, how anyone *could* be in Surrey, but hardly anyone *is*."

"That is quite possibly the least useful example I've ever heard of," she said.

"That is because you haven't heard many *koans*," Mr. Wan said.

"I guess," she said. She led him off to what had been Fyodor's room.

SOME HOURS later he found himself walking with Valentina through the roads of the Bleak Academy. She was dressed in formal blacks—not a costume of the Academy, but of Fortitude—and a small brass bell rang at her belt, and from time to time one of the dead would emerge from the grass, or the sky, or a building, or nowhere in particular, to press a small wooden box into her hand.

She would look in the box; inevitably it contained a heavy gray fume of Perdition. She would empty this into a sack she carried. Then she would introduce him to whoever it was.

"This is Mrs. Ivanova," she would tell him[19]; or, "this is Mr. Smirnov; this, Dr. Antonovich."

And to them she would say: "This is Gylbard Wan, who is learning the family magic of the Sosunovs."

"I am?" he asked, the first time, because it hadn't been made completely clear to him, but the second and later times, he confirmed, "I am."

After a time, he ventured, "You are gathering the substance of Perdition?"

"Sometimes people find it creeping in," she said. "A small amount may be caught in a dream-catcher and dumped out into the gardens; a larger amount— well. It is a nice enough night. I thought, we could walk and we could collect it for them."

"I see," he said, though he did not.

"It is something that is difficult for the ordinary dead to deal with," she said. "It can kill their—what's the thing? Hearts. It can kill their *hearts*.

---

19   ("She's alive, you know.")

Their dreams. It can ... consume them with its wickedness. Not that it is *likely* to, but if everybody banked upon that unlikelihood, then perhaps it would get its footholds here, or turn the dead into things like Glum, or inflict curses that would ring down through the generations."

"That would not happen," he said.

"No?"

"The Headmaster would not allow it."

"Well," she said, and walked a time in silence.

Eventually:

"It seems strange to me," she said, "that the world should be so orderly here; that, at the far end of chaos, we should find structure once again. It has always seemed strange to me, but I have been unable to gain a deeper understanding of it."

He did not say anything for a while. Eventually, he said, "I think that it is a matter of the focus of your gaze."

"Oh?"

"When you pull your vision away from the details," he said, "the first thing you notice is that the details become vague and confused. But in doing so you may eventually receive a sort of clarity about the whole. That is not to say that the Bleak Academy is the whole to which the Outside is simply the details, but the process is similar: as the gaze defocuses, it finds first chaos, and then a certain, different, kind of orderliness."

"Interesting," she said. "Though difficult to test."

"True," he said. "It is more in the line of speculation or eccentricity than a hypothesis."

She patted the sack she carried. "Perhaps we will make some progress towards a better understanding of it," she said, "as you combine your insights with my own."

"That is what we are doing?"

"Not yet," she said. "What we are doing is casual conversation. What we *will* be doing, however, is teaching you to dream."

He squinted at her. "Are you certain I am capable of it? Because I have never actually done so."

"I had actually meant," she said, "teaching you to dream *properly*. But if you have never done so, it is just as well; you will not have any bad habits to unlearn."

"I am familiar with the concept," he said, "of course. It is a kind of aimless fantasy by which mundane beings escape their lives, seek oracles of their future, and prevent their rest from possessing an excessive resemblance to bleak oblivion. The dead are prone to spending their time at the Bleak Academy doing so, often for months, years, or whole existences at a time, but I was not constructed to seek out such designs."

"That is a common perspective," she agreed.

"Oh?" he said. "You have another?"

"The process is miraculous," she said. "It is like the bud opening to become a flower, or the cocoon opening to reveal a butterfly. The body opens and we emerge, entering another realm. It remains behind—the body, I mean—holding open a portal for us, keeping a way for us, and standing in for us while we are away. When we have completed our business in that other world, in the world of dreams, we pack up our things, fold up our selves, and squeeze back in our body once again."

"That— I will have to do?"

"There is no great difficulty," she said. "It comes extremely naturally."

He walked in silence for a while.

"Let me tell you about dreams," she said, "so that you will be prepared.

"They are highly malleable: thus, your belief about aimless fantasies. You may impose your conceptions upon them and they will take their form. There is a vicious cycle in play here: if you catch sight of a swatch of aimless color and mistake it for an ogre, then you will doubtless begin to see other things around you as the other pieces of that ogre, and the forest that it lives in, and yourself the hero, and so forth, and the dream will take that form. If dreams were not also chaotic, you would be locked in to that initial conception; as it is, you will lurch in its direction but may still be pulled away by chaotic surges—e.g., a sudden glimpse of tree bark instead of ogre flesh confirms for you that it is not an ogre after all.

"The location for a dream is, as far as I can determine, somewhere in the Outside. —I suppose that everything is somewhere in the Outside, if you look at it properly, but this is more in the manner of a field in the forest, a creek branching off of a river, or something of the sort. It is essentially impossible to walk into Fortitude or the Bleak Academy directly from a dream but one of the greatest escapes in modern history was accomplished by walking straight from dream to the Outside."

"But," he interrupted, "the inner self— I mean, surely the body is needful?"

She waved a hand in vague dismissal. "As I have said, a placeholder. It is miraculous, to dream, but not so miraculous as the Outside is innately."

"I see."

"His name was Jack Sheppard," she said. "He'd escaped four times before, and twice from Newgate, so they bound him up with three hundred pounds of iron chains and set him in their courtyard where everyone could watch him and they swore by all the hosts of Hell and Heaven that they would finally see him hang. But they didn't think to stop him from dreaming, you see, so he went to sleep, and he went into his dreams, and from his dreams out into the Outside he slipped, and when they went to hang his body, and they did, they hanged his body, and they congratulated themselves on how they'd finally got him, that abandoned placeholder of a body that he'd left behind, it turned to crumbling leaves and it blew away."

"That is a trick I shall have to remember."

"It is difficult," Valentina admitted. "I have never actually tried it, but I have flirted with it, tried out the concept around the edges, and it is not easy. Still, possible enough.

"The last distinguishing feature of a dream is that a dream is a lonely place.

"You enter the world of dreams and you are naked and alone. No heart beats there, save for your heart. No eyes are there to see the wild chaos but your own. Each dream is as a map inscribed upon the inside of a bubble, one among the endless bubbles in the sea; there are no paths that lead between them; this may be considered the cosmos' iron rule.

"This is the law that the Sosunov magic exists to circumvent, but—let us say— it is only when circumstances allow it that it may be broken."

"This sounds less and less attractive," he said. "First I have to shuck myself like an oyster and then I have to trap myself, isolated from all others, in a world that can magnify the slightest errant thought into a private hell."

"It's not so bad," she said. "It's very convenient when you have gotten used to it."

"Said the woman on the rack."

"What?"

"Well," he said, "she could reach the high shelves now—"

"Really," she said. "You have a macabre turn of mind."

They stopped for a few minutes so she could collect another fume (and, on this particular occasion, a boxed-up pie) from a Mrs. Petrova. That accomplished, he said, "If that is dreaming, then what does it mean to dream 'properly?'"

"Do you know," Valentina said, "that it is possible to denature this stuff?"

He made a confused and drawn-out noise; perhaps, "Mnmg?"

She hefted the bag of Perdition's weighty fumes. She shook it, then lowered it to her side. "The original function of the Sosunov magic—of all the shrine family magic, really—was to deal with the dust of the Outside. It would get into Fortitude and cause all kinds of trouble, but then ... the

Kichis would cleanse it; or the Vasilis spend it; the Yatskiys smoke it; or the Sosunovs open their inner eye upon it and make it harmless.

"That is the reason that I gather these fumes—because it transpires that the same technique denatures *them.*"

"I don't understand," he said. "That is dreaming properly?"

"It is the most frightening part of being a Sosunov," she said. She rolled her neck. "More than the oceans. More than witches. It is necessary to learn to no longer be, an awareness without an observer, a body that is empty of its personhood."

"Oh," he said.

"It has nothing whatsoever to do with dreaming properly," she said, "but when you understand whence that fear arises, you are most likely dreaming well."

HE was an innocent, and Valentina did not push him too quickly.

For the first several weeks, most of his time was spent in the comfort of the library. They explored it together, walked beneath the stained cathedral of its ceiling, and Valentina gathered volume after volume for him on the recurring elements of dreams—on the landmarks, landscapes, symbols, characters, and creatures that the scholars of the dead had found to continually recur.

These were the foundation of his curriculum.

The texts were difficult—hand-copied compendia of personal observations and commentaries on prior works—but he struggled through them. Some were Sosunov texts, amended for their further studies on the dreams dreamt by the dead; these she could often elucidate for him. Others were written by various local scholars, and her interpretations were often as confusing as the books themselves.

When he was not in the library, he was typically alone in his room, processing, or he was with Valentina, who set aside at least several hours each day to speak with him about the worlds of the living and the dead—

to ensure that he would not be entirely at sea if he were ever in the living world and forced to go shopping, or to do his own laundry, or to make friends; to ensure that he was comfortable, at the Bleak Academy but not at his Headmaster's side. Sometimes she would walk with him to see the sights and wonders of the Academy; other times they would remain in, talking over coffee in the kitchen or in his room.

"There is a distinct character," Valentina said, on one occasion, "to the unknown and uncertain, separate from that which is possessed by known things, or even by that unknown thing once it is later known.

"It evokes fear," she said. "It evokes intrigue.

"It contains infinite and multivalent potential; or, if you choose to look at it thus, a diffuse fog of endless possible outcomes.

"It feeds on itself. It devours itself. It is fanged. It is clawed.

"It breathes forth a fire of inspiration.

"Such is the unknown."

Mr. Wan considered this for a while. "Having learned to confuse the matter by knowing things," he said, "you cannot help yourself, and apply the techniques of that confusion even where you know literally nothing."

"That is one perspective," she agreed.

"The words we use are usually the wrong words," he said. "The explanations we give are usually the wrong explanations. That is why I say that it is confusing the matter to know things, and why it seems to be borrowing trouble to extend the concept into the things that we do not know."

"Nevertheless," she said, "it becomes necessary to characterize the unknown and view it as a substance, if you want to engage with it in a goal-oriented fashion."

"I see," he said.

Life was full of mysteries to him; the extent of his experience was dying, repeatedly, to Glum, and what Valentina shared with him; there was little option for him at that time but to follow her leadership and attend carefully to her teachings, even when they conflicted with his beliefs, his training, or his instincts; and so he did.

Time passed, and he did not dream.

She exclaimed in delight when she found a book for him of seven impossible images—a key Sosunov primer, she explained, on the direct perception of the ambiguous and the unknown. The first illustration was a rose that could arguably also be a flame; this he instantly understood could easily be both. He named it a rose made *out* of flame and he moved on. The second illustration was a jacket with an ambiguous number of arms; he resolved this one in a matter of minutes by suspending judgment. Was it two arms? Was it three arms? It was a shape, the exact resolution of which he could hold in abeyance. Encouraged, he attempted to apply these mental sleights, or others, to the remaining five illustrations, and made no progress that day, or for many days thereafter. The rabbit-duck obstinately maintained itself as a rabbit's head or a duck's head, but never "both" or "equivocal between them;" the moon-wolf was likewise never *both* the moon rising over the hills and a running wolf; when he convinced his eyes to see the face in the flame-face he could no longer see the fire; and as for the last two illustrations, impossible geometric figures, he could not make head or tail out of them, much less, as it were, make head and tail both.

At meditation he proved more adept; and when she brought up the extinguishment of the ego as a thing that must be learned—

"It is unfortunately necessary," she said. "We are characters in a story that we are telling ourselves, and as long as our identification with that character remains total, our ability to step outside the dream-state is near-nil ..."

—he admitted that it was something in which he had already, in the Headmaster's retinue, been trained.

In the second month, they climbed a great white arch to stare out across the void at the egg on which was hosted the College of Emptiness and Dream. They were ambushed by a great dragon made of shadow while walking between two buildings and Valentina fought it off, cutting away the bright heart of it that he then proceeded to erase. They attended one of the Headmaster's lectures on the ritual strengthening of the flame.

Towards the end of that month, his dreams finally began.

They featured no spiritual evisceration, no private hells, and relatively poor fidelity.

None of the elements he'd so painstakingly studied up on made an appearance; instead, he dreamt wisps of random colors and half-formed conceptions. It made barely enough of an imprint upon his consciousness for him to realize that he'd dreamed at all.

Each morning, he dutifully recorded the experience; then, after reviewing his notes, decided that he most likely hadn't been dreaming after all. It was not until the fourth dream, and the seventh morning, that he was certain that these things *had* been dreams; he brought the matter up to Valentina.

"I have been dreaming," he said. "Only—"

He waved his notes at her.

"The most coherent thing in all four nights has been 'a hill.'"

She smiled at him. "It's all right," she said.

"Thank Heaven."

"Coherence comes," she said, "when a dream becomes relevant enough to your life—literally or on some odd symbolic level—that you pay attention to it. You invest it with your attention, and it unfolds into something closer to reality. Without that attention, it withers on the vine, becomes stifled and incoherent, and … well, you are lucky to have even a hillside to record."

He frowned at that. "Then how do I make a dream relevant to my life?" he said. "I would have thought that the very act of dreaming would in and of itself be critical."

"It will happen quite by accident," she said.

He looked dissatisfied.

"It is the only way I know how to begin this thing," she said. "It is like love or artistic inspiration. When you have felt it, you can work to refine it, but first you must stumble on it."

"The Headmaster once told me," he said, slowly, "about a man who learned to imagine whatever he liked, in perfect clarity. A strategist, you see, who used it to plan out his military engagements—a useful talent, yes?"

"Indeed."

"He won many an engagement," he said. "And eventually retired, successful and renowned, and lived in a grand manor with his wife and children, and grew old with dignity and grace. Only, one day, the fashion for women turned away from gloves, and his daughter's hands were suddenly bared to him, and he thought nothing in particular of it, until three days later he remembered that her left hand ought to have had a certain scar.

"He sought her out. He asked her about it. He thought that perhaps a doctor might have fixed it with some concoction, and she started to explain that that was what had happened; only, midway through her explanation, he realized that an alchemist's solution was more credible, and she changed her story as she was speaking it as well.

"He thought, perhaps a dragon had breathed scar-curing breath upon her, and she confirmed it.

"That Heaven had graced her with a miracle, and so she did explain.

"In that moment he realized that he had never stopped imagining what he liked to imagine, in perfect clarity, though he did not know when; instead of waking from his visions, he imagined, in perfect clarity, that he awoke. He attempted to return to his senses, but how could he? He did not even know at which time he had used his talent and then failed to awake— or was it all of them? Was he now within an imagination of an imagination of an imagination of a dream, rendered in perfect fidelity and exacting detail by the strategist's mind's eye?"

"A disturbing story," Valentina agreed.

"Sometimes," Mr. Wan said, "The Headmaster would end there; other times, he would explain, 'and thus was born reality.'"

"And you are thinking," Valentina said, "that if you stumble upon a dream that is relevant to your life, that it would be like that?"

"Mn," he said.

"It is nothing to worry about," Valentina said. "It is like reading a story; no matter how often a storybook tells you 'and then you closed the book and looked around, only to find that the monster was still there,' the distinction between the story and reality remains."

"Is there such a storybook?" he asked, in wonder.

"There is," she agreed. "I was quite fond of it as a child."[20]

"I would not dare to write such a thing," he said. "Imagine what the Headmaster would do to me if it came to pass."

"Once upon a time," she said, "but not so very long ago, there was a witch whose powers were something similar. She would lock people in their dreams and they would not wake; or, rather, they would dream of waking, without achieving it, and she would feast upon the differential between the energy of the one state and the other."

"Truly?"

"Truly," she said. "Though it was before my time, and you need not worry that she will return."

"That may be what inspired the Headmaster's story, then."

"Her punishment was ironic," Valentina said. "She was given to dream that she was dying, and that dream consumed her, and dragged her off to the Bleak Academy. Only, she was not a very strong ego, so I suspect she did not make it all the way."

"To dream that one is dying," he said, "is the same as dying?"

"Well," she said. "Not really. But she was a witch, you see, and they already break the rules."

He frowned at that.

---

20 *A Fox Book*, by Li Wei

"They are creatures that live in the space between dreams," she said. She gestured vaguely. "Or at least that is the typical arrangement. The Sosunov magic is limited because we are human; we are creatures that dream; we emerge into the world of dreams in our own little self-contained bubbles, and our dreams are bounded in that sphere. A witch is not so limited; they trample the walls between dream and reality, between dream and dream, they enter dreams and depart them, they break open that perfect containment simply by existing, and the rules as they are normally established do not always continue to follow."

"So there could be a witch," he said, "who made it so that dying in dreams brought on real death?"

"There could be a witch," she said, "who made it so that dying in dreams brought on great feasts of mangoes."

"Oh."

"By which I mean," she said, "that you need not have any such specific fear."

"Yes," he said. "I picked up on that."

"For the most part, they are entertaining stories of triumph for future Sosunov generations," she said. "So please do not let the idea of witches hinder you in your studies."

"I am not afraid of dying," he said. "Nor do I think a witch would come here. I was merely curious."

"There was a Sosunov once," she said, "who thought that dreams were better than living, and opted to stay in them forever—who cut the cord that leads back to the body, who sealed the gates of dream against the living world, and caught death, when it came for her, in a bottle, so that it could not trouble her endless stay."

"I did not realize he was in a bottle," he said.

"—that raises a question I have had," she said, interrupting herself. "Is he actually ... what's the thing, ah ... *literally* Death? Not just some glorified sort of watchdog?"

He hesitated. "I do not know what the question means," he said. "I should probably have been less casual with your anecdote. If you are asking whether trapping him in a bottle is a sufficient means of preventing one's own death, um, probably?"

"Well," she said, "I mean, our life has a natural end, when death comes for us; is that him?"

"Nobody comes for you," he said. "You go to him."

"Sure, sure," she said. "Blame the mortals."

"Death is formless," he said. "Not a thing but a word. Not a knife that cuts through the world but an experience that rises to fill it. If you stare at that experience long enough with the eyes that imbue formless things with form, he is sometimes something that it can become. I think. My own experience is atypical; when I die he is usually the one who's killed me."

She squinted at him.

"It is something he does," said Mr. Wan. "When I am too lost in incorrect conceits and ideation. Slice, slice, the scythe. Swish, the spear. Crush, crush, the fist."

"I'm sorry," she said.

"It is no matter," he said. He gave her a Wan smile. "After all, I am here now."

IT WAS in the summer of that year that a strange light wakened Valentina, and she followed it outside to find the Headmaster in the courtyard; he the lord of Death's dominion he stood before a spinning mass of unformed silver threads that gave off the light that she had seen. In those threads Valentina thought she saw echoes of human lives, but she was not sure; the Headmaster intermittently molded and tore at them with his hands.

"Valentina," the Headmaster said, without turning.

"I still think about killing you sometimes," Valentina said.

"Do you?"

She shrugged. She looked around. She kicked a pebble. She plucked a bit of grass and let it flutter away. "It seems over-dramatic."

The Headmaster set aside his work, and turned, and she marveled at the darkness of his eyes. "I am willing to grant you a visa to the far and sunless land," he said. "You may go beyond this place. I cannot promise Heaven, or Nirvana, but I *can* tell you that it is *next*, and it is good."

"And Mr. Wan?"

"He is not ready."

She thought about this for a short while. "Tell me," she said. "Have my mother and father come here? Has my Czesio? And have they gone beyond it?"

"Iskra Ermolaevna has come and gone," he said. "The rest are on their way."

She frowned. "I do not feel ready," she said.

"I urge you to think twice," he said.

She shook her head.

"Then," he said, "you have qualified, also, to begin your studies at the College of Emptiness and Dream."

"... thank you, then," she said, "I guess."

She nodded, turned, and left.

"YOU MUST GO," he said, when she told him; and she knotted her hands into frustrated fists. "There is no point in coming to the Bleak Academy if you will not learn what there is to learn here."

"But—"

"And I must go with you," he concluded.

"Oh," she said. "Of course."

"Otherwise— otherwise," he said, "that will be how it ends. You leave, and are gone forever, to the College of Emptiness and Dream."

"You are allowed, then?"

"Long since," he agreed. "It is no good for me to be a Mister Wan *forever* when I could be a Magister."

So she did not fear that she would be abandoning him, but rather felt a brightening interest in what she might learn of the True Thing at the College of Emptiness and Dream.

She tidied up her room, nodded at it, shouldered a small pack of books and food, and went.

There was a book to be signed: a sleeping functionary guarded it, and they did not bother waking him. There was a climb to be made—up one of the great arched alabaster hooks that were the anchor points for the College of Emptiness and Dream; it was wide enough for two to walk abreast, and nearly as tall as the clock-tower: up into the sky.

To its peak was tied a boardless bridge of golden ropes that glowed with an inner light.

The bridge trembled as they walked along it towards the College at the egg, and as they walked the wind whispered to her of the death of worlds. It was wordless, dark, and heady; it grew a richness inside her and made her feel delight even as it gave birth to images of cracking earth, tumbling buildings, fire, swords, and blood upon the moon.

Her eyes strayed downwards. She stopped, and clung tighter to the ropes, and she did not move until Mr. Wan nudged her.

"Don't knock me free," Valentina said.

"You were frozen," Mr. Wan said.

"I had thought we were merely at tower-height," Valentina said. "But— we are not. How far down does it go?"

And Mr. Wan drew on the knowledge that had been born in him:

"There is no 'down,'" he said. "There is only the True Thing."

AT THE College of Emptiness and Dream she studied for a time. She played with something that was like a dog, but was not a dog, on the surface of the egg. She did not keep to the academic gown, but took to wearing a long grey coat and a matching hat over her traveler's clothes.

She measured her progress by the structure that was growing for her there—a roughness in the shell of the egg that had been born as soon as she first set foot on the path of Mr. Wan's magic, that had swollen over time to the size of a sofa, and would eventually become an enclosure that she could seal away from all conceptions but her own:

An aerie underneath a private sky.

Her sense of the place deepened. She began to doubt that it was as it appeared to be; "it is, perhaps," she judged, "a writhing mass of gods, *in the shape* of a great stone egg."

Mrs. Senko, who was visiting, clarified: "And not an egg at all?"

"Right."

"Mm," Mrs. Senko said. "It is for you to judge, I think."

Valentina rolled over on her back on the grass on the eggshell hung by golden cords above the nothingness in the land that lies beyond. "So they tell me."

She stared up at a distant tower.

After a moment Mrs. Senko poked her.

"Huh?"

"You were zoning out," Mrs. Senko said.

"I was thinking," Valentina said, "how much the towers were like the tower of the gatehouse, and how much the gatehouse in Perdition reflected the condition of my soul. Do you think the whole world is like that? Do you think that it's all just an image of ourselves?"

"If only," Mrs. Senko snorted.

"Oh," Valentina said.

"But," Mrs. Senko said. "The thing you see *as* the world is in some sense an image projected from your eyes."

"When are you going to kill me, Mrs. Senko?" Valentina asked. Her arms were spread wide, her body language open. "To crack these ribs, to rip out this heart? When are you going to remove these eyes, that give forth such unsightly creations?"

"I never wanted to kill anyone," Mrs. Senko said. "I wanted to be a teacher."

Valentina huffed a laugh.

"What?"

"A 'great and terrible teacher.'"

"Yes."

"That is not, like, how it works, you know. That is not ... that is not what teachers *are*."

"Teachers are Authority," Mrs. Senko said. "That is terrifying and great."

"There is a red star over there," Valentina said, after a while. "But I never see it in anybody's eyes."

MR. WAN dreamed of the Bleak Academy; only, a Bleak Academy where he had never been lifted up from the multitude to be Mr. Wan.

He slept on a bed of smooth round stones under a frayed and ethereal sheet and blanket. He woke and he walked through the garden and plucked a strange black fruit. He cut off its top and drank its juice, wiped his mouth, and tossed the rest into the compost pile.

He took a more formal breakfast in a hall with many faceless men— porridge, a glass of water, and half an orange served on a tray. He ate in silence, though there were mutterings around him.

He did not look at the others.

He did not *want* to look at the others. His eyes slid away from their faces and their hands and hovered instead on their shoulders, on their sides.

He separated himself from the crowd as he left the mess.

He walked alone on winding paths.

He came to an old stone chapel and he knelt before a faceless statue—too worn to give any sign of its identity, save the beneficent posture of one hand—and the great window that looked beyond it, to the east, towards the dawn that would never come. There his spirit prostrated itself before the darkness that preceded all things and would follow all things while his lips murmured words of adulation whose import and sense he had long forgotten.

A timeless time later he rose.

On that particular day there was to be a lecture; his heart beat faster with it. He would interact with the Headmaster of the Bleak Academy. Perhaps they would even have a personal encounter—

He calmed himself.

Past beauteous hills and olive trees he walked until he came to the great library where he was at that time assigned. He wound his way through the groaning, teetering stacks in the lights of the brass candelabra under the great skylight that showed the red star and the endless white stars that shone above. He found his nook, he took up the book he was working from, and he began again what he had been working on before; the copying and illumination of a diagram of the ouroboros.

A black folio sat beside his desk, where the finished piece would go.

He did not know how long he worked there; it might have been a moment or a century; it ended when there was an unexpected movement and an unexpected sound.

Valentina Sosunova leaned over the low wall of his nook, peering at the diagram.

He stared at her in shock.

"That's very pretty," she told him, "but I don't understand how you're getting silver scales from black ink."

He could not believe that she was real. He reached out a hand. He touched her face. Then, because it was solid, he returned his hand to his side.

"I am not painting silver," he said. "I am removing the absence of it. I am blacking the colorlessness out."

"That has always been the most confusing side of the magic to me," Valentina admitted. "I mean: removing the absence of a thing."

He gave her a blank look. "But ... it ... is an *ouroboros*," he said.

"Er?"

"It is confusing to remove the absence of a hat," he said. "Then there is no longer not a hat, but is there a hat? Who knows?! I would not want to count upon it to protect me from the sun. But to remove the absence of an ouroboros is a different matter. It is the snake that eats its own tail; conversely, it is the snake that is constantly spitting itself out by the tail. Wherever the ouroboros is not specifically absent, surely it *must* be present; *loc. cit.*"

"I think you mean *ipso facto*," she said, and then frowned. "I *think*," she emphasized.

"I tend to imagine," he said, "in any case, that to remove an absence is to lower the resistance in the circuit of the world. Does that make sense to you? It allows the thing to spark into being with much less ontological potential. So that handles the hat—how much potential beingness does it have? And the ouroboros, whose potential is already high. In an entirely orderly world, of course, things that do not exist would have almost no potential to; but the world is, as you have doubtless seen, in some disarray."

She frowned in thought, and then nodded. "Though: I have trouble imagining that the world is seething with potential ouroborii."

"Well," he said. He smiled bashfully. "I may have overstated it somewhat. I think it may be the case that *this one* exists within this page; that I am finding it, rather than undestroying it—like a sculptor digging out the piece from within the stone."

"I see," she said. "That would explain why you seem to be inking in three dimensions."

"But surely," he said, "moving on: you did not come all the way here just to see me illuminate ouroboroses."

"What if I did?"

He looked at her. "That is a bright dream, but—"

"Yes," she interrupted; or, rather, it was not an interruption, it was spoken as if it were the harmony underneath his melody, as if it could flow in and fit beneath his words, but it did not need to break into the flow of his speech to interrupt him: the content of it was enough.

Yes.

Or, *yes; a dream.*

The concept slammed into him like a runaway carriage and in that moment the dream dissolved away from him; he could not hold it. In grasping the essential reality of the situation he entirely unmade it, and he was practically flung awake, sputtering, and from his bed.

"IT SEEMED SO REAL," he marveled, over the next morning's breakfast. It was difficult for him to work his way through his bacon. "And you were there."

"I get around," Valentina said.

"You intruded before I had the opportunity to hear the Headmaster's lecture," he said. "That is an important opportunity lost, although it is also something of a relief."

"What was the topic?"

"The reconstitution of the self," said Mr. Wan. "How to exist without being; how we can rebuild ourselves after the termination of our existence."

"How rare," she agreed.

"The problem," he said, "is that I fear he would use me for a demonstration."

"Well," she said, "you are awake now, for better or for worse."

It would be several hours before their next seminar; they moved on to a discussion of a subtle point in Gurii Iakimovich's *The Semasiology of Dreams*.

In the following nights vivid dreams did not recur. He dreamt in pieces and flashes again. When eventually he had full dreams again, they lacked the clarity and internal logic and sense of passing time that his first real dream had possessed; their plots were nonsensical, emotional significance attached to the strangest things, and the situations did not flow coherently from one unto the next.

"It is not unusual," she said.

"It is unprecedented!" he declared. He slammed a hand, though not very hard, against an open book. "Volume after volume of dream documentation agrees, not to mention your own anecdotes on the subject."

"... have you made any progress on the seven impossible images?" she asked.

He made a face at her.

She pulled her legs and feet up onto the chair that she was sitting on. She rested her chin on a hand and gave him a thoughtful look. "I should explain to you," she said, "that I was born a Sosunov, and of the Sosunovs, and accordingly from the beginning of my childhood I had dreams of the Sosunov magic."

"Can— what? I ..."

"Not *mine*," she clarified, when he found no other words to clarify his question. "Rather, the magic of others. My mother's. My father's. My cousins'. My kin. They would use the Sosunov magic to enter my dreams, and in entering my dreams they would bring my dreams into a sort of order, and I got very used to that. It is not just what one does, but what is done *to* one, that can become habitual—you see?"

"... I think so," he said.

"You are operating under a handicap," she said. "It is not possible to reach your dreams and to assist you in that manner."

"But," he said, "you did appear."

She gave him a flat look.

"You did," he protested.

"Fine," she said, relenting. "Possibly I did. But that explanation will only confuse the matter, so let us assume for the sake of discussion that I did not. Or, rather, that I can not. Or at least, not often."

"OK," he said.

"It is fine for it to be some time," she said, "before lucidity in your dreams becomes normative; if you finish your study of dream symbols to my satisfaction there are other topics yet to be reviewed. That said, if you really wish to speed the process, hmm ..."

She fished out a small mirror that she wore on a chain around her neck. She glanced into it, then tossed it over to him. He caught it, awkwardly.

"If you make a habit," she said, "of checking that you are awake, by looking in the mirror—and consciously reflecting on the matter—then it will help."

He glanced in the mirror. He frowned, but he looped the chain around his own neck.

"In the middle of an incoherent dream," she said, "you may think to check the mirror; and on looking into it, you will see not your face but your sleeping body in its bed, and you will realize, 'I am dreaming. Where are the symbols that I have read about?' and they will appear. Or, 'I am dreaming. I should take the time to see what happens if I remove my sense of self, or contemplate the impossible objects, or meditate, within this dream.' Something of the sort. Perhaps I will even show up again, impossible as it may be, and help."

He frowned. "But what if I do not have the mirror on me?"

"The simplest test is to spit in your hand," she said, "and rub it with your fingers, and see if it repulses you. But it's less gross to have your mirror."

"That it should be," he agreed.

HE DREAMT—he dreamt a thousand things, and one.

One night he dreamt the fourth impossible shape, the moon over the hills that was also a running wolf. It was very deliberate, he thought, when he woke up; it had been *intentional*, in the context of the dream.

Some unconscious will of his had thought, let us dream the moon, that is the wolf; both at once, or either.

It had howled and it had shone but he still could not grasp the shape in waking; when he wrote down his memories of the dream it seemed to him that he had dreamt it as both things at once, but that anything specific about it that made it a wolf was part of a different memory than the memories in which it was the moon.

"That is possibly your memory," Valentina said, when he showed her his dream diary. "I mean, your memory doing that, and not the dream. There are some in the family who have theorized that we dream sort of all-at-once, or at least, in an out-of-order jumble, rather than one event at a time. Then we remember it afterwards in order."

"That raises a question that has bothered me," he said. "You mentioned that a lack of attention can stifle a dream; but, when do we pay attention to our dreams? When they are happening, or upon our waking?"

She smiled. "Isidor Sosunov, so the story goes, dreamt in backwards order. Always he dreamt the ending of his dreams before the beginning of them. One night, he dreamt that he had achieved enlightenment, and had retreated to the top of a mountain to contemplate what he had learned. 'This is a secret that is like the rain,' he said. But he was awakened by a household emergency before he could reach the beginning of the dream and *achieve* enlightenment, you see, and it was not until Miruna Sosunova that anyone understood what Isidor's enlightenment had been."

"That— that is not an answer," said Gylbard Wan. "That is not even another question."

"You may pay attention to a dream at any point," she said. "Then, the next morning, a hundred years later. By doing so you give over its formlessness to form. Or, rather, you ensure that its formlessness has always been given over to form."

"Effect preceding cause?"

"Indeed."

He frowned. "That seems unnecessarily elaborate."

"It used to be that we thought it was a metaphor," Valentina said. "A way of thinking. The old books will tell you that all you're *really* doing when you write down your dreams in the morning is helping you to remember them. All you're *really* doing when you pay attention to your dreams after the fact is clarifying your memory of them.

"But then great-great-aunt Glikeriya tried taking the metaphor literally and discovered that you pretty much actually *can* fiddle with a dream long after it was originally dreamt, so we're pretty sure now that that's what actually happens every time."

"Oh," he said.

"Keep thinking about the moon-wolf, anyway," she said. "It's awfully great progress, and I'm proud."

"I don't know if you could call it real *progress*," he said, but he couldn't help it; it made his heart warm.

LIFE—OR DEATH, if that would be a better term—began to seem less frightening and his studies more stifling. He found himself venturing out of the College of Emptiness and Dream for days at a time: now returning to his old dormitory to help in its garden or gather fumes of Perdition for Valentina; now wandering the Academy for things of interest; now simply dangling from the golden cords that suspended the great stone egg to regard the darkness of the True Thing below. He grew frustrated during his conversations with Valentina because they so rarely resembled a courtship; from time to time the subject of his undying love for her would come up, but she was frankly more interested in teaching him, occasionally learning from him, and (now and then) philosophical debate.

"I would fetch down the stars from the sky for you," he said, on one occasion, interrupting her lecture on the gates of dream, and she gave him an odd look.

"That would be extremely selfish," she said. "Everyone would hate us."

He thought about that. "I would fetch down one of the *best* stars from the sky for you," he said. "If you wanted. Or the best wave from the sea."

She scratched the back of her neck, looking a little embarrassed. "That's not necessary," she said. "It is enough that you are studying here beside me at the College, and have done something so hard as learning how to dream."

"Is it?" he said.

"Evidently," she said, with a wry look that he did not understand, and then shook her head. "If you really wish to make a grand gesture, then you may do so, but I would honestly rather talk about dreams."

He subsided, unsatisfied.

"You are beautiful," he told her, on another occasion.

"You are only saying that because I stabbed the Headmaster," she said. "He the lord of Death's dominion he."

"That is probably true," he conceded. "It was an extremely beautiful moment."

"Would you say it was ... *carved* into your memory?"

He stared at her blankly.

"It is interesting," she said, after the silence had stretched, "that you can see me well enough to call me beautiful. I have never asked you about it,[21] but your eyes appear to be missing. Or, rather, to be night sky and falling stars."

"That is how it is with the Headmaster's creations," he said.

"Oh?"

"One slips up," he said. "One *means* to look at their eyes, but one looks at the night sky instead."

"But we are indoors," she protested.

"I didn't say it was a *trivial* error," he said.

She squinted at him.

He shrugged.

"Can you look into your own eyes?" she said. "I mean, with a mirror?"

"I can't," he said. "All I see is death."

"That's awful," she said.

After a long moment, he vouchsafed a confidence. "I have died quite a bit, haha."

"You have?"

"The Headmaster is not lying when he says there are ten thousand more just like me. He is not indulging in hyperbole. He is simply being cruel. If I die, you see, if, no, when I die, then he will lift up another from the faceless crowd to be me."

"I'm sorry." She asked him: "Does it hurt?"

LATER, Mrs. Senko was visiting again.

"Today I had the thought," Valentina said to her. "Why does the Headmaster allow me to study here, and yet, have you under orders to kill?"

"It would depend on what you're learning, I expect."

"To devour."

"To devour?"

---

21   she claimed, incorrectly

Valentina opened her mouth wide. She closed it with a snap. Then she frowned. "Or did I dream that?"

"That sounds like a dream," Mrs. Senko said. "But you would surely know better than I."

"It is harder to keep track," Valentina said. "And after the fact it becomes nearly impossible."

There were tears trickling from her eyes. Mrs. Senko looked alarmed.

"I am a material being," Valentina said.

"Um."

"All this way, all this way, and *still*. What am I supposed to think about that?"

"I had thought the Headmaster's curse on you had lifted."

"Lifted, shmifted," Valentina said. "A thing doesn't become painless just because you finally learn to deal with it."

"I'd think it would," said Mrs. Senko. "On account of, the fire adapts."

"Maybe," Valentina said. She reached up a hand. She snuffed out a star. "I have been taught that it is my prerogative to judge the things of the world worthy or unworthy, but I still don't know what to think of myself."

"... well," Mrs. Senko finally said, "wouldn't that be rather up to you?"

AND MR. WAN DREAMT that he checked whether the world was real, and it was not. The mirror showed him his sleeping body—on his pallet, on the great stone egg. Spit on his hand gave him no reaction at all. His thoughts were slow and clouded but they *were* thoughts; he had trained himself to take a moment each time to think upon the matter; and he realized that the world was not real. He was in a dream.

He looked around him. He was on the western hills of Fortitude, as Valentina had described them; near the Kichi pools, amongst the trees, beneath the surging sky. It was unreasonably cold, colder than it ever actually was in Fortitude; his breath fogged out before him.

He rubbed his hands together.

He called out, "Hello?"

The world was silent.

It occurred to him that he did not know what lay beyond the hills to the west—Valentina had waved her hands dismissively whenever it had come up—and he thought that he would take the trip up and then over to discover it. Between the trees and up he went, climbing awkwardly beneath the crisp air and the stars, until he reached a cleared space at the summit and could look westward out of Fortitude.

Almost he failed to catch it.

Almost he missed the process by which he dreamt the next thing. Almost he misunderstood, and thought that when he looked west to see a beauteous valley—where fruit trees grew and white stone ruins stood—that he had found it there; that he had *discovered* it. It was only by providence, by a strange mental tic, by a hesitation, that he realized what was happening instead:

That he had already anticipated its existence when he looked westwards; that it was in fact in the very moment that he anticipated its existence that he looked westwards; that he had not *let* himself dream that the view was clear until he had a sense for what would be there.

It did not satisfy him.

He realized slowly, with a dizzying sense of unreality that nearly woke him, that his dreams could not tell him what lay beyond Fortitude. The valley was ... he thought that it was most probably what the books had described to him as "Nikifor's Garden," a symbol of uncultivated richness; a dream-symbol, and not an accurate vision in any way.

It did not satisfy him, and forcefully he turned his attention away from his expectations. Forcefully he tried to see, not symbols, not valleys, not what he imagined, but what was *there*.

It eluded him.

He saw a seething nothingness—but that too was his expectation. He discarded it and saw darkness—and again.

He got no further; as far as he could remember when he woke, the dream stopped there.

"That's more or less what I'd have expected," Valentina said, when he brought it up to her later. "You'd need to condition your brain to have a concept for, a direct awareness of, a, like, *perception* of 'ambiguous, without form, could be, uhh, anything? really'

"... if you wanted to look at the unformed dream and see exactly that."

He frowned at her. "But I would be expecting that, too, then."

"If you expect to be surprised," Valentina said, "then the world does not dissolve in a mire of contradictions."

"Oh."

"In like fashion," she said, "if you have a distinct concept for the ambiguous and the unknown, and can learn to hold that in your mind with all the potential in it, or at least a multivalent potential, then perceiving that in a dream does not void either the perception or the ambiguity. You were on the right track with the 'seething nothingness' thing; it just wasn't literal enough for you."

He thought about this for a while. Then: "Does it matter?"

"It does," she said. "Hence the rabbit-duck. Hence the moon-wolf."

"Why?"

"The ability to expect multiple or ambiguous things," she said, "is the first step towards being free of the prison of one's own expectations."

AT THAT TIME, Valentina Grigorievna Sosunova did not love him.

It was something of a frustration to her. It made it difficult to teach him. She wanted to enter into his dreams and show him how things should work, *directly,* but she could not do it—or rather *would* not do it; the mechanisms she had for entering the dreams of someone that she did not love were too unpleasant.

... and she did not love him.

She was warmly fond of him. She found him engaging. She thought it extremely likely that she *would* fall in love with him, for the same reason that she wished that she already had—teaching him without direct access to his dreams was difficult, and she already knew that it was destined that she would teach him reasonably well.

Still, it was not something that she could force.

Accordingly, that winter, she judged that he had learned as much about the recurring images of dreams as he could learn without her there in his dreams to give him hands-on tutelage; she reduced that study to a monthly review, to keep it fresh for him, and set him to studying her notes on the various witches that the Sosunovs had faced.

"So that you will know what they are like," she said, "in case you are ever called to face one."

"Um," he said.

"I know," she said. "Even assuming that you will one day travel to the lands of life, the odds that there will be a witch *just then* are quite low, and the odds that it will be a witch strong enough that some other Sosunov won't have already handled it are even lower."

"Then—"

"But," she said, in mild reproach, "this is not a matter of likelihood, but of duty."

"I understand," he said.

Spring came, and he saw through two more of the impossible figures. He read the post-mortem memoirs of several of the early Sosunovs. He meditated on the story of Miruna Sosunova, who learned to see through the back of her eyes like the front of them and went out into the territory of nothingness and death.

His dreams became more vibrant; he was lucid more often during them, and could more often break them down into known elements during them or after them; he began to gain a misty awareness of the gates of his dreams and other portions of the architecture of his mind— but it seemed to him that he was still missing something vital, something core and something key that would make this *magical* rather than simply strange.

They were vibrant dreams, but ordinary ones. They had no magic in them.

It was not until the summer—when the violet trees of the Bleak Academy were in flower—that that changed.

HE DREAMT of a hut by the water, where he sat at a spinning wheel, turning fish to silver fate. Wide leaves hung low over the hut's roof. Birds cried out in the distance. It was not the Bleak Academy; it was not Fortitude; he was quite alone, and quite content in endless solitude, until Valentina rose up from the water and walked onto the shore.

"Ah," he said. He was a little embarrassed. "I was just spinning fish into fate."

She was inside. He was not sure how that happened.

She was leaning against the wall.

"They ... did not like being fish," he said. "That is probably what was happening."

"I've done weirder things," Valentina said, "in dreams."

"Have you?"

She thought about it. "Absolutely," she said. "I tend to wake myself up and take control of things before dreaming anything *really* embarrassing, but it's not like I don't let myself indulge in dreams of indeterminate numbers of horses or fuzzy bees the size of cantaloupes and the like."

"That is something of a relief," he said, setting aside the current thread and trying to figure out what to do with his hands instead.

"In fact," she said, "the matter could be instructive. Do you think that you can keep yourself from coming up with any particular theory as to *how* the fish becomes a thread, while also paying attention to the thing itself?"

"I can't," he said, and shook his head. "I already know that they're yarn dolls that are being unwoven."

"They are?"

"Not grossly," he said. "But on the molecular level."

"I see that you have given the matter some thought," she said. "Which is more than I had anticipated. Perhaps we could apply the same test to the remainder of the island?"

He frowned in thought. "You mean," he said, "refuse to know anything about the rest of the island, while paying attention to what it might actually be?"

"Yes," she said.

"I could try it," he said, and he turned his focus outwards. He struggled with the concept. He tried to see, not what was really there, not what he anticipated, but the uncertainty itself.

He saw something else instead.

He was suddenly warm inside. It was like a flower blooming in his heart. He said, "It is you, isn't it?"

"Me?"

"It is you," he said. "You are actually here."

She hesitated. Then, slightly, she nodded.

"I am not dreaming you."

"You *are* dreaming me," she quibbled. "It is just that I am *also* dreaming me, and our dreams are on this particular occasion more or less the same."

"Then," he said, "you love me."

She looked away. Her eyes were sad. "Do not make a thing of this, I beg you."

"But it is amazing," he said.

"I love you," she conceded. "And I loved you too late."

"What?"

"I do not wish to speak of it," she said. Her voice was tight. "I wish to advise you on the magic. I wish to give you a fighting chance of understanding it. If you celebrate our love right now instead then I will become upset."

He frowned at her. "You cannot expect me to comply. I have no idea what you are talking about but it sounds extremely relevant."

"Please," she said.

Slowly, he relaxed his frown. He chewed on his lower lip. He looked away. "I am not capable of seeing what you suggest. You will have to assist me."

She held up her hands, and inside them—

He blinked at it. There was a roaring noise in his ears. His vision turned speckled. His eyes attempted to follow the contours of the thing, but he could not follow the contours of the thing. It burned like a fire. It twined about itself like serpents. It moved in her hands like the shadow of something empyreal—like the thing itself, but not the truth behind it, could fit within the three dimensions of the world.

Each time he thought he had understood it, each time his eyes and his attention tracked some understanding into it, it changed. It slipped around his mental grasp like water.

"What *is* that?" he asked her, blankly.

She looked down at it. Her forehead wrinkled, slightly. "Ah," she said. "It is a snake."

It fell from her hands. It slithered away. He gaped after it.

"Or possibly an egg."

In that moment he understood it; or rather, he didn't understand *it*, but he understood *something*. He turned his thoughts away from the thing that Valentina had shown him, groped for something more approachable in the dark, and found the sixth impossible image in his thoughts: a mandala of impossible triangles and twisted curves which he pulled out of his mind's eye into his dream, seeing each line now in this interpretation and now in that one, before it could finally sink in to him what he had guessed at, what he was starting to recognize: that those interpretations lived not in the lines he witnessed but in the eyes that saw.

In that moment first one line, then another, leapt into multiple configurations simultaneously; the flat diagram seemed to buck and writhe, and then turn like the gears of a great machine; he gave a grunt of concentration and clenched both fists and there was no longer motion, but only *all things together*, and then there was no room left for consciousness, no room left for awareness of the self and of the room within his brain. He fell over and dissolved to dust; slipped into night.

IT WAS SOMETHING like progress, at last, and it kindled a great excitement in him—the more so when Valentina returned to his dreams, not four nights later, to guide him through an exercise in eliding his dream-self while remaining conscious, so as to better recognize himself as the dreamer and not the self-in-dream.

"You love me," he told her, smugly—in the waking world—and she raised an eyebrow at him. "You have said as much. It is the *implication* of your appearance."

"It was inevitable," she agreed, placidly, "but please do not get above yourself. I have not done so yet."

"I don't ..." he said, and floundered.

"One day," she said, "I take it, I shall fall in love with you. Then I shall think back to this time and say, 'I should share a dream with the Wan I knew back then.'"

She frowned.

"Though three in less than a year seems excessive. It is difficult, you understand."

"You—" He hesitated. "You can do that?"

"It is difficult," she repeated. "Please do not attempt it yourself. Meeting a younger Valentina Grigorievna would do you no good whatsoever, and meeting an older one smacks of dissatisfaction with what you have on hand."

"But this is marvelous," he said. "This is unprecedented."

"It is the very definition of precedented," Valentina argued. "Anyhow, it is the family's policy not to make a hullaballoo about the matter."

"Ah," he said, feeling oddly hurt. Then it shifted to pleasure. "Well, it means, you *shall* love me, then."

"I shall; and that day grows more remote for every minute you spend gloating over it."

"Ah," he said, subdued; and she burst into snickers at the expression on his face.

It was something like progress, anyhow, and his interest in his studies, which had faltered in the spring, grew livelier. He swept through the remaining impossible images; they no longer held challenge for him; Valentina moved him on to visualizing ambiguous objects that could not be put on paper—from "an image that looks like a vividly rendered bird, but also like a triangle" to "pick three things from the world around you, or from your imagination if you prefer, and imagine something that looks like all of them." He retained tangible momentum; the task was certainly *harder*, and easier to become confused about, but he could feel himself improving day by day.

In his dreams himself he began to see, however dimly, the application of it—

That in the dream of formless, many-formed potential there was ... possibility.

His dreams became shot through with veins of the unknown, the uncertain, the ill-defined. With Valentina's intermittent aid—and what secret, private joy that brought him!—he learned how to step back away from the dream and see the whole of it at once, to turn it over in his mental eye, and grasp the formed and unformed aspects as a whole.

"It is excellent work," Valentina told him, in his dreams; but her eyes were sad.

IT WAS in the autumn of that year that the Headmaster explained it.

"She is sad in your dreams because you have only a year," he said.

"I'm sorry?"

The Headmaster had come by unexpectedly; had been amused at the disorderly mess that filled Mr. Wan's enclosure on the egg and suggested he erase it; had dragged him to a communal kitchen for a cup of coffee; and somehow the conversation had turned to that dream.

"Perhaps a year," he said. "*Around* a year, by my guess. And after that—"

He held up the index fingers of his hands, pressed against one another. Then, making a clicking noise with his tongue, he pulled them apart.

"Parting."

"I refuse to accept that," said Mr. Wan. "I will— well, *she* will fight you on it, I'm pretty sure. And I will give her moral support."

"She is heartless," the Headmaster said. "and, I assure you, will betray you."

"... will she?"

The Headmaster gave him half a smile.

"Thank you," Mr. Wan said. He bowed his head.

"You kill a man enough times," the Headmaster said, "and you start wanting to give him advice on his love life. It's not a problem."

He drank down the last few gulps of his coffee, set his cup down, and turned, and when Mr. Wan had finished blinking he was gone.

HIS THIRST FOR life only grew.

Libraries and seminars no longer held interest; instead, he wandered the hidden places of the Bleak Academy or taught logic games to the child-dead. He was no longer satisfied to talk with Valentina about abstract philosophy and dreams; instead, he dredged up her opinions, tales of her childhood, stories from her life. They argued politics—most keenly, whether the industrial revolution, whether *progress*, had been the enemy Valentina made it out to be.

The frantic spark, the thirst in him—it was magnetic, it was compelling, but most of all it was a trial to Valentina. She was thrown off her game; she did not understand what had changed, and her attempts to return things to normal and develop his understanding of the magic brought him no further.

He did not admit his reasons for it—did not *tell* her that anything had changed for him—until one evening, towards the moonset, when she had digressed quite far, and was digressing further, into an attempt to explain the "feel" or "flavor" of a witch-touched dream. Then, it built up in him; then, it finally burst out from him:

"I don't have *time*."

It stopped her. She frowned at him. "We are not, like, on a clock," she said.

"We are," he said. "The Headmaster says we have less than a year."

"—oh."

Valentina frowned.

"Then I agree," she said. "We shouldn't be talking about this, but making new memories instead. Do you want to fight an ogre?"

"I do not want to fight an ogre."

"Let's go fight an ogre."

She took his hand.

Across the golden ropes she went, and down the alabaster arch; a quarter mile in, to burst through the doors of a lecture hall; there, as Mr. Wan and the class watched in appalled disbelief, she dragged Cornelius Krakonoš from his lecture hall podium and dueled him; but when he had beaten her ("no thanks to you," as she later said to Mr. Wan) and she lay bloody on the ground, he did not finish her.

"That's six to two," he rumbled, amused; and she wiped blood from her lip, made a face at him, and she reeled away.

SHE TOOK him to climb the Ethwray Building, which was not a mountain but was the closest that could be found to one at the Bleak Academy; and to sail the waters of the library's hidden lake; and to the gardens of Hervaeus Watson, to sit among the roses, and still she did not love him, though there was a frenzy of annoyance in her that someone that she cared for—that *something of hers*—would be taken away. She made such memories as she could, and still she did not love him; surrendered to it, finally, and accepted that she would not love him, that her student and her friend and her dear night-eyed Vanya would be stolen from her, and she would never even have the opportunity to visit him in her dreams and show him what all the lessons had been *for* because she was too stony, too arrogant, too hardened, and too fickle.

That was what had done it, of course, in the end; that unfairness, that injustice, that unreasonable betrayal was the soil in which love's seed was planted.

It was not until she had exhausted herself from grief that she would never love him that she slipped into dreams and saw a certain possibility and realized that she had come to love him after all.

It went something like this.

She dreamt that she was sinking into choppy water, the light a chiaroscuro, the water on her a heavy weight. In that moment as she was sinking she became aware of numerous details that the dream had yet to specify; where was she? Why was she there? Was she in deep or shallow water? Was she alone?

They came into the focus of her attention but she did not resolve them. She held on to the ambiguity of them.

Where was she? ... she waited. The contours of the dream shifted, like a sea urchin's tendrils in the water, with the subtle movements of her thoughts.

She *listened*.

It would not have worked without love; *had* not worked without love; a hundred Sosunovs had tried it. Dreaming, she was isolated, cut off from all others; in every direction, all around her, there was an endless, empty space—but she was connected to Mr. Wan inside her. There was a piece of him that had taken root inside her, or a piece of her that was always outside of her and with him.

Where was she? ... she waited, and she listened, and the contours of the dream slowly shifted, bit by bit, to fall into ever-greater alignment with Gylbard Wan's dreams.

Why was she there? Was she alone?

He was dreaming of a hut by the water, where he sat at a spinning wheel, turning fish to silver fate. Wide leaves hung low over the hut's roof. Birds cried out in the distance. It was not Fortitude; he was quite alone, and quite content in endless solitude, until Valentina rose up from the water and walked onto the shore.

"Ah," he said. He was a little embarrassed. "I was just spinning fish into fate."

Their dreams locked into alignment, and she was leaning against the wall.

"They ... did not like being fish," he said. "That is probably what was happening."

"I've done weirder things," Valentina said, "in dreams."

AND SO at last they could live happily ever after.

His step grew lighter and his gaze sharper and the magic in him ran deeper than it had ever done before. On a stage before seven lords of the Bleak Academy, he tore open the world; slaughtered the serpent that came through the gap; and won the title "Magister." She—lacking his literal millennia of foundational work—was a little slower; her enclosure grew too slowly for the eye to follow and a strange blind spot obscured her understanding of the deepest mysteries.

"I must hold this over you while I can," he informed her. "As I expect you'll catch up to me within the year."

That reminded him of his deadline; it sobered him; and his teasing grin became a frown.

"Whisht," she said. "*You'll* catch up to *me* when you can make a Perdition with your dreams."

At last they could live happily ever after—or, at least, happily for a very short while.

She made the most of every day of it, as did he; but in the end, it was her second-oldest enemy that got her.

BECAUSE: she was *so close.*

The fundamental insights were all right there—*all* of them. She could feel it. Everything she wanted. Everything she needed. And in the end, what was holding her back?

She was a creature of fire, but also a creature of meat and bone and hair.

She was Valentina Grigorievna Sosunova, but it was not Valentina Grigorievna Sosunova who was destined to touch upon the True Thing.

The person destined for that was ... someone better. Something better.

Something made of her, but beyond her. And she was *tired of it.* She had love, and purpose, and things to learn, and even the old curse barely mattered any more, barely made more than a twinge of illness when she reflected directly upon it—but she was so tired of being a creature of meat and bone and hair when she was meant to be the fire.

The Headmaster had been right when he said she would grow crueler; and, of course, that she was heartless.

So she sent a message and asked for Mrs. Senko to come.

And they stood at the edge of the egg, and the articulation of truth from nothingness crashed against the egg, like surf upon the shore, and limned all everything with golden light. And Valentina tossed a stone into the void.

"I understand," she said.

"You understand?"

"I understand why he told you to kill me," Valentina said.

"Oh," Mrs. Senko said, and she looked away.

"Long ago," Valentina said, "I touched upon the true thing, and I became a dark bird of emptiness in a cage of flesh. Starlight is the marrow of my bones. And this is perhaps a good thing to be and perhaps a bad thing to be but— a bird should not be caged like that. My ribs are a cruel enclosure for a wingéd thing."

"I won't do it, Valya."

"Be practical," Valentina said.

"Killing people ruthlessly when the occasion seems to call for it," Mrs. Senko, "*sounds* practical, like many things that are penny-wise and pound-foolish—but it isn't actually very practical at all. I'm not going to kill you."

"Don't kill me, then," Valentina said. Her voice was airy, fey. "Just crack my ribs. Rip out my heart. Let my body fall limp and lifeless to the ground. Let events proceed, well, *naturally*, from there. Here." She kicked a sword across the egg to Mrs. Senko. "Take it."

Mrs. Senko picked it up. She held it awkwardly. Then she put it aside.

"Valentina," she said.

"I am being quite—ah, what's the thing?" Valentina said. "'Literal.' I thought for a long time that I must surely have a heart, and that the dark bird thing was a poetic metaphor, but it shows up on an X-ray."

Mrs. Senko squinted at her.

"Did you know, Mrs. Senko?" Valentina asked. "Did you know that there's no actual rule here against being alive? I checked. When I'd seen that X-ray, I went, and I checked, I looked through all the rolls. And there's no rule at all. You're allowed to live through the Bleak Academy. There are people who've done it. There are people who are *living through the Bleak Academy right now.* There's nobody saying, 'You come to the Bleak Academy and you've got to die.' There's just the Headmaster's rule for me.

"So you can make your choice on what to believe, Mrs. Senko.

"That your own father is the sword that's going to kill me, no matter what I do. That I am mad and damned and cursed and doomed and all of this is just an awful joke and he will never let me live.

"—or you can believe, and trust, in me."

Mrs. Senko's eyes dropped to Valentina's heart. She made a dubious frown. "Fine."

A moment passed. She clicked her tongue.

Then, her eyes snapped back up; they caught Valentina's in them.

She tangled the light of her attention into Valentina's own.

"Ah—" Valentina said, in sudden regret; sudden fear; sudden concern—but it was too late.

Mrs. Senko stepped forward and as she stepped forward their thoughts flowed together; she moved a hand, and around that hand there was the pall of Glum; and, with the very substance that had kinked Valentina's *being* so long ago, she caught it, twisted it, and *unkinked* it.

IT WAS enough.

IT shouldn't have been enough, you know. It wouldn't have been enough for most people. Most people, you'd have had to go in with pliers or something, the jaws of life, wrest open the cage that was their chest by

486

hand. Most people, you'd have to *actually* rip out their heart ... and if it turned out that there *wasn't* a dark bird of emptiness in there, but just some kind of weird, I don't know, lump of beating flesh and blood, or something? You would feel really quite the fool indeed.

But there; then; in that moment; and for Valentina—

IN THAT MOMENT she was given the final license to cease her participation in the cruel façade that was Valentina Grigorievna Sosunova; and from the center of her it arrowed out:

A dark bird of emptiness; of night.

... AND SHE could have stayed, that Magistra-bird; that was the bitterness of it.

She could have stayed, and still found love, she even *wanted* to; still she dreamed of it— wore the coat of Valentina in her dreams and still she dreamed of it—

But, put another way, she couldn't.

Without the flesh, without the bone—

... it was no longer in her nature.

5MOKE AND zeppelins covered the sky. The dead ruled with an iron fist. Alexandrel Celdinar had his great and modern Night London; only, it didn't work out.

It wasn't any mistake that he'd made. It wasn't anything fair.

It was a *deus ex machina*.

Since an age before even Fortitude was founded, the demon-folk of the western hills had prayed to the gods of dream and nightmare. Night London had existed at their sufferance. This much Mayor Celdinar had known; he had always believed that they were *real*—but he had thought them dead, or sleeping like the Jotun were, or that, at worst, they'd endorsed his grand ambitions. He hadn't worried what they'd *think* of him.

Only:

If they were dead, they rose again. If they were sleeping, then they woke again. If they had once gone along with him, they no longer did ... and everything fell apart.

You could say that it was by natural processes that progress fell out of fashion.

It was something that *could* have happened. The tide of the times could have turned against it. Not every vampire could play with mortal minds, and they were profoundly outnumbered—so it could have been causality, and not providence, that made the forward march of Progress peter out; that turned his tide of immigration into a trickle fading away to other lands; that made Night London's *concept* seem ... somehow gauche.

You could even say that the earthquake was natural, although Town was hardly prone to them. The fact that it seemed to preferentially target

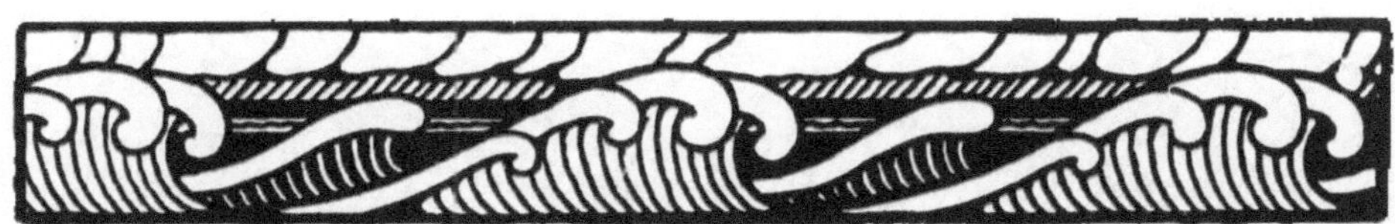

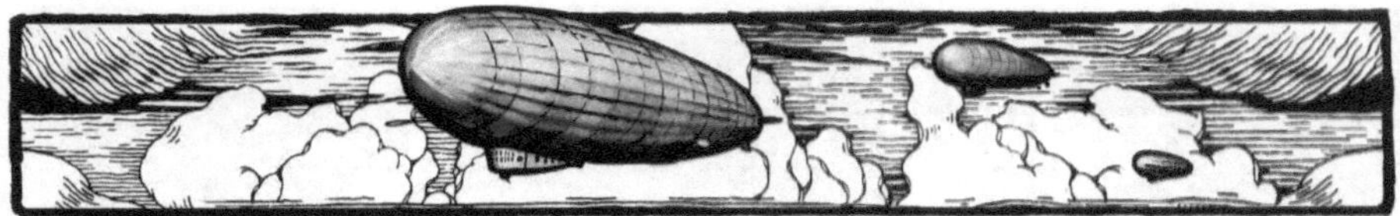

factories could have been just a coincidence, and the way they clustered, and confirmation bias.

Mayor Celdinar could have salvaged things if it were just a zeitgeist and an earthquake; he was *going* to salvage things, when it was just a zeitgeist and an earthquake; but then he started laughing and he couldn't stop, he was choking on it, it was like there was a beast inside his chest trying to burst out of him, because he *recognized* that, he *knew* that, that *light* that was limning the edge of the eastern hills—

That was *the sun*.

He gave up. He couldn't help it. Night London became "the cursed place," and people tried not to live there any longer, they drifted away to Fortitude or the Walking Fields or back to the mortal world, and in the end he gave in and did so himself; he bought a little house in Fortitude, where he could breathe the good lake air.

It was a surrender, as good as any other; he would be accepted there.

And many, many years went by.

ONE DAY the King of Evil flew down from the sky on an island on the back of a beast and built a school in the ruins of Night London. He offered incentives to people who'd come back and try living there, or send their children there to study; and, one family at a time, it worked.

Most places would have either been politely skeptical about the whole "King of Evil" thing or driven him out for it, but Town had gotten used to the strange. It became clear over time that whatever the King's game was, the school wasn't *itself* "evil," nor was it a school *of* "evil," and, even if the Principal was intensely suspicious, it was the best education a person could *get* there in Town—

So people filtered in to what had been Night London, a trickle at a time, to provide services to the students who studied there.

In time, its ruins were rechristened as "Horizon."

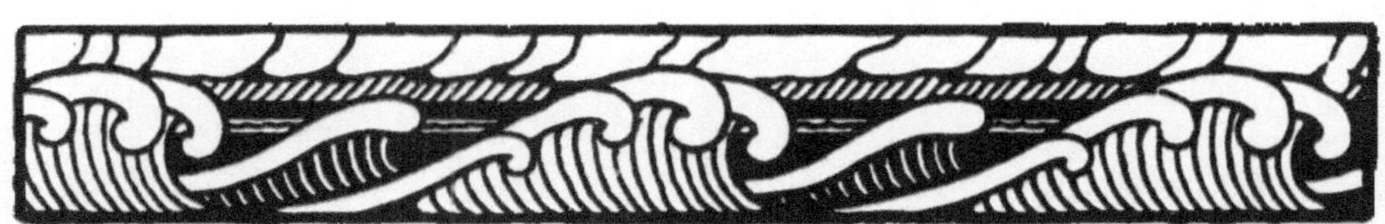

Q: Tell me then the name of that which draws the dawn
Across the lower air
And wakes the earth to red and gold

A: Shining-Mane is its name that draws the dawn
Across the lower air
And wakes the earth to red and gold

Accounted best of all horses by the heroes
And the spirits of the sky
Its course is light:

From time to time a strand of mane or tail slips
And falls upon the lower world
To exalt the spirits of the brave
To crown the sky-wise ships
And break the spell of Grayvale
On those it holds in thrall.

Q: Tell me then the name of the stream
Dividing the angel's heavens from the world ...
—from the Lay of Vafthrudnir (amended),
traditional

APROSINYA ALEXANDROVNA Sosunova grew up enfolded in love and the Sosunov magic.

She scarcely even managed to have nightmares; no sooner would one get started then there one of her family members would be, laughing—her Mom, taming the wicked wolves that were chasing her; her Dad, catching her in her fall; or even her great-great-great-great-great-&c.-grandmother Valentina Grigorievna appearing and giving the monster that was troubling her such a *look* that it skittered backwards, fell over a ledge, and exploded.

Aprosinya had to pause, after that one. She had to stare quizzically at Valentina. "Who're you?" she said.

"That's a tough one," Valentina said. "Strictly speaking, I'm not anybody any more. I only even pretend to be Valentina when I dream. But— ah, whatever. You can call me Valentina Grigorievna, child. I'm your great-great-great-great-etcetera grandmother."

"Where do you live?"

"A tree."

"You don't even!"

Valentina's eyes sparkled with mischief. Actually, there was something wrong with them. They might have just been sparkling *in general*, but it was hard to make it out, exactly, in the dream. "No? Your great-gran can't live in a tree?"

"You can't," Aprosinya said.

"Then I guess I live on a giant stone egg," Valentina said.

"No!" Aprosinya was laughing now.

"All right," Valentina said, and she knelt, and took Aprosinya's hands, and looked her quite seriously in the eyes—which just made Aprosinya's vision swim, as she still couldn't focus on Valentina's eyes at all. "All right. I live at a school that is very far away. Do you go to school yet?"

Aprosinya shook her head. "Not until I'm nine," she said.

"Well," Valentina said, *"this* school is called the Bleak Academy. But nobody will tell me why it's called 'bleak.' Isn't that funny?"

"It's funny," Aprosinya agreed. "What do they teach you?"

"All kinds of things," Valentina said. "How to make dragons out of shadows. How to turn into a bird. How to reject the appearance of reality that surrounds us and see through to the True Thing beyond. They even teach remedial classes in seeing through the back of your eyes like the front of them, though *I* learned that before I came."

"Really?"

"I did," Valentina confirmed.

"I tried it once," Aprosinya confessed. "But it just made my head funny."

"A necessary stage," Valentina said. "All must pass through it before their enlightenment."

"Do they— I mean," Aprosinya said, shyly. "Do they teach the secret that is like the rain?"

"—they certainly don't call it that," Valentina said.

Aprosinya frowned.

"I mean, maybe? But they would call it something else."

"Oh." Aprosinya looked around her at the dream. "Do you think I could study there?"

"Why?"

"I want to make monsters explode by looking at them."

Valentina made a funny face at her. "Don't go through those gates because you want to explode monsters by looking at them," she said. "It's not what they're for."

"Do you know how to play 'Sorry!'?" Aprosinya asked.

"I am a terrifying, legendary expert at Sorry," Valentina informed her. "But it's hard to do the deck properly in a dream. How about we play checkers, instead?"

And they did.

THAT WAS Aprosinya's childhood: wrapped and sheltered in her family's love, even in her dreams.

Her Da wasn't good at the magic. He'd married into the family and was barely passable as an amateur—so he only came by when he was actually asleep.

Her Mom was better. She was the heir to the family and the magic was basically like breathing to her. She'd come by once to meet Aprosinya *while still pregnant with her*, glowing with wonder at meeting her child for the first time; and the seven-year-old Aprosinya had gotten to feel her baby-self kick in her mother's belly and whisper little confidences back.

And then there was everybody else. A whole bustling house full of 'em—

And Valentina Grigorievna Sosunova, which was just *weird*.

"She's probably just watching out for her legacy," her father Alexander eventually suggested. "Say, she fell in love with the *idea* of having descendants even to our day, and for someone like Valentina Grigorievna, that might just be enough to visit little Aprosechka's dreams."

And he'd knelt by Aprosinya and said, "Be careful of her, OK?"

She'd squinted at him in puzzlement, and then shrugged. "OK."

A whole bustling household filled her dreams, a whole bustling household and Valentina Grigorievna, too; though, of her future children, her grandchildren, and her late-life loves ... there had yet to be a sign.

APROSINYA'S BEST FRIEND growing up was probably Devin Markovic, whose Dad captained one of the Sosunov ships. *Devin's* best friend, though, was almost certainly Izvivode. That was his *kaiju*—a dog he'd trained to grow bigger on command.

"Go, Izvivode!" he'd tell it, and it would glow inside with something like moonlight, and it would stretch itself out and get bigger, and its fur would soften and change color, and its teeth would curve back inside its mouth.

"It's for *kaiju* battles," he said.

This was his obsession, back then. He thought—back then—that at any moment, some great giant insect, serpent, or lizard would probably attack the Sosunov compound and the surrounding area. Or maybe a giant robot would. It would come lurching in to destroy everything, leaving it on fire, and then he'd jump out, with his dog at his side, and shout, "Go, Izvivode!" and they'd battle.

Aprosinya didn't think it would go very well. She didn't think it would go very well because, even at its biggest, Izvivode was still a pretty small monster. But it was hard to say, because the battle never wound up actually happening. And the funny thing was, the longer that that went on, the more it *didn't* happen, the more obsessed Devin became with it:

The more *certain* he was that there *would* be a big giant animal battle, or a robot vs. Izvivode struggle; that there *had* to be.

He started spending more and more of his time training for it. He bought stickers from this really disreputable magic sticker shop that didn't stay open very long afterwards and he tried to use them to level Izvivode up.

He never got over it.

This stuff went on for *years*.

ONE DAY a night-bird began to nest outside Aprosinya's window. Its feathers were shadows. Its eyes were night and falling stars. It was terribly suspicious, and it would have frightened *some* kids half to death, but not Aprosinya; between Devin and Izvivode and never having any nightmares, Aprosinya'd kind of forgotten that monsters were things a kid should be afraid of.

In *her* head they were a bit more like "pets."

Anyway, every day, throughout the day, the night-bird would sleep on the branches of the mulberry tree outside her window. At the end of the day, it would rise up and fly towards the sinking sun[22]; and perhaps it was a trick of perspective, but it seemed to Aprosinya that as the sun fell below the hills, the night-bird would snatch at it with its claws, missing it—but just barely missing it—each time.

"It's probably a witch," Aprosinya decided.

It was obvious what she had to do, once she'd decided that, and she went out to do battle with it, but it didn't do battle with her. It just flitted away when she reached for it. All she could catch was a single feather, so black that it could plunge a whole room into darkness.

The bird laughed at her. "You'll have to do better than that," it said. "If you want to catch this old bird. But if you bring me good black bread and jam, I'll do you a good turn or two."

"I didn't know you could talk," Aprosinya pointed out.

"I can't," the bird shrugged.

Aprosinya froze up for a long moment, and then she glared at the bird. "You're teasing me," she said, and her cheeks were red.

"Caw," said the bird, and groomed under its wing.

IT was harmless enough, as favors went, so she went along with it. She baked it some good black bread and took some jam from the cupboard. She thought that it probably couldn't spread its own jam so she cut a few slices for a plate and spread the jam herself. She took it out to the night-bird's nest. The bird fluttered down to the plate and began to pick at the offered meal.

---

22   —which had, as per the previous interlude, begun to show its face in Town—

After a while, it said, "Since you have been kind to me, I'll be kind to you. Watch well."

It fluttered down to land upon a garden stake. It raised its wing and the stake fell into the shadow of that wing; and then— and then— Aprosinya blinked as the bird spiraled back up into the sky. "What happened to it?" she asked.

"It receded into the primal darkness that preceded garden stakes," explained the bird.

"… I don't understand how that is supposed to be helpful," Aprosinya said.

The bird landed again in its tree. "If ever you have need of me," it said. "If ever there is something that you wish would … recede into the primal darkness that preceded it … then you must take the feather in your hands and whisper your wish to it, and if I can hear it and heed it I shall."

"I don't think I'd ever need anything like that," Aprosinya said.

"Caw," the bird said, dismissively.

It tucked its head beneath its wing and went to sleep.

THE NEXT EVENING she watched as the bird seized at the sun again; and the evening after that; and the morning after, when it had straggled back to the nest from parts unknown, she went down to the sleepy bird and asked it, "Why do you do that? Why do you snatch at the setting sun?"

"I'm a sun-eating bird," the bird explained.

"That's not really a reason," she said.

The branch on which the bird stood bobbed. "Well," it said, "imagine a maze that is full of wind, and that wind is always knocking you about, so that it's hard to keep track of which direction you are facing, so you're always getting turned about. Imagine that people keep jumping down from the walls of the maze to pull canvas sacks over your head and beat your stomach with iron rods. Wouldn't you be a little angry at them?"

"I would be terrified," Aprosinya said.

"I saw the True Thing that is behind all things," said the bird, "and in that moment, I felt myself to be upon a raft in white waters, constantly battered about by the lies that are the world. I felt myself to be in a maze of wind and canvas-sack-rod-jumpers. I felt like—like that story, where the emperor has no clothes, only it was the opposite:

"Like beside me was the most precious jewel in all creation, only, no one would believe that it was anything but a clod of dung.

"It made me angry," said the bird. "It made me angry at many things, but my chosen scapegoat is the sun."

"You shouldn't do that, miss witch," Aprosinya said.

"... please don't call me that," said the bird. "I am ... you may call me Kusha. Magistra Kuwa Grigorievna Kanna. I think. I have not actually had a name before."

"You haven't?"

"For a long time," the bird said, "I was just a bird that lived inside somebody's chest and beat my wings to keep their blood flowing. Or maybe I was a person with a bird in my chest? I'm not sure. But I wasn't a bird with a name, anyway."

"Well, it's nice to meet you," Aprosinya said. "And you may call me Aprosya."

THE BIRD grew thinner and thinner, and tireder and tireder, even though she brought it bread and jam and other treats every now and then. She was a little sad for it, except for the fact that it was trying to catch the sun. She thought that if it withered and died before it managed it, it was probably for the best. She didn't change her mind on that until her father Alexander grew sick.

"Best you say goodbye," her mother said, and Aprosinya's face was suddenly a mask of tears; and she slipped into his room to say farewell, but she didn't. She wouldn't. She called to that old black bird instead.

She held the feather to her lips and said,

> Night-bird, night-bird, fly to me!
> The world is wretched, cold and cruel,
> The gods they laugh, the priests are fools,
> And you alone have ne'er lied to me—
> And you have offered solace; then:
> Cast this sorrow that I see
> Back to th' primal dark again!

The window shattered and the dark bird landed on her father's desk. It shook glass from its feathers. It looked around. It said, "—oh."

"Please," Aprosinya asked.

The bird stretched its shoulders and neck. It tilted its head. "You need not ask me twice," it said. "Observe."

The lantern closest to the bird seemed to sway. The bird's feathers, the color of shadow, seemed to stretch out; they swept across the sleeping Alexander. In that moment, Aprosinya almost understood it; she almost saw:

It was as if that sickness had been a stage convention—an actor, denoting it with a taboo-sign for sickness on his clothing—and Magistra Kanna had refused to get it. As if she had shouted from the audience, "Why in the world are you wearing that thing, you ridiculous man?" And, "you can't be sick here, it isn't in the script!"

It was as if everything in the world were mere artifice that existed only while Magistra Kanna consented to it; that if she were to shake her head and clear her eyes and look beyond it, the façade of that false truth would fade away.

It was not at all clear to her whether Aprosinya Alexandrovna Sosunova could do the same.

She thought it likely that she couldn't—that she was a character and not an actress, inasmuch as the analogy applied—and couldn't decide whether she was glad or sad of it; because it would certainly be *handy* if she could make things go away whenever she wanted to, but she thought it must be super, super disconcerting to live without a world, but just a stage.

Her mother was bursting into the room behind her; her father was stirring, and it was becoming rapidly more difficult to imagine him as being sick at all; and the bird was swirling out of the room again, in a great fluttering of wings.

AFTER THIS Aprosinya spent much of her time sitting beside the tree. She talked to the bird, read it stories, and brought out bits of her own meals for it. She complained about the difficulties of learning the Sosunov magic, but the bird was unsympathetic.

"You've just got to stick to it," said the bird.

"Oh, what do you know," Aprosinya sighed.

"If you were uniquely terrible," said the bird, "then I'd smell that on you. I'd be, 'ah, here's a great fool. I bet she'll bring great luck to me!' But you're not. You're not any worse than anyone else at this, and that means that if you work hard enough then you'll get better."

"Really?"

"... yes?"

"I mean," Aprosinya said, "you'd really know if I were bad at this?"

"That is just one of my special talents," said Magistra Kuwa Grigorievna Kanna.

SHE DREAMT that she was walking with Valentina.

She brought it up to her:

Something she wouldn't talk to her mother, or even the *bird*, about.

"You know," she said, "nobody ever comes to talk to me from the future."

"Oh?"

"My Mom visits," Aprosinya said. "My Da visits. My grandparents. Even you. But never my kids. My grandkids. My husband. Or even a great-grandniece."

"That bothers you?"

"Unh," Aprosinya confirmed.

"When *I* was your age," Valentina said, "I didn't even know what the future *was*."

"That's silly."

"I didn't! We didn't have days and nights. Our understanding of time was very limited and was mostly constrained to making sure people mostly were asleep at the same time and having clocks because everyone over in Europe was doing it."

"Well, it worries me," Aprosinya said. "And it's kind of lonely."

"Well, you don't need to be lonely," Valentina said. "You have me."

"Yeah," Aprosinya said. "But you're dead."

"Nothing wrong with dead people," Valentina said. "Most of the *family* is, ah, what's the thing?— dead. Right? And *they're* pretty good people, too."

"It's not the same."

"Well," Valentina said, "I'll just have to be alive, then, won't I?"

Aprosinya's thoughts flickered onto a new track. "What is it like there?"

"Where?"

"At the Bleak Academy?"

"It is darker than it is here," Valentina said. "Though not as dark as you'd expect. And very pretty. The paths are wide and there are gardens in abundance and the buildings are inspiring. There are fruits like olives and apricots there that you cannot find in the mortal world, and the waters are clear. Most of the dead drift through their time there in a daze, and most of the students wind up sequestering themselves in one way or another, so it is very quiet despite how very many people there actually are.

"There are ruins that give it a sense of history, but I do not know if there is an actual history.

"It is a place where you may deepen in yourself. It is a place where you may ... find an inner darkness? Does that make sense? But not wickedness, not sadness, though that darkness may be wicked and it may be sad. I mean the cool refreshing darkness of a starry night."

"It sounds nice," Aprosinya said.

"Does it?"

"Do you think I could go there?" Aprosinya said.

"Why?"

"Sometimes I feel dark," Aprosinya said. "Sometimes I feel dark, and it would be nice if it could be a great and shadowy thing."

Valentina's eyes rested on her for a while, but she shook her head.

"Don't go through those gates because you're a little sad, sometimes, Aprosya. ... That isn't what they're for."

And whether she'd understood Aprosinya well or not, Aprosinya didn't know.

LIFE WENT ON and the bird continued to wither. Aprosinya took a blanket out to cover it, even though it was autumn and it wasn't even cold yet; she brought it herbal teas that it refused and cider that it drank down.

"At least," Aprosinya said, "if you *are* a witch, you're really easily defeated."

"Kuh," laughed the bird. Then she thought about it. "It'd still count, though. I'd go down to your credit. Even though you could be described more as feeding me than fighting."

"I'll look forward to that," Aprosinya said.

And things continued in such a vein until her cousin Anton Sosunov's ship went down.

There was nothing that the bird could do. Aprosinya knew that there was nothing that the bird could do. The ship was missing for six days before they were certain Anton was dead; twelve before they'd guessed the ship was lost; fourteen, before they broke the news to her, when no hope at all remained—

But still she called to it.

> Night-bird, night-bird, fly to me!
> T' unrip the sails, t' unturn the wheel—
> T' unchurn the waters of the sea.
> T' uncrack the keel, t' unblow the gale!
> T' unbreak the mizzen and the main:
> ... and let the sea-lost live again.

She had not waited to be alone, and her mother turned to her in some alarm as she said this; but through the small skylight crashed a black bird. It shook off the glass. It looked at her. "These things I can do," said the bird, "save one; I cannot make them live again."

"But—"

"I can make them *not dead*," said the bird. "If that is all you like."

"Listen," Aprosinya's mother said. "You mustn't. Aprosya, you mustn't; bird—we have let you spend time with our daughter, with a child of the Sosunovs, but you *mustn't*—"

"*Yes*," Aprosinya said.

And the bird rose up, and its shadow began to move; but Aprosinya's mother interrupted it: "What does that mean, 'not dead?'"

"On this matter there is some question," murmured the bird. Its shadow receded back into its wings. "But fairly asked, and I shall fairly answer. We are that which *looks*, and we are that which *is looked upon*. Once the fire of consciousness has been freed from the curse of flesh and the mortal life, I cannot force it back again; it must take up that burden on its own. Once the fire of consciousness goes *out*, I cannot make it burn again; I can only create the conditions by which it *may* relight itself."

"So they may return, for instance, as hideous mockeries of life?" Aprosinya's mother offered.

"Your pessimism is exaggerated," said the bird. "That would hardly ever happen."

"We do not wish your aid, good bird."

"That is for Aprosya to determine," said the bird.

"She is a child!"

"A child who feeds me," said the bird.

"Come now," said Aprosinya's mother. "Who do you think buys the flour and the salt?"

"That is a fair point. ... so I will warn her further: Aprosya, do not fear death; I have seen many smile, even at the Bleak Academy, and *it* is only a stopping place on the way to a far and a sunless land."

Aprosinya hugged herself. Finally she looked away. "Tch," she said, conceding the point.

The shadow of the bird swept out, and Anton's empty ship sailed in.

NOW Aprosinya turned nine, and went to School, and learned of many things; and while she was gone her mother brought the bird food on her behalf. And the bird was as thin as sticks, but still she clawed for the sun each night.

And she turned ten, and still she went to School, and still she learned of many things; and while she was gone her mother brought the bird food on her behalf. And the bird was as thin as a copper wire, but still she clawed for the sun each night.

And she turned eleven, and still she went to School, and still she learned of many things; and while she was gone her mother brought the bird food on her behalf, but that summer when Aprosinya came home, the bird was gone. There were only feathers in the nest, and uneaten loaves beside; it had flown up to snatch the sun, and for three whole weeks had not returned.

"I'm sorry," her mother said.

"I'm going to go and look for it."

"Aprosyusha ... you're awfully young for a job like that."

Aprosinya considered this. Finally, she said, "I'm the only friend it's got."

Her mother bowed her head.

NOW APROSINYA thought that while the bird only had a single friend, it also only had a single enemy, which is to say, the sun; so it was to the land of the sun that she had to go. She thought about meeting it at the western hills when it sank below them, but it might burn her up; she thought about climbing the cliffs at the northern beach, but they could be awful sheer; so finally she decided to head to the mountain Kailas Mantra, past the Walking Fields, and ascend it to the sky.

Her mother packed a magical tablecloth, a survival kit, and several changes of clothes for her; thus bolstered, she set out.

A dirt road took her out of Fortitude and up the western hills into what had been Night London (and had later been "the cursed place," and was finally named "Horizon.") From there she went further west, out into the Walking Fields, and turned north to follow the Track to the Outside.

Many times had this road been traveled, until not even the Outside could cloud it entirely. In the chaos she became disoriented, she became confused, the world around her and the sun above her became distorted and strange, but the road remained—now a broad highway, now the faintest animal trail; now a trickling silver river, and now a slippery line of light. From time to time there would be a road sign or trail marker; the words on these would be ambiguous symbols that could have meant anything at all.

Because there was a road, as confusing as things were, she didn't lose her way—not even in the chaos of the Outside. It was hard, and once she was swarmed by little flying snakes, and once she had to resolve a dispute between a tiger and a bear, and once a stone that she sat upon turned into a wicked man, but the road led ever always on towards distant Kailas Mantra.

From time to time she spread out the magic tablecloth and a feast appeared. There were two kinds of borscht, five kinds of bread, lentils, potatoes, vushka, cod, cabbage (stuffed with various wonders), honey, herring, knish and salad, sweet grain pudding, sauerkraut, mushrooms, fried cheese, fried eels, and pickled eggs, and uzvar, coffee, and wine for her to drink. There was even a bite of chocolate by the side!

She'd eat and drink and then put the tablecloth away.

From time to time she'd sleep, fitfully.

From time to time she'd stop to watch the view.

She'd do these things—and then she'd get back to her long trudge along the road.

It was there, upon that road, that she first met Valentina's witch.

She had dozed off again—not that it was safe to do so, but what choice had she? If she paced herself and didn't exhaust herself, it was a four-day trip—and she was dreaming that she was in a movie theater with her father. They'd been watching one of her friend Devin's imaginary *kaiju* battles. But dreaming in the Outside is dangerous, and the dream kept fritzing out.

Everything kept turning into multicolored static, and visions of something *else*.

A heron beat its wings.

And then quite suddenly, she was in the movie theater, only, the sound was off, and the movie had gone into the end of reel, and the theater was empty, and her father was gone.

Instead there was the heron-witch.

"Ah," said the heron. "It's a Sosunov. I've found me a Sosunov at last."

"Oh," Aprosinya said. After a moment, she said, "You're a talking heron. But you've got a bad vibe to you."

"I do," said the heron. "It's because I'm a witch."

"No," Aprosinya said.

"No?"

"Rejected," Aprosinya said. "My life is already too complicated."

"It's not up to you, sweetling," the heron said. "If this were the old days, I'd have already cast you under the shadow of my wing and you'd have gone to sleep forever, right where you are, and I'd have nourished myself in your dreams like an egg.

"Except that doesn't make me happy. It turns out. It turns out that that isn't what actually makes a witch like me happy."

"I'm in the middle of rescuing *another* witch," Aprosinya explained.

The heron-witch hesitated. "Really?"

"Yeah."

The heron-witch thought about this. "Damn," she said. "I guess that I probably shouldn't fill your dreaming brain with obsessive thoughts of your own worthlessness, then."

Aprosinya's thoughts were derailed. "*That's* what makes you happy?"

"I liked it when Valentina was moping around being all 'woe is me I am a creature of meat and bone and hair,'" said the witch. "I didn't like it at first but later on when I was bleeding and bleeding and nobody would help me I started thinking, yeah, this is the only redeeming feature life has got."

"Oh."

"And you smell like Valentina," explained the witch.

"Wait," Aprosinya said. "*Valentina Grigorievna?*"

"Yes?"

"I don't smell *like* her," Aprosinya said.

"You're just like her."

"No, it's just— I mean, you're smelling *her*. Not me being *like* her.

She's, she was like—" Aprosinya held up a hand way above her head, then jumped a few times to make her point.

"Exaggerated," said the heron-witch. "She was a bloody-minded thug."

Aprosinya thought about this. "That's even worse," she said.

"Tell me about this other witch," the heron-witch said.

"—oh," Aprosinya said. "Well, when I'm awake, I am traveling to Kailas Mantra, to go up into the sky, to try to rescue a dark bird that is trying to eat the sun. And I don't even know if she's there, I just don't know anyone who would actually try to capture a bird like that and keep her from me if it *wasn't* the people of the sun?"

"Could you tell me in order, maybe?"

And Aprosinya tried. "Well," she said. "She lives outside my window. And she flies up every night to try to catch the setting sun. And she's a witch who can make gardening tools vanish and bring back the dead, only they come back wrong. And I bring her bread and jam. And then she vanished, and here I am."

"All right," conceded the heron-witch. "I'll help you rescue her, and *then* I'll torment you."

"Thank you," Aprosinya said.

The witch wandered down the aisle to the movie screen. She poked it with her beak, and Aprosinya felt a horrible pain in her left eye. The witch poked it again, and again, and then it tore, and with a scream, Aprosinya woke up.

"There," said the witch, climbing out of her eye and unfurling into the world.

"Ow," whispered Aprosinya, rubbing at her face.

"YOU MUST GO FASTER," said the witch.

"I am pacing myself," said Aprosinya. "My mom made me promise."

The witch stared blankly at her.

"If you push too hard," Aprosinya said, "instead of succeeding in whatever you're trying to do, you can actually make everything worse. If I get bad blisters or hurt my legs I can probably still make it to the mountain but how am I going to get all the way up to the sky?"

"Fine," sighed the witch. **"You are puny and pathetic. You can ride on my back."**

"You're not big enough," Aprosinya said, but the witch was already shaking herself all over, and as she shook herself, she was growing larger; or, rather, it became increasingly, eerily clear to Aprosinya that the witch had been further and further away than she'd thought. A half-minute later and it was done—

There was easily enough room for her to climb onto the witch's shoulders and sit there, below the neck and above the great wings.

"You will have to balance yourself carefully," said the witch; and she lurched upwards, and flew.

Twenty times swifter than the swiftest horse she went; the world blurred by beneath them, and in the time it would take for a kettle to boil, they had reached Kailas Mantra; and still, the witch flew on. Their ascent should have been even faster—for Kailas Mantra is no match for its elder namesake in Tibet—but instead, as the witch went higher and higher, aiming for the sky above the mountain peak, it seemed to resist growing closer; the muscles of the witch were surging, the world was shaking with each great wing-beat, the witch's body was stretched out long against the air, and they had risen so high that anxiety clawed at Aprosinya's heart and lungs, but still the mountain peak seemed far away. The wind whipped at her clothing; stole her spare shirt which had been sticking out of the flap of her pack, ripped it out and billowed it out and turned it in moments into a distant dot in the air behind them, and still they rose.

Her ears began to ring. A subtle pressure mounted around them, and then grew less subtle; the air became viscous, gelatinous, heavy first with metaphysical and then with literal weight; breathing became laborious, and she could not imagine how the witch continued flying—

And finally, they broke through; the mountain peak surged closer, then passed beneath them; and the sky was like a syrup-lake, a glassy medium through which they burst, that fountained up behind them as they rose above the sprawling airy kingdom where dwelt the angel of the sun.

For a while, quiet reigned.

The heron drifted low, then came in for a landing on a cloud— beneath the spreading branches of an apple tree that was growing thereupon. **"Here,"** she said. **"If she has been taken by the people of the sun, she'll be held here."**

Aprosinya slipped off the heron's back and collapsed onto the cloud. She shuddered, pressed her face into the spongy white, and then, reluctantly, stood up again. "What must I do?"

The heron tilted its head and pointed with its beak. **"There,"** it said.

She followed its gaze and saw a great palace-yacht upon the clouds— saw that it was cutting its own course across the glassy medium, and that fine cords dragged a handful of other clouds, including the one on which she stood, erratically in its wake.

"There," said the heron-witch, **"you will find her, in a wrought-iron cage, if she is here; take her, and leave the cage behind."**

From one cloud to another she leapt; and again; and a third time. There she failed, and fell, but one hand caught the line that went between two clouds; the line sank an inch, and the great bulk of the clouds drew closer together, and her foot brushed the glassy medium, but it went no further.

She was dizzy with panic, but it slowly receded:

The glassy medium had held beneath her weight—or, if not quite held, was sucking gently at her foot rather than letting it fall through. Hand over hand she went, on the cord between the clouds, not fearing *too* terribly that she might lose her grip; and at last she fell face-first against the bottom edge of the palace-yacht's cloud.

She hugged it. She crawled up it, and up the soft and foamy palace wall, and into the palace garden.

There three cages hung: one of wrought iron, one of silver, and one of gold. In the golden cage was a fiery bird and her eyes drank up its beauty; but, she was not there for a firebird. In the silver cage was a veery thrush, singing softly as she came; but, she was not there for song.

In the final cage, the wrought iron cage, she saw her withered old black bird.

"Oh," she said, in sorrow. She rushed to it. "Oh. What have they done to you, Kuwochka?"

"Hubris," cackled Magistra Kanna. "Too close unto the sun I flew."

Her cackle turned into a weak cough. She turned her head.

"Here," Aprosinya said. She unlocked the cage. She slipped the bird out. "Here, you are safe now. You will come with me, and we will return to the lands below."

"Kuh," whispered the bird. "I had rather try again, while I'm this close, but wasting a rescue *would* be rude."

"It would," Aprosinya confirmed. She turned to go. Then she paused. "That cage—it has the power to hold a witch and nullify her powers?"

"…evidently."

Aprosinya stood there, lost in thought. *You smell like Valentina,* the heron-witch had said. And, *I'll torment you.* Almost without her conscious intent her hands reached out for the cage; went to unlatch it from the hook on which it hung—

But the instant she took hold of it, there sounded throughout the garden a great noise of clanging bells.

"Agh," Aprosinya said, recoiling, and dropping the cage. She turned to run, but she did not make it up the wall before the hand of a palace guard did seize her.

Let us not speak of the nature of those guards; let us draw a veil over the people of Celestia; let the light of the sun behind them render them as silhouettes, for they would only confuse our tale. It suffices to say that they brought her before the captain of the palace-yacht, who sat lazily upon a golden chair, and he looked her up and down and said, "Who are you, to come to my palace-yacht, and commit such a shameless crime? From what country do you hail? Of what father are you a daughter, and what is your given name?"

"I am Aprosinya Alexandrovna Sosunova," she said. "And I am that witch's friend."

"Which witch?"

"The— well, um. Really, just Kuwa Grigorievna," Aprosinya said.

"Oh," he said, because it was not the custom in the kingdom of the sky to refer to random malicious magical birds as witches. "The prisoner."

"Yeah."

"I was not aware that she had any friends," he said. "Are you aware that she sought to extinguish the sun, which is to say, the light of the world, the light of hope, and day, and all tomorrows? That she sought to snatch the heart of the angel of the houses of the sun and bury herself inside her chest that there should be only night thereafter?"

"When my father was sick," Aprosinya said, "she made him bett— well, *not* sick, anyway."

"I see," the captain said. He thought about this. "That is a good enough reason for you to come here and attempt to steal her back, but it is not a good enough reason for me to set her free. But perhaps you may do a favor for me."

"… that is acceptable," Aprosinya allowed.

"There is an evil island that flies around the sun," the captain said. "There the King of Evil rules from his palace of black glass. Shining-Mane the horse, who leads the horses of the dawn, ran free, and his run took him to that island, and he was taken; now he is a prisoner there. If you can fetch him back from the King of Evil, and if Kuwa Grigorievna promises not to snatch the sun again— or, at least, not for a year and a day— then I will release her into your custody."

"What option do I have?" Aprosinya said. "I will attempt it."

She left the palace-yacht and returned to the heron-witch. There she related most of the tale. **"Foolish girl!"** the witch berated her. **"You had her rescued, and you risked it all for an iron cage?"**

"I am guilty before you," Aprosinya admitted.

"Well," said the witch. **"I will help you again. Climb up upon my back, and tell me where we must fly."**

"To an evil island," Aprosinya said, "that circles around the sun."

THE WITCH was large enough now to carry two grown men upon her back and flew fifty times swifter than the swiftest horse; blurringly through the sky they went, past the palaces and great arched halls of the kingdom of the sky. At last it came into sight, on the back of something that resembled in parts a blowfish, catfish, eel, manta, and whale: the evil island of an evil King.

The tendrils at the creature's mouth reached for them but the heron-witch whirled through and among them, and out over the creature's back, across forbidding jungles, down towards a palace in the center of the evil island, a palace of black glass.

There, on a great balustrade she perched and let Aprosinya down.

"Go now," said the witch, **"swiftly, swiftly to the stables. Take away the horse with the shining mane—but, if you love me, leave the cruel hooked bridle that hangs beside the beast behind."**

"... but I don't love you," Aprosinya said. "I'm, um, extremely grateful, but—"

"Figure of speech," the witch said airily.

Aprosinya went.

The palace was like a maze inside; many times she heard footsteps approaching and had to duck into a room, into a cupboard, or behind a door. She did not see what made the steps, or the skittering sounds, or the booming crashes, but only grew more and more frightened as the hours passed. Eventually, though, she found it, right down the hall from the witch in a direction that she hadn't gone—

A stable where the King that on that island ruled kept his flying beasts.

She was sickened by what she saw there. They were hideous—horrifying on deep, primordial levels. They had too many mouths, too many eyes. They did not have the consistency of flesh. Some were almost beautiful, but even those were awful to her; they seemed to look at her and judge. She was staggering onwards as if caught in a nightmare when she finally found the stall that penned in Shining-Mane the horse.

He was woefully out of place. He did not belong there; he was normal, or even *holy*. The cage that penned him in was cruel, with metal fencing to every side and inward-pointing hooks. She gasped as she saw him, fetched down the keys, and rushed to unlock his enclosure.

"Oh!" she said, and hugged him—she could do nothing else—and buried her face against his side.

He nosed her. He gave her a curious, hopeful look. She backed away to let him from his cage. Then she stopped, and her eyes fell upon the bridle that hung beside it, and she thought *I have ridden the witch thus far; what if it would let me tame her?*

And again it echoed in her mind: *You smell like Valentina. And I'll torment you.*

Her hands moved as if in a dream. They took the bridle down; only, no sooner had she done so than there rose a great clanging and thundering, as of instruments of brass.

"Oh my," she said. She looked frantically around her, then tried to climb up onto the back of Shining-Mane the horse; but he shied away from the bridle in her hand, and her opportunity for flight was lost.

The hair of the stable boy, who had been sleeping, was fanged tendrils; they groped blindly around the room; they seized her; and before she could say another word she was wrapped in his great horned fist.

She thought that was the end of her; she thought she would be eaten, and could not even draw the breath to scream—but the stable boy brought her before the King who ruled in that place instead. He was a noseless man in ornate robes and crown; his hands dripped with a sourceless blood.

The stable boy forced her down onto her knees before the King; she did not dare look up.

"It is rare," said the King, "to see a child of Fortitude upon my isle, much less committing theft."

"Your majesty: it is not theft, if the horse was already stolen."

"Hush," he said, and an invisible vice tightened around her throat, and she could not speak. "Had you come to ask for him, I might have given him back to you with all honors. But instead you would take him from me, and my bridle and my tack? I should have you fed to the tsuritsenekele and the drambele. At the very least I should feed the beast Sa'a your soul. But I will not do this thing. Do you know why?"

Words were not available; she shook her head.

"Because it is not convenient for me to have Shining-Mane in my stables. I do not want that horse wandering my island and getting up to who knows what mischief, but keeping it is only asking for a better hero than you to come along. Therefore, you have a chance at survival. Find me—" The King considered. "Fetch me the daughter of the Headmaster of the Bleak Academy, and I shall free the horse to thee."

After a moment, she realized that she was no longer being held; no longer being silenced. She straightened. She rubbed her throat. "Ah, your majesty," Aprosinya said, "what do you *want* with the Headmaster's daughter?"

"Do you think to judge my intentions?" said the King. "Are you in a position to do so?"

She shook her head.

"Lest you become confused," said the King of Evil. "Lest you be there, and find that your conscience cripples you; or lest you prove unable or unwilling to abscond with her by force—rest easy. I have a School in Horizon below; I believe, in fact, you are attending."

Aprosinya gulped.

"And she, I think— there is a faculty position she would be perfect for."

"Oh."

"Now: go."

She left.

Walking slowly, she returned to the heron-witch. There she told her most of the tale. **"Foolish girl,"** said the heron-witch. **"You had the horse, and you risked it all for an iron bridle?"**

"I am guilty before you," Aprosinya said.

"Well," said the witch, **"I will help you again. Climb up upon my back, and tell me where we must fly."**

"To the Bleak Academy," Aprosinya said, "that is beyond the end of life."

A HUNDRED TIMES FASTER than the swiftest bird the heron flew— faster than you could tell of in a tale; faster than you could write of in a book. Like an arrow she tore through the Outside, and it broke before her in a wave, bound itself to solidity through the power of her *looking-upon*, until they had pierced it through entirely, torn through the veil of Perdition, split the gates, and like a thunderbolt come down to land in the gardens of the Bleak Academy—

And, oh! How those gardens stunned her.

The experience of them froze her, there, on the witch's back. As her vision settled from the swiftness of the flight, the Bleak Academy rippled through her—filled her senses past the limits of them. She was overwhelmed by unexpected beauty; her heart was shaken; she looked at ancient walls and fruited vines and thought, *I could drink of this place, like a giant drinks a lake.*

Water flowed across the tiles of a fountain, and she had a dizzying image of it:

The Academy would fill her up, until inside her was a sea of darkness, darkness piled on darkness, like deep black ink, and all the world upon it. She would know the secrets of the heart, and pluck the stars down from the sky. She would wear glasses and a feathered coat and be an axis of the world—

Aprosinya, Magister.

It rattled her, how intense the yearning was; it held her for minutes, and it could have been hours ... only, someone was poking her.

Her vision swam, came into focus.

"*There* you are," said Mrs. Senko. She was standing below the heron, poking up at Aprosinya with the end of her umbrella. "It's an ill-mannered child who rides a giant heron into someone's garden while they're in the middle of a particularly good book and then goes catatonic for no particular reason."

"... yes," Aprosinya conceded. "That would be the case."

"Well?"

Aprosinya hesitated. She tried, "I'm sorry?"

"Mm, yes," Mrs. Senko adjudged. "Sorry, stubborn, and self-important to boot; but I suppose you *are* trying."

"... thank you?"

Mrs. Senko rubbed at her forehead, as if to soothe a headache. "Well," she said. "Out with it, child. Why are you here?"

"I'm looking for the Headmaster's daughter," Aprosinya said. "… is that you?"

"Mm."

Aprosinya refocused on her purpose—

After all, her family was still waiting for her at home; and her witch was still a prisoner. She licked her lips. She held out her hand.

"Please, then," she said. "Climb on behind me."

Mrs. Senko's eyes flicked up and down the heron. "You *may* have accidentally skipped a portion of your explanation, dear. What exactly is the emergency?"

Aprosinya reviewed it in her mind. "The King of an evil island," she said, "that flies around the sun has demanded I bring you, in exchange for a horse with a golden mane. The lord of a cloud-yacht palace in the kingdom of the sun has demanded the *horse* in exchange for a bird that is my friend. I do not know how long either the bird or the horse will endure. Please get on."

"—I've never heard such nonsense in all my life," Mrs. Senko said.

"*Please.*"

"Just for *starters*," Mrs. Senko said, "What would people think, if I went around being traded for horses?"

"They would think you exceedingly lovely and intelligent?" Aprosinya tried.

"Hmph," Mrs. Senko snorted. She opened a locket-mirror, held it up and considered herself, and then closed and dropped it again with a nod. "If anything, it would diminish their appreciation for my better qualities. What does this King want with me?"

"It's about a job," Aprosinya said. "… at his School."

"Oh," Mrs. Senko said. She closed her eyes for a moment. "That *would* be different, I'll admit; I hadn't realized that my reputation had preceded me.

"… Very well. You may tell him I am open to a lateral career move. — but I'm afraid I can't just hop on a heron and fly away; there is no way a heron that large can even support its *own* weight, much less ours too."

"I am not actually all that large," the heron-witch admitted. **"It is a trick of perspective."**

"My declaration redoubles," Mrs. Senko said. "I must also pack a bag, complete my current assignment, and await the completion of the train route to Schism; so, tell him I will arrive in the next three to four years."

"*Years?*"

"If it helps," Mrs. Senko said, "there is no such thing as evil."

Aprosinya stared at her for a long time.

Then she clicked her tongue and leaned forward, shaking her head convulsively, and the witch took off into the sky.

"WE should go back," Aprosinya said, an hour later.

"We shouldn't go back," said the witch.

"I can't possibly tell the King of Evil that we fetched her, but on a four-year time delay. At *best* he'll keep the horse that long. At worst he'll *eat* me."

"Kuh," laughed the witch as she flew. **"I have done so much for you, but I will do this one thing more. I know how she looks. I know how she sounds. I know the manner in which she speaks. When we reach the palace on the evil island, I will leap into his eyes and make him see her there. Then you must ride Shining-Mane until you are far away, and I will catch up to you there."**

"He's really scary," pointed out Aprosinya.

"I've fought scary people before," said the witch. **"I took on the whole Sosunov family once."**

"I mean, *really* scary."

"Hush, child, or maybe I won't."

Aprosinya quieted. The bird flew in for a landing, and walked beside her into the King of Evil's court. Now, as soon as they were brought before the King, the heron-witch darted forward, and flew into his eye. The King shook his head uncertainly, once, twice, thrice, but then when he looked upon the room he saw Aprosinya leading Mrs. Senko in. "Child," he said, "you have done well; and I shall free the horse into your keeping. Here is my mark, that the stable boy will know to release him to you."

He stepped down and walked to Aprosinya and brushed a bloody finger along her brow; and for a moment, everything in the world was evil. A wordless shout of rejection welled up in her, and despairing helplessness; the harmony of the cosmos was *engineered*, she suddenly understood, to grind out suffering from those who lived upon it. Because it was easier, in some ineffable sense—because it saved some demiurge a hint of effort. Because it was interesting to see how much awfulness could be wrung out from the mortals before they gave up completely. Because to watch them suffering was *fun*.

The scales fell from her eyes and she knew, in that moment, that she had been so terribly blind, like a dog that didn't understand that its master hated it. That each day when she went about her day, living an ordinary life, the ordinary life that she saw was just a construct—a *daydream*—put together to hide from her the true nature of things, which she still could not see, which she was still *blind* to, but which she now imagined as an ineffable world of the spirit where she, the true self of her, was constantly torn and ripped apart by spinning hooks.

That even the false hope of the false reality was doomed to fade in time; that despite the lies of science, faith, and sorcery, people would not meet meaningless fates or meaningful ones, but would rather each come down to a poetic, artful, and personally tailored demeaning, dishonorable, and tragic end.

That she had somehow *missed* the fact that as she went about her life she was contorted into a shape that was the uttermost and starkest betrayal of herself—

The finger left her brow, and the moment ended, leaving only a burning pain that would recede and a red mark, like a horse's hoof, that wouldn't.

"There is a seed of evil," the King said, casually, "in the human eye; or rather, in the human *power to perceive.* It lives there, squirming uncomfortably because it must share that space with you. And from time to time—when it is dark; when you are frightened; when you are proud—it shines forth from your eye to project itself upon the world. Then, for a moment or for eternity, you are no longer in Fortitude or upon the Earth but on my evil island.

"Thank me for this lesson, Aprosinya."

"... thank you," she said, and bowed to the King of Evil, and shivering, she stumbled away.

The guards had to help her stand several times as she made her way to the stables. She brushed her hair back away from the mark and the stableboy let her take out Shining-Mane. She mounted up and rode him out onto the balcony, from which she could reach the sky.

She did not have as long as she had hoped.

The heron-witch's deceit did not last; the King of Evil was trickier than she imagined, or the witch was not quite so clever as she'd thought. He slipped out from under her mirage, realized that Mrs. Senko had not come at all, and snarled in his rage.

Aprosinya looked back as Shining-Mane spiraled upwards and away from the evil island to see a swarm of horrors flying after her and gaining fast.

A devilish thought occurred. She pulled her bag around to one side and felt around in it until she had her hands on the tablecloth. There, in the sky above the evil island, she unfurled it.

In the very moment she unrolled the tablecloth a feast faded into view upon it!—and flew away into the wind. There were two kinds of borscht, five kinds of bread, lentils, potatoes, vushka, cod, cabbage (stuffed with various wonders), honey, herring, knish and salad, sweet grain pudding, sauerkraut, mushrooms, fried cheese, fried eels, and pickled eggs, and uzvar, coffee, and wine for her to drink. There was even a bite of chocolate by the side! These things fell onto the horde below in a steady rain—replenishing whenever the last one disappeared—but there was more.

As the tablecloth flapped and fluttered it began to generate too the monsters' food: noisome goop, startled chickens, eccentric solids, and human bodies began to fall.

The monsters below were battered and struck about by the endless feast; they slowed, some wounded, some skittish, some distracted.

Nevertheless Aprosinya began to regret her plan the instant the first *living* human fell screaming to the horde.

It had to be a magical fake. She reassured herself of that. There was no possible way she was conjuring one, two … five, eight … dozens of *real people* and throwing them to fall through a crowd of monsters and then down, for what was at least three quarters of a mile now, onto an evil island.

Her face set in an expression of horror. She tried to fold the tablecloth back up but it resisted her, flapping ferociously in the wind. She thought about dropping it, she nearly *did* drop it, but she feared what would happen if it *landed* on the island.

Behind her as they flew there was a screaming rain.

Shining-Mane burst through the bottom layer of a cloud; the tablecloth folded up; and there was silence.

"Oh my God. My *God*," Aprosinya said, and leaned against the horse's back, before finally adding, "Home. You can go home."

EVENTUALLY the heron-witch joined her.

"I apologize for that," said the witch. **"He was a slippery fellow."**

"I nearly died," said Aprosinya. "Along with an unknown number of possible people."

"I have made sufficient apologies. You are fortunate that I am helping you at all. —Should I pretend to be the horse, do you think, so that you can keep him?"

Aprosinya sighed.

THE HERON-WITCH LANDED, and this time stayed behind—for Aprosinya had demurred—as the girl returned to the palace-yacht upon the clouds.

It was not the captain of the palace-yacht who met her, though, but the Queen of all that land—the angel of the houses of the sun. It was that angel who stepped forward and let Shining-Mane nuzzle at her hand; who soothed the horse and ruffled his mane before turning her gaze to Aprosinya.

"Child," she said, "you have done a great service; for the dawn has been less since Shining-Mane was lost. But I see that you have suffered for it."

In the presence of the angel she was tongue-tied: "I was— it was— OK."

"Here," she said, and she bent down to kiss Aprosinya on the forehead, half-upon and half-beside the King's red mark; and in that moment, there was nothing in the world remaining.

There was only the light of the sun.

In that moment, as she stood before that endless light, as there was nothing before her *but* that endless light, she came to understand the nature of the fire. In that moment, as the darknesses inside her became crenellations, distortions, and recesses instead—as the darkness itself drew back from them, leaving only uneven patches in the contours that were she—she came to understand the fierce power of the fire of consciousness, came to believe that it could not merely find but shape the world with the power of its *interest*. She came to believe that the world was not as she found it, but as she *made* it; that from her eyes she cast forth sight to ignite what she saw with the forms that she desired for them. She came to believe that even the worst of torments could be untangled with that—that the light of interest could recontextualize even the most brutal awfulness, catch hold of it by its weak point, and allow the application of conscious force to turn torment into opportunity.

In the face of that endless light, she learned, there could be no hopelessness. In the face of that golden brilliance, no situation could e'er be without recourse; no power nor curse could e'er imprison her in impenetrable literal or figurative walls—were she immured in a cage of bolted sheets of iron, the fire of her could buckle that encasement, rip out its bolts, and bend a portion of it inwards towards her, that she could seize it and pull it in and open up the world within to the lush viridian richness that had lain beyond.

In the face of the sun there was no awfulness:

There was only value as of yet unfound.

It was incandescent. In that moment she felt a surging confidence, a certain knowledge that she could transform any situation into something hopeful simply by seeing it properly; that she could *find* that way of seeing it properly—because she was Aprosinya Alexandrovna Sosunova. Because she was herself.

The angel stepped back, and Aprosinya found herself on her hands and knees, panting, fallen as she had not fallen even before the King of Evil's touch. A circle of gold gleamed on her forehead, where the angel's lips had been.

"I have been told," said the angel of the houses of the sun, "that when I look into a person's soul, the light I see is my own light. That I chase away the darkness with that light, and that is why I see imperfection but nowhere anywhere darkness. That I have made you bright, but that when I look away, you all become chiaroscuros once again.

"I cannot say if this is true. I cannot say if this is not true. But I may commend to you this rule:

"If you wish to be as I have seen in you, then, when you look inside yourself, seek to cast such light as I have done."

"Thank you," Aprosinya said.

"It is nothing," said the angel. "Bring me that old black bird."

Swiftly it was heeded; swiftly it was done; the captain of the palace-yacht presented the caged bird to her from one bended knee. The angel opened up the cage. She took the night-bird out and let her grip upon her arm.

"As for you," she said. "If you continue, you will only get caught again. And if you do not get caught again, still you will only get weaker and weaker until you die. And if all of this is false, and you manage to seize and swallow the sun before you die, then it will burn its way out from within you. Give it up."

"It's a lie," croaked Magistra Kanna. "How can I? It's a lie."

The angel stared thoughtfully down upon the bird.

"Before the coming of the sun," said the bird. "Before people started seeing whatever they damn well liked: everyone saw by the light that there was in things *because they are themselves*."

"Ah," the angel said softly.

She closed her eyes for a moment. Then she opened them.

"I will tell you a secret," said the angel of the houses of the sun.

SHE BENT DOWN her lips to the bird's ear.

SHE WHISPERED THERE the secret that is like the rain; that is like a cloud passing over nothingness:

"..."

AND THE BIRD drew back from her.

It stared at her for a long time.

THEN IT shook its head, once, twice, and it flew away.

AND AS for what that secret was—

Well, her exact words won't fit in the language you're reading this in, and revelation always seems a little silly when you write it down. It won't have the same impact on you if you haven't eviscerated Glum, if you haven't touched on the True Thing, if you haven't picked up the bone-deep knowledge along the way that you are the fire of *looking-upon* as much[23] as the thing that that fire sees.

If you aren't angry at the sun for showing up in Town and changing everything you knew; for the way everybody around you looks at everything *differently*, now, and yet the same. If you didn't look at the sun and feel, instinctively, like it were *arguing* with you about the starlight that was in your bones—like, just as you had come to grasp the True Thing and be lifted up by it, just as you had started to take flight, somebody had come along, this great big ball of fire in the sky, to *quibble* about how that ought to be.

If you hadn't turned around in your head, at least one time, to see the night and the stars that were behind you. That *were* you. That had filled you up.

It won't be as big a deal to you, in short, if you're not *Magistra Kuwa Grigorievna Kanna*—

But I think that you could boil it down to this. That

> *Some things may be, and some things may not—*
> *... but it's up to you what you will think of them.*

And once upon a time, you see, Miruna Sosunova learned to see through the back of her eyes like the front of them. She raised up the curtains of the self and she went out beyond them, into the territory of nothingness and death, and there she found the secret that was like the

---

23   or more

rain, that was like a cloud passing over nothingness; and she, who was a fire of looking-upon, but also the thing *that* that fire was looking upon, lit up the void like a candle in the darkness, and she understood in that moment that she was beautiful.

... because she *could.*

Because that was an *option.* All she had to do was choose.

ON A CLOUD Aprosinya and the witch descended to the ground; the cloud dissipated; and **"here we part ways,"** said the witch.

Aprosinya hugged the heron-witch around the neck. "Thank you," she said.

"Kuh," said the witch. **"I didn't do it for *you.*"**

"Even so."

"The next time we meet," warned the witch, **"I will torment you."**

"Couldn't you reconsider that? Aren't we friends now?"

"You have won a place in my heart," agreed the witch. **"But I am a horrible person, and that only makes me want to torment you more. I don't like people who I care about. They make me feel twitchy, angry, and afraid."**

"That is not what caring about people is," Aprosinya said.

"Whatever," said the witch, beat her wings powerfully, and flew away; and Aprosinya walked back to Fortitude.

Time passed, and the witch did not keep her promise. *Years* passed— And she did not torment Aprosinya.

She skulked around the edges of Aprosinya's dreams. Once she stalked into them on taloned feet, tore away the meadow that Aprosinya had been dreaming, and told her viciously, **"You are the eidolon through which I shall have my vengeance on that Valentina."**

... but she did not *do* anything to Aprosinya; and finally, she gave up.

"It is too hard to torment someone I know," concluded the witch. **"And if I put you to sleep forever you will lose your only friend."**

"Um," Aprosinya said. "I think you mean *you* will."

"The distinction is irrelevant," said the witch. **"I surrender. I give in."**

And she set aside her wicked plans and schemes; surrendered all her wicked dreams; and pierced Aprosinya's eye with wicked beak, to crawl inside, to nest against her brain, and huddle there against the dark and wait for something in the world to change ... and piled mounds of fluffy down against her ears to drown out Aprosinya's rude, unwarranted, unruly screams.

It was possible—she tasted Aprosinya's sensations briefly, then shuddered and turned away—that her nesting place, chosen purely for personal comfort and nostalgic flavor, was poorly conceived; or, that she should have waited for Aprosinya to be asleep before she went a'poking at her eye and brain; but still the screams, she thought, *were* quite discourteous, since she *had* been very explicit that it was not *intended* to be a torment, after all.

IT'S LIKE: *come on.*

NOW, there are a number of virtues that Fortitude will cultivate in its children. They are, as a general principle, respectful, diligent, joyful, earnest, honest, and kind.

... they are not, however, terribly open, or terribly good at going to others for help.

When the heron-witch forced her way into Aprosinya's mind, her brain burned with it. Her soul ached with it. Her existence felt thereafter ... *thin;* as if one heart, one spirit, were not meant to support two such beings, particularly not without the intercessory medium of an egg.

It did not matter that the witch was not drinking of her dreams to feed herself.

It did not matter that there was no real *action* on the witch's part at all.

The witch's mere *presence* there, unsheltered, left her strained and hollow; bent her mind, as if beneath great burdens; pushed her tolerance of existence to the edge.

… and she did not go to her parents about it. She did not go to her family.

She did exactly what you'd expect a child of Fortitude to do, what only the very wisest of Fortitude's children know better than to do:

She bore it all privately, and in solitude.

Some of that was her shame. It was an unworthy shame, of course. It was no crime of *hers* that she had been broken; nor no crime to *be* broken, in any case. It was no fault of *hers* that she had been weakened; for that matter—even had it been—being weak, being brutally depleted and lacking capacity, is a kind of suffering and not a category of crime.

Nevertheless.

She was ashamed that she had screamed, when the witch bored her way inside her.

She was ashamed that she could not find her bearings; that she could not grasp the world around her firmly; that her thoughts skipped and stuttered and she staggered simply getting through the day.

She was ashamed that she might fail in the face of a witch.

Conversely, some of her solitude came from something like pride.

It was *her* witch that was doing this to her.

Her witch: she felt fiercely possessive. It was a great challenge that *she* was meant to face.

She kind of thought, on some deep level, that she didn't have much in the way of a future; that if she had any kind of prospects worth thinking of, they would have shown up in her dreams. She was a *dead end*, someone to die young or maybe old, unloved, and forgotten—but here, here was her chance to seize a destiny *now*. Right here and right now, she could be someone important, a Sosunov for the stories; she could go down in legend.

So wrapped up was she in this pride and this shame that she almost forgot to beg the witch to get out; to snarl at her, to tell her that it *hurt*, only to be met with complaints that it could not possibly be so—because of how precious the pain and the struggle was to her; because of the sense that *this* was the challenge at the heart of her story, the thing that she'd been born only to face. She almost forgot to scream in the witch's face that she was *failing* at her decision not to torment her, because the Aprosinya that she thought she *should* be could bear up under the burden of it all and do ... something else.

It was *her* witch; her *second* witch, if she were counting, which put her ahead of Valentina *herself* at her age.

And perhaps the very attenuation she was facing gave her a certain inwards-turning tendency that warred with any intention of reaching out.

"Move," she told the witch. "Get out of me. It is *hurting*."

"... I ... had, originally, meant to hurt you," said the witch. **"So arguably this is a fortuitous and blessed event."**

"That is the worst justification ever."

But that time, and many similar others, the witch merely pulled deeper into her nest; curled more tightly into a ball in the center of the mind's eye of Aprosinya—like a blind spot around which every thought and sensation had to go curling—and said, **"You whine too much."**

And she screamed and threw pointed dreams in the witch's direction; but she didn't even really expect it would help.

SHE KIND OF got used to it.

She flung herself against the witch, in dreams. She gathered up her will, when she could, and battered it against the nest. She tried to come up with *something*.

But most of all, she got used to it.

She became *accustomed* to it, like a broken sink; like an aching back.

It was always possible, notionally, that if she worked a little harder, or a little more reliably, or went a little further, she could fix the situation. It was always possible that it was just a failure of her imagination, or her will, or her perseverance. Or possibly it was not, and nothing she could have done would conceivably have helped.

Possibly her family could have saved her, if she had told them.

—and, just as possibly, not.

She grew *used* to it, grew accustomed to the burden faster than she grew desperate, and by the time that she'd accepted that she had no hope left, by the time she'd accepted that she would *have* to find some external power to assist her, she'd lost the momentum that would push her outside herself to try.

She looked through the Sosunov libraries, perfunctorily. Prayed to Miruna Sosunova. Invoked the feather of the night-bird—but the Magistra had flown away.

Perhaps if she'd tried it more than once, the bird might have heard her.

Perhaps if she'd searched more deeply, the library might have had an answer waiting for her in its depths.

... if it were certain, though, or even all that likely, she would have mustered up the will to try. It wasn't, so she never actually did.

A year and change passed, and she grew ever more broken; most nights, she had no dreams at all.

IT WAS AROUND THAT TIME that the first trains began to run between the Bleak Academy and Schism Village, and Mrs. Senko took the train—and then a carriage, through fifteen untamed but relatively stable miles of the chaos—to Horizon, in pursuit of an opportunity that a witch-riding girl had at one time mentioned.

She presented herself to the King of Evil; or, better put, to the Principal of School.

"I'm told you have a position available," she said.

If he was surprised to see her, he did not let it show. "I do," he said. "I have too many students. It's difficult to tell where I should direct my resources. I need educators who can help me winnow the herd."

"I see," she said.

"I need you to break them," he said. "Show them the terror that is Perdition. Ruin their hearts. Crush their dreams. Empty them out, make them hollow skins. If they can survive that, if they can *endure* that and come back stronger from it, then they have a greater likelihood of being useful to me."

She squinted at him. "Is such survival likely?"

"It would be— ah, one could say, a miracle," he said. "Perhaps."

She hissed out air through her teeth, even though she herself had seen more than a few suchlike events. "Really," she fussed. "You're putting an extremely negative spin on teaching. What is the compensation package?"

He raised an eyebrow at her. "I am offering, void-child, to grant you license at my School; to let you teach, to interact with, to *predate upon ... my* students. You would ask for more? You, who can build servants out of river mud and palaces out of air? What even more *is* there?"

"I want to pick my own students," she said. "Seventy-five thousand cash a year. And full benefits."

Disappointment flickered in his eyes. "The façade of normalcy is conducted through Administration," he said. "You may freely write your own ticket; I'll have nothing to do with it."

She frowned at him. "It is best to observe the forms," she said, sulkily; then shrugged. "But such an offer is not one that I can reject."

WHEN APROSINYA finally reached out, it was not to anyone she'd ever have to face in person.

Her hungry eyes latched on to Valentina Grigorievna Sosunova in her dreams.

"Tell me," Aprosinya said. "Tell me, if— if the heron-witch came back— how would you— I mean, can you tell me how to fight her?"

"I may have thought about it," said Valentina Grigorievna Sosunova; "somewhat, yes."

"DID SHE?" Valentina asked. "Come back, I mean? Then?"

Her voice was low and fierce, but Aprosinya did not answer her; she looked away.

And Valentina's shoulders slumped. She sighed. "All right," she said. "I will tell you what I can."

Softly: "thank you."

"There is the weakness that you must know," Valentina said. "That if she binds your family to sleep, she will accumulate the sum of their affections. I assume that is not useful to you at this time."

Aprosinya shook her head.

"And another: you can tell her that I will flay her from the inside out— no?"

"She knows you're dead."

"That wouldn't stop me, you realize," Valentina said. "And besides, it isn't true."

Aprosinya just shook her head again.

"... here is my thought, then," Valentina said. "What I would try to do, were she to come at me today, and I a child and not her match, again.

"She is a witch of *looking-upon,* as you must know; of *the eyes that see.*

"And ... we spend a *lot* of time, don't we, shoveling awfulness into our own *looking-upon?* We are constantly dwelling on things that are unbearable to us. Things that we do not want to see."

... the King of Evil brushed his finger across Aprosinya's brow ...

"And it struck me," Valentina said, "that there's no reason *we* should have to deal with all that garbage, shovel it into our own *looking,* if there's a witch *right there.*

"So that's what I'd do. I'd stuff her to the gills with rot—

"With the things that I can't bear to see."

SO SHE took it to herself—that red and crystal moment, that finger brushing along her brow. She dragged herself awake from nightmares that left her dry-mouthed and shaken. She went deep into her own mind and dug out so much more of it than she wanted to remember, than she wanted to see or think about again. She held up the *awfulness* of it, the sheer unbearable horror of it, up before the witch, and felt her world perverting, felt it twisting; then, like she was vomiting it, or disgorging it, or, maybe, swallowing it up with her eyes, she wished it out onto the witch ...

But the witch just stared into the monstrous meaninglessness of life and hope, and laughed.

"Once upon a time," the witch said, **"while I hung there, still dying, ... Valya showed me a thing that should not be.**

"And I think if she had understood that I was still alive, there, then, as I hung there motionless and helpless like dry kindling, she would have killed me, she *could* have killed me; because o, it was impossible to accept that thing she saw. Impossible to look upon a world that had that in it. *That* was a thing, Aprosya, that I couldn't bear to see.

"But this—

"This one, is *fine*.

"I don't know if evil *does* rule the world, Aprosya, but that it *might* ... is the most natural thing of all."

Aprosinya stared at her bleakly, her hand slowly lowering.

"But *I* don't want to look at it," she pled.

"Kuh," said the witch, and her feathers fluttered. **"I'm not the witch of looking-upon the things you *like*."**

THE RUMORS that spread through School about the new teacher were varied.

Some said that she was wicked. Some said that she was the daughter of the Headmaster of the Bleak Academy, there to fetch souls out to Death's dominion. A few said she was an angel, or a transformed bird. But Devin Markovic, to Aprosinya, gave *this* report instead:

That *she* said she could teach you how to live, how to *prosper*, even when your heart was dead; your dreams were dead; and your whole world gone all lifeless, cold, and grey. She'd written it on the blackboard, even, on the first day of her class:

Survival, in Perdition.

Aprosinya heard those words, and went still with hope.

… she doubted that it was true, of course. She thought Devin's fantasy life was quite active; quite possibly, Mrs. Senko's was as well—

But, if it were true …

If only it were true …

So she went to Mrs. Senko. She stared blankly at her.

"Close your mouth, dear, a fish will fly into it."

"It's you," Aprosinya said.

"I have been myself on every previous occasion," Mrs. Senko agreed. "And you are also yourself, I see. But not riding on the back of giant birds this time. I approve."

"I mean—you really *are* the Headmaster's daughter."

"Ah. Yes. Is that all, dear?"

Aprosinya shook her head. After a long moment, she stammered, "I want into your class."

"Really?" Mrs. Senko eyed her. "I *had* meant to look at your file, at some point, anyway. But there are so very many to go through and grading papers takes up all of my time. Well, mostly, I just stamp them 'failed,' but then I must engage in a philosophical contemplation as to what it *means* for somebody to fail in my course."

"Um," said Aprosinya.

"Of course," said Mrs. Senko. "I am quite happy to give you a test for admission."

She tossed Aprosinya a locket. Inside the locket was a mirror, or something *like* a mirror, anyway. In it, when Aprosinya looked into it, she saw that she was just a creature of meat and bone and hair. She saw that her eyes twitched in their sockets like two little fish darting about. She saw that her muscles lay long against her bones. She saw that her thoughts were like ants tracking filthy mud across the floor that was her brain. She saw, in short, that she was a monster, a worthless heap, who had no business taking up anybody's time.

Slowly, licking her lips, she handed the locket back.

"Well?" Mrs. Senko prompted. "How'd you do?"

And Aprosinya lied: "I ... passed?"

THAT WAS HOW she found herself in the class when Mrs. Senko finally put a stop to Devin's Izvivode fixation. It was the middle of class, and somehow things had gotten around to Devin bragging about how there was going to be a giant insect, serpent, lizard, or robot attack on the School, and how he was going to call out Izvivode to stop it, and how this was going to be the big decisive moment of his life, how this was "the story of a man," and all the while Mrs. Senko's left eyelid was twitching in irritation, and finally she said: "Mr. Markovic."

"Yes?"

"If your magical dog continues to disrupt class like this," she said, "I will have to confiscate the creature."

"Ha," he said. "And leave School defenseless when the giant enemy attacks?"

"I will just have to deal with the giant enemies," she said, "myself."

He squirmed a little at this notion. He sat upright. Then he gave her a challenging stare. "OK," he said, "then. Try it."

He took his hand off of Izvivode's ruff. He sat back, calmly.

"Confiscate," he said, "away."

This turned out to be a mistake.

It was the first year that Mrs. Senko was teaching, and she'd hand-picked the students that she'd teach, so hardly anyone was actually in her classes. She hadn't had time to meet people, to bump into random students and decide to hand-pick them. She hadn't had time to *hear* about students of interest from the rest of the faculty, or to do a full and complete review of the Principal's files. So there were just the eight of them back then, seven personally selected and one tested in, to learn the unusual things she taught. Back then, for instance, they were studying what she called *Contextual Self-Betrayal*, or, the tendency that a person has—when pressed and belittled—to emulate others' worst expectations of oneself:

To *snap*, and in snapping, to become what one has been told, repeatedly, one already is.

It was a weird topic, but the class had seen much weirder things, like the way the dog came to Mrs. Senko when she held out her hand. Like the way she was able to *take* Izvivode, with this bright open-maw smile, the way she called the dog to her, the way she put Devin's creature away.

It stood in the corner for a while, right where she put it.

And after that even Devin kind of lost track.

"MR. MARKOVIC," the teacher said, a few days later, "you are sulking."

He gave her a look.

Then he said, "I am thinking about how the School is going to be attacked by giant monsters, and then we're all going to die, and you're going to be so terribly sorry. Or possibly how you will realize at the last moment that you should have let me have my dog all along, and everything will be all right, except for your own tragic ending. You will apologize, weeping, on your death bed, and I will probably apologize too, saying, 'if only I hadn't given you such lip, Mrs. Senko!'

"But, 'it's all right, Devin,' you'll tell me. 'You were right all along.' And then you'll die."

"I see," Mrs. Senko said.

"It's just a theory," he said. "You might not be enlightened enough for such a deep and meaningful dialogue."

"I am fairly certain," said Mrs. Senko, "that if something like that were to happen, a rather large dog would not be sufficient to save us."

"No," he agreed.

He looked away.

"It's a one in a million shot," he said. "A heroic tale. A dog and its master, as powerful and awesome as they might be, far overmatched. But there is the touch of destiny upon it."

"... I can't accept that," Mrs. Senko said, "Mr. Markovic, for several reasons."

There was something in the way she said that. It made him sit up, instead of slouching further. It made him lean forward, and took a bit of the anger from his eyes. It wasn't obvious what it *was* in the way that she said it. It was just that *something* was there.

"First," she said, "the word 'destiny' is a dangerous one. It is as treacherous as it is glamorous. I have found that it usually indicates— well."

She squinted at Devin for a moment.

"Let's say, it's a word used to patch the holes in something, to make something seem just or correct when it is false and wrong, a word used to give a false concept *authority*. But let us leave that aside for now; more importantly, Devin, if you're going to fight giant monsters, why in the world would you send a dog?"

"It's a magic—" he started.

"*Even so*," she rapped out.

She paused. She turned. She stared aimlessly at her chalkboard. Then she said, "Let's try this another way."

She scrawled across the top of the board, REMEDIES TO GIANT MONSTER ATTACK.

Underneath she wrote a few bullet points:

- *Sappers*
- *Snipers*
- *Larger giant monsters*
- *Hero teams*

SHE PAUSED THERE. She turned to the class. "Class," she said.

"You could confiscate them," said Devin, bitterly. "Maybe they'll come to you when they *should* be listening to their evil master."

"Young man," said Mrs. Senko, "I am hardly the kind of person who could go around confiscating giant monsters."

Aprosinya had her hand raised. When Devin failed to speak further, Mrs. Senko called on her: "Aprosinya."

"What do the giant monsters want?" Aprosinya asked. "If you could find out what they wanted, you could maybe get them to go away."

"Oh," Mrs. Senko said. "That's a good one."

She put it up there:

- *Exploit psychological weaknesses*
- *Leverage motivations*
- *Manipulate the situation in general*

"THOSE," she said. "Those are always good."

"You could say, 'Go! Izvivode!'" Devin said, bitterly, "and send a giant dog to deal with the monsters directly."

"Mm," said Mrs. Senko. She added:

- *Feed the giant monsters large, arguably tasty snacks.*

"THAT IS NOT the *reason*," stressed Devin.

> *Shout magical phrases at the monsters, in the hopes that their hearing is so sensitive that this will wound them.*

"MRS. SENKO," said Devin, "how do you expect class participation if —"

> *Whine like a puppy in the general direction of the giant monsters.*

HE SANK BACK in his seat, fuming.

"Mr. Markovic," said Mrs. Senko, and she could not quite resist a smile, "as many issues as there may be between us, you may rest assured that I do not fear an absence of class participation from you."

Aprosinya had her hand up again. Mrs. Senko looked at her.

"I'm sorry," Aprosinya said. "It's not a suggestion. But 'sappers?'"

Mrs. Senko started to answer, but Aprosinya was still struggling for words, and managed to get a noise out first—so Mrs. Senko waited, instead.

"I mean, I get it," Aprosinya said. "I get, I mean, you dig under them and they fall or something, but why is that *first?*"

"Ah," Mrs. Senko said. She looked at the board for a while. Then she said, "It is because of something which occurred to me, but which I wanted to wait out the class' ideas for before I noted it."

She was thoughtful. Then she wrote:

> *Allow them to collapse under their own weight, unable to breathe or move, owing to square-cube law considerations.*

"MR. MARKOVIC," she said, "could you tell me how you first came to possess a magical dog?"

"I told you," he said, irritated.

"Remind me."

"I had trouble breathing," he said. "As a child. I'd be OK in the daytime, but at night Izvivode would come in and sit on my chest. Pin it. Make it harder and harder to breathe. Sometimes Izvivode would even grow, just, bam, the moonlight would fall on it and it would swell up to like three times its size and I thought I was going to die."

"Then you understand," she said.

"It's a good dog!" he protested.

Patiently, she said: "That it can be hard to breathe, with too much weight pressing on the lungs."

"Oh," he said.

"This," she said, and she tapped at the board, "is the fundamental reason why I am not terribly concerned that in the absence of your magical dog giant monsters will overrun the School. I can question the entire scenario as much as I like, Mr. Markovic; I can say, but these monsters have never attacked before; or, I am fairly confident that 'battle a giant lizard with your dog' is not *actually* your destiny. I can say that there is an aggravating mysticism pervading the entire concept, and that in the clean bright light of science the notion dissipates—but in the end, this is what it comes down to: such an attacker would defeat *itself.*"

"Izvivode," he said, "is able to breathe when larger—"

"Oh," she said. "If you're merely concerned about a lizard the size of a bear, then?"

"Well," he said.

"Because that would be somewhat frightening," she said, "although I can't see how it would require your personal assistance to deal with. We *do* have, for instance, Hugh."

Hugh Rosewood taught gym to the upper classes.

It didn't really seem possible for a gym teacher to *actually* beat a gigantic lizard, but the more Aprosinya thought about it, the harder it was to imagine him *not.*

"There could be a robot," Devin said. "Robots don't have to breathe."

"Mm," Mrs. Senko agreed.

 ❧ *Casually create a giant robot capable of moving at that size, and use that robot to defend us.*

"UMMM, AH?"

"I don't actually know the mechanical details there," Mrs. Senko admitted. "You could look into it, if you had a mind. I'd *think* it'd be as impractical as a living thing, at that scale. But, if it's not, if it's just *that easy* … well. I don't understand your attachment to throwing away the life of your magical dog, then, when you *could* be building a giant robot instead."

He stiffened. He was getting ready to be angry at the idea. He was getting ready to defend himself, to say he wasn't *throwing away* the life of his dog; but he stopped.

And it seemed to Aprosinya that maybe it was a little like this:

That somewhere at the back of his mind, he'd always thought that Izvivode would get terribly injured, when the battle finally happened. He'd always imagined himself weeping, racing desperately to the side of his injured, raggedly breathing dog, after the battle; imagined himself thinking, *Oh, God, is it dead? Don't be dead!*

And maybe he'd also thought, of course, that it'd be OK. That there'd be this surge of amazing, magic relief, that everything *would* be fine.

But it was enough. It was close enough. She could feel the spear of guilt slamming through him.

For what might have been the first time, Devin questioned his destiny, and it was cold in him, he felt his intestines twist with it, and so he couldn't quite manage a protest.

And in the quiet where his angry shout wasn't, Aprosinya could hear Mrs. Senko muttering, "I can't see why there has to be a fight with them anyway, I mean, seriously, what would the giant monster even be *thinking?*"

SOMEWHAT TO APROSINYA'S SURPRISE—somewhat to *everybody's* surprise—he actually did it.

He'd been burned into everyone's mind as that strange boy who was always going around with (and bragging incessantly about) his magical dog, but now—

People saw him hanging out with the mecha club sometimes.

He argued with Mr. Skivens in Physics.

And one day Aprosinya suddenly realized it, she suddenly *understood* it: he was actually doing it. He was actually trying to figure out if a giant robot was a feasible thing. No, more than that. When she saw him staggering to the cafeteria one day under the burden of a metal arm the size of a dresser she realized: he was trying to *build* one.

She caught Mrs. Senko after class the day after she saw that. She told her, "You should give Devin's dog back."

Mrs. Senko looked at her with a hint of pity.

"He's an annoying magical dog shouting boy," Aprosinya explained, "but that's better than being a *broken* annoying magical dog shouting boy."

Mrs. Senko coughed.

Then she said, "People break, Aprosinya."

Aprosinya stared at her blankly. Why would someone even *say* that? She said, "But he's ... he's *magical dog boy*."

"Mm," Mrs. Senko said. She shuffled together some papers. She looked up at the ceiling. She thought. "Aprosinya," she said, after a while, "in the end, people aren't really anything. In the beginning, sure, we might think that we are. We might form these ideas about who we are. But the most important thing about growing up is, we understand that we're not."

Aprosinya didn't get it. "Not?"

"Not anything," Mrs. Senko said. "In the end all our delusions, all our conceptions, all our—all the things that we give to ourselves, as our names, as our truths, they all flit away. They fade from us, and we're left just ... more faceless, more empty, more of the shuffling masses. The spark in us goes away. He thought he was a magical dog boy, but that was only because he had a magical dog."

"You can't—"

Aprosinya frowned at her.

"You can't take away somebody's magical dog," Aprosinya said, "and then say, 'that means that you're not actually a magical dog boy at all.' That's ..."

"That's?" Mrs. Senko waited.

"That's *awful.*"

"Well," Mrs. Senko said, "I don't know what to tell you. Should I go with 'awful things happen, Ms. Sosunova,' or should I try 'judgment only works when applied to someone of lower power and authority than yourself?'"

"Those aren't the answers I am looking for," Aprosinya told her. Then she poked her. She poked her on the top of her breastbone, just under her throat, and felt bone through her blouse and her skin. "You're *unrighteous,*" Aprosinya said.

"Oh, yes," Mrs. Senko agreed. "Quite so."

DEVIN TOOK to fiddling with a circuit board in class. It was really improper, but Mrs. Senko didn't stop him. In fact, now and then, she'd stop and she'd ask him questions about it.

"It's no good to build a giant robot," he said, "if you can't control it."

"That's so," she agreed.

"I mean," he said, "if I were to make one, and it went wild, out of control, and attacked the School, and I didn't have a magical dog to defend me *and* the giant robot was evil, then that would be the worst."

"Don't lets make everything about your magical dog," she said.

His eyes were almost feverish.

"But," she said, "I'm surprised. Do you actually think you can accomplish anything?"

"It's been done," he said.

A pleased tone: "Oh?"

"It's been done," he said. "Twenty years ago. That's why there's the mecha club. Some girl down at the Steamworks *managed*."

"Mm," said Mrs. Senko. "Did she?"

"Forty-seven feet," said Devin. "Height, not, ummm, ah," and he waved his hand towards what Aprosinya really hoped was his feet. "But then she scrapped it."

"That's unfortunate," said Mrs. Senko. "I'd like to see a thing like that."

"Yeah," said Devin.

He looked down at the circuit board. Then up at Mrs. Senko. He glared at her. "I don't like you, though, so I won't show it to you. If I make one."

"If I may ask," she said, "she scrapped it ... for what reason?"

"It wasn't practical," he said. "It was ... it needed to be plugged in. It had a very limited battery life off the plug. Everyone teased her and told her she'd gone over the verge. Eventually she went on a rampage and proved it."

"Ah."

The class slipped by and, towards the end, she asked him, "You *do*—I mean, I *have* taught you to know better, haven't I, than to go on a rampage, Mr. Markovic?"

"Yes, Mrs. Senko," he said.

"I understand," she said, "that that is a temptation for those who practice unorthodox science."

"I know better," he agreed.

IT MAY SEEM from all this like her life was cheery; disturbing, perhaps, but a bright enough thing.

... but this was not so.

Being alive:

It *hurt.*

Aprosinya was squeezed to a corner of herself; under the constant pressure and the burden of the witch. Her very *being* had been stolen from her; her mind, her heart, her dreams, it all *existed,* but there wasn't *room* for it.

And she was broken.

At nights, she struggled to build a thing inside herself that the heron-witch could not bear to look upon; and each failure did more harm to her than the last. She consulted with Valentina, learned that the witch *must* have been referring to the Headmaster's curse or the thing that lived in Evdeniya Kaneko's house when she spoke of the thing that could have *actually* killed her, and tried to construct a thing like that within the fraying fabric of herself. The image training that she undertook towards this end was not so bad, nor the meditation, which touched as often on the angel of the houses of the sun as on King Evil—

But ultimately, to make progress, to build a *thing that the witch could not bear to look upon,* was a process of farming her own despair up, like it was a crop; and such self-treatment took its toll.

It took its toll; and months slipped by, and it was yet to help.

Months slipped by, and it hadn't helped; months slipped by, and she began to grasp that it *wouldn't* help; that it would never help; that she would never get there. That driving off the witch this way was possible, perhaps, it might be possible, but that one small Aprosinya was not sufficient to the task.

"Can't I come to the Bleak Academy?" Aprosinya pled. "Can't I leave all this behind?"

"You can't," Valentina said, and she brushed the hair away from Aprosinya's forehead. "You can't run away to the Bleak Academy. You can only be running towards."

... or, "don't go through those gates because you're hurting."

... or "live your life first. There's still time."

"Don't go through those gates, Aprosinya, just because you're *lonely*."

"What, you think the Headmaster would *help?*"

It was honestly, sometimes, she thought, as if Valentina thought the best use of a place like the Bleak Academy was to learn the secret of immortality, or the secret that was like the rain; to break the cage of false conceptions and make the world like grass; to punch out the Headmaster, maybe, or to share his wine; to learn the ancient secrets of the dead; or, to find new wings—not to *escape*. And that would have all been well and good, that would have seemed very solemn and believable and imposing and adult to her, had her need to *escape* and the Bleak Academy's breathing presence in her life not been so *acute*.

Except, they were.

Mrs. Senko, weirdly enough, was nicer about it—one of the very few things she *was* nice about, really. She *wanted* her students to go to the Bleak Academy one day; was quite up front about this, even if it wasn't quite clear if she was planning to murder them all, or wait out their lives, or get them in on some kind of alternative enrollment for the living; and she was quite obviously thrilled, as much as she tried to hide it behind her pressed-thin mouth, that Aprosinya was interested in attending.

... but even *she* didn't think Aprosinya could just *go* there; she acted like Aprosinya had to, somehow, "prove" herself first.

So it was kind of inevitable, really, given everything, that asking Mrs. Senko for help would go poorly. It ... wasn't demonstrating herself worthy of the Bleak Academy. It wasn't rising up from the pack. It was kind of the *opposite* of proving herself worthy, really, on top of every other thing that it was:

... but one day, Aprosinya just got desperate.

She told Mrs. Senko about the witch; and Mrs. Senko's lips went white with anger. She told Mrs. Senko what the witch had done to her; and Mrs. Senko glared at her; and for a moment, Aprosinya thought, or perhaps just hoped, that she was *actually* glaring through her at the witch.

The truth, perhaps, was somewhere in between.

"Even your imaginary friends," Mrs. Senko said, "Ms. Sosunova, are delinquent."

It was a bucket of cold water. Ice. "... what?"

"Seriously," Mrs. Senko said. "Squeezing into your brain? Stealing *my* hard-earned teachings?"

"Uh—"

"She isn't even properly enrolled."

SO THAT WAS THE DAY Mrs. Senko would set metal staples into the walls, by the old bloodstains—thick and old and there were two them, set up as if to pin or hold a spread-armed student's wrists.

That was the day she would put in two anchor spikes, not far above that, as if to hold a rope.

And that was the day, as well, that she would feel around behind Aprosinya's eyes and rip the heron-witch away; and the end of the witch's haunting of her, too—or, rather, *almost* the end of the witch's haunting of her; almost the end of that story, but not *quite*.

Three days later the class got its ninth member.

A heron-witch nervously, shyly, walked into the class to learn. She'd taken Mrs. Senko up on an *invitation*, apparently, to pick up her education the *right* way, rather than stealing it from her students; she introduced herself, softly, as **"Hi; I'm, um ... I don't really have a name ..."**

And Mrs. Senko pinned her to the wall, and cut her throat in flesh as it had been cut in dreams, and turned her head towards the blackboard so that she could follow the class while she still lived.

"Behold," said Mrs. Senko. "An important lesson about life."

She wrote it again on the board, as she had written it before: *Witches do not exist.*

AND APROSINYA was down in East Commons, one day, and Devin dragged it in, clanking. He was walking backwards, operating the remote, and behind him followed a metal man, eight feet tall if it was an inch.

It stooped, it bent its head, as it passed through the door.

He was *such* a geek.

"Good *lord*," Aprosinya said, but he only beamed proudly:

"It's for *kaiju* battles!" he said.

She made a face at him.

"Listen," he said. "I mean, listen. Obviously I'm going to get Izvivode back. She can't just *keep* him. But for now, for *right* now, for this year?"

"She's keeping him *all year?*"

"For right now," said Devin, as if a dog could sleep on his chest keeping him from breathing for most of his childhood, and then become a steadfast ally in his early teens, and he could just *forget* it—"I'm going to use *Botvode*. Look, he grows bigger!"

"No," Aprosinya said. She shouted. She half-shrieked, desperately cringing back in her chair and wishing it weren't a sturdy chair and there wasn't its great cushioned back behind her. "Don't—"

"Go, Botvode!" he shouted.

It didn't glow from within with something like moonlight. It didn't expand to triple its size! It just let out some steam with a great valving clunk and then its middle section—torso, arms, and head—rose up on a steel three-inch post.

Devin was giggling helplessly. He was shaking his head. "God, Aprosinya," he said, "your *face*," but she was already up and stomping away. And she told him from the door:

"You can't just forget your dog like that!"

And he blinked a bit at this, shook his head once or twice, as if in confusion, and said, "You can't really fight giant monsters with dogs."

CHOICE

"**S**TILL," MRS. Senko said. It was three months later. "Still. I let you into my class. I remove your witch. And *still*... you are not content with your lot as a faceless minion of society."

The middle of Mrs. Senko's class was always a blur. Aprosinya didn't know how they got to that point in the story. She didn't know how she could have possibly brought up the topic, or how anyone else could've; there was no causal chain that seemed to lead there.

One could call it a miracle, perhaps—that articulation of the fire, in the absence of the self, that brings the self back to existence. One could call it a miracle; or a *something in the world, that moves;* or the characteristic action, at the minimum, of someone predisposed through training[24] or heredity[25] to evoke their own existence should they ever find that it isn't there:

Ab initio, and with poor timing, Aprosinya was.

Mrs. Senko was looking at her. Mrs. Senko was *squinting* at her, *leaning forward* at her, locket-mirror spinning and dangling.

"What exactly," she said, "do you mean, Ms. Sosunova, when you say you're a 'dead end?'"

Horror and embarrassment froze Aprosinya. She tried, desperately, to figure out how she'd gotten there; what Mrs. Senko had been talking about, what she *herself* had been talking about, what she had *said*, but—

Her best guess was that Mrs. Senko was cheating somehow.

She grasped at that history but it was like air, and the longer she tried, the weightier the unanswered and unanswerable silence became. She squirmed under it, realizing it had been too long since Mrs. Senko had spoken, and afraid of what Mrs. Senko would do if left too long without

---

24   like Aprosinya

25   like Mrs. Senko

Aprosinya replying; it was personal, she didn't want to say anything, but without knowing what she had said to bring it on, she couldn't exactly refuse.

And so finally it ground out from her, the words slipping free:

"Mrs. Senko," Aprosinya asked, "what would you do if you knew the future?"

Mrs. Senko tilted her head like a bird. She didn't blink. "Make a series of highly leveraged bets," she said. "Perhaps. Twist things to my own advantage. It depends on the model of causality in play: are we speaking of alterable or inalterable time?"

"No," Aprosinya said.

"No?" Mrs. Senko's eyebrow twitched. "Those are the only options, Aprosinya."

"No," Aprosinya said. "It's not like that. I mean, what would you do if you knew the future, and it was bad? What if you could dream the future and, only— what if you *knew?*"

"Mm," Mrs. Senko said. "I would feel a compelling confidence, Ms. Sosunova, that I do *not* know the future, and would face down that *weird* or sense of doom by reflecting upon all of the past occasions where I had been absolutely certain of a thing and yet it had not come to pass."

Devin's hand shot up.

Mrs. Senko glared at him.

"Past occasions," she said, "which we shall absolutely not be discussing at this time."

His hand, slowly, inched back down.

Aprosinya said: "But if— if you *did* know?"

Mrs. Senko thought on it. She said, finally, "then I would ask myself, Aprosinya, 'what value does this knowledge have to me?' And I would see a counselor, I think, because it would not be the kind of knowledge that my mind would handle well."

ALL HER LIFE Aprosinya'd known that Sosunovs were a community across time. All her life she'd lived with a richness of the past, and known that that past had a richness of the future. Her grandparents had spent time with her, even though one was dead. Her Mom visited her from the future and past. Valentina had reached forward from, presumably, long, long ago.

To be in a Sosunov was to be in a community that stretched across time; only, one day, Aprosinya had noticed that she wasn't like that.

She wasn't like that, and it didn't make sense.

She never met her future husband. And that was fine. Maybe … maybe he was like her Da. Maybe he couldn't walk through time. That was possible. That was why, she thought, you don't usually meet your … your just *passing* lovers, your boyfriends, your dates. They don't ever learn the Sosunov magic at all. And if you wind up falling for someone who can't learn the magic, or if you marry out of the Sosunov family or something, or, more likely, both—

Well, all things put together, it was *sort of* a big deal never to get visited by the person she was going to marry, but, honestly, there were a lot of reasons for that.

That wasn't surprising. That wasn't a reason to be a dead end.

But she never had any visits from children. She … if she became good enough, if she was strong enough, if she learned enough, then one day she could go back and bug her Mom as a child. She could tease her about being her own daughter and yet even bigger and older than her. She could help her with her childhood math. And she could play around with her little kid Da, and maybe play matchmaker for the two later on. She could peek in on one of those dreams that her great-gran Valentina had had. And she guessed she probably didn't do that, since nobody ever mentioned it, but maybe she'd done and they just forgot. She thought …

She would *expect* to get visits. If she had children. At least, if she had more than one. If they lived long enough. If the line passing through her didn't die out. Grandchildren.

And more.

Loosely, she knew that not all people have children. Loosely, she knew that wasn't enough on its own. But ... there could have been nieces and nephews; cousins once, twice removed; the children of the family Sosunov, had she none of her own. Friends with the magic, from the family's more distant branches, that she'd make years and years in the future. People she'd *know*.

There should have been *someone* who'd love her, someone strong in the magic, whom she didn't yet know; she couldn't plausibly live out the rest of her life, as a *Sosunov*, in *Fortitude*, and *not* have that happen; only, there wasn't.

That's how she realized it, one day, that—

That that never happens. That she wouldn't make a mark. That her future just *ended*, it just dead-ended somewhere, it *had* to, because nobody later on ever cared. She could explain away little bits of it, sure, she could say, oh, they don't know enough magic, not her husband, her daughters, her sons. Maybe she didn't live long enough to see any grandchildren, or maybe their magic was just too weak as well.

But *someone* would have come by. If not beforehand, then ... when she *realized* that she was a dead end. If not when she was a happy kid, roaming the beaches, streets, and the temple in Fortitude, then *later*, once she'd started to figure this out.

Someone would have come by and said, "Your life will touch mine, Aprosinya."

They'd say *your future won't just die out.*

It was obvious, when that didn't happen, why it wouldn't. She was going to die before she ever mattered. She was going to die unloved and unmourned, and probably—

She was going to make her own family hate her, somehow, or die in such an awful way that they couldn't even bear to visit her to say goodbye.

In her dreams at night, she rode ships at sea with her Mom and Da and her cousins. She played alone in the dream-worlds that she built. She had tea and cakes with her great-gran Valentina, and listened to her stories of the Bleak Academy. And then she'd wait for her death when she woke.

Sometimes she thought that she had gotten used to her despair, when the witch was in her; had gotten used to her little island of despairing, and could not leave it easily just because her world had changed.

Other times she understood that her fundamental situation had not altered:

It had been writ in stone, her ending had, and long before the coming of the witch.

SHE THOUGHT she was saying this. She thought she was talking about it. She didn't know why. She was gesturing broadly. And Mrs. Senko's mouth was just a thin, angry line.

"Truly," Mrs. Senko said, "how *any* of us can slog through the mire of this world without the validation of fleets of future wizards lauding us across the span of time I can't imagine; it is a mystery."

Aprosinya sputtered.

"Setting aside for the moment the underlying ...*folie à plusiers*—" Mrs. Senko said.

"You can't assume that *every* multiply attested belief you disagree with is a shared delusional disorder," Claire objected, without even raising her hand. "No matter *how* many chapters you devote to rhapsodizing about the subject."

Mrs. Senko gave her a considering glance, then ignored her. "*Setting that aside*, as previously stated:

"Ms. Sosunova, for God's sake: just *move to Boston.*"

"... Boston?" Aprosinya asked.

"They have a pie that is not a pie," Mrs. Senko said. "I've always wondered— Aprosya, Aprosinya, if we cut through the trappings of dreams and prognostication, what you are telling me is that you cannot survive a life entangled in the stifling embrace of your family lifestyle and superstitions. The answer is transparent; move, or die."

"You don't understand," Aprosinya said.

"Oh?"

Aprosinya's jaw worked.

"Am I really to believe," Mrs. Senko said, "then, that this is *actually* about prophetic dreams? That it is genuinely your *belief* in such things, your dedication to the *reality* of this delusional construction, that is bringing you such distress? That has disrupted *my* class? Brought you to sputtering ruin, and Claire here to the point of interruption and—"

A glance. A contemptuous sneer.

"*Levitation?*"

"... yes."

"Then I must take it from you," Mrs. Senko said, simply.

"Ah?" Aprosinya said. She shrank back in her seat. "Ah. No. That isn't necessary. Wait, but, you can't—"

She did.

Mrs. Senko held out her hand; and—as to such matters as her dreams—Aprosinya lost all interest.

IT IS COMMONLY understood by practical adults that if one can only remove a child's dreams, they will immediately redirect the freed-up mental energy into more respectable and desirable pursuits. Free of the burden of being autonomous individuals, they will immediately conform with brilliance and rigor to the desired program and flow like molten steel into their mold.

In Aprosinya's case, at least, this did not transpire.

As a pallor spread across her dreams, she did not become cheerful and obedient. She fell into a bleak delirium, instead; her spirit sank into Perdition. Her dreams were dead—or, at least, inaccessible to her. Her hopes were dead. All things were lifeless, cold, and grey. There was no *agony* in this, for her, no pressing despair; in fact, arguably, her despair had lessened, as the withholding of her dreams immediately and directly averted the prognosticated doom:

Without dreams, no further evidence of disaster could conceivably appear.

She could have future children, future grandchildren; she would not dream of them. More than that—it was as this new, dreamless Aprosinya that they would come to know her; naturally, they would not choose to visit the dreams when she was someone else. Perhaps whole future *societies* would otherwise have dreamt their way back through time to praise her; she could miss out on that, now, as easily as on an incoherent dream about a bee.

In one act, Mrs. Senko had stripped her of the future that had doomed her—as far as she knew, at least; and technically, the weight on her had lifted.

Only, nothing actually mattered any longer and everything was a meaningless cavalcade of forms.

She'd attended that class so she could learn to live without a heart, or dreams, in a world that was lifeless, cold, and grey; in case she got there, in case her heart finished dying, her dreams finished dying, her world finished *going that way* ... and now it all had, she was fully in that dead world, and she hadn't learned how to live there *at all*.

Mrs. Senko would lecture on probability, and Aprosinya would record the lesson, and do the homework, but it did not register on her. Mrs. Senko would speak at some length on identity, and it would fall into the grey fuzz of Aprosinya's head; the concept of identity had become elusive.

Bits and pieces of life drifted past her in the fog. At one point she caught Mrs. Senko's eyes on her, and they seemed sad. She tried to be angry at that. She tried to say, "Well, it's your own fault, isn't it?"

But she couldn't.

"Mm, pity," Mrs. Senko said.

There was one point where she realized that Devin Markovic was staring at Mrs. Senko every day, every minute of the class, just *staring*, and Mrs. Senko followed her attention, and said, "Mr. Markovic, what *are* you doing?"

"I am attempting to encase you in an egg," he said.

"An egg."

"That is the rule here in Horizon," Devin said. "When a monster is studied sufficiently, they become an egg. Then what comes out is just a person. Won't you go into an egg for me, Mrs. Senko?"

Her feathers were ruffled: "Certainly not."

"You're nervous," he said, as if it thrilled him, and a little spark of schadenfreude woke in Aprosinya's heart. "You're nervous. You know I'll get you eventually."

"I'm aggravated," Mrs. Senko said. "The entire idea is absurd."

Slowly Aprosinya grew more distant from existence. She watched her body go through the motions of the day. She listened to Claire's arguments with Mrs. Senko over whether there were such things as ghosts, and thought, a ghost is what I am. She listened to Devin boasting about his robot, and thought, a robot is what I am. And the fire of her looked upon the fire of her and it made these things ever closer to the truth.

She sank deeper and deeper until she touched bottom at last.

Then one day Mrs. Senko was speaking on the topic of identity. "What is the self?" she asked. "It is not immanent in the flesh. Nor is it immanent in the fire. It is, rather, a conjure-beast—a thing that the fire sees into the world."

"Mrs. Senko," Devin said. "You have digressed into mysticism."

"Mr. Markovic," Mrs. Senko said, "when lesser minds digress into mysticism, they are obscuring the topic; when I do, it is to elucidate it. The matter is entirely different. If you insist, then I can reframe this in terms of developmental psychology—"

But the empty nothingness was curious about these conjure-beasts; and so Aprosinya whispered, "Aprosinya."

Mrs. Senko went still, like a hunting hound.

Devin turned around in his chair, craned around to see what she was looking at. The class was, for a moment, silent; then a small brown bird on a branch not far from the classroom window took off, in a dizzying, pattering flutter of its wings.

"Do you have something to share with the rest of the class," Mrs. Senko asked, "Ms. Sosunova?"

It was awkward.

Aprosinya did not want to admit it—that for just a moment, she had wanted to be a thing again. That for just a moment she had been curious, because hope was, after all, dead, and not *inconceivable*, about what seeing herself into existence would be like. If she were truly a ghost, she would have shrieked and fled, rather than admit that she had considered personhood. If she were a robot, she would have sent herself in to be reconfigured. As pure emptiness, she would simply have decohered:

It wasn't like she'd even seen anything grand! There was just one small, gross Aprosinya.

She wasn't *literally* emptiness, though. Not literally a ghost, or a machine.

The option of lying, or staying silent, was at the far end of a tunnel dizzyingly long.

So:

"I am trying to see myself," Aprosinya said.

"Interesting," Mrs. Senko said. She was by Aprosinya's chair, half-kneeling to look up into her face and catch it in her hands. "There is light in your eyes. Do continue."

"Stop it," Aprosinya said, and wriggled away.

"Oh, no," Mrs. Senko said. "No, I won't stop it. You have chosen to regard yourself and interrupt *my* lecture, so I will have the details. You look upon yourself with the fire of yourself; and, what do you see?"

Aprosinya gave her a haunted look.

"Tell me, Aprosinya," Mrs. Senko said, "is it worthy of me? Are *you* worthy of me? Are you something lustrous, something jeweled, something that can grow beyond the petty bounds of this mortal earth and spread your wings above the Bleak Academy?"

Aprosinya, jerkily, shook her head.

Don't be ridiculous.

"Oh," Mrs. Senko said. Her face fell, and she looked down. "Well, that is, of course, your choice."

She rose to her feet, creakily, bracing herself with her umbrella. She walked back to the front of the classroom. She took a breath to resume the lecture.

"Wait," Aprosinya said. "Wait. Wait. I ... I get to *choose?*"